One Knight ENCHANTED

CLAIRE DELACROIX

NEW YORK TIMES BESTSELLING AUTHOR

Books by Claire Delacroix

Time Travel Romances
ONCE UPON A KISS
THE LAST HIGHLANDER
THE MOONSTONE
LOVE POTION #9

Medieval Romances
ROMANCE OF THE ROSE
HONEYED LIES
UNICORN BRIDE
THE SORCERESS
ROARKE'S FOLLY
PEARL BEYOND PRICE
THE MAGICIAN'S QUEST
UNICORN VENGEANCE
MY LADY'S CHAMPION
ENCHANTED
MY LADY'S DESIRE

The Bride Quest
THE PRINCESS
THE DAMSEL
THE HEIRESS
THE COUNTESS
THE BEAUTY
THE TEMPTRESS

The Rogues of Ravensmuir
THE ROGUE
THE SCOUNDREL
THE WARRIOR

The Jewels of Kinfairlie
THE BEAUTY BRIDE
THE ROSE RED BRIDE
THE SNOW WHITE BRIDE
The Ballad of Rosamunde

The True Love Brides
THE RENEGADE'S HEART
THE HIGHLANDER'S CURSE
THE FROST MAIDEN'S KISS

THE WARRIOR'S PRIZE

The Brides of Inverfyre
THE MERCENARY'S BRIDE

The Champions of St. Euphemia
THE CRUSADER'S BRIDE
THE CRUSADER'S HEART
THE CRUSADER'S KISS
THE CRUSADER'S VOW
THE CRUSADER'S HANDFAST

Rogues & Angels
ONE KNIGHT ENCHANTED

The Brides of North Barrows
SOMETHING WICKED THIS WAY COMES
A DUKE BY ANY OTHER NAME

Short Stories and Novellas
An Elegy for Melusine
BEGUILED

Dear Reader;

One Knight Enchanted is a medieval fantasy romance, featuring a knight cursed to become a wolf by day and the maiden who breaks the spell with her love. An earlier version of this story was published under the title **Enchanted** in 1997. I've always liked this story, partly because of the fairy-tale feel to it and partly because I just love Rolfe and Annelise. Many readers have written to me over the years to tell me how much they loved the story, too. I was excited to have the chance to publish it in a new edition and make it available again.

My original plan had been to simply re-publish the book, but when I read through it, there were things I wanted to revise. Once I started to make changes, the project snowballed into a much bigger job. My challenge was to create a version of the story that made me happy, but not to sacrifice anything that readers liked about the original. Although the basic story is the same, the telling is so different that the book's been given a new title to distinguish it from the older version.

One Knight Enchanted is also the launch title of a new series, which will include both revised books and new ones. In this new version, Rolfe is part of a company of knights who fought together in the First Crusade and who call themselves *Rogues & Angels*. That's the new name of the series—all eight of these knights will have their stories told and find their HEAs back in Europe. In **Enchanted**, Rolfe had purchased the mysterious bottle as a gift for his brother: in *Rogues & Angels*, all of the knights receive parting gifts from an ally in Jerusalem. The gifts are a bit enigmatic and challenge the knights' various expectations. There are also connections between the knights of this company and my other medieval romance series: many of them are the forebears of later protagonists, and I'll tell you more about that in each book. On my website, these stories are all under the *Sayerne* tab, because that's the world they share.

The next story in the series will be **One Knight's Return**, a revision of **My Lady's Champion**. In this book, both Quinn and Bayard find their happy endings. There's an excerpt from the new version of Quinn's story at the end of this book.

I hope you enjoy this new version of Rolfe and Annelise's story, and also the companion knights of the *Rogues & Angels* series.

All my best
Claire
http://delacroix.net

One Knight Enchanted

PROLOGUE

May 1101—Jerusalem

e could join the Lombards and this new crusade," Thierry Douglas suggested, his opinion of that strategy clear in his tone. "If we want to fight with peasants."

The eight knights who had become friends, as well as comrades, sat in the tavern they favored and drank young red wine. They had each ridden to crusade and had met in Outremer, ultimately joining forces to fight together. Rolfe de Viandin liked to jest that his friends were rogues and angels, for it was true that their natures could not have been more varied.

Thierry and Luc Douglas were twins from the north of England, and Rolfe still found it uncanny how well they anticipated each other's thoughts and movements. The sole difference between them was that Thierry's eyes were green, a striking contrast to his black hair, while Luc's remaining eye was hazel. They, too, had ridden in pursuit of adventure and Rolfe admired that neither hesitated to engage a foe.

Rolfe had met the twins at the siege of Antioch four years before, when both he and they had noticed two other knights being struck down and taken captive. Rolfe, Thierry, and Luc had rescued Quinn and Bayard, which had formed the core of their company. Luc had lost an eye in that battle and had worn a patch ever since.

Quinn de Sayerne, with his auburn hair and amber eyes, was the most thoughtful of the company, as befitted an older son and heir. He often fought back-to-back with Bayard de Neuville, dark-haired and dark-eyed, a younger son with no claim at home, much like Rolfe. Bayard was quick with a jest and quicker yet to strike a killing blow, which was a good balance to Quinn's temperance. They had met shortly after arriving in Palestine and become close companions. Rolfe thought that Quinn had joined the crusade for experience and pursuit of justice while Bayard sought adventure and opportunity. They might have been lost without such timely intervention.

Never mind the aid of Lothair. Lothair, who they called the Viking, was taller than any of them and more ferocious in battle than any knight Rolfe had ever known. He was also a talented healer and had ensured Quinn's survival, thereby bonding those two together. Lothair had blond hair and green eyes and must have hailed from some frozen northern land. He was inclined to be enigmatic but there was no doubt of his ambition—he had joined the fight for plunder.

The company was completed with two handsome knights, both with a measure of charm. Amaury de Montvieux was another with a legacy he had only to ride home to claim. He had joined the crusade out of a conviction that it was right, and was an excellent fighter. He was affluent—no surprise, given his status as heir to a prosperous holding—and inclined to be a little proud. His heart was of the best and valiant, too. Because of his connections, the company had been shown favors in Outremer by the king himself.

Finally, there was Niall MacGillivray, a Scottish mercenary with a fondness for damsels in distress—with his fair hair and blue eyes, he easily gained the favor of any lady he sought to woo, though he vowed that he would never lose his own heart. Although he was even more shameless in his pursuit of women than Rolfe, he listened well and often learned details from the ladies that were of advantage to them in battle.

It was after sunset by the time they had all gathered at the tavern and had their first sip of the wine. Although they met most nights, on this night, they had a decision to make. Lothair had pronounced Quinn to be fully healed, and Quinn had received a message from his overlord that he was now Lord de Sayerne. Would Quinn leave? If so, there was no doubt that Bayard would accompany him. But what of the others? Should they join another battle, like the one mustering in Constantinople, or should they dissolve their company?

The wine had become sharper than had previously been the case and Rolfe de Viandin found it less palatable.

Not as unpalatable as Thierry's suggestion, though. He had endured enough war.

"I failed to bring my plow," Rolfe said, then quaffed the rest of his wine. He recalled, not for the first time, the rich wine made at his home estate and felt his yearning to return grow stronger.

Niall grinned, his blue eyes dancing. "I forgot mine, as well." He filled Rolfe's cup and the two toasted each other before drinking anew.

"They killed Alexios' pet lion," Lothair said grimly. "Regardless of their social status, they lack sense in any measure."

"Allying with fools will see a man dead quicker than any other choice," Luc, the strategist, agreed.

There was a murmur of agreement to that.

"I see little to be gained by remaining in Outremer, but much to be lost," Rolfe said. "Jerusalem is taken and secured. We have gained some riches, which could be lost."

"Just as our health could be," Lothair agreed. "We have sufficient injuries between us, to my thinking."

Again, there was assent.

"It is said that other forces arrive," Quinn noted, speaking with his customary calm. "Knights among them. Raymond IV of Toulouse is said to be arriving at Nicodemia with troops."

"He turned back from the first crusade before the battle was won," Amaury scoffed. "I see the reason they already call this the crusade of the faint-hearted. I am not hungry to join such company. They might falter in battle, which would lead to no good result."

The knights nodded at this.

"They come to reap the spoils now the hard labor is done," Bayard muttered. When Quinn might have protested, he gave his comrade a hard look. "We only lingered so long in Outremer because of your injury. Now you are not just healed, but heir to a holding! I say we ride for Sayerne, pray at your father's grave, and find you a wife." They drank to Quinn's health and congratulated him again.

Quinn did not reply to that, merely sipped of his ale. Was it possible he was not happy with these tidings? Rolfe wondered if he had been close to his father and mourned his death.

"But not all of us are so fortunate as Quinn," Thierry noted. "Not all of us have a holding that merely awaits our arrival."

"Although some of us do," Luc said, giving Amaury a nudge. That knight only smiled, for the truth was indisputable. "Perhaps we shall all come with you and live off the fat of the land at Montvieux."

"God spare me the expense of a company of hungry mercenaries!" Amaury said and they all laughed. "And then there is my fair cousin. No, no, no. You will not be welcome at Montvieux." He pointed at Rolfe. "Not you." He pointed at Niall. "And especially not you."

"How fair is she?" Niall demanded with a grin. "I might make her happy."

"For a night," Rolfe teased.

"Then you will make her happy for the next," Niall agreed easily.

"Do not provoke me in this," Amaury retorted, his eyes flashing blue fire.

"You can all stay away from my sister, as well," Quinn added.

"Then we shall have no place to sleep," Niall complained in good temper.

"I say we visit both Sayerne and Montvieux and confirm the beauty of these ladies," Rolfe said. Niall chuckled.

"I say you will sleep in the stables if you cross my borders," Amaury said and Quinn agreed.

"The fact remains that not all of us have a destination where we will be welcomed," Thierry noted.

"We have need of a company of heiresses," Lothair declared. "Beauties, every one, burdened with wealth and property and ripe for the plucking."

"So long as you do not dream of too much good fortune," Rolfe said to much laughter.

"Now there is a fantasy worthy of a tale!" Thierry said with a laugh. "Keeper! We shall have more wine, if you please."

"I say we shall make our fortunes at home," Bayard argued, raising his voice over the merriment to sound a more somber note. "Outremer has been divided and allotted. There are few futures to be made here now and, indeed, I fear the Latin Kingdoms will not remain stable for long." He shook his head. "There are few prospects for us here."

"It was a blow indeed that Godfroi died last summer," Lothair contributed with a shake of his head. "There are few leaders his equal."

"Though his brother promises to do well as king," Quinn said.

There was another grunt although it was harder to determine whether the greater mood was skepticism or agreement.

"Here is a suggestion," Quinn said. "Let us leave Outremer. As Bayard notes, there is little opportunity for good here and more for peril. Let us ride home together. My holding might be besieged, seeing as it is without a lord. I might have need of your expertise." He fixed a stern gaze upon Rolfe and Niall. "You are all welcome to visit Sayerne, so long as you pledge to leave my sister and other women at Sayerne untouched."

Niall and Rolfe agreed with a show of reluctance, for they knew it was a generous offer and one they welcomed—they would both tease Quinn about his sister, though Rolfe knew Niall would also keep his pledge.

"So, we have a destination," Luc said with satisfaction.

"And must choose a route," Thierry added, turning to Quinn. "Where is Sayerne?"

"North of the Alps, east of Martinach. We rode south through the great Beauvoir Pass with Robert Courteheuse, then down to Brindisi, sailed to Greece, then rode through Byzantium to

Constantinople." He shook his head. "We will reach the pass in winter, though, if we depart now. I would suggest Godfroi de Bouillon's route, through Byzantium and into the Holy Roman Empire, then approach Sayerne from the north in the spring."

Thierry, who remember a map of all the world, shook his head. "I would ride for Acre and sail for Venice, avoiding these newly arrived crusaders and whatever trouble they would make. It would be quicker..."

"But still you will reach the Alps in winter," Quinn said. "I will not undertake that ride again."

"We could linger in Venice," Luc suggested.

"Too expensive," came a chorus of protest. The Venetians were reputed to charge visitors richly.

"But if we do not depart soon, we might be swept into this new battle, the fight of fools," Rolfe noted. "I, for one, would be glad to reach home for the Yule."

Marcus, the keeper, arrived with another pitcher of wine as there was a chorus of agreement. He glanced around at the knights as Quinn's squire Michel took the pitcher to fill the knights' cups. "Is there some cause for celebration?" he asked politely.

"Perhaps for you," Lothair said with a smile. "For you will finally be rid of us."

"Say it is not so!" the keeper protested, and Rolfe knew the man had come to rely upon their regular custom. When the knights insisted it would be, he raised his hands in surrender. "I have long feared that this day would come, so I have prepared gifts for you all."

"Marcus, there is no need," Quinn began to protest.

"You have defended my home," Marcus said to Quinn and Bayard, recalling an incident in which they waylaid a thief. "You have given me coin to build an olive press," he said to Amaury who nodded acknowledgment of that. "You have aided in the healing of my son," he said to Lothair, who knew more of herbs than any man Rolfe had ever known. "You have brought *Franji* to my door who had need of hospitality, and you have ensured that they paid," he said to Luc and Thierry. They hadn't all been from France, but the occupants of Outremer called all the crusaders

Franji. Marcus smiled as he turned to Rolfe and Niall. "And you have left my daughters untouched." He bowed as the knights laughed together at his jest. "I will thank you all."

Marcus hurried from the common room as the knights exchanged glances. "Provisions for the journey ahead?" Quinn guessed.

"Nieces and daughters," Niall suggested with a wink.

"More wine!" Luc said.

But Marcus brought gifts. He set them upon the table in the middle of the room and the knights leaned forward as one, their squires appearing from the shadows to peer at the small heap of presents, as well. There were several wooden boxes, a collection of small bags of velvet in different colors, a small glass vial, and a large dark decanter. "My wife is said to have the gift of seeing the future, a gift from the angels themselves. When I spoke to her of all of you, she prepared these gifts, telling me which was for each of you and why. It seems my wife knows something of your reputations."

Smiles were exchanged as Marcus chose a small red velvet sack and presented it to Amaury. At his nod, Amaury opened it and poured its contents into his palm. It was a stone the size of a very small egg of a mottled green color. He raised his gaze to Marcus, his question clear.

"A stone to detect poison, found in the gullet of a winged lion," Marcus said. "Place it in any food or drink that you fear to be poisoned. If it remains the same, all is well. If it turns black, do not consume that substance."

Amaury nodded, hiding his skepticism. "I thank you, Marcus."

"My wife says you will face treachery upon your return home, and you will have need of it."

Amaury's eyes narrowed and he tucked the stone away with care after thanking Marcus again. Rolfe wondered if there was someone at Montvieux who Amaury did not fully trust.

Next was a glass vial with a swirled stopper, sealed with wax. "A perfume that will win the heart of the most reluctant maiden," Marcus said. Niall grinned and stretched out a hand, but Marcus scoffed at him. "You have no need of this gift!" he said, then passed it to Bayard. That knight flushed, for his clumsy manner with women was a jest with the others.

"I have no need of a maiden's heart, so long as I have no home of my own," he said.

"You will have both, otherwise the gift would not have been meant for you," Marcus replied.

Bayard bowed and thanked the keeper, his appreciation clear.

Rolfe knew he was not the only one whose curiosity had been whetted. It seemed the gifts gave some hint of their respective futures.

Marcus handed Quinn a small box with a pattern of small flowers inlaid on the lid. He made to open it but the keeper stopped him. "You must keep it. When you have found the residence where you mean to remain forever, then open it and have your home blessed forevermore."

Quinn frowned a little, then smiled and nodded. Rolfe's sense redoubled that Quinn believed some trouble awaited him at Sayerne. Perhaps the overlord's messenger had told him more than he had shared.

Another velvet sack was given to Lothair, this one made of dark green silk. At Marcus' nod of encouragement, Lothair opened it and spilled the contents into his hand. It was a gold coin, but one unlike any Rolfe had seen before. It had a square hole in the middle and a swirling design that might have been script in another language. "A coin, stolen from a dragon's hoard, and one that can buy your very soul," Marcus said.

"Though none of us are surprised that it is for sale," Niall muttered, earning a quick look and a grin from Lothair.

The Viking thanked the keeper graciously and tucked the coin away.

A blade in a heavily ornamented sheath was passed then to Luc, who regarded it with awe. "A dagger that always strikes true," Marcus said. "For it has a hilt of dragon bone."

"So it can see where you cannot," Thierry said, making a reference to Luc's injured eye.

"A welcome gift. And a fine blade, as well," Luc said, turning it so that it caught the light. "This is fine steel. I thank you, Marcus!"

Thierry was given another of the small velvet sacks, this one being blue. He opened it and immediately light flooded from inside it. He removed the contents with care and the knights gasped as one at the stone that hung like a pendant from a fine silver chain. It was as clear as a drop of water, but it shone with inner light. The squires nudged each other and pushed closer to see it better.

"The Virgin's Tear," Marcus said softly. "Said to have been gathered from a maiden when the unicorn that had laid its head in her lap was snared and slaughtered." He nodded. "Its luminosity indicates the future of the bearer. When it is radiant, as it is now, all prospects are fine. But when it clouds over or turns dark, take warning."

"Thank you, Marcus," Thierry said, the awe in his voice echoing what Rolfe felt. "I will treasure this forever." Rolfe guessed he was not the only one glad to see the light shining brightly from the stone.

"This is for you," Marcus said, offering a smaller carved box to Niall. At his nod, Niall opened the box, revealing black seeds as large as a man's thumbnail. "The red bloom of passion. It grows only when a destined lover appears in the life of the bearer. Plant it and it will grow, a mark of your heart's true impulse."

"It will wait a long time for Niall to experience true love," Lothair teased. "Do the seeds become infertile in time?" The knights laughed at this.

"Whatever do you mean?" Niall asked in mock outrage. "I feel true love daily. Hourly! Each woman I meet, I cherish from the depths of my soul!"

They laughed again and Marcus shook his head. "There will be one, and you will have need of this gift to win her to your side."

"If she is clever, that will certainly be so," Niall agreed easily. He bowed. "I thank you, Marcus."

There was only one gift remaining on the table, the tall stoppered bottle of deepest black. Marcus touched it with a fingertip, then turned and presented it to Rolfe.

"This rich gift cannot be for me," he protested.

"It is," Marcus said and smiled. "For it alone has the power to make dreams come true."

Rolfe took the bottle with care, surprised that it was so heavy. It was blacker than obsidian and its surface danced with strange opalescent lights. Its slender neck curved gracefully to a bulbous base, which was etched with unfamiliar designs. It was mesmerizing to gaze upon the vessel, and even more enticing to speculate upon its contents. The stopper was made of the same dark material, its heavy cork jammed solidly into the neck. A fine silken cord of silver and gold was knotted around the stopper, then secured to the decanter's neck with a healthy dollop of red wax.

"It is too small to have a woman in it," Niall teased and Rolfe grinned.

"Let alone half a dozen," Amaury agreed.

But Rolfe knew that his dream did not involve a woman. He stared at the bottle and knew that the one thing he desired above all else was a home of his own.

It was so simple and so true.

He would be content to have a place to defend, perhaps a border territory sworn to Viandin. Five years of travel had taught him the merit of having a place to call home. This remarkable bottle, presented to his older brother Adalbert as a gift, might be rich enough to earn his brother's favor.

Adalbert, after all, had a taste for the exotic.

"I thank you, Marcus," he said with a deep bow. "I am honored by your generosity."

The knights thanked Marcus again and toasted his welfare. They remained at the tavern to eat a hot meal and plan for their departures, Thierry tracing routes on the tabletop as they debated the best way to ride. In the end, their ways did part: Rolfe, Thierry, and Luc would ride for Acre and the quicker route via Venice. Quinn and the others would ride for Constantinople. They agreed to meet in Sayerne in a year, then gathered a collection of coins for Marcus and his family.

Rolfe was packing his belongings to depart at the dawn when the bottle rattled just a little, moving on its own. He wondered what could be inside it.

Had it moved? Or had he simply indulged too much in the wine?

It did not matter. This gift was for Adalbert, and it would make Rolfe's dream come true, just as Marcus had vowed.

CHAPTER ONE

November 1101—in the forest south of the Beauvoir Pass

olfe felt the cold as never before.

The wind wound its way beneath his heavy cloak, its fingers creeping under his tabard to chill his flesh. He shivered as he rode, knowing that winter had only just bared its teeth. It had not even snowed as yet.

Clearly, his years beneath Outremer's sun had thinned his blood overmuch.

Wolves howled, their voices at greater proximity than Rolfe might have liked. He was in the forests that covered the flanks of the Alps to the south of the Beauvoir pass, and he knew it would become colder as he climbed higher. He regretted leaving Thierry and Luc in Milan, for he would have welcomed their company, but he was determined to arrive at Viandin well before the Yule.

He refused to think of the cheerful inn in Milan, or of the comfort of his fellows there. Instead, Rolfe thought of the greeting he would receive from his brother and mother, as well as the satisfaction of warmth and plentiful food. He had grown lean in his time away.

It would be worth this weather to be home.

Rolfe was keenly aware of his solitude as he rode onward. He had forgotten that a winter forest like the one surrounding him could be so bleak. He was certain there were no other men within earshot. The trees' barren branches seemed to scratch the dark bellies of the clouds scurrying across the sky. A few dry leaves scuttled over the ground, their rattle like a muttering of unwelcome intruders.

Not a creature stirred; not a bird sang.

Rolfe huddled lower in his cloak, wishing he had not taken the short cut he thought he recalled. The path had been clear at first but had dwindled. He had the odd sense that the forest was reluctant to let him pass. His way had been obstructed multiple times and he wondered if he had lost the path completely. He eyed the faint glow of the sun and hoped he had not lost his direction. On an overcast day like this one, it would be an easy error to make.

He deliberately thought of Château Viandin. His older brother, Adalbert, should feel secure in his seat as Lord de Viandin by now. He would have the administration organized and the tithes collected. He would have made his bonds with local overlords and undoubtedly be in the confidence of at least one king. Perhaps Adalbert would have a bride, even a son. Rolfe permitted himself to hope that his brother might be inclined to be generous.

He did not wish for much: just a small property to manage. Perhaps one that Adalbert wished to see securely beholden to his hand. Perhaps there was a holding on the perimeter of Viandin in need of vigorous defense. One with a bridge or a toll. Rolfe would be ideal to oversee the defense of a border, in his own opinion. It would put his experience to good use.

Adalbert, of course, might not share his view.

Rolfe's gaze fell to the black decanter lashed to his saddle. He had itched to open it since Marcus had placed it in his hands, but he was determined not to insult Adalbert with a used gift.

That would not make his dream come true.

Yet the months and the miles had fed an imagination Rolfe had not known he possessed. He had grown more certain that there was a treasure inside, simply waiting to be discovered. He imagined a rare liqueur created from pomegranates, or an exotic healing potion, or even a perfume the like of which had never been smelled west of Byzantium.

Rolfe ran a finger down the neck of the decanter.

It was then that he noticed that the wax seal had lifted cleanly away from the bottle. He was certain it had been firmly adhered before. But now the glittering cord swung free and the seal was still whole upon it.

Perhaps the cold had lifted it from the bottle.

He could satisfy his curiosity without Adalbert ever knowing the difference.

Rolfe did not need to consider the matter twice.

He pulled his destrier to an unceremonious halt before he could question his impulse. Mephistopheles' ears flicked, as though the beast made a comment about stopping where there was no sign of shelter, but Rolfe ignored him.

He freed Adalbert's gift from the lashing with impatient fingers, then halted in wonder once the weight of it filled his hand. The dark bottle fit perfectly into his gloved palm, and he sat, turning it and transfixed by the lights reflected from its surface, for a long moment. A fresh gust of wind swirled around him, lifting the ends of his cloak, and Rolfe shivered.

He tried to twist the cork free, but it was more resolutely anchored than he might have expected. Rolfe grimaced as he pulled, but to no avail. Mephistopheles nickered, impatient with their delay, and when the beast danced sideways, Rolfe's grip on the bottle slipped. It leaped from his grip and for a terrifying moment, it was loose in the air. Rolfe managed to snatch it out of the air before it fell to the ground, and he closed his eyes in relief.

It was obvious he needed a sure footing for this task. He dismounted then twisted the dark top with all his might.

The cork popped with sudden vigor, its release sending Rolfe sprawling backward. When he fell, the bottle danced from his grip.

"Fool!" he muttered and lunged after the bottle. To his relief, it hit the ground and rolled without breaking. It stopped an arm's length away, apparently undamaged.

Perhaps it was charmed. Rolfe exhaled shakily and reached for the bottle. Nothing had spilled from it either and he wondered if it might be empty after all.

No sooner had his hand closed around its base than something began to spew forth from its mouth. It was neither elixir, nor liqueur, nor exotic scent.

As Rolfe stared, a dark cloud billowed from the bottle with alarming speed. It was unnatural, to say the least. He dropped the decanter and stepped backward, staring in awe at the erupting cloud. What had he released?

How would he get it back inside for Adalbert?

The dark mist swirled into the shape of a tall woman with long dark hair. She was before him, yet she was not. Her features were clearly visible, but Rolfe could also see the trees through her form. His heart skipped in fear as she loomed high above him.

It stopped when she fixed her gaze upon him.

Rolfe swallowed. This sight could not be real.

The vision leaned closer as he struggled to make sense of what he saw. Obviously, this was some trickery, like that caused by certain mushrooms.

It was an illusion, if a very detailed one.

"You!" the shadow roared and pointed a finger at him.

Rolfe jumped at the volume of her voice.

As far as he knew, visions from mushrooms were silent.

But he was not the only one to have heard the vision's cry. His palfrey, usually content to follow Mephistopheles, whinnied in fright and tugged vehemently at its reins. It snapped the leather from Rolfe's astonished grip and bolted into the woods.

Curse the skittish creature! His supplies were in the palfrey's saddlebags! That fact recalled Rolfe to his senses. He called after the palfrey, but she did not halt.

He turned angrily on the vision responsible for his woes. "You have frightened one of my steeds and now my supplies are lost!"

"Me?" she purred, and Rolfe shivered. The specter leaned closer suddenly and he was granted a view of wickedly sharp teeth.

Perhaps he should have worded his question more politely.

The scents of saffron, cinnamon, cloves, and ambergris flooded Rolfe's nostrils as her dark cloud surrounded him. He struggled to explain the presence of smells that had no place in this northern forest and failed.

Losing his palfrey might be the least of his problems.

"Confess to me your name, mortal," she growled.

"Rolfe de Viandin." He answered before he could question the wisdom of doing so. He was dismayed to find his voice no more than a shadow of its usual bold tone.

"So, it is Rolfe de Viandin who condemns me to leave my beloved palace in this place. Trust a mortal man to complicate matters!"

The specter spat. The ground melted with a hiss where the missile landed, just to Rolfe's left. He watched in alarm as a cloud of steam rose from the spot.

He should have set that old cheese aside at midday, he reasoned wildly. Clearly, the cheese had been past its prime. He had suspected as much at the time but hunger had compelled him to avoid wasting it.

He would discard the rest of it.

Rolfe eased a little farther away from this manifestation of a sour stomach.

Caution was the better part of valor, after all.

Before he got far, the vision flung her arms wide with a bellow of astonishing volume. The cloud, still erupting from the bottle, boiled angrily beneath her.

"A curse upon you, Rolfe de Viandin!" she cried, pointing a finger directly at him. The fury of her gaze made him tremble in his boots, despite all he had faced in the past few years. "A mortal man is at the root of my woes and you shall pay the price of the faithlessness of your kind!"

That did not sound promising, but Rolfe had little time to reflect upon her words.

The dark cloud began to swirl like a tempest, picking up dirt and leaves, gathering them in a spinning column. Rolfe's cloak whipped around him, its hem snapping across Mephistopheles' side, and his hair blew across his brow, obscuring his vision.

He snatched at the cloak, closed his eyes, and lifted his arm over his face to protect himself from the unexpected assault. He leaned his face against his destrier, who snorted indignantly and lowered his head. Rolfe was halfway certain that every scrap of clothing he wore would be ripped apart. He did not dare to consider how cheese could manage such a feat.

Then, as suddenly as it had begun, the raging wind fell silent.

Inexplicably, Rolfe heard a bird sing.

His garments seemed suddenly too warm and he felt the heat of the sun upon his head. Rolfe lifted his head and blinked in shock at the sight that greeted his eyes.

He stood in a garden surrounded by lushly fragrant and exotic blooms, although that seemed decidedly against the odds. Was this an illusion, as well? He stared in disbelief. Golden sunlight poured on the blossoms around him and the air was alive with the hum of insects. The bleak forest where he had ridden just moments past was nowhere to be seen.

Truly, the cheese had outdone itself.

Surrounding the garden was a high wall made of an unfamiliar white stone, artfully fitted and gleaming so brightly in the sunlight that it might have been made of silver. A low palace stretched out behind him. A long pool lined with blue tiles guided the eye directly to its doorway, and the scent of Eastern cooking teased his nostrils.

Rolfe blinked, but the illusion stubbornly remained.

As did the specter before him. She folded her arms across her chest, dissatisfaction clear in the harsh line of her lips.

Rolfe licked his lips. He had hoped for a home and now he stood in a palace. She had said she would surrender it to him. He had been cold and yearned for warmth.

Was this vessel trying to make his dreams come true?

That was beyond belief.

It had to be an illusion or a jest. Rolfe braced his booted feet on the ground and faced the vision. "What manner of trickery is this?" he demanded. "I insist that you return me to the forest and restore my palfrey."

She arched a brow. "Make no mistake, mortal, my palace is as real as you are."

Rolfe eyed his surroundings. He shed his gloves, sniffed a bloom, fingered the leaves of a shrub, and found nothing amiss. A type of insect he did not recognize ambled along the shrub's leaves and he touched it.

It stung him. Rolfe cursed and leaped backward, shaking the creature from his hand.

He eyed the specter. "Where are we? What have you done?"

"You are precisely where you were before," she replied. "It is my palace that has moved here, to satisfy the curse laid upon me." Her eyes narrowed to fierce slits and her voice dropped low. "Now it is yours. I hope that you are satisfied." There was no denying her bitterness, which made Rolfe wonder if she told the truth.

Wolves bayed in the distance, their howls carrying over the walls in support of her claim.

There were no wolves in the East, from whence this palace seemed to have sprung. And he had heard wolves in the forest just before opening the bottle.

This must be a deception, and he had only to figure out how it had been accomplished.

"I do not understand," Rolfe said, although he thought he might. "What have I done? If this is your palace, take it where you will. It is not my fault that it is here."

The spirit granted him a chilling glance. "Of course, it is your doing!" she replied. "Do you imagine that I would *choose* such a dismal locale?" She shuddered and eyed him with accusation. "It was you who opened the bottle and you to whom I am indebted for my release."

"You seem less than pleased," he replied. "Surely to be released from confinement is no small thing?"

"Perhaps it would be a relief if I did not have to pay such a heavy price! Who would be pleased to give their greatest treasure to a mere mortal?"

At that, Rolfe was insulted. Mere mortal? "I asked you for nothing!"

The specter bent down, her eyes flashing with fury. "And what you want is of no consequence! Trust me, mortal, if I could betray my obligation, I most surely would, for no being ever deserved such a gift less than a mortal man!" She folded her arms across her chest once more. "But a curse required me to grant possession of my palace to whoever freed me from my prison. Even a djinn must adhere to some code of honor."

A djinn? Rolfe had heard of those beings but had never believed they existed.

She glanced about herself, her displeasure more than clear. "Though nothing was said of doing so with grace."

But no one would surrender such a palace willingly. A tale too fair was seldom true. This had to be a trick, a trick designed to rid him of his possessions. The palfrey was already gone, and with it a goodly quantity of his supplies.

Rolfe glared at the inexplicable being before him. He had heard of such deceptions. Bayard had been cheated of his coin upon arrival in Outremer, having been convinced to pay for a saddle for a steed that he could have free of charge. He had paid for the saddle, then both steed and saddle had vanished in the night, leaving him penniless and without a mount.

Rolfe's grip tightened on Mephistopheles' reins. No one would take from him what was his.

"You grant nothing to me," Rolfe argued. "This is merely a trick."

The djinn's eyes blazed. "A trick? You spurn my glorious gift?"

"I have no need of your spells and sorcery," he retorted. "Return my palfrey and let me continue on my way."

"No need?" the djinn echoed. Another wolf howled beyond the walls and a glint lit her eye. Dread trickled down Rolfe's spine, and he took a step back before he could stop himself.

The djinn pursued him with terrifying speed. Her face filled Rolfe's vision, and when she smiled, he saw that her teeth were not just sharp, but points of brass.

"Perhaps you will soon see the need of spells and sorcery," she hissed. "I reserve the right to reward ingratitude." She drew herself up taller and flung her hands skyward, her growing size making both Rolfe and his black destrier ease toward the gates.

Rolfe wondered if they could flee while her attention was averted.

"Rolfe de Viandin," she roared, and the ground trembled at her words.

*"Ingratitude for my gift has earned you this strife:
as a wolf, you will live out your life!"*

A wolf!

Despite his conviction that this was nonsense, Rolfe waited for a moment, holding his breath. When nothing changed, he dared to feel relief. His relief was quickly followed by scorn.

Spells and sorcery were fables.

"A wolf?" he repeated, his tone skeptical.

"You do not believe me?"

Rolfe shrugged. "I believe in what I see, as well as what I can hold in my hands. I see that nothing has changed. I suspect that you and this—" he gestured to the palace "—are a reminder that the cheese I ate at midday was past its prime."

"Cheese?" the djinn echoed. Rolfe jumped at the volume of her voice and even Mephistopheles' eyes widened. "You dare to attribute my presence to cheese?"

Her eyes flashed as the clear sky was abruptly obscured by dark clouds. Thunder rumbled overhead. Lightning crackled and the ground stirred beneath Rolfe's feet. The black destrier stepped sideways with a skittishness more typical of the lost palfrey.

"I am more than mere cheese and you will see the truth!"

"Perhaps I should have been more tactful," Rolfe murmured. Mephistopheles flicked one ear, as if to agree. The djinn grew to the height of a mountain before them and Rolfe could not help but dread her pronouncement.

Cheese. Rolfe repeated the word like a litany, but as he watched the ominous cloud grow, his conviction faded.

When the djinn spoke again, her voice made the ground shake. The trees quivered from the tumult of her breath. The flowers abruptly closed against the storm.

*"Powers vested beneath the earth,
Hear my words and attend my curse.
Teach this one to respect my powers;
Leave him trapped outside these towers.
Condemn him to howl and prowl near,*

This place a reminder of all he held dear.
Mortal ways he shall pursue no more,
Doomed to remember forevermore.
Let the one who crosses this threshold first,
Be condemned to wed him despite his curse.
And let the one in whom he confides,
Lead a killer to his side."

The wind ripped at Rolfe's cloak again as her voice fell silent. When the wind stilled and he opened his eyes, he was outside the smooth white walls. The silent forest surrounded him again, and snow fell thickly around him. There was no sign of the djinn, although winter had fallen with a sudden vengeance. At least Mephistopheles was still by his side, perhaps because he still clutched the reins tightly.

"May you be as miserable as I have been, mortal!" The djinn's voice came from every side, though she was not within view.

Rolfe spun around, but he could not see her.

Or the bottle for Adalbert.

Much less his palfrey.

"Look for your change by nightfall." Her laughter filled the forest, coming from everywhere and nowhere at all.

Rolfe shivered, telling himself it was only the unexpected change of temperature he felt. The sky was darkening, though he refused to let himself dread the night.

"Cheese," he said to Mephistopheles. Although he spoke to the destrier, he knew his words were meant to reassure himself as much as any.

"The vision is clearly over," he continued with a resolve he was far from feeling. "We are in the forest, just as we were before and, undoubtedly, just as we have been all along. It is not surprising in the least that I did not see this palace wall, for it is as white as the falling snow."

Rolfe waved his hand, deliberately ignoring the fact that it had not been snowing earlier. "Perfectly logical," he concluded. "We will seek the palfrey and continue our journey home. Perhaps Adalbert will be indulgent even though I have lost his gift."

Mephistopheles gave his knight a glance that might have been skeptical, had it come from a man instead of a beast. Then the horse's gaze fell pointedly on the space behind Rolfe. Mephistopheles snorted and tossed his head, backing away from his knight.

A curious tickling sensation made Rolfe dread what he might see. He turned and caught a glimpse of a silver-gray tail.

Rolfe twisted, and the tail danced merrily out of sight as he turned in ever tighter circles, trying to get a better look at it.

He grabbed at it, his eyes widening in shock at the answering tug he felt. The tail trapped within his grip was long and quite firmly affixed to him. It was graced with thick silver hair that shaded to white at the tip.

Precisely like that of a wolf.

Before he could utter another sound, Mephistopheles nickered a warning.

Rolfe swiveled to see the bottle rolling across the ground, seemingly of its own volition. Where had it come from? What would spill from its mouth now? More trouble, to be sure, but Rolfe could not see the cork anywhere.

He knew he should flee, but he could not tear his gaze away from the bottle. It rolled first this way and then the other, leaving a trail in the thickly falling snow. He was struck by the conviction that something was trying to get out of it.

Where was the cork?

He had seized a fistful of snow, hoping to jam it into the vessel, when a voice spoke from its interior. He dropped the decanter in surprise.

"A curse upon this bottle! In all truth, one would think that to be free of her company would be blessing indeed, but no! This wretched bottle has to hamper my departure in a most uncomfortable way. Too many centuries waiting for rescue has a way of going to one's hips, I suppose, but *truly...*"

Rolfe's eyes widened. Mephistopheles stamped his hooves when the feminine voice squeaked.

"Oh! I never thought I had indulged that much. Certainly, she consumed twice what I did, if not more, but perhaps malice is better for the figure in the long run. Would that not be a sad statement on the world, if such were the case! I cannot imagine it, but certainly, it would appear to be so."

It was another djinn.

Rolfe had had enough of djinns and their interference for this day.

"Away with you!" he shouted. "Trouble another if you must, but leave me be! I have had my share of djinns and their curses to last a lifetime!"

The voice fell silent, but Rolfe intended to put as much distance between himself and the vessel as possible. He flung the bottle through the air, no longer wanting to take it home. It did not travel as far as Rolfe might have hoped before bouncing in the snow. Another muffled squeak had Rolfe reaching for his saddle, tail or no.

He had no intention of waiting like a fool to see what this djinn's response might be.

A rosy cloud unfurled from the bottle's mouth this time, making the air around Rolfe and his destrier glow like the first light of dawn.

It was not unpleasant.

Rolfe found himself glancing back over his shoulder in curiosity, one foot in the stirrup.

"Much better, oh yes, much better indeed," that feminine voice declared. "What a relief it is to have room to stretch."

The glow grew high and wide, stretching out to encompass all of the surrounding woods, before rolling back into a tight orb. That sphere radiated an opalescent light, but beyond its periphery, the sky grew steadily darker. It was as if the moon floated before Rolfe, or a small version of it.

Rolfe leaned closer then there was a loud crack that made him jump.

A plump woman of indeterminate age sat on the upturned bottle. She smiled at Rolfe and propped her chin on her hand to study him, as if there was nothing unusual about her sudden appearance at all.

Rolfe blinked and she smiled at him.

She wore the sheer trousers and upturned leather shoes like those he had seen in Outremer, topped by a high-necked, heavily embroidered tunic. Her hair was dark and hung on either side of her face in thick braids. She wore a round fur hat with red woolen balls dangling from its rim, and those balls danced as she moved her head. A broadsword much like Rolfe's own hung by her side.

She returned his regard intently for a moment then suddenly stared down at herself.

"Oh, my," she whispered and one hand rose to her lips.

A shimmer of light blinded Rolfe for a moment. He blinked, and incredibly, in that short interval, the woman's garb changed.

She wore a fitted blue kirtle over an undyed chemise and a fur-lined cloak that fell all the way to her boots. She looked like any noblewoman Rolfe might have seen before, with the exception of her strange hat which remained.

She touched it and smiled at Rolfe's glance. "It is warm," she informed him. She had a certain girlish charm, but he would not be swayed from his suspicions.

"Are you another djinn?" he asked, realizing that his tone was hostile.

"Yes, that I am." She drew herself taller. "I must say your manner is decidedly forward, if not rude."

"My manner is nothing compared to that of the last djinn I met," Rolfe declared. "How many of you are in there?"

She looked startled by his question. "Only two, mercifully, for she was company enough for me." She sighed. "I can tell you that centuries take considerably longer to pass than one might think when the company is less than ideal."

Rolfe had no idea how to reply, but she continued as if not expecting him to do so.

"I am so relieved to be released. I should even grant you a wish." She frowned and tapped one finger on her lip. "Was that how it worked?" she mused to herself. "One wish? Three wishes?" She flicked a glance at Rolfe. "One must follow the rules, you know."

The last djinn had spoken similarly just before she had taken her vengeance upon Rolfe.

Clearly, it was time to leave.

"It does not matter," he said hastily. "I thank you, but have no need of any favors from djinns." He took several quick steps backward and reached for his saddle once more. Could he mount and ride away without her stopping him? It was certainly worth a try.

"Oh, but I must insist—"

"No, it is best saved for another. If you will excuse me?" Rolfe pivoted and had one foot in a stirrup before she clicked her tongue.

"Oh, she is good," she said.

Rolfe knew this djinn had spotted his tail and he felt his neck heat in embarrassment. Something tingled at his fingertips before he could speak, and he glanced down to find his nails had turned dark.

Like claws. Panic made him spin back to face the djinn, for lack of other alternatives.

He was changing to a wolf!

Right before his own eyes.

Perhaps spells and sorcery had their uses, after all.

"You said you could grant me a wish?" he asked. The djinn nodded. "Can you undo her spell?"

"Undo?" The djinn shook her head. "No one can *undo* anything. That is not the way."

"Then you cannot help me?"

The djinn sat up straight. "I did not say that," she replied. "I will help you, despite your manner, because I think she was ungracious in cursing her liberator. We had hopes, you know, that time would cure her of her malicious tendencies, but it seems she has only become more vengeful." The djinn fired a glance at Rolfe. "And I was always taught that there was no excuse for rudeness, under any circumstance."

Rolfe averted his gaze, for he knew his own manners had been decidedly lacking.

Even if there were extenuating circumstances. The wind riffled through his new tail as though to remind him of the precise nature of those circumstances.

"I do apologize," he said. "I have never encountered a djinn before, much less two in rapid succession."

"Of course not," the djinn replied. "We are somewhat rare, although I have always been burdened with an inexplicable affection for mortals."

Rolfe did not miss her slight emphasis. He felt himself color and decided his charm had picked a poor time to desert him. "I apologize for my earlier manner..." he began, trying to make matters right.

The djinn, however, seemed to have forgotten his presence. "Let me see..." she mused. She tapped one fingertip against her lips, clearly thinking.

Suddenly, Rolfe's ears felt odd. He lifted one hand, hoping that he would not find what he feared, but fur greeted his touch. His ears were pointed and covered with fur.

The djinn did not appear to notice, and frustration filled Rolfe.

Was he to be no more than a pawn in these djinns' foolish games?

What had he done to merit such a fate?

"God's wounds, woman!" Rolfe cried in his impatience. She jumped in a most satisfactory way. "Think if you must, but do it quickly! I will be all wolf before you are done!"

The djinn's gaze landed on him and her eyes widened in surprise. "How very quickly she works," she murmured. She pursed her lips, looking all of six summers old as she concentrated.

> *"Powers above and powers below,*
> *attend my words as never befo'e.*
> *Cursed by day is enough to pay..."*

She hesitated and nibbled on her bottom lip as she clearly fought to make a rhyme.

It said something about Rolfe's fortune that the malicious djinn had possessed a greater gift with words.

"Befo'e?" he echoed.

The djinn shot him a hostile glance. "Spells are not my greatest talent," she informed him archly. She closed her eyes before Rolfe could respond. "Now, I have forgotten where I was." She frowned, and he did not dare interrupt again.

"Alakazam, by night be a man."

She nodded with satisfaction at her own conclusion.
Rolfe caught his breath.
He waited.
He watched.
Nothing changed.
If anything, his tail seemed a little more thick.
This djinn's powers were apparently less than compelling.
And little wonder, given the quality of her rhymes.
"Alakazam," Rolfe repeated under his breath. "Now there is a spell." He rolled his eyes, then was took such a blow to the shoulder that he nearly fell to his knees. Rolfe staggered to regain his balance and glanced about himself. There was no one behind him.

The djinn smiled at him with such serenity that he knew she had somehow struck him without moving.

"A completely inexplicable affection," she reminded him. Any urge Rolfe might have felt to apologize was swept away by her next words. "But quite a nice spell, I think, all the same."

"That is all? You intend to do no more?" Rolfe was astonished. "What manner of solution is that? Being a wolf by day is little better than being one all of the time! With all respect, I must say that I had hoped for more!"

The djinn rose to her feet. "I told you that I could not undo the charm," she said. "In truth, for spontaneous work, I thought it was not at all bad." She eyed him, as if this situation were all his own fault. "My best work is not performed under duress."

Rolfe fought to maintain his temper. Half his time as a wolf was better than all the time.

Maybe she could do better yet, if his manner was sweeter than it had been so far. His charm had brought him good fortune in the past, if not the grace of more than one maiden's favors. He might do well to spare some of his charisma for this djinn.

Mindful that he could easily make his situation worse, Rolfe bowed to the djinn. "You have indeed outdone yourself in aiding me on such short notice."

The djinn eyed him, clearly skeptical of his change of tone, and Rolfe spared her his most winning smile. She thawed a little, though her gaze flicked away. The feminine gesture was familiar and fed Rolfe's confidence as nothing else could.

It was reassuring that djinns and mortal women were not that dissimilar.

"Make no mistake, *madame,*" he continued. "I do appreciate your endeavors. Undoubtedly, the shock of this change made me speak in haste." Rolfe held her gaze when she turned to him, and deliberately let his voice deepen. "I would thank you with all my heart for your assistance."

The djinn granted him a smile. "I could try again," she offered.

"You cannot imagine how greatly I would appreciate your efforts," Rolfe said. Encouraged by her offer, he dared to suggest once more, "Perhaps we could remove the entire curse?"

"Oh, no." The djinn dismissed his suggestion without giving it the consideration Rolfe thought it deserved. "It is not the way. You must earn your salvation with the conditions you have been granted. I cannot change that, but I can grant another point in your favor."

"Earn?" His temper flared. "I did nothing to earn this curse!"

A tingling sensation halted his protest. Rolfe looked down to find silver fur sprouting all over his flesh. He gasped aloud, but his voice sounded more like a muffled yelp.

He appealed to the djinn, but she only shrugged.

She shook a finger beneath Rolfe's nose, which he was alarmed to see had turned black. "*You* opened the bottle," she explained. "Do you not see? That deed earned you this."

"But can you not do something? I beg of you, *madame,* help me however you can!"

"Well, perhaps a little more," the djinn mused, her expression considering.

"Then hurry! Please!"

"I told you that I do not like to be pressured."

Rolfe was going to interrupt her, but his voice was a bark this time. Panic flooded through him, but the djinn merely closed her eyes again.

> *"Though when cursed by day,*
> *in the garden he cannot play,*
> *let him in at night*
> *to avoid the forest's plight.*
> *And whether he feel good or ill,*
> *the palace shall reflect his will.*
> *Finally, by grace of the powers above,*
> *let this curse be broken by the blessing of love."*

She opened her eyes and smiled with satisfaction. "That was rather a good one, was it not?"

Rolfe could not confess to be in the least pleased by the djinn's intervention. He thought he had won her assistance! Forest's plight? Blessing of love?

What manner of solution was this?

He did not believe in love. That was a whimsy favored by women, and truly not a condition for his release that would suffice.

There was a shimmer beside him and Mephistopheles disappeared. Rolfe had been deprived of his possessions, after all.

He barked in frustration, but it was too late. He ran upon all fours in the snow around the djinn. He could see that the sun was sinking and the shadows were growing longer.

How could that be? What about her spell? Night was falling and he was still a wolf. Rolfe howled deliberately at the stars overhead, then fixed the djinn with an accusing glance.

The djinn's lips twisted as she considered the hue of the sky overhead. "It is just a question of timing," she assured Rolfe but he knew he was not the only one who was not convinced. "That is far and away the most complicated part of casting spells."

Rolfe had thought it was the rhymes she found troubling, but he could hardly argue with her.

He heard his destrier nicker from inside the walls of the palace, then the stallion kicked the gates from the other side. How did the palace reflect his will if his horse was inside and he was outside?

The djinn smiled tentatively. "He is safe from wolves," she suggested.

The palfrey neighed then, the sound also coming from inside the walls. He had been robbed of both of his steeds.

The djinn shrugged. "Both safe," she offered. "You wanted a home." She smiled. "We do advise that one should be careful of making wishes."

Rolfe snarled for the first time and liked the feel of it.

He enjoyed the way the djinn jumped when he did it. She retreated behind her bottle, as if that small vessel could defend her, and watched him warily.

"You know, it is not very fitting to have her flying freely," she said. "There was a reason why she was confined to this bottle in the first place, as you can well imagine. It might be wise to see her thus confined again. You could help..."

That was enough. Rolfe was finished with djinns and their curses. He could see no benefit to furthering their association.

There was one good way to express his opinion.

He lunged toward the djinn and bared his teeth. He snapped, and though his jaws closed on empty air, he was convinced he had made his feelings clear.

"Well, well." The djinn sniffed from several feet away. "I see I shall have to find someone else to assist me. It is a most inexplicable affection." She snatched up the bottle she had vacated, then pivoted and stalked off into the forest. The red balls on her hat bounced indignantly as she walked. Her footsteps left no mark upon the surface of the snow, and in the twinkling of an eye, she had disappeared completely.

Rolfe was left alone in the forest outside the first djinn's palace.

Were it not for his changed form and the palace wall behind him, the entire incident might not have happened.

Wolves howled again, although they were closer, and Rolfe felt a primal urge to lift his voice along with theirs. The forest was more alien to him than it had ever been. He was snared and he was cursed.

Marcus had been wrong. This was a far cry from making his

dreams come true.

Although Rolfe was uncertain what he could do about it.

And the knowledge that he was powerless in this situation was what bothered him most of all.

CHAPTER TWO

December—Beauvoir Keep

nnelise's worst nightmare was unfolding before her very eyes and, worse, there was little she could do about it. She had already been chided once for not paying attention to her embroidery.

"Yves, the most sensible course would be to wed your sister to Hildegarde's son." Bertrand de Beauvoir clapped Annelise's younger brother on the shoulder as if they were comrades. Though his manner was friendly—more friendly than he had ever been to Yves in the past—Annelise wondered why the old mercenary was so certain what choice Yves should make.

She was not certain that Bertrand had ever before spoken directly to Yves before. Her younger brother was a bastard, true enough, but their father had let him be raised within the walls of Château Sayerne.

Indeed, Jerome de Sayerne had not been without his own motives in that choice or any other. It had been her own father who had taught Annelise to look behind a man's smooth words to the truth of his intentions.

What would Bertrand gain from this proposed match?

"I am not certain Annelise should wed a man I know so little about," Yves replied calmly.

Annelise cast him a look but he ignored her. Why would he not ask her opinion? She parted her lips to protest but Bertrand's wife shushed her.

Again.

That woman's agitation convinced Annelise to be silent. She had a good idea why the other woman might fear her husband and had no desire to make trouble.

Was it so unreasonable to want to wed for love or not at all?

With their father deceased, Yves was all the family she had left. It was annoying that a half-brother, who had not seen her in years, would be asked to decide her fate while she would not be permitted to comment. Indeed, it seemed the place of women in the wider world was not so different from that of the convent. Frustration roiled within Annelise.

She had a legitimate brother, Quinn, though she had never met him. Quinn had left Sayerne to earn his own way before Annelise had even been conceived. No one was certain of his location and Annelise was glad of it. She would never forget the tales her father had told of the cruelty of his first-born.

Considering the source, Quinn was not a man she ever wanted to encounter.

That was why they were at Beauvoir. She knew they had been right to leave Château Sayerne when they had heard that Quinn would soon return home again. It suited Annelise's sense of justice to leave the man who had inherited her father's cruelty a second worthless legacy.

Château Sayerne, the traditional holding of Annelise's family, might once have been a prize but was so no longer. Jerome had let the estate fall into neglect and, with his death, the last of Sayerne's tenants had fled. This past year, not a single seed had been sown in Sayerne's fields. The holding had declined so greatly from its original state that Annelise and Yves had not even needed to discuss the merit of leaving once they learned of Quinn's pending return.

Neither of them had looked back.

Beauvoir was, in marked contrast to Sayerne, a comfortable

keep, despite its remote location. Bertrand, the new Lord de Beauvoir, had been entrusted with the strategic task of guarding the Beauvoir Pass by their overlord, Lord de Tulley. At this pass, the old Roman road passed out of Lord de Tulley's holdings on its route south to Rome. Château Beauvoir was perched on the apex of the pass and built across the road itself. No one could cross the mountains without paying the toll.

Beauvoir's tower was as narrow as a needle, like a finger pointed to heaven, its construction having been restricted by the rocky terrain on all sides. There were windows only at the very top of the tower, in Bertrand's solar and the guard's watch above. To say that the keep was heavily garrisoned would have been an understatement. It was the most military keep in all of Tulley's holdings, which said much about its strategic location.

On this night, Annelise and Bertrand's wife were the only women to be found within the walls. Annelise had been keenly aware of the soldiers' gazes following her every move and could not wait to leave Beauvoir behind. She felt like prey or like a prize to be seized.

The question was where she and Yves would ride.

The chamber that Bertrand used to administer his holding was adjacent to the great hall. It was a sparsely furnished room, although the pieces there were fine ones. A merry fire burned in the brazier and the air was smoky but warm.

Silver-haired Bertrand sat in a high-backed oak chair that faced the fire, its wooden arms worn to a smooth patina. The lines on his face were etched into a severe expression, and he looked every inch the experienced commander that he was.

His wife perched closer to the fire on a three-legged stool, much like the one Annelise used, although the lady had a cushion of wool dyed richly red. A mousy woman with almost no color in her complexion, Bertrand's wife bent over her embroidery, her shoulders rounded, her demeanor meek. Annelise had yet to hear her speak a word unbidden.

The way she looked at her husband was enough to chill Annelise's heart.

Annelise, in contrast, was seldom so quiet. Her outspoken

nature had been the greatest challenge of her time at the convent dedicated to Ste. Radegund and their vow of silence had been one reason she had so despised her time there.

The golden light from the fire cast what was a tense discussion in a falsely warm glow of intimacy. The light burnished Yves' mail to silver and cast mysterious shadows in the secret corners of the room.

"She must wed, though," Bertrand said to Yves as if Annelise was not even present. "A man cannot make his way dragging a sister by his side." The older man's silver brows drew together sternly. "You did ask me for advice, after all, and this is the only option that makes good sense. I know of no other suitable men seeking a bride at this time."

"Perhaps someone might ask my opinion," Annelise murmured. "After all, it is my future that you discuss." Bertrand's wife shot a warning glance in her direction, but both men continued as though she had not spoken.

Yves tapped his toe. "Perhaps the Lord de Tulley should be consulted about this match," he mused. "I would not want to offend him by taking the matter into my own hands."

Since their father's demise, Yves had shown a decisive side that Annelise had barely glimpsed before. She did not really care for this aspect of her half-brother, for it reminded her of her father's determination.

Annelise was forced to acknowledge that she truly did not know Yves that well. She had returned to Sayerne from the convent only a year before Jerome's death, after all.

"Nonsense!" Bertrand dismissed Yves' comment. "Tulley has too much on his board these days to trifle with the match of a noblewoman without a dowry. You must make a match where you can and see the matter resolved with haste."

Annelise felt her color rise at being discussed like some baggage to be forced on another.

"But who is this Hildegarde?" Yves asked, only the first of many questions Annelise had.

"Hildegarde de Viandin, an old family friend. Her husband, Millard, and I trained together. Sadly, Millard passed away some years ago."

Annelise licked a thread and fed the floss through the eye of the needle. *A lady should hold her tongue.* She repeated the nuns' admonition to herself silently.

Bertrand cleared his throat. "She wrote last summer to ask whether I knew of a suitable young woman to marry her second son. The eldest, of course, is the heir, but Hildegarde might be persuaded to ensure that the younger son be granted a small holding."

Yves said nothing, and Bertrand continued. "Annelise cannot expect to do much better, you know, given her lack of dowry. And everyone knows about the curse of her forthright manner." He fired a glance at Annelise that kept her from protesting the accusation.

The nuns would have been proud of her, she thought, and jabbed the needle into the linen.

"The timing is most opportune, Yves, and the family is a good one. Their holdings are prosperous, and your sister would have a most satisfactory life."

Annelise could keep silent no longer. "Satisfactory by whose standards?"

Bertrand visibly gritted his teeth. "It is a curse," he muttered, and Yves' lips tightened.

"It is not a curse to know one's own mind," Annelise argued, ensuring her tone was polite. "I fail to see how my opinion could not be relevant. You are discussing my future and marriage to a man with whom I would be destined to spend the rest of my life."

"Annelise, can you be silent for once?" Yves said impatiently. "You know that this decision is not yours to make."

"I do not like it."

"It does not matter what you like," Yves retorted in a sharp tone he had never used with her before. "A sensible choice must be made and I will make it."

"You might ask me..."

"I know what you will say. You are not in love with any man, so far as I know, so you would remain unwed," Yves replied. He flung out a hand. "Where will you go, a maiden with no dowry?"

"I thought I would stay with you."

"You were wrong."

Annelise's conviction that Yves would do his best for her faltered.

Yves paced across the wooden floor in the shadows beyond Bertrand, his hands clasped behind his back, his bright blond hair catching the light. His expressive amber eyes, so like her own, were hidden from view, and Annelise felt that her brother had become a stranger.

He straightened, and before the words even fell from his mouth, Annelise saw that Yves meant to agree with Bertrand. She tossed the needlework aside, hating Yves for betraying her treasured hopes.

How dare he cast her desire aside for his own convenience?

Before she could utter a word, though, there was a knock on the door.

"Lord Enguerrand de Roussineau to see his lordship," Bertrand's manservant announced.

Bertrand winced, then composed his expression and beckoned with one stately finger. His wife set aside her embroidery and scurried to call for refreshment. Annelise watched as a young man of whom she had heard much—and little of it complimentary— swept into Bertrand's chamber.

Enguerrand was dark-haired, and more lavishly dressed than Annelise would have expected he could afford. There was a dusting of snow across the heavy green cloak tossed over his shoulders, and more snow on his boots. He brought a whiff of the night into the chamber and she guessed that he had just arrived. His gaze flitted over the room and she knew she did not imagine that his eyes gleamed when he spotted her.

That made her dread his mission.

Enguerrand smiled then, bowing low to Bertrand, as if Annelise was not there. The older man tolerated the gesture, although he arched a brow at Yves over the new arrival's head as though he, too, wondered at Enguerrand's purpose. Enguerrand accepted the welcome cup offered by Bertrand's wife, although he took no notice of the woman herself.

He did not even show the courtesy to thank her.

Annelise was glad to bend over her needlework rather than to speak with this man.

"It is long since we have had the honor of your company," Bertrand said with a coldness that could not be missed.

Enguerrand spoke warmly, in contrast. "Bertrand, neighbor of mine, I come for tidings. Do you know the whereabouts of Annelise de Sayerne? I have just found Sayerne deserted and Tulley is away at battle."

"Why do you seek my sister?" Yves demanded.

Enguerrand jumped as though he had not seen the younger man, that ruse making Annelise distrust him even more. His eyes narrowed as he surveyed Yves. "Sister?" he asked. "I had thought Jerome de Sayerne had only two children."

"Two legitimate children," Yves confirmed, his stance proud. "I am his bastard, although my father spoke of giving me legal status as his son."

"But he did not?"

"No."

"Ah!" There was no mistaking the relief that swept over Enguerrand's features. His gaze slid to Annelise once more. "Might this be the fair Annelise herself?"

Annelise rose to her feet and set her handwork aside. "I am Annelise de Sayerne," she admitted. "Why do you seek me?"

Enguerrand sank to his knee before Annelise and lifted her hand to his lips. "Fairest Annelise," he murmured against her fingers. "I am most charmed to make your acquaintance."

"Indeed?" Annelise should have returned the compliment and she knew it.

"Indeed," Enguerrand confirmed, undeterred. "Your beauty is more than I might have hoped for when I set out to seek your hand in marriage."

"Marriage?"

That the subject should come up twice in such short order was beyond belief. Annelise had always been told how unsuitable she was for marriage, both by her father and by the nuns. Too outspoken, too poorly skilled in household tasks, too tall. Her auburn hair was a liability—it had to mark a fearsome temper and, worst of all, she was without a dowry.

Yet two offers for her hand were to be heard on the same day, within moments of each other.

Why would this man seek her out? Annelise wondered whether Enguerrand believed that Quinn would not return home. Perhaps he desired Sayerne for himself.

Was that also Lady Hildegarde's motivation? Did she seek a holding for her younger son outside her elder son's legacy of Viandin?

Would either of them be pleased with the reality of Sayerne's impoverished state, even if Annelise did inherit it? This knight did not look like one inclined to work hard to gain his desires.

And what if Quinn did come home as Tulley insisted he would? Annelise would bring nothing to any match, then, and might find herself in a similar position as her mother.

The prospect made her heart chill.

"Yes, my lady," Enguerrand continued with confidence in her acceptance. "You will be fairer than fair as my bride."

"I thank you for the proposal, but I will not be your bride."

"Of course, you will," Enguerrand insisted.

"Of course, I will not!" Annelise tugged her hand out of Enguerrand's grip and backed away.

"Annelise!" Yves chided.

Bertrand's wife gasped, and Bertrand fired a reproving glance Annelise's way.

Enguerrand straightened and brushed off his cloak as if unconcerned. Annelise was not fooled. She could fairly smell the anger in him and it terrified her.

"Do not concern yourselves," he said in a low voice, his gaze rising to fix on Annelise. "I have always enjoyed women of spirit. I am certain the lady can be convinced of my...ardor."

Annelise swallowed but did not flinch.

"Perhaps you will have no such opportunity," Bertrand said.

Enguerrand tossed the weight of his cloak over his shoulder as he turned to Bertrand. "What do you mean?"

"Hildegarde de Viandin seeks a wife for her son. Yves and I

were discussing the terms of our agreement that Annelise should be that bride."

Already he spoke of it as an agreement! Annelise kept silent, though, wondering if it would be better to wed a stranger than Enguerrand.

"Who is this son?" Enguerrand asked, his manner haughty.

Bertrand consulted the missive, though surely he knew the answer. "A knight who has taken up the cross—the younger son, name of Rolfe."

"So, he is in Outremer?" Enguerrand scoffed. "This lady has no need of a spouse far away in the Holy Land."

Annelise arched a brow that this knight was so convinced of her needs, without knowing any detail of her beyond her name and origin.

"He is expected home soon," Bertrand said. "He sent word to his mother from Outremer that he rode for home."

Enguerrand threw out his hands. "But if this Rolfe never returns, then where would our fair Annelise be? Do you imagine Hildegarde would show compassion for a mere fiancé? Their match would not even be consummated!"

Bertrand bristled. "How dare you imply that Rolfe will not arrive home?" he demanded. "How dare you imply that Hildegarde's intent is less than honorable?"

"Admit the truth, Bertrand," Enguerrand replied. "You do not even know whether this knight still draws breath. There have been many casualties in the East, and this man might well have been among them."

"Rolfe is bold in battle!" Bertrand insisted. "He is the son of a noble and esteemed family who will treat his intended bride well. He is on the route for home!"

But he would marry the bride his mother had chosen for him, without a word of protest. Annelise did not make the protest. She realized that she wanted to wed for love and to wed a man who could make a decision for himself.

She would have a husband who believed in the merit of love.

Her father might have told her that she wished for too much and she guessed that Bertrand would agree.

"Enguerrand's concern is not unfounded," Yves said to Bertrand. Enguerrand smiled. "My only goal is to see Annelise safe in my absence. Perhaps it would be best to await this Rolfe's return before committing to the match. She could remain here, at Beauvoir, under your protection."

Bertrand shook his head. "What if your brother Quinn returns home first? We have all heard the horrible tales of his cruelty. Surely you cannot imagine that he will have any concern for your welfare or that of your sister? She would be a pawn to him and no one would be able to protest his legal right to do with her as he chose." Annelise locked her hands together, thinking of this prospect. Bertrand was firm. "The lady's future must be assured immediately."

"In contrast to this possibly deceased man," Enguerrand said, "I am here this very day, bearing gifts for the delightful Annelise. Surely, Yves, my offer bodes better for the future of your lovely sister."

"We all know the handicap of Roussineau," Bertrand noted. "Even the second son of Viandin would be better situated than the heir of Roussineau."

Enguerrand flushed, which told Annelise that Bertrand was too close to the truth for comfort.

"Roussineau is a holding of much potential," Enguerrand argued.

Particularly, Annelise concluded, if he could marry into a larger and better-situated holding. Sayerne had been badly abused in the last years of her father's life, and certainly had been poorly managed, but at least the fields were fertile.

Unlike Roussineau. Annelise had heard about its setting in the foothills, rife with boulders and stones. There was precious little soil between the rocks, and even less sun, with mountains surrounding Roussineau to the west and south. She knew that the vein of silver mined there in the past had been depleted.

"Have the tithes improved at Roussineau of late, Enguerrand?" Yves asked.

Annelise cast a glance across the hall that her brother chose to ignore.

Enguerrand smiled. "Roussineau may be a small holding, but it is adequate to see to your sister's needs and safety. I am not without ambition, though, and imagine that your charming sister will be more finely housed within short order."

"Housed like some steed acquired at the market," Annelise muttered. Bertrand's wife was the only one who heard, evidently, and her lips thinned.

"Adequate?" Bertrand retorted. "Roussineau is hardly adequate for any manner of lady. Yves, do not be a fool! Accept Hildegarde's offer and see Annelise's future assured."

Yves' manner was thoughtful, and he flicked considering glances at the two older men as he paced. He did not, Annelise noted with rising anger, even so much as acknowledge that she was in the room.

"Yves!" Enguerrand appealed. "See Annelise wedded now, to me, and know the matter is resolved. We can exchange our vows this very night and ride to Roussineau in the morning, man and wife."

"I say she should wed Hildegarde's son!" Bertrand declared. He pounded on the arm of his chair, clearly not accustomed to being challenged in his own home. "There can be no other sensible choice."

"And I say she should wed me!" Enguerrand replied, taking a step forward.

"Perhaps we could leave the matter for a few days," Yves suggested.

"No, Yves, there is no need to wait so long," Annelise said firmly. All three men glanced her way then, their expressions surprised. "There is nothing to decide," she declared. "I shall wed neither of these men and that is final."

"Annelise!" Enguerrand whispered as if she had wounded him. Bertrand's face set in anger, and Yves watched her with open curiosity.

At the very least, Annelise had their attention.

"What manner of young woman would show such audacity to her seniors?" Bertrand demanded. "No wonder your father saw you cloistered for most of your years. It is your place to be silent, woman!"

"As Hildegarde's son's place is beneath her thumb?" Annelise retorted. "I cannot imagine what I should want of a man wrought of such mettle."

"And I cannot imagine how a woman of such sweet countenance could be cursed with a viper's tongue," Bertrand retorted.

"Then we are agreed that the match would not be a wholesome one," Annelise concluded sweetly, then gestured to Enguerrand. "What do you know of this man, Yves?" She already knew the answer, but she wanted her brother to say the words.

"Only what he says and the rumor I have heard," he admitted.

"Consider, then, that you would grant my hand to a stranger whose repute is less than ideal." Annelise forced herself to continue in an even tone. "I would not slight another guest of our host, but it could well be that this gentleman's sights are set upon Sayerne itself."

Enguerrand's lips set in a thin line, but Annelise ignored him.

"And of this younger son of Viandin, you know nothing at all. Am I right?"

Yves agreed with reluctance.

"He is another stranger."

"I know his family," Bertrand began.

"I will have neither of them," Annelise said, then met Yves' gaze. "You know that I am determined to wed for love alone."

"Love needs only time to grow," Enguerrand murmured.

"Love?" Bertrand protested. "Trust a woman to be guided by such whimsy."

"It is not whimsy," Annelise replied, knowing the truth from her own experience. "It is a guarantee for a woman's future, and I will not exchange marital vows without it."

"You will die a maiden then," Bertrand replied, his tone practical. He turned to Yves again. "If a valiant knight like Hildegarde's son does not meet with her favor, then none will satisfy. You must choose for her, Yves."

"She will undoubtedly find marriage has much to commend it, once she has a babe or two." Enguerrand lent his voice to persuade Yves.

Annelise bristled and did not take her seat again.

"You cannot take Annelise with you while you seek your fortune, Yves, and I will not have her remain here unwed," Bertrand stated flatly. "This keep is too full of warriors and it would be unfitting for me to accept responsibility for a maiden. Annelise cannot return to Sayerne, so she must go somewhere, under some man's defense."

"Surely you do not desire to see sweet Annelise left alone, without husband, hearth, and protection?" At Enguerrand's question, Yves' shoulders sagged.

"Annelise," he appealed. "You must make a choice and make it this night."

Her heart softened a bit that he finally appealed to her. "You could take me with you."

Yves shook his head. "No. I must see you safe before I depart to seek my own fortune." He held her gaze resolutely. "I must insist that you choose one suitor or the other. I bid you decide immediately, before Quinn returns."

"Choose from these two men, Annelise, if you insist upon making your own choice, but do it now and see the matter resolved," Bertrand added. "You do not grow any younger and soon your appeal will diminish even more."

Annelise lifted her chin, knowing that there was only one way to compel Yves to understand how serious she was. "If I must choose a spouse this very night, then I choose to return to the convent. I will become a bride of Christ." She held Yves' gaze, knowing that resolve shone in her own.

Yves knew how much she had loathed the convent. Surely, once he saw that she would rather return there than marry, he would abandon the argument?

Her threat hung in the air. The fire crackled, and all eyes were fixed upon her.

To her astonishment, Yves nodded calmly in agreement.

"So be it," he said. "We ride for the convent of Ste. Radegund at first light."

Annelise's lips parted in shock.

Yves arched a fair brow. "It was you who named the price, Annelise," he reminded her softly. "I must have you safe before Quinn comes home, and you have made your choice."

Then he turned away, accepting Bertrand's invitation of a cup of wine. Enguerrand stared at her, but Annelise did not acknowledge him.

She had thought she could trust Yves.

But she knew her own desire and it was not folly. Should the convent be the price she was condemned to pay for her convictions, then pay she would.

The sky was pearly when Annelise descended to the bailey just before dawn the next morning. The snow was already falling thick and fast. The wind was cold enough to chill right to the bone, and she shivered as she mounted her palfrey.

She had hoped that Yves would change his thinking. She had expected him to meet her this morning, or halt her on her way to her palfrey to declare that he had relented. Yves knew how she had hated her years in the cloister. He knew that life would never suit her. He had to realize she had made the claim to show him her determination to avoid these matches.

But he had not come to her.

Annelise's gaze flew to him as he stepped out of the hall, apparently preoccupied with donning his gloves. Was this the moment of his capitulation?

Without even glancing her way, Yves strode to his destrier and mounted.

Fear rose within Annelise. Perhaps he only waited until they were upon the road to speak to her. He would not want to back down before all these soldiers and Bertrand.

But there was a resolute set to her younger brother's lips that troubled her.

It would be the convent for her.

The horses snorted, their breath making clouds in the cold air. Squires blew on their hands to keep warm, and the gatekeeper looked to be wearing every garment he owned.

Another burly man stamped his feet as he paced back and forth in the tollbooth, although at this early hour, no traveling merchants had yet reached the pass. Annelise was not surprised that Tulley—and Beauvoir—had no intention of failing to collect any coin due.

The portcullis protested with a squeal as it was hauled skyward. Yves cast a stern glance over his party, but did not meet his sister's gaze before leading the group toward the gate. Bertrand and his wife had not even come to say farewell. Annelise's heart felt as cold as the snow around her.

Unlike the last time, when she had been sent to the nuns for her education, Annelise would never be able to leave the cloister again.

She would be consigned to a lifetime of silence.

She would be alone, entrusted to the care of an abbess who was a complete stranger, surrounded by yet more strangers.

And there would be no hope of respite.

It had been the hope of a future beyond the convent walls that had made the cloister bearable before. That and the dreadful secret Annelise had confided in none, a secret that held no fear for her any longer, yet still left its legacy in her thoughts. Her throat tightened that once again she would be banished for being an inconvenience in the lives of men.

The choices were impossible, though. As sad as it was, the convent was the best of the array of poor choices.

Annelise lifted her chin as their little party left the shelter of Beauvoir. The portcullis dropped behind them with a clang that echoed in Annelise's own bones. Outside the gates, the wind was strong and cold. It burrowed beneath all the layers of clothing she wore.

Pine trees covered in fresh snow flanked the road. Rocky cliffs above disappeared into the low clouds. The morning was as colorless and cold as a tomb. The party was silent as the wind cavorted about them, and the horses bent their heads as they headed southward.

Curse Yves! Annelise thought as she blinked back angry tears. Curse Quinn! Curse one brother for making her choose and the other for ensuring that she could not remain safely at home! Curse these meddling men who would dictate her fate!

But they were not the ones who would be condemned to live

their lives in silence and prayer.

The house of the Sisters of Ste. Radegund was outside Tulley's lands, nestled in the forest on the south face of the mountains. It was a secluded place, well away from the traffic and temptations of the secular world.

Once through the pass, the party turned away from the straight Roman road, onto a track that trailed eastward through the woods. The horses' hooves stirred the snow as they proceeded. Annelise took little interest in their direction, although Yves and the men frequently dismounted and conferred over the trail.

The snow had hidden much of it and Annelise took a grim satisfaction in the inconvenience of delay. She was not in a hurry to begin her life as a bride of Christ, even if it meant spending more time in the cold.

The sky was darkening when Yves drew his steed to a halt once more. Annelise, riding directly behind him, slowed her own beast. Although it had been two years since she had ridden this road, she knew that they had ridden far too long.

She would have expected them to arrive after noon, with plenty of time for the men to ride back to Beauvoir.

But twilight was falling and only snow and leafless trees greeted her sight in every direction. She should have seen the roof of the convent or the plume of smoke from its fires. She might have heard the bells. But only the clatter of barren branches in the wind carried to Annelise's ears. She shivered and huddled in her cloak, feeling the chill more deeply now that she knew there might not soon be any relief.

"We could return to Beauvoir," she suggested.

One of the knights snorted and Yves ignored her comment. "I think it must be this way," he said, and Annelise heard the doubt in his tone.

It was then that the wolves began to howl.

One howled first, far to the left of the path they followed and they all froze at the sound. The call was chilling, and the men exchanged glances of concern.

Then another wolf responded from the right side of the trail. Its cry was much closer than the first and made the hair on the back of Annelise's neck prickle.

She looked to Yves in alarm. "Surely the convent cannot be far?" she asked. "We could at least seek haven there."

"In truth," Yves confessed heavily, "I do not know." He pushed his hand through his hair, which made him look very young. "The snow upon the path must have led us astray. We should have arrived hours ago."

"Could we have passed the convent by?" one of the other men asked.

Two more wolves howled. They were even closer, and Annelise could not tell whether they were the same as the first two or not. The sky darkened an increment more.

The autumn had been unseasonably cold, with much early snow. The wolves would be hungry.

All knew they were bolder in darkness.

"Surely, Yves, you have some plan in mind!" protested the third man. "We cannot take shelter in the woods with wolves abroad!"

"I cannot lead you to a hearth without knowing where we are!" Yves flung out his hands in frustration. "Tell me in which direction you would head. My choices have led us far astray."

They all peered into the woods about them. Annelise caught her breath, for she saw the silhouettes of the wolves between the trees.

Their eyes glowed in the shadows as they watched the party.

She might be fortunate to even reach the convent alive.

At Yves' command, the men rallied their steeds hastily about Annelise. The horses snorted nervously, well aware of the scent of wolf in the wind, and stamped with fear.

A wolf howled to its brethren. The horses shied away from the sound. Annelise stroked her mare's ears, but the beast was oblivious to her touch. Its ears flicked, and its dark eyes were wide. Annelise felt the creature shudder.

"Surely there must be somewhere we can take shelter," she said, fearing it was not so.

The man beside her drew his blade. "It is too late now, my lady. They are all around us and hungry, unless I miss my guess."

Annelise looked into the woods, at the pacing shadows of the predators. "We should flee!"

"To where?" the man beside her asked. "Wolves are possessed of an unholy cunning and stamina beyond all. They will separate us and dog our steps until our horses fall from exhaustion. At least one of us will pay the price, to be sure."

That one of their party—if not more—was doomed to become a meal for these beasts made Annelise's heart race.

Yves gathered his reins in his gloved hands. When he spoke, his voice was grim. "We must try to outrun them, even knowing that one of us may fall. I remind you all that you have already given your pledge to protect Annelise."

The men grunted in assent.

"Shall we draw lots or allow Dame Fortune to make the choice?" Yves asked.

The men barely glanced at each other before responding.

"Dame Fortune is my choice," the man beside Annelise replied. "And let our fates fall as they may. May she not be a greedy wench this night and see us all taken."

The other two men nodded their agreement, drawing their blades as they watched the wolves' shadows under the barren trees.

Yves put a gloved hand over Annelise's and their gazes clung. "I bid you good fortune, sister of mine," he said softly, "lest I not have the opportunity to do so later."

Annelise's heart clenched at the import of his words. She felt the full weight of her guilt. She should never have chosen the convent, not if it meant any of these men should die. "Yves, I never thought..." she began, but Yves tightened his grip over her fingers.

"It is not your fault," he said, interrupting her with resolve. "I erred in being as stubborn as you in this. In fact, I erred more by leading us astray this day." His gaze turned resolute and he was once again the young man she had come to trust. "I wanted only to ensure your safety before I left and I was too stubborn to wait for finer weather." The corner of his mouth lifted in a smile, making the dimple that graced his chin deepen. "Fare thee well, sister mine," he whispered.

"And may you fare well, also." Her voice broke, but Yves had already moved away.

"I cannot even count their numbers," whispered one man.

"And they are gaunt from this cursed winter," muttered the third. "Mark my words, they will be bold."

"As shall we!" Yves bellowed. The wolves halted and eyed him warily, their eyes glinting silver. "Away to the right with all speed! We circle back to the road. And mind the lady!"

All four men shouted and gave spurs to their horses at that moment. Their steeds were only too glad to obey the command to run. Annelise's palfrey raced in their midst, surrounded by the larger horses. The wolves howled and she did not doubt they were fast in pursuit.

She crouched down as her mare plunged into the forest. The snow crunched underfoot as the horses broke trail, their breath billowing steam into the air. She could feel that her mare was running with all her might.

The palfrey understood instinctively that whichever horse fell back would be the first to fall.

Several wolves bayed, and there was the sound of breaking branches. Annelise glanced over her shoulder to see four wolves close in pursuit. She clutched her mare's reins, her heart in her mouth. Her heels dug into the horse's side as the wind ripped her hood from her head.

The mare bolted forward and ran alongside Yves' steed at breakneck speed, her fear ensuring that she left the other three horses behind.

"Flee, Annelise!" Yves cried when he saw her. "Do not wait— our armor will be our doom!" He did not wait for her reply. His hand smacked heavily on the mare's rump.

It was all the encouragement that horse needed to race even more quickly into the forest, leaving Yves and his men behind.

Annelise was alone!

CHAPTER THREE

olfe heard the party of knights in his woods and was relieved by the sound. He cared little about their mission—it was enough for him that they were here, close enough to aid him in gaining his freedom.

This last month had shown the curse was real, indeed. Rolfe's skepticism of djinns and their powers had been eliminated by the experience of changing from man to wolf and back to man again with a relentless repetition that echoed the sun's rise and fall each day.

The second djinn had proven to be right about the timing. He had spent that first night as a wolf but not another since. Perhaps because night had been falling when she cast her spell, its effect had to wait until sunset the next day. Rolfe did not know.

He only knew how profound his relief had been when he changed back to a knight.

And how devastated he had been at the dawn to feel that silver tail again.

Each night since, as soon as darkness fell, he found himself a man again, but confined inside the palace as surely as he was locked out of it by day. Within the palace, he had every luxury. There was fine fare and a soft bed, a garden of pleasures and his horses to tend. Outside, there was the wilderness and the wolves.

Each day since, he had taken the form of a wolf and found himself outside the palace walls. He feared to leave the area as a wolf, for he might be hunted and his horses would be abandoned. He dared not leave as a man, for he knew it was several days riding to any abode. He had no desire to be a man alone in the forest at night.

It was a vexing situation.

The other wolves avoided him, although the djinn's acceleration of winter had made them gaunt with hunger. It was as though they knew him to be different, though Rolfe had little desire for their company.

His life, such as it was, was a lonely business.

The familiar sound of men and horses brought him running, but not before his fellow wolves had attacked. To Rolfe's dismay, the largest and meanest wolf had separated one rider from the group.

A noblewoman. And on a small palfrey. Though the horse was quick-footed in terror, Rolfe knew the lady had no chance against the wolf's determination.

The oath of knighthood he had sworn years before burned in his heart. Though he might be condemned to look like a wolf, Rolfe was yet a knight to his marrow.

There was only one thing he could do.

He gave chase, hoping that the large wolf would be satisfied with the horse. Somehow, Rolfe would save this woman, even if he had to pay the price with his own miserable existence.

There was nothing else a man of honor could do.

The palfrey ran like the wind. The stark silhouettes of the trees danced past in endless succession as Annelise sought some glimpse of a sanctuary ahead. She would call back to Yves if she found one. She would see them all saved.

But the carpet of snow appeared endless.

The sounds of the other horses faded behind her, but she could not have slowed her palfrey to save her life. The beast was possessed of such terror that it might run to Outremer. It cared little for its footing and Annelise feared she would be thrown, that both of them would be injured. She tried murmuring to the horse and stroking its neck, to no discernible effect.

When she heard an anguished cry, her mouth went dry.

Had one of the men fallen prey to the wolves?

Surely it could not be Yves.

Annelise dared to look back, but she could not see the other riders. Their shouts carried to her ears and she was certain they fought a battle. She tried to turn her horse about, but then she saw a lone wolf loping through the forest directly toward her.

It had separated from the pack. It was large and its gaze chillingly cold. Too late Annelise realized that she had only a very small eating blade with which she might protect herself.

Then she saw that a second wolf dogged the footsteps of the first, and her heart sank to her toes.

Even if she defied the odds and outran the first wolf, the second would still claim her life. Annelise clutched the reins. The palfrey ran on, as yet unaware of these two wolves in close pursuit.

The sounds of the men faded even more.

Annelise was alone.

She glanced over her shoulder just in time to see the first wolf leap clear of the forest. It trotted in the tracks of her horse, not more than ten paces behind. It neither drew closer nor fell farther back.

Just as the man-at-arms had said, the beast would follow her until the horse collapsed.

What a patient and cunning creature.

Perhaps she could outrun the fiend. Annelise dug her heels into her palfrey's ribs. The mare's nostrils quivered in fear and a shudder ran over its flesh. It must have smelled the wolf, for it spurted ahead more quickly at Annelise's command.

The wolf loped behind, keeping the same distance, as though aware that it was only a matter of time.

Annelise was unnerved to know the wolf's intent and be powerless all the same. She leaned over the mare, urging the creature onward, but the horse stepped suddenly on a patch ice.

It whinnied in terror and threw back its head as it slipped.

The wolf did not miss a moment.

Annelise looked back to see long white fangs bared all too close. She screamed. The horse fought to regain its footing, but fell on the ice. It landed hard on its rump, hooves flailing as it slid further on the ice. Annelise only managed to jump from the saddle in time, then she slipped on the ice, as well. She fell, realizing that the ice covered a small creek. At the perimeter, there were small stones and she crawled toward them.

She looked back in time to see the wolf jump. Annelise screamed again and threw a stone at the wolf. The stone hit its back but the beast was undeterred. The mare shrieked as the wolf's claws dug into its rump, and the wolf bared its teeth again.

Blood flowed from the mare's flank and Annelise seized another rock. She flung it at the wolf and hit the back of its head. It raised its head to snarl at her and the horse struggled to rise. Annelise fought to her feet and lunged at the wolf, her eating knife in her hand.

"Not my mare," she whispered with heat and lunged for the wolf. The wolf's eyes were so cold that she knew she would be next and she did not care. It snarled and eased closer to her, choosing its moment. Annelise held the knife before herself, not even daring to blink. The mare stumbled up the bank of the stream, blood running from its flank, and Annelise hoped it would escape.

She feared they would both die.

The wolf suddenly jumped toward her, its jaws stained with the mare's blood.

There was a blur of silver fur as the second wolf attacked the first, taking it to the ground. Annelise stared as the two rolled on the ground, biting and snapping, battling for supremacy. The second wolf paused and lifted its head, then barked at her, baring its teeth.

As if it meant to tell her to run.

The first wolf snarled and the pair fought again.

Annelise fled after the horse, seizing its reins and urging it onward. She did not know where they ran, and the trail of blood that the mare left in the snow would certainly send any wolf quickly after them.

They had a reprieve and she hoped it would be enough.

She was not surprised some time later to hear the soft patter of his footfalls in the snow behind her. She cast a glance over her shoulder to find the second wolf close behind. He was large, too, but of a paler hue of silver than the one that had attacked her first.

The mare smelled him and whinnied, charging onward despite her injuries. Annelise ran alongside the mare, certain the predator waited only for their inevitable exhaustion.

The sight of a path ahead gave Annelise new strength. She cut between the trees, plunging through knee-deep snow. She fell once, trapped by her skirts, but her grip on the mare's reins pulled her to her feet. Her hair fell loose about her face as her veil was ripped away by low branches and she risked another backward glance.

The wolf, she saw, took a more roundabout path.

Annelise caught her breath that she had gained a bit of time. She stumbled onto the path and ran blindly as she shook clumps of snow from the hem of her kirtle.

The mare nickered and Annelise looked up to see walls.

The convent!

Her knees nearly gave out beneath her, though they were not safe as yet.

It was not the convent she knew, for its walls were only as high as Annelise's shoulders and made of rough stone. These walls were white and smooth and soared high.

As she hurried closer, Annelise knew she had never seen the like of these walls. The stone was fitted with such skill that the surface appeared to be as smooth as a sheet of silver. She approached a castle, although Annelise could not guess why it was in this remote spot.

Nor did she care.

The wolf behind her seemed to have slowed his pace.

Perhaps he feared whoever lived at this palace. Annelise ran for the gates and the mare needed no encouragement to hasten onward. The wolf loped after them, keeping his distance, and Annelise had the curious thought that he guided her toward the palace.

The gates were closed, but at dusk, she would have expected nothing else. She had only to awaken the gatekeeper. She pounded on the wooden portal with first one fist, then both.

The mare's ears flicked and her nostrils flared.

"Who knocks?" demanded someone within.

"Annelise de Sayerne." She spared a glance over her shoulder at the wolf. He drew yet closer, his proximity agitating the mare, and she pounded again on the door. "I beg you for sanctuary! A wolf pursues me!"

The keeper's words were spoken with a slow precision that seemed inappropriate to the circumstance. "A price must be paid for your entry to this place."

Surely such details could be settled once she was inside?

"Anything!" Annelise declared. "I will pay anything if you let me in."

"The price of your finding sanctuary here," continued the voice slowly, "is that you wed the lord master of this abode."

Wed?

Annelise stepped back from the portal, shocked at the curious request. She frowned, wondering what manner of ogre the master of this fortress must be to gain a wife in such a manner.

A snarl behind her recalled her to her senses.

The mare tugged at the reins as if she would flee. Annelise backed into the gates, unable to tear her gaze away from the wolf, who steadily stalked closer, his head lowered and his gaze fixed upon her.

"Let me in!" she cried. "The wolf is close!"

"You must give your pledge," that voice intoned. "You must promise."

It was madness.

Marriage to a stranger or death.

With such stakes, Annelise could only set her resolve aside.

"I promise! Open the cursed gates, I beg of you!" she cried.

The portal abruptly fell open behind Annelise and she stumbled backward, nearly losing her balance completely. The mare cantered through the gates, hastening past Annelise.

The wolf leaped, as though he, too, would enter.

Annelise screamed in terror. As his jump brought him closer, she caught a glimpse of the wolf's eyes.

One was blue and one silver-gray.

The heavy wooden doors abruptly slammed shut—leaving the wolf trapped outside.

He howled, but he was on the other side.

Annelise shook as she caught her breath, unable to believe her good fortune.

They were safe.

She had to find the mare and tend to her injuries.

Rolfe paced outside the palace gates, watching the setting sun with even more impatience than usual. He had heard the gates make their request and was startled by the reminder of the first djinn's curse.

> *Let the one who crosses this threshold first,*
> *Be condemned to wed him despite his curse.*

How could he have forgotten that detail?

A noblewoman was within the walls of the palace that had been granted to his keeping. Even more remarkable, she had agreed to become his wife, without ever laying eyes upon him. Rolfe's month of solitude had made him grateful for whatever blessings came his way.

He admired her boldness in defending her steed.

She was pretty, too.

She would be his wife.

Who could have imagined that a curse could have brought him such fortune? Rolfe would woo this woman destined to be his bride. He would win her heart. They might have children. He had a palace and they could live well here, making a home as he had hoped.

It seemed that Marcus' gift was making Rolfe's dream come true.

His excitement made him pace more quickly. He would build a partnership like that of his parents' marriage, in which each trusted and relied upon the other. He would pledge himself to this woman's happiness...then he recalled the rest of the spell and halted.

And let the one in whom he confides,
Lead a killer to his side.

But what would happen when this mysterious noblewoman learned of his situation?

Rolfe halted.

It could not take her long. At morning's first light, he would be expelled from the palace and find himself a wolf again. He did not doubt that she would have the wits to notice his absence, even if he managed to hide the transformation from her.

What would she do when she learned that this palace was nothing but illusion, that it existed on no map and that her husband could never leave it?

She would laugh, as the fair Rosalinde had once laughed at Rolfe for his expectations. That lady had welcomed his affections until she had learned Rolfe was the younger son, without a holding to his name. Then her charm had fled and he had seen her nature for what it was.

She might summon a more favored suitor, one who would sacrifice Rolfe for his own ambitions. Any man could desire a palace such as this. What was Rolfe to do?

Finally, by grace of the powers above,
let this curse be broken by the blessing of love.

There was the second djinn's spell, as foolish as Rolfe thought it to be.

He had never seen the merit of love himself. Rosalinde had pledged her love until she learned he had no wealth. Love was capricious and fleeting, if not a lie. Trust could be shown and deserved. Even honor was proven by deeds, but love was a tool plied by women like Rosalinde.

Rolfe stared at the gates and thought.

Then he had a thought. Love was also a physical act and one natural between husband and wife. That was it! He would wed the lady and he would love her abed. The physical expression of his admiration for her, and the cultivation of her pleasure would satisfy the spell.

He had learned from Rosalinde, that intimacy was negotiated. Some women wanted gifts. Others wanted only pleasure. This one agreed to be his wife, and Rolfe would marry and defend her. They would have an arrangement to their mutual benefit.

She had sanctuary and would have pleasure. As a result, he would see his curse broken.

It would be a simple transaction.

No more and no less.

"Gatekeeper!" Annelise cried after she had caught the reins of the mare. She led the horse back to the gates and only then realized they were alone.

Where was the gatekeeper? The gate could not have opened by itself.

But there was no one in sight. The walls were as smooth on the inside as on the exterior. She could not even see a mechanism to open them.

Ridiculous. Gates did not open themselves.

"Hello?" she called again. "Gatekeeper? Are you here?"

Nothing moved. Goose pimples rose over her flesh at the silence but Annelise refused to be daunted.

There was a gatekeeper. He had talked to her. He could not have gone very far.

Annelise examined the walls on either side of the heavy gates more closely. They were as smooth as glass, without so much as a nook for a keeper to hide within. She tipped back her head to eye the height of the walls and admired them again. There was neither a ladder nor a stair, nor so much as a walkway. Nary a lookout along the entire wall, as far as she could see.

There was not even an opening in the portal to let one peek outside the heavy walls. Did the lord have no interest in seeing who approached his gate? It made no sense to need to open the gate to see who knocked.

Yves was still in the forest. Annelise knocked once more on the solid door. When there was no response, she knocked harder.

"My brother also needs sanctuary," she declared.

There was no reply

Annelise pushed at the gate but it might have been part of the wall. She spun around, but could see no other break in the walls. She eyed the empty arched windows in the strangely low-built keep, with its sparkling blue pool.

Those windows were most impractical, without so much as a shutter across them. The hall would be cold as cold could be in these winter months. Obviously, those skilled masons had not possessed a speck of sense...

In that moment, Annelise realized that the air in the bailey smelled like summer. Indeed, her wool kirtle and cloak with its squirrel-fur lining were so heavy that she felt a trickle of perspiration on her back.

Annelise looked about herself with wary eyes. What manner of castle had she entered?

And what manner of man would be its lord?

One thing was certain. Annelise was effectively his prisoner, and she did not care for that in the least. Surely the keeper could not have truly meant that she would have to wed the lord?

What manner of man was he?

It was clear that Annelise and her host must talk. He had not made an appearance to greet her, so she would seek him out.

But first, she would tend her mare's injury.

Her nose told her that she would find a stable to her left.

It was a relief that in one matter, at least, her host's abode was predictable.

Annelise's nose was right. Hidden along one side of the palace were the stables. The wooden doors were cast open and straw was strewn on the ground. The pungency of the smell left no doubt as to the building's use. Annelise's footsteps quickened with the hope that she would find someone there.

The gatekeeper, or at least an ostler. A stable boy might even be of aid.

"Hello?"

She peered into the shadowed stables and a horse nickered from within. Her own mare replied. Annelise stepped into the darkness. Her eyes adjusted enough so that she could make out a pair of low-built stalls and she made her way toward them.

The first was occupied by a chestnut palfrey. It was a large stall and as her mare seemed glad of the companionship of one of her own kind, Annelise tethered her there. She washed the wound upon the mare's hip, which was not as deep as she had feared. There were brushes and cloths in the stable as well as the trap for the palfrey and Annelise's confidence returned as she found these familiar items.

Annelise removed the mare's saddle and brushed her down, noting how the creature calmed beneath her touch. The mare drank of the water already left for the other palfrey and ate of the oats. The chestnut palfrey nibbled on Annelise's hair, making her laugh, and she resolved to return in the morning when there was more light. She could not see a lantern, but she was sure she heard another horse in the stables.

The mundane task brushed aside her own uncertainties. Annelise made her way back to the gate, but it was still sealed and there was still no sign of a gatekeeper. She strode through the lush garden and under the broadest archway of the palace. It was impossible not to notice the richness of her surroundings or the complete absence of any other being.

The keep had to be a palace. Once the gates were breached, it had no defenses—though those gates had been a formidable obstacle.

Even so, it was unlike any abode Annelise had ever seen. The walls were white stone and the floors tiled with intricate mosaics of stones in varying shades.

Annelise called repeatedly for her host or someone in his service, but no one answered. She felt that she should be greeted and not simply enter the palace, but she would not find her host in the garden. She had already ascertained that she was alone there, so she entered the palace, knocking on doors and calling as she continued. Surely, she would find him soon enough.

His abode was a marvel, seemingly containing every luxury. The rooms were large and uncluttered, the size of the windows indicating that the interior would be bright in the daylight. Luxuriously thick rugs in shades of red and ochre were scattered across the floors. Oil lanterns glowed at regular intervals, so many of them that Annelise knew the lord of this palace had to be wealthy, indeed.

She might be trapped inside but, as prisons went, this one was exceptional.

No one demanded that she keep her silence, either.

Perhaps she might like being wed to her mysterious host. The notion made Annelise shake her head at her own whimsy. He could not wish to wed a stranger any more than she did.

But she was unlikely to be able to ask him soon. The palace seemed to be deserted. It was odd to find no other person. Who had lit the lanterns? Annelise continued in wonder, certain she would find her host sooner or later. Finally, she stepped into a room flooded with candlelight and halted in awe.

The room faced onto a small tiled courtyard, where a fountain splashed. It was open to the sky and she could see that twilight had fallen and that the first stars shone overhead. The walls of the chamber were hung with rich tapestries resplendent with exotic flowers she could not name. So many carpets were flung on the floor that they overlapped two and three deep. Annelise's feet sank into their softness when she crossed the room.

Hundreds of candles covered storage chests and were scattered across the floor right out into the courtyard. The smell of beeswax was inviting and the flickering golden light picked out the mother-of-pearl inlay on the chests.

In the middle of the room was a low table, evidently set for a meal. An embroidered cloth covered it with tassels wound with gold and as thick as Annelise's wrist hanging from its four corners. Three brass salvers reposed on the table, glinting in the candlelight.

Annelise glanced over her shoulder, but she already guessed that no one would serve her. She caught a delectable whiff that was enough to make her stomach grumble.

She could at least see what the meal was.

Who would know if she looked?

A waft of steam was released when she lifted the first lid, and Annelise inhaled the rich smell of a savory meat stew. Her stomach growled openly, defying her to believe that the crust of bread she had eaten at Beauvoir that morning was enough to sustain her.

The meat was venison, the gravy thick and crowded with tiny onions, and the serving was the precise amount she might eat. Annelise felt herself salivate as she eyed her favorite dish.

How had her host known she loved venison stew?

He could not have.

They must have this taste in common.

Although, if a man had ever been bent on earning Annelise's favor, he would be wise to offer food. More than any woman she had met in the convent or Sayerne, Annelise possessed a love of good, hearty fare.

But it was impossible that the lord could have known her taste, let alone that he might have cared to court her approval so soon after her arrival. This was but a coincidence—otherwise, it was sorcery. Annelise knew that she was being presumptuous to think this feast was laid out for her.

It might be his meal.

Then where was the man?

She had seen no other soul within the walls.

Just as there had been no one to open the gate.

Annelise discovered a loaf of fine white bread with a perfect golden crust under the next salver. A knife reposed on the wooden plate beside the bread.

It was enough to drive her mad with hunger.

The third sheltered a cheese of sufficient tang to make her lick her lips, as well as a pot of freshly churned butter and a bowl of olives. She had not tasted olives in a long time, though she loved them dearly.

She glanced about herself, then quickly took one, closing her eyes as she savored the taste. She made that one small olive last as long as possible, certain that no one would guess at her indulgence.

When she had swallowed it, the others looked even more

enticing.

There was a single spoon for the stew on the table, Annelise noticed. There was also fruit, a chalice, and a decanter that proved to contain red wine.

A meal laid for one.

As a lord might eat in solitude?

Or as one might offer a guest?

Annelise surveyed the room again and noticed the large tub steaming in the comer. Her skin itched at the very idea of a bath and she immediately investigated. The water was hot and the tub was full enough that the bath would be deep but not overflow the tub. Rounded flower petals the size of her thumb floated across the surface of the water and their unfamiliar scent was heavenly.

Feminine.

This was no lord's bath but one prepared for a lady.

A guest who was a lady.

Annelise knew she was the only woman in this palace on this evening. She smiled at her host's generous hospitality and decided she would not insult him by letting it go to waste.

She dipped a finger into the scented water and decided it was too hot as yet.

But if she ate first, it would be near perfect. Annelise considered the chamber even as her heart told her to believe her suspicions.

If this enigmatic lord meant to court her favor, she would not decline.

Indeed, if she was going to argue with him over his odd stipulation of marriage, she would do well to be at her best.

Rolfe's sense of purpose deserted him when he rounded a corner in the palace and saw the candlelight pooling on the stone floor ahead.

The noblewoman who held his fate in her hands was only a dozen paces away.

If she had any sense at all, she would have one question—if not a hundred—and he had no explanation for any of it.

At least not one that any sensible person might believe.

Perhaps she was a fool, but that would be a cruel fate indeed.

And not his dream come true.

There was no point in delay, though. The noblewoman had given her agreement, and Rolfe was anxious to break the curse. One night of loving might well solve his dilemma, if the second djinn had been right.

Perhaps some wondrous explanation of their entwined fates would pop into Rolfe's mind before he confronted her.

Perhaps not.

Perhaps matters would be simpler once the curse was broken.

There was a thought! He strode onward with purpose.

Then he halted on the threshold of the chamber he favored. For the second time in rapid succession, the palace had taken him by surprise. Rolfe had hoped that the lady's desires would be met, but he had never imagined his will had this kind of power.

The room he preferred had been transformed. It was filled with a glow that exceeded every other chamber, as if it had been summoning the lady. Rolfe could smell food and the warm sweet scent of a lady risen from her bath. He took an appreciative breath and caught the tang of a robust cheese.

The lady, though, was nowhere in sight.

Feeling like an intruder in his own palace, Rolfe stepped into the room. Emboldened by the silence, he continued until he was staring down at the remains of her meal.

The lady had an appetite, to be sure. He smiled his approval of that.

A bowl that looked to have contained stew was empty, the spoon licked clean as though every mouthful had been savored. Crumbs littered the dish, evidence that the lady had wiped up the gravy with bread. The pitcher of wine was empty, though there was still a quantity of bread and a piece of cheese.

Rolfe was certain he had never known a woman to enjoy food more or eat with such enthusiasm. Had this savory meal truly been her heart's desire? He could not believe a lady would eat so simply if she had the choice. Rosalinde had picked at her food and preferred ornamental fancies that did little to fill a man's belly. Women in Outremer oft wanted wine or rhapsodized about favored meals that were unavailable.

Maybe the magic had inflicted Rolfe's own plain but hearty tastes upon this stranger.

He truly knew nothing about this woman he needed to take to wife.

But then, many were betrothed to those they did not know. His own parents had found trust after their marriage had been arranged by their parents.

Rolfe suddenly heard the soft whisper of her breathing and spun on his heel, alarmed that he might be discovered.

The lady was unaware of his presence, however. She slept in her bath as wisps of steam rose around her.

Rolfe exhaled in relief then inhaled deeply of the scent of roses. He had never smelled roses of such fragrance before encountering the red roses of the East. He had never thought to smell them again once he had crossed the Adriatic.

Yet they grew in the gardens of this palace. Even better, there were hundreds of rose petals scattered in the lady's bath, teasing him with their glorious feminine scent.

That was nothing compared to the lady's own charms.

The candlelight caressed her bare shoulders and touched the curve of her cheek. Rolfe swallowed and eased closer for a better look. Being in attendance while a lady bathed recalled past pleasures with lightning speed. He savored the sense that he had stumbled into some forbidden bower as he surveyed his guest.

Though the water obscured the sight, the lady had to be nude in her bath.

Her head leaned back on the rim of the wooden tub and her ripe lips were parted. One hand hung limply over the side of the tub while the other was lost in the water that rose to her collarbone. Her garments were discarded, not folded, as though she had been impatient to bathe.

Rolfe smiled, well familiar with that desire.

Her long auburn hair was twisted up on top of her head, evidence of that same haste in the loose knot she had actually tied in the tresses. Rolfe found his smile broadening, again sensing that they had something in common. Rosalinde would have summoned a maid to pin her hair up prettily, regardless of the time involved. She had mocked him once for noting how he nigh dove into a bath after a long ride.

But this lady would probably agree with him.

Rolfe was curious about her. He took a tentative step closer, half expecting her to awaken and cast him out. When the lady neither stirred nor vanished in a puff of smoke, he could not resist temptation. Rolfe stepped to the side of the tub to gaze upon his bride-to-be.

Hers was not a conventionally pretty face, he noted with interest—not as Rosalinde's had been. This woman's lips were too lushly curved and her eyes would be too large and wide for her to be a man's ornamental prize.

Yet despite her differences from the woman he had once thought perfection in flesh, Rolfe was intrigued by the voluptuousness of this woman's features. Her cheekbones were prominent and she possessed a dimple in the center of her chin. There was a sensuality about her face that suggested an intriguing beauty of an entirely different sort.

She looked like someone who smiled often, who laughed frequently, and who savored the joys of life. Ye gods, but he would welcome such a companion after the battles he had fought in Outremer.

The lashes that swept over her cheeks were luxuriantly thick, tinged with the same reddish tone as her hair. Her complexion was creamy, her lips a ruddy hue, her throat and shoulders as smooth and pale as the finest silk. Hers was a face that spoke of passion, of the same zest for life evidenced by the remnants of her meal.

The hand that languished on the side of the tub was long and slender, feminine despite the short, cropped nails. Sadly, the quantity of rose petals floating on the surface of the bathwater obscured everything else and foiled Rolfe's rising curiosity. He folded his arms across his chest and stared down at her with satisfaction.

His bride.

The notion of sealing their vows with a kiss, perhaps immediately, made his chausses seem snug. Indeed, the night ahead held considerable promise.

Rolfe wondered what color his lady's eyes would be. He recalled that she was tall and wondered whether she would be slender or as voluptuously curved as her lips.

She had called herself Annelise, but he had not been able to hear the rest of her name. Where was she from? Who were her family? Why had she been abroad on this winter day, so far from any destination? Had she been alone? It made no sense. If she had not been alone, what had happened to her companions?

And why would she have agreed to wed a stranger?

He supposed the wolves might have encouraged her agreement, but still. As tempting as this lady's form might be, Rolfe forced himself to face the fact that he knew nothing about her character.

With the exception that she devoured stew like an over-worked villein.

And that she had defended a horse without fear for herself.

And let the one in whom he confides,
lead a killer to his side.

The recollection of the djinn's words chilled Rolfe to his marrow.

He could not trust her.

He dared not trust her.

Rolfe took a step back from the enticing beauty in her bath. He could not risk sharing his name with this maiden. He should not let her see his face, not until the curse was broken.

The loving he needed to dissolve the curse must be accomplished as soon as possible. Somehow he would have to wed the lady before she could reconsider the wisdom of her choice, and he had to consummate the match this very night.

On the morrow, Rolfe could explain everything to her, if indeed the lady was even remotely interested in the tale. What would happen to the palace when the curse was broken? He might have as little as he had had when Rosalinde had spurned him. She might insist upon an annulment.

Rolfe would not think of it. He had to break this curse.

He would come to her in the darkness and do whatever was necessary to earn his salvation. He would love her until dawn.

Rolfe's pulse began to thunder at the prospect.

But she had to know that his intentions were honorable. Rolfe pulled the heavy ring his mother had given him when he departed for Outremer from within his tabard. A cabochon garnet reposed in the gold setting and winked in the candlelight, still secure on its chain.

It was the only piece of jewelry he owned and his mother had declared it to be a talisman of luck. Rolfe did not believe in luck, but he had to admit that nothing ill had befallen him in the East. He had feared the ring lost when the djinn cursed him, but had found it inside the palace when he became a man the next night. He had secured it on the chain then, not wanting to count on it being returned again as a manifestation of his will.

A bride had need of a ring and Rolfe chose to give his bride this one. It was a token of his family, after all, and an indication that he had need of all the good fortune he could find.

He removed the ring from its chain, but lost his grip before he could decide how to offer it to her without revealing himself. The gem danced on his fingertips as he struggled to catch it, then fell. Rolfe watched in horror as it fell into the lady's bath.

It landed below her throat, then rolled between her breasts and disappeared into the water.

The lady's eyelashes fluttered and Rolfe's heart leaped.

As much as he wanted to know the hue of her eyes, she could not see his face, not yet.

He pivoted and raced from the chamber, his heart in his throat.

CHAPTER FOUR

omething warm landed between Annelise's breasts and awakened her with a jolt. A small, smooth shape splashed into the bath, rolled over her belly, and was lost in the depths of the tub.

The lord of the palace had arrived!

Annelise sat up abruptly then realized her host would see her nude. Her hands flew to cover her breasts as she eased down in the bath water again and surveyed the chamber.

The room was deserted, though the candles had burned much lower since she had stepped into the inviting bath. It was too dark outside to see the fountain in the courtyard, but she could hear the water flowing.

She was still alone.

How could that be? Annelise felt around the bottom of the tub for whatever had awakened her. Her fingers closed on a hard, round item and she pulled it to the surface.

A man's ring reposed on the flat of her palm. It was made of gold, so of no small value, with a red stone set into it.

Annelise's mouth went dry. He had been here, looked upon her, and left this token behind. It was clearly a reminder of her promise to wed him.

But she had not even seen him. Why had he not spoken to her?

There could be only one reason for him to be so reticent and, indeed, it would explain his strange condition for entry. Her host might be unattractive. He might have been scarred or otherwise injured so that people feared to look upon him. She felt sympathy for him, for she doubted he could have so fearsome an appearance as that. People should be kinder and look beyond the surface to a man's truth. If she was to wed him, she must look upon him at some point.

She wondered if that would be soon.

Soft music carried to her ears from another part of the palace. Was it a lute? Did he play it? There had been no music before. Was this his way of summoning her to his side? Was he inviting her to dress and join him, because he had been surprised to find her at her bath? Annelise's heart softened toward a man who showed such thoughtfulness.

Perhaps he would insist they wed when they met. Annelise knew she had to convince him that such an arrangement would be foolish, given how little they knew of each other.

She doubted he would be readily convinced.

Annelise rose from her bath with purpose. There was no time for hose or headdress, she decided. It would be false modesty to fret about appearances when the man had already looked upon her while she bathed.

And truly, she wished to speak to him as soon as possible. Annelise braided her hair quickly and laced her kirtle, pushed her feet into her shoes and went in search of her host.

Annelise followed the sound of the music, her leather shoes tapping lightly against the marble floor. She ducked through a wide archway and found herself alongside the pool in front of the palace.

The moon painted the garden with silver light. The scent of the same unfamiliar flowers that had graced her bath filled the air. The perfect stillness of the pool reflected the stars overhead. The music was louder, but she still could not see the players. She might have walked in a dream.

Annelise halted when she noticed a figure wrapped in a dark

cloak awaited her beside the pool. A man, by his height and the breadth of his shoulders. Her heart fluttered.

Her host.

Her husband-to-be.

It could be none other.

The shadow of the hood hid his features and the indigo cloak fell to his ankles. Annelise caught the barest glimpse of his boots, which did not begin to satisfy her curiosity. She tried to discern his features in the shadows of the hood as she approached him, but to no avail.

He was completely concealed from her.

Silent and watchful.

At least he was tall and broad of shoulder, although Annelise would have preferred to look him in the eye to explain why she could not possibly wed him.

But she was clearly not to have that chance.

She halted before him and felt the weight of his gaze upon her. He did not speak.

Annelise saw no reason to be shy. She curtseyed before him. "Good evening. I trust that you are the lord of this estate?"

"Indeed, I am," he responded. His voice was deep, and Annelise thought she could hear a smile in his tone. "And you are the lady who sought refuge here this day?"

"I am."

"And your name?"

"Annelise. Annelise de Sayerne."

He moved as if startled by the confession, although Annelise could not imagine why. "I am most pleased to make your acquaintance." He bowed slightly, but contributed no additional information.

"I apologize, but I did not note your name, sir."

"That was because I did not mention it."

"And you are?"

"A man with no name, as far as you are concerned."

Annelise caught her breath in surprise and he chuckled at her response.

"You laugh at me," she charged and he did laugh then.

"I am delighted by you. It is different."

Annelise found herself blushing, because she could not forget that he had looked upon her in her bath. "I fail to see any source of amusement in our situation..."

"I am not amused, Annelise. I merely enjoy your company." He reached out and touched her chin with a gentle fingertip. Annelise hated that even his hand was gloved, though the leather was soft upon her skin. "Your spirit is beguiling, my Annelise."

Her mouth went dry. Her name sounded like a caress on his tongue. "I am not your Annelise, sir."

"But you soon will be."

Annelise shook her head. "No, I will not."

His tone hardened. "But you promised..."

"Anyone would have agreed to any term to escape the wolves!" she protested. "But the condition is absurd. You cannot intend that we should marry, simply because I came to your gates in search of aid..."

"But I do."

"That makes little sense, sir. I would choose to wed a sensible man."

"Do you not believe in destiny, my Annelise? Perhaps the Fates brought you to my palace, because our futures are entwined."

She eyed him, sensing that he did not believe his own words. "I do believe in destiny, sir, and in love, but I think you do not."

He laughed again. "And what need have you to see my face, my Annelise, when you can see my heart so easily? You are right about my skepticism."

"Then why would you make such a demand?"

"Perhaps I have no choice." He leaned closer and she could almost discern the gleam of his eyes in the shadows.

"Why not?"

"I cannot confide that in you, not now."

"Not ever?"

"Not now." His voice dropped low. "Do not tell me that you are inclined to break your word, now that you are safe and warm and fed?"

Annelise felt flustered. "I keep my word, always."

"And I keep mine." There was satisfaction in his tone. "And so we begin to find common ground, my Annelise. We can both be trusted to keep our pledges. Is that not a fine cornerstone for a match? Many wed without such assurance."

The truth in that made Annelise flush. "I fear you play a jest at my expense, sir. I fail to see the humor in it, I must confess." She held out his ring. "Please take your ring back. I have no intention of marrying a perfect stranger."

"I am far from perfect, my Annelise." The humor in his tone weakened Annelise's resolve.

She liked his voice.

She wondered about his smile.

She was enjoying their discussion, even though they disagreed. "You understand me well enough, sir. We are complete strangers."

"Yet with every passing moment, we each learn more of the other." He folded his arms across his chest, showing no inclination to take the ring.

What if he refused to let her leave?

"I do not wish to be rude, sir, but I do not wish to marry you. Indeed, I cannot."

"Why not?" His voice sharpened. "Are you betrothed to another?"

"No, not that. I vowed long ago that I would wed only for love."

"Now there is a folly unworthy of you," he said softly, his tone making her feel flustered and uncertain. Truly, her host possessed an unholy charm. "Love is a caprice and a whim, not a feeling upon which a woman should make her choices."

"Love is the voice of the heart, of intuition and instinct and destiny."

"Surely reason should have a place in the choice of spouse? I have given you sanctuary." He gestured to the palace but sadly, the movement did not make his hood move so that she could see his features. "I have ensured your comfort. I will continue to protect and fulfill your needs when you are my wife. Is that not of merit?"

"It is, sir," Annelise was forced to concede.

"And more of a guarantee than many other maidens have upon

taking their vows?"

"More, indeed."

"Then, let us wed." His tone indicated that he thought the matter resolved. "Let this love you desire grow in time, after we are wed."

"Sir, my notion is not whimsy. I do not even know your name! I have never looked upon your face! I know little of you, beyond the fact that you have treated me well on this day. That is not sufficient!"

"But if you thought you loved me, that would compensate for all else?"

Her conviction sounded foolish when he expressed it thus, but Annelise lifted her chin. "If I believed we loved each other, that would, sir."

"Shall I try to change your thinking?"

His low voice had awakened a tingle in Annelise that was not unwelcome. She was keenly aware that she was alone with this man, in a palace seemingly made for pleasure.

With a man who spoke to her as if she were his equal.

She swallowed. "I think not, sir."

"Whyever not?" he murmured. He raised that gloved hand to her cheek, letting his fingertips trail across her skin. Annelise shivered despite herself. She found herself leaning toward him, wanting to feel his warmth—and far more. "Many ladies prefer to be convinced," he said, his voice almost a whisper.

"Not me," she said with haste and stepped away. "I know my own thinking, sir, and often express it with vigor. Indeed, most men see that quality as a liability."

The smile was in his voice again. "While I am intrigued. I have a great affection for honesty, my Annelise, and have never desired a wife who would tell me what I sought to hear. You see? Our match becomes more potent with every moment."

Annelise felt that she was being overwhelmed by his surety. He had a reply for every objection and, worse, she found her wish to deny him fading quickly. "I am certain, sir, that the novelty would fade. Marriage to me would suit you less well than you believe."

He laughed then. "Do not have such little confidence in your charms, Annelise. I am convinced otherwise, that further acquaintance would only add to your allure."

Annelise flushed then, because he had to be mocking her. No man had ever spoken to her thus. "I fear you mock me, sir."

"I know you are mistaken."

"All the same, I would abandon your hospitality, sir. I thank you for offering me a haven, but would prefer to leave."

"You choose the wolves over marriage to me?"

Annelise nodded. "Certainly," she said, although she did not feel so resolute. "I shall leave first thing in the morning."

He did not reply, but she felt his gaze upon her.

"With my horse." Annelise swallowed. "Thank you again, sir, for your hospitality. Perhaps the next maiden will welcome your offer."

Still he did not speak.

She held out the ring again, but he did not move to accept it.

Had she injured his feelings? She felt a twinge of guilt then. He must truly be a fearsome sight. He must be lonely. While Annelise could feel compassion for him, she would not wed a man who refused to even show himself to her. She placed the ring on the flagstones between them rather than approach him again, then turned to leave.

Why had her heart clenched so tightly?

Why did she fear that she erred? Annelise knew she was right.

She was Quinn's sister.

Rolfe was well aware of his comrade's demand that Rolfe and Niall keep away from his sister. It had become a jest, but also was about seduction and not marriage. Rolfe had been resolved to abandon his ways with the exchange of marriage vows, but knowing that Quinn would take poorly to any slight suffered by his sister only redoubled his determination to court the affection of his lady wife alone.

Annelise was even more lovely when awake and Rolfe found her unspeakably alluring. Though he could see the resemblance, she was vivacious while her brother was more somber. She had amber eyes like Quinn's, but while the knight's often glowed with deadly intent, the lady's eyes flashed with a fire that heated Rolfe's blood. He had no doubt that her passion would extend to all facets of life and that she would embrace every pleasure. He had vastly enjoyed their conversation and the speed of her wit, and already anticipated a merry union.

But she meant to leave.

She would depart the palace and abandon its comforts rather than marry him. Perhaps she shared her brother's skepticism of his intentions.

Perhaps Rolfe's charm had faded.

It was clear he needed to be more persuasive with Annelise. She must agree to wed him on this very night.

He let her take a dozen steps before he spoke. "Not in the morning," he decreed.

Annelise glanced over her shoulder and Rolfe shook his head. "If you leave, my Annelise, you will leave now."

Her dismay was clear. "It is the darkest hour of the night!" she protested, turning to appeal to him. "You could not be so cruel!"

"I fear I must be firm, Annelise," Rolfe insisted. "You gave your word that you would wed me in exchange for being granted admission to my palace. Is that not true?"

Annelise exhaled and her lips set. "It is, sir."

"And now you would rescind your pledge."

Annelise flushed. "You cannot wish to wed me, either, sir, not on so little acquaintance..."

"But I do." He shook a finger at her. "I would excuse you from your vow, but only if you left this very moment." It was a risk, but he doubted she would take it.

He hoped she would not.

Wolves howled in the distance, as if to remind them both of the perils of the forest.

Rolfe continued, speaking with a confidence he did not entirely feel. This lady, he suspected, was unpredictable—which, in truth, only added to his interest. "But if you remain within the walls until the morning, you must wed me first. I would not have it said that I had despoiled a maiden so lovely as yourself."

Annelise strode back toward him, those eyes flashing with a

vigor that made him want to kiss her senseless. "But I cannot leave now! You know the wolves would attack again."

"You gave your word," he reminded her.

Annelise halted before him and lifted her chin, clearly intending to look into his eyes. "Please do not be insulted. My choice has nothing to do with your disfigurement, however horrific it must be." Rolfe frowned in confusion as she continued. "I can never marry a man who does not love me. It is that simple."

"And how," Rolfe murmured, "would you know whether a man loved you to your satisfaction?"

"I would simply know."

"How? Give me a tangible example of a man's love."

"He would protect me from harm...."

"Save you from hungry wolves, perhaps?"

Annelise glared at him. "Perhaps."

"What else?"

"He would ensure that I was sheltered and fed."

"Ah!" Rolfe pivoted to survey the palace.

"Gifts," Annelise said, sounding as if she had gritted her teeth. "A man smitten with his lady would bring her gifts."

Rolfe could not resist reminding her. "Perhaps like a hot bath when she most desired one."

Annelise exhaled in such evident frustration that he almost laughed. "You twist my words, sir! You cannot love me. We have known each other mere moments."

"Yet it is said that the greatest journeys begin with a single step."

Annelise eyed him, apparently having no argument to make against that.

"Perhaps," Rolfe continued, "the truth of a man's affection might also be found in the marital bed." He saw her swallow as he raised his hand to her chin and felt her shiver beneath that light touch. "Your position is precarious, my Annelise," he murmured. "You would neither wed me nor leave my abode before morning. Surely you know that I could take whatever I desired of you, with no nuptial vows between us. Who would come to your aid?"

Annelise caught her breath but did not retreat. "But you would not."

Rolfe was intrigued that she was not afraid. "How do you know?"

"You are not that manner of man."

"How do you know?"

She frowned. "You would have done your worst already. You might not have offered me sanctuary. You showed me kindness when you did not need to..."

"And you come to trust me. I think we already take steps upon our journey together."

She flicked a glance at him that was so filled with vexation that Rolfe did smile.

"But we both know that you cannot possibly love me," Annelise insisted.

"Yet the end result is the same, is it not?" he whispered. "Surely love, like all matters of merit, manifests in tangible results?"

Annelise opened her mouth to argue, then closed it again.

Rolfe was close to triumph. He dropped to one knee before her and saw her try to spy something of him as the cloak parted. Her gaze flicked over his bent knee, then dropped to his gloved hand. She was curious about him, which could only be progress.

Of course, she had concluded that he was disfigured.

Perhaps that worried her, as well.

Rolfe straightened and doffed his glove. He held the ring out to her, the circle of gold pinched between finger and thumb of his right hand.

She looked and he knew what she saw. His hand was tanned, the palm broad and fingers strong. There was a callus on the palm at the base of his smallest finger. Her gaze lingered there, then she glanced suddenly at him.

"You are a knight."

"Intent upon winning a lady's favor so that she agrees to become my wife."

She reached out and touched the white band on his finger. "You wore this ring until you gave it to me."

"It is the only ring I possess, and a wife must have a ring."

She caught her breath, her eyes darkening.

"Take my ring, Annelise," he said softly, a thread of command in his tone. "Keep your vow."

Rolfe saw her panic, but then she was cornered. What would she do, this unpredictable lady? She would not flee. Not Annelise. No, she would try to expose him, Rolfe guessed.

Indeed, she reached abruptly for his hood, clearly hoping to surprise him.

Rolfe's other hand emerged from the folds of his cloak with lightning speed and locked around her wrist. She looked down at his hand, and Rolfe knew it was the supposed scar that she feared. His left hand was gloved, but clearly intact. Rolfe felt her pulse flutter beneath his thumb.

"I made myself a promise," she whispered.

"And you made another promise to me." Rolfe shed the other glove, watched her look, then captured her wrist again. His thumb slid across the inside of her wrist in a gentle caress, and his voice dropped as he continued. "The two are not necessarily incompatible."

Her pulse leaped, the lady flushed, and Rolfe was reassured.

She peered up at him, and he saw that her resolve wavered. "How could they not be?"

Rolfe felt protective of her and wished he did not have to press her so on this matter. In the morning, the curse would be broken and he could confess all of the truth to her. There would be no cost in confiding in his wife then. "The two goals can be as one," he said with conviction. "Your needs were met before you even stated them. I promise to you that will continue."

Her eyes flashed and her next words were tart. "I expect more than a meal and the occasional bath from marriage."

Rolfe smiled despite himself, liking her spirit. "And perhaps you are overly ambitious for that," he chided. "Many women are abused or ignored by their spouses, kept in dismal conditions and forced to bear countless children. It is not so uncommon as a sheltered woman like yourself might think."

Annelise was so impassive that Rolfe wondered if that was her fear.

"You will experience none of that at my hand and will be better situated than most," he said. "I swear it to you, Annelise, that as my lady wife, you will be protected and defended to my very best ability. Indeed, you will have the benefits that you consider to be a mark of a man's love."

"But there would be no love between us," she said.

He clicked his tongue. "Can you divine the future, my Annelise?" He began to trace larger circles against the soft inside of her wrist as he spoke and felt her sway toward him. That was promising, indeed. "Who can say what will grow between us over the years?"

Annelise peered up at him, again trying to catch a glimpse of his face. "Tell me your name," she insisted. "Give me this much."

Rolfe shook his head.

"That does not bode well for this pretty future you promise."

"You must not look fully upon me before the morrow."

She frowned in confusion. "What will change by the morrow? It is already late...."

Rolfe chuckled and she gasped with a maiden's surprise.

"But without my looking upon you? How could we..." She flushed and he admired that she had the courage to ask what she clearly believed to be a very bold question. "Is this to be a consummated match, sir?"

He moved so that they stood toe-to-toe. Her breasts were but a finger's width from his chest, and he looked down into the glory of her widened eyes. He could smell the scent of the roses from her bath, mingled with the lady's own sweet scent, and his anticipation of their union rose. He would introduce her gently and sweetly to the arts of love. He would seduce her. He would ensure her pleasure. And he would do as much as many times as she desired. He would win her with his touch. "This match will be complete in every sense of the word," he assured her.

Her flush deepened to a darker hue of crimson. "You looked!" she whispered.

He shook his head and lifted her hand to his lips. "No, but I wanted to. You are alluring in sleep, my Annelise, but the honor of a lady must not be compromised."

He kissed her fingertips, well aware that she strained to see his mouth.

He continued with resolve, using her apparent concern as an excuse. "We must consummate in darkness so that you are not burdened with the sight of me."

Annelise bit her lip and he guessed that her compassion for him grew.

"What about the morrow? Why did you say I could look upon you then?"

"Perhaps my situation will have changed."

She frowned, but Rolfe silenced her question by raising the ring between them again. The garnet snared the moonlight and glowed a dull red. "Do we have vows to exchange, Annelise?"

"There is no priest," she whispered, though the heat was gone from her protest.

"Marriage is the only sacrament for which one does not need a priest," he reminded her. "Annelise?"

She stared at the ring. She bit her lip. She sighed and Rolfe had a moment to fear that she would still decline him. What would he do then? A panic rose within him for he could not take what she would not give, or compel her to accept him, yet the breaking of the curse relied upon her agreement. How could he persuade her?

Then Annelise lifted her left hand toward the ring, sending relief surging through Rolfe. "I will, sir." She sighed. "I concede defeat."

It was not the most encouraging agreement of a proposal, but Rolfe was heartily glad of it.

He brushed a fingertip across the end of her nose, unable to keep from teasing her. "Ah, my Annelise, why do I suspect that you never truly admit defeat?"

Her eyes sparkled then, filling with a merriment that stole his breath away. "Perhaps we do come to understand each other, sir."

Rolfe laughed as the lady smiled up at him. "I might have to believe in destiny, after all, since the Fates brought me such a bride," he said, then bent to claim her ripe lips with a kiss.

She would be his bride and his salvation, and Rolfe would ensure she never regretted this choice.

Annelise had no time to feel disappointment in her choice, for it had not truly been a choice at all. She knew her host had cornered her with logic and she took encouragement from his determination to hold her to her word. She liked that he coaxed her smile, as if he had feared she would still decline.

She had not anticipated his triumphant kiss.

He bent quickly and touched his lips to hers, then when she caught her breath in surprise, he slanted his mouth over hers and deepened his kiss. The hood of his cloak shrouded her face from even the light of the moon. One of his arms was around her waist, drawing her against his heat, while his other hand held hers.

Annelise had never been kissed like this before.

It was a marvel.

His kiss was sweet, coaxing her response, inviting her to participate instead of claiming his due. He did not force himself upon her: instead, he persuaded her to respond in kind. His kiss was a marvel and a delight, one that set her pulse racing and her anticipation rising. Her very flesh was on fire and she found herself rising to her toes, wanting only more.

It was a persuasive kiss and one that fed her confidence in her choice as nothing else could have done.

When he lifted his head, Annelise found herself struck to rare silence.

Her host led her to the bower of flowers, then turned to face her again, holding both of her hands in his own. His hands were warm and strong, unscarred, and his touch was gentle. Annelise thought about them upon her flesh and her toes curled in her shoes. He began to recite the familiar vows in his wonderfully deep voice and she was amazed to find herself in such a situation.

But not unhappy with it. He had listened to her concerns and tried to reassure her. He had promised to treat her well, and she was inclined to believe him.

"I take thee, Annelise de Sayerne, to be my wedded wife..."

Annelise made her vows in turn, her voice growing in conviction as she spoke.

The lord slid his ring onto the middle finger of her left hand. It was heavy and still warm, a weight to remind her of her pledge.

Annelise glanced up when he kept a grip on her hand, wishing she could see his eyes in this moment.

"With this ring, I thee wed," he said huskily. "With my body, I thee worship, and with all my worldly goods, I thee endow."

It was done.

She was married.

Annelise stared down at the ring, the red stone almost glowing in the moonlight, and thus missed her new husband's quick movement.

He caught her nape with one warm palm and pulled her in his embrace with gentle force. His kiss was gentle, cajoling, yet more resolute this time. He held her against his strength and she felt both cherished and protected.

An unfamiliar longing was awakened within Annelise, its embers stoked to a flame as his kiss deepened. She found herself melting against him, surrendering to his touch, mimicking him and wanting more.

So much more. She could feel no imperfections in his form, although something decidedly hard pressed against her hip. She ran her hands over his shoulders and soon forgot her exploration, for she liked the feel of him so very well.

She tasted the hunger in him and knew that she was not powerless in this exchange. That, above all else, gave her hope for their future.

Finally, he lifted his head and cupped her face in his hands. "Well, wife of mine," he whispered. "Shall we retire to our nuptial bed?"

Annelise had never expected she would be so willing so quickly, but she was. Her flesh tingled in the aftermath of his touch, and though she did not know precisely what would happen abed, she was anxious to learn more.

She wanted his hands on her.

She wanted his lips on her.

She was a wanton of the first order, yet in this moment she did not care.

Annelise nodded, not trusting herself to speak. Her husband swung her into his arms and carried her back to the palace with such ease that she dared to hope he had no flaw at all.

What if this might prove to be the match she had always desired?

Annelise's kiss had set Rolfe's blood afire. That she had learned so quickly to mimic his movements, that she should so readily entice him with ardor was far more than he had expected.

She would have him in her thrall if he were not cautious.

Rolfe could think of nothing but the consummation before them as he carried her back to his favorite chamber. She kicked her feet playfully and stole glances at him, her expression a mix of anticipation and maidenly concern. He would see those fears banished and pleasure found in their stead.

The palace offered an abundance of pleasures but he wished that they might have had a solid bed. There was nothing in his opinion that could compete with the comfort of a massive bed, rooted to floor and ceiling with four oaken pillars and hung with heavy draperies to block the cold. His parents possessed such a bed, and he had not seen the like since he had left for Outremer.

It was at moments like this that Rolfe disliked the exotic tendencies of the palace. Likely, they would have to make do with cushions, leaving them with aching backs on the morrow.

Even that prospect could not dampen his ardor. One night of loving—one night of loving a woman whose allure grew by the moment—and he would be free of the curse that bound him. Finally, it seemed that Rolfe's good fortune had returned.

He stepped into his favorite chamber and froze in his steps.

To his astonishment, there was a bed precisely as he had imagined against one wall of the room. The tub and the low table where Annelise had eaten were both gone, although the fountain still danced in the moonlit courtyard beyond.

He stared at the bed and Annelise slipped from his embrace. She crossed the chamber and gave one post a shake, as though she doubted the evidence of her own eyes. Then she turned to him, those eyes flashing. "How did you cause this to be here?" She gave the bed a hearty shove, then glanced back to Rolfe. "It is fixed to the floor as solidly as though they were made together. This was not here earlier. Is this the same room?"

"Yes."

"Then how can this be?"

Rolfe understood that it was because he had wished for it. He recalled the second djinn's spell.

And whether he feel good or ill,
the palace shall reflect his will.

How much could he wish for? Clearly, he could not wish to break the curse, and his desire to win Annelise's agreement had not readily overcome her reluctance to wed him. This was a matter to be considered later, perhaps on the morrow when he could discuss it with Annelise.

He did not dare to confide in her just yet.

Not give the rest of the curse.

"Servants," he said with a wave of his hand. "I am fortunate to have some gifted ones here."

"Servants." Annelise echoed, her doubt more than clear. She folded her arms across her chest and granted him a skeptical glance. "No servant, however diligent, could have built this bed in the time I was gone."

"Never underestimate the skill of a talented craftsman." Rolfe felt the weakness of the argument but he had no other.

Annelise's lips tightened and he knew she would not abandon the issue so readily.

Indeed, he looked forward to hearing what she would say.

"Which reminds me," she said with another survey of the chamber. "I have not noticed anyone here since I arrived. Not one other mortal soul." She turned to look at Rolfe, her manner expectant. "Only horses. Where are your servants, sir?"

"Oh, they are here. Perhaps you have not looked in the right places," Rolfe replied. Unable to hold her gaze—even though he knew she could not see his own eyes—he turned to snuff the candles.

There was a matter requiring their immediate attention. The more he spoke to Annelise, the more she intrigued him and the more he was tempted to confide in her. They had to break the curse as soon as possible.

Annelise did not move, Rolfe noted. Nor did she undress. He paused before extinguishing the last candle. "Do you need assistance?"

A gleam lit her eye. "Will you summon one of your servants to assist me?"

Rolfe bit back a smile, knowing he should have anticipated her. "No. It is too late to trouble them."

"You are a thoughtful master."

"I do try."

She tilted her head to one side. "But it is evidently not too late for them to build a bed."

"It is precisely because of such diligent labor that I would let them rest now."

"Indeed," Annelise murmured, eying the bed again.

Rolfe saw that her concerns were returning, and knew they had to get to bed with all haste. "Perhaps I should help you disrobe."

The lady flushed scarlet. "I shall manage on my own. I am not accustomed to having a maid, after all."

Why not? Why would she not have a maid? Rolfe did not ask because he had no desire of more conversation.

When Annelise did not make any move to unknot her laces or even remove her shoes, he prompted her again. "Are you going to disrobe, my lady?"

Annelise lifted her chin and turned to face him. "If I cannot see you, sir, then be assured that you are not going to see me. I shall await the darkness. "

There was much to be said for the lady's spirit. Rolfe smiled as he pinched the last wick and plunged the chamber into darkness. The moonlight did not illuminate beyond the courtyard, which defied belief.

But then he realized that, too, was a mark of his will. He wished for complete darkness and so it was.

He cast his cloak aside, discarding boots and shirt. The garments fell audibly to the floor.

Annelise was breathing quickly, but he could not discern that she had undressed. "God in heaven, but it is dark," she whispered, agitation in her tone.

"Are you afraid?" he asked when he was beside her.

"Of course not!"

Rolfe said nothing, guessing that the heat of her reply meant otherwise. He waited, giving her the time she seemed to need.

When the silence stretched between them, Annelise sighed. "I am, perhaps, a little uncertain, sir," she acknowledged in a small voice that he already knew was uncharacteristic. "What exactly should I expect to happen this night?"

Rolfe imagined that she had tilted her head to look where she thought he was, and he could easily picture her amber eyes bright with curiosity.

He reached for her cheek and stroked it gently. "More like the kisses in the courtyard. Did you not enjoy them?"

"I did. But the other..." Her voice faltered. "Will it hurt?" There was a slight tremor in her tone.

Rolfe could think of nothing but reassuring her.

He slid his fingers along her jaw and cupped her face in his hands. Her skin was softer than the finest silk. Rolfe could feel her racing pulse under his thumb and took encouragement from it.

"It may hurt," he murmured, brushing his lips across hers. She trembled but did not retreat or pull away. "But only for a moment if it does, and only this first time." He felt Annelise swallow. "I vow to you that I shall be gentle."

"You like to make vows, sir."

"I like to keep them even better."

She took a quick breath. "Of course, for you are a knight."

"I am, lady mine."

He felt her straighten beneath his hands and his heart soared at her boldness.

"And I am your lady wife," she whispered. "I trust you in this, sir, and I will be your wife in every way by morning."

The conviction in her words stole the breath from Rolfe's lungs. Her confidence touched him to his heart and redoubled his determination to do his utmost to please his Annelise.

She would have no regrets. Rolfe would ensure as much.

He bent and captured her lips, liking how she rose to her toes to meet him, and his surety that this match would be a good one grew stronger again.

He would spend the night convincing his lady of the same.

CHAPTER FIVE

I do not know what to do," Annelise admitted when Rolfe broke his kiss.

"Nothing," he murmured against the softness of her cheek. "Simply enjoy."

She took a deep breath and released it slowly, and he felt the tension ease out of her shoulders. He took one himself, wanting to be sure to seduce her slowly.

"Very good." Rolfe whispered the words into her ear.

Annelise shivered then giggled. "That tickles!"

It was as good a place to begin as any. "And this?" Rolfe pressed a slow kiss into her ear. The lady quivered again, as he had guessed she would.

"That is a tickle of a most wicked kind," she said, her words breathless.

"How so?"

"It awakens something deep within me."

"Something good?"

"Yes, my lord."

To Rolfe's surprise, this time it was Annelise who stretched to brush her lips across his. He liked that she wanted to participate and deepened their kiss, even as he planned how to encourage her. He trailed kisses down her cheek and she tipped her head back with a purr of satisfaction. He ran his teeth across her earlobe. "And this?"

Annelise gasped. "I do not know what to call how that feels."

"Good or bad?"

"Oh..." Her laugh was throaty. "More than good."

Her enthusiasm made Rolfe chuckle again. "Then perhaps we should try the other ear." He took his time with that kiss, savoring the way she melted against his chest. The darkness made the scent of her skin seem more potent.

More beguiling.

Annelise locked her arms around his neck and kissed him fully, showing an expertise unexpected. He caught his breath that she learned so quickly. The night promised to be even more delightful than he could have imagined.

Her breath tickled as it fanned his ear. "Good or bad?" she whispered, mischief in her tone.

"More than good," Rolfe growled, liking her playfulness as well. He ran his hands down her sides and feigned surprise. "You are still fully garbed, my lady."

As though she had just realized that he was not, Annelise's hands moved from Rolfe's neck to touch his bare skin. Her fingers fanned out as she tentatively ran her hands across his shoulders. Rolfe let her explore, sensing that she needed to know something about him before they were intimate.

He heard her take a deep breath as her hand slid downward. When she found the mat of his chest hair, she bounced her fingers playfully upon it, then slid them through its tangle.

"Furry," she pronounced, then skimmed her fingertips over his nipples. Rolfe inhaled sharply at her light touch and Annelise, noting his reaction, paused to caress his nipples. "You like this," she whispered.

"As I expect do you." Rolfe cupped her breast in one hand, then teased the nipple with his fingertips. Even through the heavy woolen cloth, he felt it tighten to a peak.

"So I do," Annelise admitted, then stepped back from him, her hands stroking him. Rolfe closed his eyes, awash with pleasure from her touch. Her fingertips eased lower, where the hair thinned near his waist, then halted at the drawstring of his chausses.

She hesitated.

"My turn," Rolfe whispered. Before Annelise could protest, he bent and rapidly unlaced the sides of her kirtle. He lifted the garment over her head and cast it aside, then the chemise she wore beneath it. The warmth of her skin greeted his exploring fingertips and he slid his hands over her upper arms.

"Your hair," he whispered, knowing that he would never find all the pins in the darkness. Rolfe heard them tinkle to the floor as she removed them quickly, then the heavy mass of her hair fell over her shoulders and his hands.

It was thick and almost straight. Rolfe could imagine the shimmer of it and remembered its rich auburn color. He buried his hands in its thickness, then pulled her into his embrace.

With those amber eyes, she should be garbed in emerald green, in samite and satin heavy with golden embroidery. She needed veils of the finest cloth of gold to highlight the richness of her coloring.

Indeed, her worn travel garments scarcely did her credit. With such vivacity and life, Annelise dressed as a queen would be a stunning sight.

The fullness of her breasts pressed against his chest as he explored her. Her waist was delightfully narrow under his hands, her curves ripe enough to fill his hands. Rolfe's heart leaped when her hair moved over his hands, evidence that she had tilted her head back. He bent and captured her tempting lips beneath his own, swallowing her sigh of satisfaction.

Rolfe kissed her gently, savoring her. He felt Annelise catch her breath, then caressed her bottom lip with his tongue. She parted her lips, welcoming him, and Rolfe sampled her deeply, loving the taste of wine mingled with her own honeyed sweetness.

She was all sweet curves and femininity, her skin soft no matter where he touched her. Rolfe kissed her leisurely and thoroughly, taking his time with the feast she offered. Annelise was his wife and his salvation both. He could give her no less than his all.

His hand moved in her hair, caressing her jaw, tracing the curve of her ear. Annelise shuddered and her hands locked around his neck. He lifted her to her toes, cupping her buttocks with one hand and pulling her against the heat of his arousal. She moaned softly and rolled her hips against him with a need that thrilled him.

Desire surged through Rolfe. He kissed Annelise with new fervor, fearing he would spill his seed early if she rolled her hips again, but he could not step away. He would have liked to have seen her but the darkness was complete.

"Oh," Annelise whispered as her lips moved against his throat. Her voice was unsteady.

It amused Rolfe that this woman of so many words could only conjure that one small exclamation to describe this. "Oh?" he repeated with a smile.

"I...I had no idea."

Rolfe could not help but chuckle at the wonder in her voice. The affection he already felt for her surprised him with its intensity. Rolfe could not recall ever being so aware of a woman so quickly before.

"And still you have not, wife of mine," he murmured. "We have only begun."

He bent quickly and took one of her feet in his hands. It was so slender and small, so delicate compared to his own, that he halted for a moment in silent appreciation.

Annelise's hands landed on his shoulders, and Rolfe quickly unlaced her shoe. He discarded it, noting with interest that she did not wear hose.

She had been in a hurry to seek him out. That made him smile.

Her foot fit perfectly in his palm and Rolfe could not resist caressing its arch. The darkness served only to heighten his awareness of her.

The other shoe was shed and Rolfe paused with both hands wrapped around the lady's graceful ankles. He glanced up and her fingers dug slightly into his shoulders.

"There must be more," she whispered, her impatience urging him on.

Rolfe eased his hands slowly up her calves, feeling the shape of her. His lips followed suit, tasting and caressing as he progressed. Had she worn stockings, he would have removed her garters with his teeth.

Her thighs were slender, and when he approached her hips, the sweet perfume of her arousal tempted him. That mingled with the scent of the roses was more intoxicating than the finest wine. Rolfe filled his lungs with the heady scent and caressed her as his lips meandered onward.

She gasped when he reached the apex of her thighs and Rolfe buried his nose in the nest of curls. His tongue danced against her and he knew he had found the prize he sought when Annelise gripped his shoulders.

"Oh!" she gasped. "Sir!"

Rolfe pulled her closer, one of his fingers rising to caress her even as he continued to tease her with his tongue. Her enthusiasm fed his own passion as nothing else could. He wanted more of Annelise; he wanted all of her. He wanted to make her collapse on top of him. He wanted to feel her wrap herself around him and demand more. He wanted to hear her cry out as she found her release and know that he was responsible. He felt her skin heat and her pulse race. A quiver passed over her flesh, but she did not pull away.

She trusted him, which was the finest aphrodisiac Rolfe had ever known.

He gripped her waist, loving how his hand spanned her back there, and held her captive to the pleasure he intended to give. The woman would drive him mad with desire. She writhed against him, her fingers digging into his shoulders, her wet sweetness flooding his senses.

When her hips began to buck, Rolfe held her more resolutely. He drove her higher, demanding more, caressing her with more vigor.

Suddenly, Annelise arched back. She gave a little cry as she strained for the heavens and found her release, then wilted and sagged against him, her breath coming in quick spurts.

Luckily for the lady, Rolfe was not finished pleasuring his bride just yet.

"That was a marvel," Annelise whispered, unable to believe the power of the tremor that had nigh overwhelmed her.

"That, wife of mine, is only the beginning," her husband murmured then he ran his tongue over her tenderness once more.

Annelise gasped, then laughed a little. "You know my sources of pleasure better than I do," she charged and he chuckled.

"Should a husband not do so?" He trailed kisses across her skin. He tickled her navel with his tongue but Annelise was impatient to grant him pleasure, too. She caught his head in her hands and pulled him upward. He caught the weight of her breasts in his hands and turned his attention to her nipples, teasing them with his fingers and lips until they were aching and taut.

Annelise moaned softly as she rocked on her feet, powerless beneath his touch. The man was a sorcerer. He wove a spell to enchant her completely. He would make her a slave to the pleasure that only he had ever given her.

And Annelise did not mind.

Indeed, she was increasingly certain that her husband bore no disfigurement at all. His hands were strong and well-formed. She felt no scar on his chest or his shoulders, and the sole thing unusual about his mouth was its unholy power to give pleasure. His legs were muscular and he possessed both of them.

Was it his face that was scarred? It could not be fearsomely so, not from what she had felt. He possessed both ears and they were shaped as they should be. She felt no scar upon his jaw or his cheek.

Was it his nose?

One eye?

He pinched her nipple so that she gasped in pleasure then swept her into his arms. She guessed that he strode for the bed, but had no opportunity to ask for he kissed her. His tongue danced with hers, his kiss shaking her to her very marrow—as she already came to believe that every good kiss should. She felt her desire rising again, that seductive shimmer beneath her skin making her anticipate whatever would come next. They tumbled onto the mattress which was soft and thick.

Annelise landed on her back with her husband beside her. He held her fast against his side and leaned over her. If not for the darkness, she would surely have seen his face. His hand swept over her thigh, then found the spot where his caress had given her such pleasure just moments before. He eased one knee between hers, and she wrapped herself around him, wanting him to be closer.

She could not help but note that every bit of him she touched was perfectly normal.

Then his fingers and their wicked dance obliterated all such concerns from her thoughts. Annelise felt that she was a slave to sensation and she adored it. She arched against her husband's strength, rubbing her breasts against his chest, feeling his heart beat faster. He emanated a heat that seemed to hint at his own excitement. She pressed kisses to his chest, then grazed his shoulder with her teeth. He growled with satisfaction and she bit him a little, making him chuckle in a way that thrilled her.

He shifted her beneath him and eased between her thighs. Annelise felt a hardness against her thighs as he braced his weight above her, and wished mightily that she might be able to see him in this moment. She parted her thighs to welcome him, for theirs was an agreement made, and heard him inhale sharply.

"Annelise," he whispered, his voice hoarse. "My lady Annelise."

He eased inside her, moving slowly and pausing often to kiss her temple. Annelise held on to his shoulders, waiting for the anticipated pain. She felt full and stretched, but also so very close to him. It was an intimacy beyond anything she had experienced before and one that made tears rise to her eyes. They were two become one, their flesh pressed together from shoulder to toe, their lives bound together until death did they part. Annelise lifted her hips against him, then realized he moved no deeper.

"And that will be the worst of it," he murmured to her, kissing her lips quickly. "How does it feel?"

"Wondrous in a new way," she confessed, feeling that there could be no secrets between two people who had joined thus in the night.

"Did it not hurt?"

"Only a little, sir," she confessed. "Will you show me more?"

"Of course, my lady. Your wish is my command." His voice sounded taut and she wondered if he held something back to ensure her pleasure. Then he moved and she heard herself gasp aloud at the brush against that sensitive spot. She squirmed beneath him and he groaned, a most delicious sound of surrender and one Annelise wished to hear again. She locked her knees around his waist, pulling him closer, and on his next thrust, he sank more deeply inside her. Annelise tightened her arms around his neck. Her breasts were crushed against his chest, and her nipples were teased by the hair on his chest.

He moved slowly, then with increasing speed. Annelise felt his pulse increase and his skin heat. She heard the rasp of his breath and felt an answering arousal within herself. They moved together, driving each other on to some crescendo she could not name but did not want to abandon.

All too soon, the heat rose furiously within her again. He rubbed against her and Annelise cried out in pleasure. She knew that her nails tore into his back as she arched against him and found her release once more.

"Sir!" she cried, feeling she had betrayed him somehow.

But her husband roared with a pleasure that could not be feigned. He reared back, clutching her buttocks tightly as the heat of his seed poured into her. He was strong and taut, a perfect warrior in every way, and his release made Annelise feel that they had tasted magic together.

"Oh!" she said softly and heard him chuckle.

He rolled to one side, landing on the mattress beside her, and held her fast against his side. "Oh!" he mimicked, then kissed her temple.

"Did I do what I should?" she asked.

"You were perfection itself, my Annelise," he said, satisfaction resonating in his tone. He brushed the hair back from her face with his fingertips, and she wondered if he could see in the darkness for his touch was unerring. "Did I do what I should?"

"I am not certain, but it was quite a marvel," she admitted and he laughed.

Annelise liked that sound well. She propped herself up on one elbow and touched his shoulder, peering down to where she knew his face had to be.

What would she have given to have seen his eyes in this

moment of moments?

On the other hand, it was easier to ask bold questions when she did not have to look him in the eye.

"Is that how other people consummate their marriages?" she asked.

"That has always been my understanding," he confirmed, amusement in his tone.

Annelise leaned over him, pressing her breast against Rolfe's ribs. The tumble of her hair landed on his chest and she felt his hand move into its length. She liked that he was not immune to her charms, such as they were, and dared to ask an even bolder question.

"Can we do it again?"

He laughed more heartily than he had yet and Annelise smiled at the sound. "It would be my pleasure, my lady," he replied and rolled her to her back before he claimed her lips once more.

His kisses proved to be more powerful each time. Annelise was breathless when he raised his head and her heart was thundering. She stroked his broad shoulders and smiled with satisfaction. "Perhaps it would be mine, sir," she replied and he laughed again.

"I wager we will both be well pleased, my Annelise."

"I would not wager against you on such terms," she said, prompting his laughter once again. His kiss was quick and thorough.

"Then you have no complaints, my Annelise?"

"Not about this, sir," she began but had no chance to continue for her husband kissed her to silence.

And within a heartbeat, Annelise did not care.

Rolfe awakened before the dawn, eager to begin his first day free of the curse. He would be a man in daylight again and could explain all to his marvel of a wife. They could decide whether to remain in the palace or ride for Viandin.

The fountain tinkled merrily in the courtyard and the chamber was still dark. Annelise burrowed against his side. He could feel her hair strewn over her shoulders and savored her sweet warmth pressed against him. He eased a tendril away from her cheek with a fingertip, affection swelling within him.

What a wife this palace had brought to him! Rolfe was jubilant that they had sent his curse on its way in such a resounding fashion. He would never have anticipated finding a woman of such passion as Annelise simply by chance, much less having such a woman as his wife.

The bottle truly had made his dreams come true. He had a palace, a wife and obvious wealth. They could raise a family within these walls, if she desired. They might like to return to Viandin, but it was a relief not to be reliant upon Adalbert's good will to build a future.

On this morning Rolfe would eliminate the secret between them and share his truth with Annelise.

It was possible that she might hold a small grudge. Rolfe considered that her eyes might flash that he had not initially confided all of the tale. He kissed her forehead and decided he would ensure she was in a receptive mood for his confession.

Flowers were a well-established path to a woman's heart. Reluctantly, Rolfe slipped from the warmth of the bed. The palace was filled with the warm air of a summer morn but it was his wife he did not wish to leave.

He walked to the garden without donning a chemise. In truth, there was advantage in having no servants or others in the palace. He cut more of the same red roses that had perfumed her bath. Their scent already evoked the sight of Annelise's smile to Rolfe and the taste of her skin. He smiled in anticipation of the aftermath of his confession.

Their celebration might be an exhausting proposition.

Rolfe could hardly wait. Even the memory of Rosalinde's scorn could not color his optimism this morn. Annelise was different, Rolfe was certain. They would make a good life together, here in this remote palace. He would invite friends and artisans, perhaps establish a village with a mill. Their children would prosper in this place.

He hurried to arrange the roses in the chamber where Annelise slept, determined to surprise her when she awakened. Rolfe surveyed the result and decided he needed more blooms. The dawn drew near as he hastened back to the garden one last time.

The first rays of the sun lit the roof of the palace and Rolfe watched the sky lighten in the east. For the first time in over a month, he could savor the dawn without fearing the curse. He smiled as the sky lightened and took a deep breath of the morning air.

He savored his first day as a man again.

Then the morning breeze slid through his tail.

Rolfe spun around and his heart sank when he saw the truth.

How could this be?

Even as he struggled to understand why the change was occurring, an unseen force propelled him across the garden toward the gate. Rolfe fought against it every step of the way. He knew he was not permitted within these walls in wolf form, but he should not have become a wolf this day. He should have been able to remain with Annelise and tell her the truth!

Love was supposed to be his salvation.

What had gone awry?

Rolfe quickly found himself flung through the gate. When he landed on his four paws, he ran toward the open gate, but they closed against him.

He sat down in the snow, perplexed.

The curse had not been lifted by his efforts.

Had the second djinn been wrong? Had he misunderstood her terms? Or had she deceived him, promising a reward then stealing it away when he had earned it? There was a lesson there on the deceptiveness of women, mortal or djinn, of which Rolfe should not have needed a reminder. Rosalinde had taught him that lesson, after all.

He was a fool to have trusted the djinn and a worse fool for beginning to trust Annelise. And now he would have considerable time to consider his error.

Alone.

In the snow outside the palace walls.

He lifted his head and howled in frustration.

Annelise awoke feeling warm and content. She snuggled beneath the coverlet in the great bed and let her fingers ease between the linens in search of her amorous husband.

He was gone.

She sat up in surprise, her hair falling over her shoulder as the linens dropped to her waist.

"Sir?" she asked, then shouted more loudly. "Sir? Where are you?"

There was no reply.

Annelise was alone.

She got out of bed to look for him, noting that there was no sign of his clothing. That great cloak was gone and so were his boots. She wondered how he could have abandoned her after the night they had spent together.

Then she noticed the flowers. They were scattered all over the bed and cast across the floor surrounding it. Annelise smiled with the certainty that her husband had left them for her. Their scent was familiar, both from her bath and from the garden last evening, but still she did not recognize the blossoms.

For an ogre who used such unusual means to find a wife, Annelise's new husband had a definite measure of charm.

She picked up one blood red bloom and fingered its soft petals. She buried her nose in it and closed her eyes in recollection of the night before.

Just the day before she had left Beauvoir's bailey with the dawn. Had she truly wed the lord of this palace since then? Or had it all been a dream?

The red stone winked in the ring on Annelise's left hand as though it would confirm the truth to her. She supposed it must be a garnet, which was a valuable stone, and knew it was as real as she.

She noticed the dried blood stain on the linens and considered it. It was clear she was a maiden no longer and she had not dreamed it.

She bent and smelled her husband's skin upon the linens, then shivered in recollection of his caress in the darkness.

She was wed.

The match was consummated.

Her husband had promised to reveal himself to her this morning. Annelise was more than ready to learn the worst about him and to see his truth. She would look upon him and not give any sign of revulsion, no matter how scarred he might be.

He had been tender with her. Gentle. Kind. Her heart swelled. The measure of a man was not in his features but in his heart. She would tell him so, if he doubted the truth.

But where was he? Annelise considered the empty room again, then smiled as she guessed.

It was his chivalry at root again. He had let her sleep and was waiting for her to join him to break their fast together. He could not yet know that she was inclined to rise with the dawn. That he did the same was yet another trait they held in common.

That realization was all the encouragement Annelise needed to rise, wash, and dress.

Draped across a chest was another surprise. The kirtle of emerald green was so dark and rich that Annelise had never seen the like. She touched it tentatively, guessing that it must be a gift for her. There was no other lady in this abode, after all. There were fine ochre shoes of smooth leather fit for a queen, a sheer chemise embellished with fine embroidery, a cloud of cloth of gold for wimple and fillet.

Annelise found a steaming bucket and a cloth, and smiled. She washed then donned her new garments. They fit perfectly and were of such fine material that she could not believe her good fortune. She spun happily in the middle of the room. She could easily become accustomed to her husband's generosity.

It seemed she had not made such a bad match, after all.

But there was a great deal Annelise wanted to ask her spouse. She certainly had not felt any evidence of disfigurement the night before and she thought she had made a fairly thorough investigation.

It was time to find him and learn the truth, whatever it might be.

The palace proved to be as deserted as it had been when Annelise arrived. No matter how loudly she called, only the echo of her own voice sounded in response.

What of the servants her husband had mentioned? She found no sign of them.

Had he lied to her?

Annelise did not like that prospect at all.

And where had he gone? The pleasure of her surprises dissipated when she could not locate him.

She did find a simple meal, left for one. The scent of fresh bread drew her to a room alongside the chamber they had shared. As before, there was butter and cheese, as well as a rosy apple and a cup of golden ale. She ate, assuming that he had already done as much. Then she embarked on a thorough investigation of the palace, resolved that she would not rest before she found her spouse.

The palace was not infinite. She was certain she could explore every nook before midday.

The sun was high by the time Annelise had explored all of the rooms of the palace.

She had not found another living soul.

Where had her husband gone? Where could he be hiding?

She wondered whether there was only one gate in the entire circumference of the surrounding wall. There might be another gate for the servants to use. There might be a watchtower at some point where she could overlook the grounds and see what she had missed. She decided to walk the entire circle of the wall.

It was not long before she reached the stables once more and she hurried into their shadows. Her husband might have taken refuge here, in the company of his horses.

The palfrey she had ridden the day before nickered at the sight of her. She greeted the beast and checked its flank, relieved to see that the wolf's bite was healing already. The other palfrey in the stall greeted her with enthusiasm and she gave each of them a brushing. They had been tended very well, but she knew that horses enjoyed the attention. There were oats aplenty for both horses, and water, as well.

As she worked, she recalled the day before, which seemed like a distant dream. What had happened to the rest of the party? What of Yves? Had he been taken by wolves? Annelise recalled hearing one man's scream, although she could not have identified the voice.

She should have spoken to Yves instead of trying to provoke him into granting her desire.

She should have sought him out instead of waiting for him to cede to her.

Annelise had been so certain that she could accompany him, but he had been adamant. She had to admit that Yves would know more of what lay before him when he rode to tournament than she could guess. She had been raised in the shelter of a convent, while he had trained with men of war.

All she had been able to think was that she had not wanted to wed either Enguerrand or Hildegarde's son.

And now, Yves might be lost. She might have no one in her life, save her elusive husband.

This palfrey nuzzled her hair and Annelise wiped her tears. She had been right in that, at least. She could not believe that either of those suitors would have made her first mating as pleasing as her husband had. They had been men with their own objectives—or their mother's—who cared nothing for her.

Whereas the husband that Annelise had gained by fate was one who desired her for herself.

She was not solely responsible, after all. If nothing else, Yves and Bertrand had played a part in what had happened. Either could have listened to her. Yves had admitted as much himself.

In future, though, she would try to discuss matters openly.

Annelise scratched the palfrey's nose and peeked into the other stall. The largest destrier she had ever seen occupied it, his coat blacker than midnight. He flicked an expressive glance her way and stamped a hoof.

"Well, hello to you, sir," she said, giving him a pat, as well.

Her husband had admitted to being a knight, and here was the evidence.

The stallion's ears flicked and he nosed the contents of his feed box impatiently. It was not empty, Annelise noticed. He could not be hungry, although she wondered if he might be bored. He snorted and scattered oats about the stall, then glanced back at Annelise.

He was probably used to activity. As though to reinforce her thought, the destrier stamped his feet restlessly.

Annelise folded her arms across the top of the rail and dropped her chin on them. She watched the horse toss his head. "You seem to need a run. Does my husband not ride you daily? My father oft said that a good steed should be ridden frequently."

The beast nickered and tossed his head as though approving of the notion. Memory sobered Annelise and she stepped back from the stall.

"Before you decide that my father was a wise man, you should know that he applied the same axiom to women. Whether they were good or bad was not a consideration for him."

She frowned at the straw on the floor, determined not to recall another troubling incident so quickly. Still, she had broken her own pledge to wed only for love. Her husband could not love her, but he had been kind to her. Would that last? Would it be sufficient to spare her the fate of her own mother?

Annelise did not know and she would not find out by standing in the stable all day.

She looked about herself with curiosity. What else could she learn about her husband from the stable? The horses were well-tended, a sign of the same generosity and kindness he showed to her. The stable was neat and the stalls had been swept out, even though there was not a soul to be seen. The destrier's trap was hung along the opposite side of the stable, and her gaze danced over the familiar gear.

She refused to think about Yves.

If this was her husband's horse and his equipment, she reasoned, certainly there was nothing about the saddle to indicate any deformity. The stirrups were hung at precisely the same length.

A glint caught her eye and she ventured deeper into the stables. A knight's mail was carefully stored there. It was in excellent repair and polished to a gleam. Annelise squinted at it, trying to envision the height of the man to whom it had been fitted.

It could readily belong to her spouse. He was, after all, lord of the keep, and this mail was finely wrought. It was the armor of a knight and nobleman.

Annelise knew that there were not two noblemen inhabiting this place.

Feeling as though she was prying, but continuing nonetheless, she examined the mail. There were a few nicks and scratches, as one might expect from equipment used in battle. On one shoulder it looked to have been repaired with newer rings.

But its silhouette was that of a perfectly normal man.

Remembering her theory that he might have a scarred but previously handsome face, Annelise examined his helmet. It was without blemish beyond the usual scratches and minor dents. There was evidence of nothing that could have granted him a major disfigurement.

Was it possible that there was nothing amiss with her spouse?

Why would he hide his identity from her?

Annelise drummed her fingers on his helmet. The nuns had taught her that every riddle had a key, and she knew she could solve this one. Her husband could be a villain, an outlaw wanted for some heinous crime. That would explain his reluctance to reveal himself until after the match was consummated.

No. Annelise shook her head firmly. The man who had treated her so kindly could not have a black heart.

Could he be married already? Snared in a loveless match? Annelise considered that possibility for a long moment even though she disliked it intensely. It would mean that he had tricked her—but why? No man had need of two wives.

Unless his wife was barren and he was without a son and heir.

Annelise bit her lip. But then, where was this barren bride? Surely she would be resident at his home? Annelise knew she was alone in this palace.

She refused to consider other possibilities along that line. Her host and husband could have simply seduced her, if he had been driven by desire alone. It had not been necessary to marry her, much less to surrender his ring to her.

No, she refused to believe that he was already wed.

He could be falsely accused of a crime. That was a promising possibility. But who might bring a false charge against a man evidently so honorable?

Perhaps a woman spurned.

If so, her spouse might not be certain which side she would take in the fray.

But she was his wife. And he had ensured that she had no grounds for an annulment. Annelise's skin tingled with the memory of his touch. Her spouse had seen to her earthly needs in a way far beyond any expectation and had given her hope for a marital future blessed with love.

Annelise was wed, for better or for worse, yet she would not abandon her hope of love in marriage.

Indeed, if he feared that she might recoil from some truth in his nature or his past, she could prove otherwise to him. His battle could be hers. What better way to earn his love than to banish whatever demon haunted him? She would aid him, clear his name, appeal to the king, do whatever was necessary to have him fully as her spouse.

But first Annelise had to discover precisely who her husband was.

She examined his belongings, telling herself that the greater cause justified the intrusion. He could have simply confided in her, but clearly had chosen not to do so.

He had promised to tell her the truth this morning and had not.

Annelise was in the right—even if she felt that she was wrong.

His tunic was rich indigo and trimmed with white silk that looked somewhat the worse for wear. There were the caparisons of a size to garb the destrier in the same fabrics and colors.

Annelise recalled the callus on his hand. Clearly, her spouse was not just a knight. He was a warrior who actually engaged in battle. As she ran a fingertip over the scarred leather scabbard of his sword, she wondered where he had fought.

His shield was emblazoned with a white griffin on the navy ground. One of the beast's claws was extended as though the talons would shred an attacker. Its wings were spread high, its scowl fierce.

A silver branch embellished with what Annelise thought were oak leaves hung from the griffin's beak. A row of tiny silver-and-white *fleurs-de-lis* ran along both top and bottom edges of the crest.

She traced the emblems with her finger, noting the nicks and scratches upon them. She did not recognize his insignia, but that said little, for Annelise paid scant attention to such matters of war. If nothing else, she recognized that the *fleurs-de-lis* signified his family's pledge to the king of France. He was far from his origin, then.

How had he come by this palace in the forest? Who was his overlord?

His packs were virtually empty, with the exception of various masculine miscellany that told her little. She touched the dagger and spare shirt, found his comb, his flint, a small and very sharp knife, a coil of rope, then grimaced when she discovered some cheese that he had evidently forgotten.

Annelise disposed of the cheese and surveyed the stables again. Clearly, she would have need of her ingenuity to discover the identity of her enigmatic spouse.

"Would you like to go for a ride?" she demanded of the destrier.

His ears flicked with what Annelise chose to regard as interest. She lifted the saddle to his back with some difficulty and harnessed the large beast. For once, she was glad of the days she had hidden in Sayerne's stables to avoid her father.

"We shall check the wall," she informed the destrier.

What Annelise had to do was concoct a plan and she knew that the most successful plans were reliant upon the most complete information.

Before the sun set, she would know every secret of this palace.

Perhaps there was an advantage in her solitude within these walls: there was no one to stop her from her quest.

CHAPTER SIX

After a day in the forest, Rolfe could make only one conclusion: it was clear he had not loved Annelise with sufficient ardor.

Perhaps his long run of celibacy had weakened his skills of seduction. Perhaps the lady had not been as pleased as he believed. Perhaps they had not adequately explored the range of lovemaking possibilities.

Whatever the issue, it was clear to Rolfe that the only possible recourse was to return to the great bed and seduce his lady wife again.

As many times as necessary.

The promise of that made him even more anxious than usual for the day to end.

He knew his anticipation could only be due to the prospect of breaking the curse. It had nothing to do with Annelise herself. As charming as she was, he was in no peril of forgetting the truth of their match.

Their marriage was a bargain, no more and no less. On his side, there was a curse to be broken. On Annelise's side, there was the prospect of comfort, security and a spouse who would treat her well.

Their marriage was an example of duty, honor, and a measure

of trust. The fickle emotion of love was of no relevance.

Rolfe was pacing outside the gates of the palace long before the sun finally dipped toward the horizon. He was determined to put every moment of the night to effective use.

Let the one in whom he confides,
lead a killer to his side.

The curse had echoed in his thoughts all day, feeding his resolve.

As soon as he became transformed, the gates opened to him. Rolfe strode nude into the courtyard and they closed behind him silently. He crossed the garden with long steps and discovered Annelise in the shadowed foyer. Mercifully, her back was to him, for she had lit a lantern. Even the darkness in the courtyard was not complete.

Rolfe crept up behind her silently. He wished that he had a silken handkerchief and immediately spied one upon the floor. He blinked, then realized he should put the palace's inclination to serve his will to better use.

Annelise's kirtle was new—and it could not be coincidence that it was of the same deep green he had envisioned upon her. She had possessed no baggage when she entered the palace gates, so this, too, was a manifestation of his desire. The kirtle clung to her curves in a way that made him all the more intent upon his nocturnal quest.

He snapped the handkerchief over her eyes, blindfolding her, and she gasped. "You!"

"Yes, it is me, my Annelise."

"Where are you? Where have you been today?" Annelise reached for the knot in the handkerchief, but Rolfe gently grabbed her wrists.

"You will not look upon me."

"You promised to tell me the truth this morning, but you have been impossible to find."

"I changed my thinking."

"Perhaps I will change my thinking and look, then." It was a shame that he could not see her eyes, in a way, for he knew they would be flashing with fire.

"Perhaps you would be foolish to do so." He dropped his voice low. "Trust me, Annelise. I will show you all as soon as I can."

"You deceived me."

"Not by any scheme of mine. You must believe me, Annelise. I was deceived myself."

"How cruel," she said, her tone wary.

"Indeed. I spent the day trying to make amends." He stole a quick kiss. "Believe that I would never break my word to you willingly." Her annoyance seemed to be melting and Rolfe wished to avoid more questions he could not answer. He spun Annelise around and around, easily evading her searching hands as he ensured that she kept her balance.

To his delight, she began to smile, then to laugh. "You will make me dizzy!" she accused. Her laughter made Rolfe smile himself and he wished they did not have to play such games.

What if he did confide in her?

The possibility was tempting.

But no. He should persist in his scheme first. When the curse was broken, he would be able to defend them both from whatever threat might result from confiding in her.

When he stopped her and held her shoulders in his hands, Annelise still wavered unsteadily. She reached up with one hand and claimed one of his, as if he were her anchor. Her lips parted and her cheeks were flushed, and Rolfe could resist her no longer.

He bent and kissed her sweetly, then stepped back. Annelise tried to grab him, but her hands closed on empty air.

Rolfe chuckled and she spun to face the sound. "I will find you," she threatened, then headed toward him. Rolfe stepped silently around her as she walked toward the place he had been, and instead was behind her. She reached out, found nothing, and pivoted at the sound of his foot dislodging a small stone.

"I thought you scarred or maimed, sir, but so far I find nothing wrong with you. Perhaps there is nothing amiss."

Rolfe's heart stopped. "Perhaps you have not looked closely enough."

"Perhaps you fear that I will recognize your face," she continued and he might have cursed her cleverness if he had not admired it. "Perhaps that is why you keep your name secret."

"Perhaps you should not ask such questions." Rolfe circled her silently, intent upon surprising her.

"What else am I to do all day alone?" she asked, flinging out her hands. "You said you would confide in me, sir. This is a poor start for our match."

Rolfe stepped closer and abruptly caught her shoulders in his hands. "I thought we began quite well," he whispered and kissed her throat. She sighed and leaned back against him, her lips parting. "Catch me if you can," he whispered and darted away again.

"Devil!" Annelise cried. Rolfe laughed. She pivoted and headed for his voice. "You change the subject, avoiding my questions."

Rolfe eased sideways, knowing that her hearing would be sharpened.

"Over here!" he murmured, hastening the other way when she turned. "No, here!"

"You are wicked, sir." Annelise propped her hands on her hips. "Perhaps you never intended to confide in me at all. Perhaps that was only a ruse to seduce me. Perhaps nothing changed this morning at all."

He crept up behind her, caught her waist in his hands, and bent to kiss her ear. "I thought it was my kiss that seduced you?"

Annelise shivered then spun in his embrace. She wrapped her arms around his neck and he bent to kiss her again. "It is the truth that I find most seductive, sir," she said just before his lips touched hers. "Tell me yours and I shall be yours this night."

"I believe you will be mine regardless, my lady wife," Rolfe replied, then captured her lips. He kissed her slowly, holding her close, enjoying how she responded to his touch. She opened her mouth to him and leaned against him, her surrender so complete that his blood heated.

Then her hands roved across his shoulders and down his arms and she broke their kiss. "You are nude, sir!" She was blushing.

"Surely you are not shy this night, Annelise? I was warmed all day by the memory of your passion."

"But not compelled to share my company." Annelise spun out of his grip and reached for the knot in the handkerchief. "Is this match about desire alone? I had understood that marriage was a greater union than that."

Rolfe ran for the bed chamber as soon as she lifted her hand and ducked around a bend in the corridor just in time. "It seems, my lady, that you welcome my touch."

"Yet I would welcome more than pleasure, sir."

Rolfe eased deeper into the shadows as Annelise pursued him. He wished for darkness and the corridor became as dark as night. He stood, veiled in shadows, and watched her approach.

"What if I refuse your touch until you tell me more of yourself, sir? What if I demand a confession for each night abed?" She reached out to the wall with one hand, letting it guide her as she continued toward him.

"You would not manage the feat, my Annelise."

"Would I not?"

"I come to believe that you were made for passion." Rolfe dropped his voice low. "Or perhaps you were made for me."

She caught her breath. "Yet I am certain, sir, that my passion would be greater with the exchange of confidences." She smiled. "Is that not a prospect worth your consideration?

It was. Indeed, Rolfe could not imagine Annelise showing greater passion than she already had. The possibility of more almost tempted him to confess the whole tale.

Rolfe bit his tongue and did not reply.

He knew better than to be hasty with trust. He reminded himself of Rosalinde.

"And so you fall silent," she said. Rolfe flattened himself against the wall, but she came closer, evidently assuming that he had continued down the hall to the bed chamber. She shook her head. "Straight to the bed, as though there was nothing else of import in this match than pleasure. I had expected more from you, sir, and do not mind confessing as much—"

Annelise passed him, just steps away in the darkness, as she chastised him. Rolfe waited a moment, then snatched her from behind, spun her around, and kissed her. He poured all his desire into his embrace, hoping to convince her that his scheme of seduction was best.

When he lifted his head long moments later, Annelise leaned against his chest. "You are persuasive, sir," she whispered.

"I would make your surrender worthwhile," Rolfe whispered and caressed the soft curve of her cheek.

Annelise laughed. "You make me forget my plans and my resolve far too easily. I think you do not fight fairly, sir."

"Would you rather I abandoned the battle."

"No, sir. In fact, I pray that you do not." This time, she stretched to touch her lips to his.

Rolfe was aroused that she initiated the kiss. Indeed, the lady showed more ardor than even he had come to believe and when he next had the chance to speak, Rolfe's voice was husky. "I am not too proud to confess that I sorely missed you and your touch this day, Annelise."

"Then you should not have left me."

"Would you believe me if I said I had no choice?"

"Where did you go?"

"I had an errand that could not be delayed."

"But where?"

"Beyond the walls."

"But where? You did not take your destrier or palfrey. How could you have gone any distance without them?"

Rolfe's heart chilled. "My destrier?" he echoed, realizing that she had not been idle during her day alone. "You were in the stables?"

Annelise laughed a little. "I searched every corner of this palace for you, sir, though the only living souls I found were in the stables." She must have interpreted his silence as surprise. "Even I have the wits to recognize the steed of a knight, sir, as well as his armor and weapons. He is quite a lovely stallion."

Rolfe did not know what to say. How would he explain the absence of servants? What could he say about his absence? He did not wish to lie to Annelise, but her curiosity was confounding.

"Will you not tell me?" she asked quietly.

"I cannot." Rolfe sighed. "I would if I could, but I cannot." It was true and he hoped she understood as much. Rolfe was certain that Annelise was trying to study him, seeking a glimpse of his expression. When she sighed, he wished that he could see her expression. The shadows were as much a curse as a benefit.

"It was disappointing to find you gone this morn," she said, leaning her brow upon his chest. She was so close to him that he could feel her heat and her hair fell over his hands. He bent to kiss her brow and was inundated by the scent of her skin. He wondered if the scent of Annelise would always be such a potent temptation to him. "Although the flowers were beautiful. Thank you for them."

"They are roses," Rolfe said, feeling a wave of gratitude that she had accepted his meager explanation.

"Roses are not so large and lush as that!"

"They are in Outremer. Do you like them?"

"They are magnificent." She touched her lips to his throat and heat emanated from that spot, making Rolfe hold her more closely.

"I would love you again this night," he whispered. "Perhaps more than before, but only if you agree."

"Of course," she replied, her breath fanning his skin. "Of course, my lord husband. My passion abed is yours to command."

Her agreement was all the encouragement Rolfe needed. He swept Annelise into his arms and strode for the bed chamber, determined to ensure that the lady learned even more of pleasure.

One more night.

A more thorough loving.

And this time, the curse would be broken.

On the morrow, he could confess the truth.

The man was persuasive, indeed.

Annelise had never experienced such pleasure as her husband granted to her. He knew more of her body than she, it was clear, and he could conjure passion that she had never imagined might exist. He set her very soul on fire, cast her to the stars, then did it all again. It was too easy to surrender to the sorcery of his kiss, too easy to forget her own resolve to uncover all of his mysteries. He could make her forget her plans with a touch.

And worse, she did not regret a bit of it.

He was vulnerable only in one moment. Annelise realized as much after he had pleased her twice and had his own release. Immediately after their mating and his release, he was spent, just as he had been the night before. He almost dozed and it was in this brief interval that Annelise knew she must try to discover more of him.

He had promised to tell her more this day. It was only fair to her thinking that she actively seek the truth that he had declined to share.

When he fell back against the linens, his breath coming quickly, she recognized her chance.

Annelise propped herself on her elbow and looked down upon her husband. It was darker than dark, for he had drawn the drapes around the bed, but she knew where he was. She set her fingertip upon his lips and felt him smile beneath her touch.

"Were you pleased?" he murmured, his voice a low growl of satisfaction.

She smiled herself, liking that he was concerned for her welfare. She came to believe that he was a good man, if a secretive one. "You know I was, sir, and twice so."

"Good." He captured her hand and kissed her fingertips. "I would not see you disappointed." It was a sentiment that pleased her, but Annelise refused to be swayed from her plan.

"Who are you?" she asked.

She felt him stiffen. She felt the skip of his heart and knew he was shocked.

"I beg your pardon?"

Annelise dropped her chin onto his chest, her fingers tapping against his shoulder. "Who *are* you?" she asked again. "I capitulated to your touch," she reminded him. "Now you could offer a morsel of truth in exchange. Surely you already know that I am cursed curious. You promised to tell me more on this day, and though I understand circumstances can change, you could share some detail."

He took a quick breath and she heard the change in his tone. "I am lord of this palace, of course." It was evident that he wished to flee from her questions.

Annelise angled her weight over him, knowing she could not stop him if he chose to leave, and tried to charm him. She gave his shoulder a playful poke. "Your name, sir. I wish to know your name." When he did not reply, she shook her head. "I begin to wonder, sir, whether you wed me only for your pleasure. Perhaps I am to be a courtesan, with only one purpose in your life."

"Do you not wear my ring on your finger?" he asked, and she heard that he was insulted. "Did I not pledge myself to you?"

"Yes, but without offering your name." Annelise tapped a finger upon him. "Are you a villain or an outlaw, sought far and wide for your crimes?"

"No!" That he was insulted was a good sign, in her view.

"Have you a wife already then, and you fear that I should discover the truth of it?"

"No!"

"A betrothed?"

"I have no wife and no betrothed," he said, sitting up as he spoke. "Indeed, I had no intention of wedding until I came to this palace, and then..." He fell silent just as his confession became interesting.

"And then?" Annelise prompted.

"And then I changed my thinking."

"Why?"

"I cannot tell you."

Annelise considered what he had told her. "But you came to this palace. You did not inherit it from your father?"

"Not from my father, no." His reluctance to share even this was evident in his tone.

"Are you an imposter? Have you usurped the true lord of this palace?"

"No!"

"Then how did it come to be yours if not from your father?"

He got out of the bed and paced, and she knew he was deciding upon his reply. "It was a gift," he said finally.

Annelise felt her lips part in surprise. "A gift? From whom?

What did you do to earn such a rich gift?"

"You could say that I won a lady's favor." He sounded to be exasperated but Annelise was not precisely reassured.

She swept from the bed to pursue him. "Sir! Where is this lady?"

"Gone."

Annelise could not believe it. He had seduced the lady who owned this palace, then the lady had left him in possession of it. While she already had great admiration for her husband's amorous skills, the tale was unlikely to be true. "I would have a more plausible explanation, sir."

"And you will have it, when I can share it."

"When will that be?"

"I hope on the morrow." His doubt was clear and Annelise recalled his conviction that he would be able to tell her more on this morning. Who had deceived her spouse? Was it this lady who had given him the palace? Was she capricious in her whim?

A thought assailed her and she flung herself at him. "Did you visit this lady on this day? Is that where you were?"

"No!" He seized her shoulders and she knew he was looking down at her. "Annelise, please trust me in this. She is gone, I hope forever, but her injunctions still govern my own choices. I hope that you and I will change that, together."

His appeal was irresistible, though still Annelise worried what she did not know. "But you will confide in me when you can?"

"I will." He pressed a kiss into her palm. "I ask for your patience until I can do so."

Annelise frowned. She was being swayed by his touch and reminded herself that her request was fair. "Why will you not let me see your face?"

"You guessed it yourself. I do not wish to distress you with my disfigurement."

Annelise shook her head "I was wrong," she said. "There is nothing wrong with you that I can feel." She ran her fingertips down his chest. "And I can see nothing amiss with your mail. If you were missing a limb, your armor would have been modified."

"My mail?" His voice was strained. "You have found my mail?"

"Of course, I was in the stables."

"But it is at the back, out of view."

Annelise bristled at the implication that she had been nosy. "It is in plain view for anyone who looks. What else would you have me do all day?" she asked. "A prisoner can at least explore her cell." She sensed that he was shocked and caressed his shoulder, wanting there to be harmony between them. "I took your destrier for a ride today, by the way. He seemed impatient for a run, although we could only canter in the courtyard. It was better than no exercise at all."

Her husband made a choking sound. "You rode Mephistopheles?"

"Mephistopheles?" Annelise blinked. How curious that he confessed the name of his destrier before his own. "Why would you give that fine creature such a dreadful name?"

"It was the breeder who named him—he named all his black foals after demons, it seemed—and I saw no reason to change it."

That was more of a confession than Annelise had expected.

She decided to challenge him more, in the hope of more detail.

"No reason?" she scoffed. "Such a name could bring you the worst fortune imaginable. You invoke a demon each time you utter his name. It is folly, sir."

"Is it?" He sounded amused again, which was good.

"How long have you had him?"

"Five years."

"And your luck in that time?"

"No worse than that of any other man."

"You have this marvelous palace. That is better fortune than most could boast."

"Is it?" he asked tersely.

Annelise made a guess, purely to provoke him. "Did you summon a demon and make a wager? Was that the lady you seduced to gain this prize?"

"Annelise!" He turned away from her as if he would leave. "You must cease your questions."

She considered that her guess might have been close to the truth. "Do not leave me so soon, sir," she urged, sliding her hands around his waist. She pressed a kiss between his shoulder blades. "I do not believe we have loved enough this night."

She felt him glance back and his hand rose to cover hers.

He did not speak, and she dared to be encouraged. She eased back, drawing him after her. "You should ride your destrier more often, for he was restless," she chided gently, then kissed his cheek. "It is not good to treat a steed thus. I can only guess that you have a sizable investment in such a fine beast."

"Yes. He cost me dearly."

"Where did you find him?"

"In Outremer."

He had been on crusade then. Pride filled Annelise that her husband had been so brave as to render such service. He was a man of honor, just as she had believed. "If you acquired this destrier in Outremer, you must have ridden another to the Holy Land. Surely not the palfrey in the stables?"

Annelise was silenced when her husband rolled suddenly atop her and he caught her shoulders in his hands. "You have erred seriously this day," he informed her, his tone forbidding as it had not been thus far. "Do not question what is around you, Annelise."

"Whyever not?" she dared to say. "I must do something with my time and every puzzle has a key. If you will not tell me about yourself, sir, it is only reasonable that I try to divine the truth.

He shook her and she fell silent, feeling his will bearing upon her. "Look only at what you are shown."

"But—"

"But *nothing*," he whispered, dropping his thumb over her lips. His tone was fierce as it had never yet been and Annelise feared suddenly that there was true peril for him in this place. "It is imperative that you follow my dictate on this. All could be lost, Annelise. *All.*"

Her heart skipped then, for she feared for her husband.

But surely, if he was in danger, he had greater need of her assistance? She did not truly believe in demons, despite what the nuns had taught her, and she knew there had to be some reasonable explanation for all that she had seen in this strange place.

His voice was low when he spoke and his words were hot. "Never betray me, Annelise."

"Of course not," she agreed, though she could not imagine what he meant.

She would not betray her spouse: she would save him.

And that would earn his love forevermore.

It was not precisely how she had hoped to wed a man who loved her, but the end result would be the same.

Whatever threatened him and their future would be her challenge to resolve.

Then his lips closed over hers, obliterating all such considerations from her mind. There was only her husband in the darkness, her husband and his seductive touch.

Her husband and the pleasure only he could conjure.

And for the moment, that was more than enough.

Annelise had never believed in magic, but awakening to find her husband absent again compelled her to reconsider her perspective.

Where could he have gone?

And why?

There was a new kirtle laid out for her, and her linen and stockings had been washed. She knew her husband had not done that—even if he had been inclined to do such labor, he had had no spare moment the night before. A meal awaited her pleasure, just like the day before, although once again, she could not detect another person in the palace.

The servants might use hidden passages, but Annelise doubted they could remain so completely out of sight. Surely she would catch a glimpse of them?

The horses had been fed and brushed, and their stalls swept out. She was certain the weeds in the garden had been pulled and the dead blossoms had been trimmed. The palace was perfectly clean and organized—as if it had several dozen servants.

If there was a rational explanation, Annelise could not think of what it might be.

And why was his palace in such a location? There were no fields for crops, no villeins as at Sayerne, no road or bridge that might bring tolls as at Beauvoir, not even mines as were reputed to have been at Roussineau. As far as she knew, the palace was lost in the forest to the south of Beauvoir, just as she had been.

He said he had won the palace from a lady. Why had she built it in this remote location? Had she been hiding from some vengeful individual or evading the consequences of some foul deed? Even that made little sense, since the lady was gone. Why had she bestowed the palace upon Annelise's husband? It seemed a whim beyond all expectation, especially if she yet drew breath.

Could her husband be responsible for his benefactress' demise? Annelise paused in the act of taking a piece of bread, then shook her head. No. He was kind and generous. Not violent.

She recalled his vehemence the night before and set aside the bread. She would believe the best of him until she had evidence to the contrary. His kindness to her had to have some reward.

If the lady had brought a fortune from Outremer, where had she found the craftsmen to build the palace and those high walls? Someone would have heard rumor of it. Annelise had to believe that Tulley would have known of it and come to see it for himself.

She stepped into the courtyard and considered the clear blue sky. The weather was the most perplexing detail, and the one she could not explain at all. She knew there was snow on the other side of the gates, yet within the walls, it was as warm as a summer's day. Even the most perfect location could not have ensured that.

No, there was something greater afoot.

She could not dispel her own suspicion that a demon had been invoked. She had never given credit to the notion of them existing in truth, but here was evidence aplenty.

If a demon held her husband in thrall, that would explain his heated reaction the night before. He had shown time and again that he was protective of Annelise, and it made sense he would fear for her welfare. Of course, he would not wish her to invoke the demon or be compelled to face his wrath.

It would also explain why her husband had not been able to confide in her as he had promised he would. Yes, a demon might refuse to keep his word. They were reputed to be untrustworthy.

But why was he so adamant that she not see his face? He was not scarred or disfigured.

He must fear that she would recognize him. Annelise could not imagine that might occur, but if her husband feared as much, he must have good reason. Perhaps he recognized her.

Annelise blinked. She knew few knights, to be sure, having spent so many years in the convent. But perhaps he had seen her at Tulley's château or had ridden in the company of Yves. They did resemble each other.

By the time she had broken her fast, Annelise was resolved. If there was a spell or a curse laid upon him, she would have to break it and free her husband. She would spend the day exploring the palace again, seeking hints that might be of aid.

And she must see his face. If she knew something of his origins, that might aid in her quest. He could only be hiding himself from view because she might well recognize him, and Annelise needed every bit of assistance she could find to win her spouse's freedom.

Rolfe was more vexed than he might have believed possible. Despite the fact that he had loved Annelise more thoroughly, he yet again found himself transformed into a wolf. He could have shouted in rage that day in the forest, but instead, his protest came out as a howl. He hated that he had been unable to keep his pledge to her and felt like a cur for deceiving her at all.

It was wrong.

He paced all of that day, wanting only to be back at his lady's side.

Yet Annelise was not slow of wit. Her guesses showed a fearsome accuracy. She might guess all the truth without him confiding in her at all!

Rolfe halted in the forest and looked back toward the palace. She might guess his truth. What if she learned of the curse, but not from him? What if the palace revealed his situation to her? He would not have confided in her directly then, so perhaps she would not lead a killer to his side.

Even if she did, even inadvertently, if he was his own self all of the time, he could defend them both from any foe.

Rolfe eyed the palace. He thought of Annelise, her fire and passion, her loyalty and her persistence.

Then he wished.

I wish that my lady wife should find something in the palace that would help us to break the curse.

It was done.

The sun was already setting, so Rolfe hastened back to the palace.

He strode through the gates as soon as they opened and turned his steps toward the stables. He had not seen Annelise in the garden and he wished to greet her fully dressed this time. There was a bath awaiting him in the stables, yet another reminder that the palace served his whim.

The water was hot and he welcomed the sense of being clean again. He wished he had not left his clothes and the cloak in the bed chamber, only to see that they were folded and clean, waiting on the bench with his mail and armor. He dressed with satisfaction, taking a moment to rub his destrier's nose and talk to the great beast. Judging by the position of the saddle and the gleam of Mephistopheles' coat, Annelise had ridden him again today.

The horses had plenty of food and water, and he noted the presence of a second palfrey stabled with the first. She was a pretty mare and friendly, the healing wound on her flank telling him of her identity.

Rolfe left the stables with purpose, wondering what his inquisitive wife might have found. He pulled up his hood as he walked, hoping he would not have to hide from her much longer.

Perhaps some puzzles did not have a key.

Annelise returned to the palace, exhausted and discouraged after another fruitless hunt. She had ridden the destrier again because he seemed to expect it, but she had not addressed the horse by name. The sun was setting and she expected that her husband would appear soon. She hurried to the chamber, hoping there might be a bath waiting for her.

But there was a book on the low table, one that had not been there before.

Annelise stood on the threshold of the chamber where she found her meals thrice a day and eyed the massive volume.

No, it had not been there before. She would have remembered a book of such splendor. Even the nuns had possessed few so wondrous as this one.

The book was bound in dark green leather and adorned with elaborate gold filigree. On closer inspection, she realized it was more lavish than any book she had ever examined before.

But books, particularly weighty ones, did not simply appear out of thin air.

Of course, many other things did in this palace.

Annelise crossed the chamber and tried to pick it up. It was a heavy tome, as thick as her hand was wide, and layered with dust. It was large, as well, its height more than the distance from her elbow to her fingertips. She blew the dust off the cover and sneezed as the resulting cloud enveloped her.

She opened the book cautiously, then grimaced. Its contents were inscribed in a beautiful but unfamiliar script. She could not read it.

Who could read it?

Was this the script of the infidels? Annelise had no way of knowing for certain. She might have had a moment's uncertainty, but she already knew that her husband was no infidel. He had ridden to Outremer on crusade, with the insignia of the King of France on his standard. He was as Christian as she—perhaps more so, if the opinion of the nuns was solicited.

Had the lady who had given him the palace been an infidel?

There was an interesting notion and just cause by every law in the land for him to have dispatched the lady as a foe. Annelise hoped he had not done as much, all the same. Were knights not sworn to defend women and children?

She frowned and closed the book, hearing his step behind her in the courtyard.

She turned and her heart skipped at the sight of him, even though his hood was drawn over his head and she could not see his features.

She would exhaust him, she decided in that moment, exhaust

him and steal a look at him in the night before he could stop her.

"What is that?" he asked as he came to a halt beside her. His arm slid around her waist and Annelise turned to him, lifting her face for his kiss. He did not disappoint but kissed her with sweet heat, his tenderness convincing her even more that he was a man of great merit.

"I meant to ask you as much. I found it here, just this moment."

He leaned over and opened the book, scanning its contents. "Ah, written in the script of the infidels."

"Can you read it?"

He shook his head. "Not me." She felt the weight of his glance upon her. "Can you read it?"

"I can read Latin, thanks to the nuns, but not this."

"The nuns," he echoed. "Tell me about the nuns."

"There is little to tell. I was sent to the establishment of the Sisters of Ste. Radegund for my education."

There was laughter in her husband's words when he replied. "And who was taught to consider the world in a new way? The nuns or you?"

"You mock me!"

"I tease you, my Annelise. I cannot imagine that you found it easy to be consigned to silence and obedience."

He did not say that as if it was a bad trait.

"I did not. I despised it there."

"Yet you were intent upon returning to that cloister when you arrived here."

"I meant to escape an arranged marriage," Annelise admitted. "We departed from Beauvoir keep at dawn, but became lost. The path to the convent was obscured by the snow." She shivered in recollection. "Then the wolves attacked."

"And instead of escaping an arranged marriage, you were required to accept another one."

"That is true, sir." She spared him a smile. "Though the terms were not marriage or death the first time."

"Which explains your change of perspective." There was no condemnation in his tone and Annelise thought perhaps he sympathized with her plight. He gestured and she sat down, then he sat opposite her. "And what do you mean to do about that, if ever you leave this palace?"

"Do?" Annelise frowned in confusion. "I do not understand."

"Will you seek an annulment?" His tone was light, but she felt his intense interest in her reply.

How strange that she already came to rely upon his presence in her life, even after so few days, even knowing so little of him. She spared a glance to the palace and tried to imagine being without her enigmatic, resolute, passionate spouse. She failed.

Did he mean to abandon her?

"Our match has been consummated, sir," she said with care.

"You could accuse me of claiming what was not mine to take."

"I would not do as much!" Annelise was appalled by the suggestion. "We are wed. We have exchanged our vows. We are bound to each other, sir, until death us do part."

The words seemed to startle him rather than reassure him, much to her surprise. "But there are no witnesses of our vows, Annelise, and no record of them in any parish church. You could deny them and it would be only my word against yours."

A lump rose in Annelise's throat. "I have your ring, sir," she reminded him tightly.

"And so you do. I wonder only if you might choose to lose it once you know more of me."

Annelise understood then that her husband's secret was a fearsome one. Perhaps his caution was deserved. Perhaps he did not understand that she took her vows most seriously, whether there had been a witness or not.

"There is only one way to know for certain, sir." She dared to reach out and put her hand over his. "You could tell me of yourself."

He recoiled, but she continued before he could protest. "I am a prisoner within these walls. Regardless of what you confide in me, I cannot flee. I cannot share such tidings with any other soul." She shrugged. "Well, I could tell the horses, but I doubt that they care."

He laughed then, laughed as if she had surprised him. She

thought that he was not displeased. "You are right, my Annelise. Your thinking is most clear." He laid his hand upon the book again, turning it so that he could open it once more. "How curious that you should find this today."

His tone hinted that he did not find it curious at all, which made Annelise wonder.

"Perhaps someone left it for me," she said, convinced that it had been him. "But that makes no sense as I cannot read it."

He was turning the pages and paused at an elaborate spread. "Look at this," he said with awe. "These calligraphers possessed such skill." And he touched the script with his fingertip, as if to caress it in admiration.

The letters shimmered for a moment. When the light faded, they were different. Annelise hastened to her husband's side to look down at the book. It was written in the Latin script with which Annelise was familiar.

"How did you do that?" she demanded.

He shook his head. "I do not know." He closed the book and opened it again, but the script remained legible.

"I suppose nothing should surprise me any longer in this palace," she murmured and her husband chuckled. He cleared his throat and began to read.

There were, there were not, in the oldness of time, twin daughters born to a djinn and his wife. Herein lies the tale of Leila and Kira, twins born to Azima and Azzam. They were matched in looks but not in manner...

"A djinn and his wife?" Annelise let her skepticism show. "This is no more than a fable for children."

"Is it?" her husband asked in a low voice.

"Clearly, it is, and as such, it is of no use whatsoever."

"How so?"

"We have no children and I feel no inclination for idle entertainment."

He considered her for a long moment and yet again, she wished she could have seen his eyes. The book must be of import.

Before she could reach for it and read more, he swept to his feet and caught her hand in his. "Come for a stroll in the garden, my lady. I would talk to you while dinner is prepared."

"But the book..."

"Will remain at your disposal, should you care to entertain yourself during the day." He spoke with a resolve that surprised Annelise, as if he was giving a command. When she looked back, the book had been moved to another table and a cloth had been spread upon the low table.

Dinner was being prepared.

"I still do not see your servants," she noted.

He tucked her hand into his elbow and led her into the garden. "I misled you, my Annelise. I have never seen servants in this palace either, though it seems they must exist."

Annelise caught her breath, sensing that something had changed. Her husband was not avoiding her questions but seemed inclined to answer them this night.

That could only be an excellent portent.

CHAPTER SEVEN

he lady was right. Rolfe could not believe his own folly.

Annelise could not lead a killer to his side when she was trapped within the walls of the palace. And even if she left, where could she go and who might she summon? There was forest in every direction.

Not to mention the wolves.

By her own admission, Beauvoir was a day's ride away and she did not know the route. He heartily doubted that she would even attempt such a long journey alone after her experience with the wolves.

No, he could tell her of the spell and she could help him to break it. They would solve this conundrum together and that would be the foundation of their match. Rolfe felt like a fool for not realizing the truth sooner.

He would not tell Annelise all of the details, of course, for that might make him vulnerable, but he believed he could share the root of the trouble.

She inhaled deeply beside him, glancing back toward the chamber. "Venison stew," she said with satisfaction.

Rolfe wondered at her tone, even though he recalled her enthusiasm for the fare on her first night in the palace. "Do you not like it?"

"I adore it! It is my favorite meal, and I do not mind if it continues to be dinner every night."

"It probably will be, then," Rolfe acknowledged.

"How so?"

"The palace serves my will and my desire is that you should be pleased."

She blushed a little then and he wondered how often any one had put her desires first. "Why were you raised in a convent?" He knew little about Quinn's family history, only that his comrade had a sister.

"My mother died," she said quickly, so quickly that Rolfe thought there might be more to that tale. "The overlord decided a young girl would be better raised in a convent than in a household of men."

That sounded reasonable enough. "Have you siblings?"

"An older brother, said to be a wicked tyrant and cruel beyond compare," she said with a shiver. Rolfe frowned at this description of temperate Quinn. "And a younger one, my father's bastard. Yves was just awarded his spurs by the Lord de Tulley. He intended to fight in the tourneys and earn his fortune."

"But?"

"He was escorting me to the convent when the wolves attack. I do not know his fate." She bit her lip then, looking so uncertain that Rolfe wished to ride out immediately and find the truth. Then she took a deep breath and glanced up at him with a smile. "And you, sir?"

"One brother, no more than that."

"Older or younger?"

"Older and heir to our family holding."

"Which is why you rode to crusade."

"Indeed." They came to a halt beside the bed of roses and Rolfe picked one lush blossom, cutting the stem with his knife. He presented it to his lady with a little bow, and she buried her nose in it, abandoning herself to the pleasure of its scent. He watched her, his chest clenching that this lady was his wife.

"They smell so wondrous."

"Aye, they do." Rolfe turned and offered his arm again, liking how she leaned against him as they walked back to their chamber. "Perhaps we should grow them wherever we live."

"But this is your palace. Do you not mean to remain here?"

Rolfe did not truly know what would happen to the palace when the curse was broken. "I had hoped to return home for the Yule."

"We had best depart soon, then, sir," she replied, showing a welcome practicality. "Depending on the distance, we might already be too late."

Rolfe took a deep breath. "There is something we must do first, my lady. You guess aright that I have been cursed. We must break the curse before we can leave this palace together."

"A curse? I knew it!" She rounded upon him, a marvel in her concern for his welfare. "You must change the name of your destrier, for invoking demons is folly beyond all else..."

Rolfe dropped a finger to her lips to silence her. "It was no demon," he whispered. "It was a djinn."

Annelise gasped and her eyes widened. "This is a djinn's palace," she whispered. "She was the lady who built it."

"And she was compelled to give it to me, which did not please her."

"So, she cursed you!" Bright color burned in Annelise's cheeks and her eyes flashed with fury on his behalf. "What a wretched deed to do!" She clutched at his hand. "Can the curse be broken? What must we do?"

Rolfe smiled that he had made the right choice. Annelise was devoted to his cause already, and their working together could only improve matters. "Here is the part about breaking the curse," he said, then recalled the precise words uttered by the second djinn.

> *"And whether he feel good or ill,*
> *the palace shall reflect his will.*
> *Finally, by grace of the powers above,*
> *let this curse be broken by the blessing of love."*

Annelise laughed. "But you, sir, do not believe in love."

"We have loved with vigor each and every night..."

"That is the act of love," she said, interrupting him. "And it is common enough that it cannot be the means to break a curse. No, sir, you must open your heart to me as I must open mine to you."

"But that makes no sense. What will be the tangible measure of that love? How will anyone know when it has been achieved?"

She thought about that for a moment, looking around the courtyard. "Perhaps this strange palace will know when I lose my heart to you, sir." She lifted her gaze to his, her eyes shining with delight. "But I will know, sir, when you surrender your heart to me."

Before Rolfe could think of a reply, Annelise closed the distance between them. She slipped one hand around his neck and pulled his head down to her kiss. She was in his arms, pressed against him, her kiss demanding more from him than she had thus far, and he forgot djinns and curses and everything except the lady in his arms. He was breathless when she broke her kiss, awed by her passion, and his heart thundered that she could be both wife and ally.

"Let me seduce you this night, sir," she whispered, her words husky. "Let me share with you all that I have to give."

It was an invitation Rolfe could not refuse.

Annelise had not intended to seduce her husband so thoroughly and she certainly had not intended to delay their evening meal. But his fledgling trust in her had so pleased her and she had wanted to reward him in a way he understood.

She would leave him in no doubt that she was delighted by his confidence.

Their mating was wild and thrilling as it had not been before. It clearly pleased him when she took the lead and so Annelise did, touching him and tasting him, teasing him as he had teased her, until finally the fury of desire claimed them both.

She fed him in the great bed, finding his lips with her fingertips. When she missed and dripped the sauce upon his chest, she licked it off, leading to another enthusiastic bout of lovemaking.

The third time was slow and sweet, so intense that Annelise almost wept. She felt that their bodies and their souls had merged, that they were each part of the other, that it was impossible to think of being without him. Night had fallen completely by the time she nestled in his embrace, dozing against his warmth.

He was protective.

He was gentle and he was kind.

He liked her impertinence and her passion, instead of finding fault with her nature.

He was the perfect man for her.

Annelise smiled as she heard his breathing slow. When had he slept since their marriage? Where had he slept? It was only right and good that he should sleep here, in their nuptial bed, with her. His heartbeat slowed beneath her cheek and she was glad to have offered him a haven, even for the rest of this night.

But Annelise was wide awake. She thought of his confession that he was cursed. She thought of the book. She thought of his fear that she would change her thinking about him if she looked upon him, and she knew she had to be certain.

In a way, it felt wrong to look upon him in his sleep.

In another, Annelise knew one peek would bolster her confidence to argue against his concerns.

She would be so quick. He slept so deeply. He would never know.

Before she could reconsider, she eased from his embrace. His hand fell heavily upon her hip when she rolled to her side, as if he would stop her. Annelise jumped, certain he had guessed her plan, but he nuzzled against her back, drawing her against him again.

"Rosalinde," he mumbled.

Rosalinde? Who was Rosalinde?

Was he thinking of another woman while he loved her?

Was this why he feared that love could not save him? Because he loved another woman?

Annelise was outraged. That single utterance was all the encouragement she needed to slip from the bed. She fetched the candle and struck the flint. The wick sputtered to life. She caught her breath and cupped her hand around the flame. She swallowed then turned to face her spouse.

There was nothing wrong with his face.

Quite the contrary, in fact.

God in heaven, but he was a very handsome man. His wavy hair was as black as jet, and his brows were dark, too. His face was tanned, as his hands had been and his jaw was square with determination. His nose straight and narrow, his lips full enough to make her flush in recollection of his kisses. There was a faint shadow upon his jaw and she reached to touch his cheek, half-fearing that her eyes deceived her.

He awakened with a cry of alarm.

His eyes were of different colors. One was blue and one was silver-gray.

"Annelise!" he cried and snatched the candle from her grasp. He cast it onto the floor and the chamber was plunged into darkness again.

Annelise's heart stopped cold. Only in hindsight did she realize what she risked. His fury reminded her of the incident she struggled to forget.

She was once again a little girl who had seen too much.

"Annelise," he whispered, disappointment in his tone. "You promised."

Annelise could not reply. She cowered at the foot of the bed and trembled in terror.

Now he would beat her.

In the darkness, when she could not see his face.

Would he kill her?

Who would ever know her fate?

Annelise's heart raced and her mouth went dry. She wished, too late, that she had curbed this particular impulse.

"You said you would not betray me," His voice was low, and Annelise shivered at the danger in his tone.

Now she would pay the price.

He had encouraged her confidence. He had prompted her trust, by showing her such kindness and gentleness. Because of what she had learned of her husband, Annelise had not believed he would respond in anger.

But she had erred and he would teach her another lesson. She covered her face with her hands and awaited the blow.

Her spouse swore with vehemence, but then shoved himself from the bed. She heard him snatching up his garments, moving quickly in the darkness. It was a curious choice, but perhaps nudity made him feel vulnerable. No doubt he would turn upon her once he was dressed, beat her senseless and leave her weeping on the floor.

But he simply marched out of the chamber.

Annelise lifted her head in shock and peered after him. She saw his cloaked silhouette as he entered the courtyard, then he rounded a corner and disappeared from view.

He would come back. Certainly. He only fetched a switch.

But his footsteps faded to silence.

And he did not return.

Long moments later, she exhaled.

Her husband had simply turned away. Words had been his weapon of choice.

What manner of man had she wed?

A man who was gone. Annelise swallowed.

He had left her because she had broken her word.

She left the bed, her knees trembling, and donned her chemise. There was no sign of him, not in the chamber beyond, not in the garden.

Certainly, her spouse appeared to be of a different ilk than her father.

Indeed, Annelise could think of no one who had ever treated her with such kindness. She had been fed, sheltered, protected, introduced to lovemaking with a tenderness unexpected in marriage to a stranger.

And how had she rewarded his kindness? A lump rose in Annelise's throat. She had defied the request he had made of her. She had known he would see such a small thing as a betrayal. She had believed she knew better. She had believed she made a choice for the greater good.

But he had left and she would have no opportunity to argue in her own defense. She looked down at his ring, still upon her hand. They had exchanged marriage vows, but there had been no witnesses. Would he deny her after all they had done together?

Would she be cast from the gates of his palace to fend for herself? She was a maiden no longer—what if she bore his child?

Annelise sat on the side of the bed, more fearful of the future than she had ever been.

What would be her fate now?

Betrayed!

Rolfe was furious, though his anger was directed as much at himself as his wife. He paced the length of the stable and railed at Mephistopheles.

"Seven kinds of fool!" he said. "How could I have trusted her? I should never have trusted her! I should never have trusted anyone! Have I learned nothing in this life?"

Mephistopheles rummaged in his feed bin. Rolfe strode to the side of the stall and leaned over in an effort to catch the beast's attention. He had to talk to someone or go mad, but Mephistopheles seemed indifferent.

"Was it not enough for me to be cursed?" he demanded. "No, I had to insult a djinn and have the curse redoubled. It is one thing not to believe in the unseen, quite another to tell a djinn as much!" He shook his head. "And was that enough? No, even once warned, I had to trust Annelise that I might be betrayed!"

Mephistopheles continued to chew complacently.

"One might argue that I believed I had a good reason to trust her." He folded his arms across his chest. "Oh, yes, it was a fine reason, and I shall share it with you. The lady is attractive and possesses a rare passion." Rolfe turned on his heel to pace the length of the stable again. "Is that not adequate reason to entrust my life to her keeping?"

He waved a hand. "Oh, yes, lest I forget, she also appreciates a venison stew." He shoved his hand through his hair, sick with the knowledge that he had been his own worst enemy in this.

The sad truth was that he did not know enough about Annelise. He could unerringly find every mole upon her flesh in the deepest darkness. He knew precisely how to caress her to send her scaling the highest cliffs of pleasure. She had a passion for life and a sharpness of wit that captivated him. Rolfe liked how she laughed and appreciated that she was the first woman with whom he had ever been able to talk.

His mother would have noted that he did not know sufficient about the lady's history and family to take her to wife.

Rolfe enumerated what he did know. She was Quinn's sister. She had been raised in a convent after her mother's death. He could not imagine that she had enjoyed her time there. Yet she had chosen to return to the convent rather than accept an arranged marriage, proof of her determination to keep her vow to wed only for love.

Where had she come by such a conviction? Certainly, no father or overlord would teach a daughter such a notion, and Rolfe doubted the sisters of Ste. Radegund would have endorsed such a view.

Was he right that she had been afraid when he snatched away the candle? To be sure, he had been angry, but he had never injured her. Why would she fear him?

She had broken her promise to him, but Rolfe wanted to return to the bedroom, to console her and make her smile. Annelise had a power over him that was not entirely welcome, for it reminded him of Rosalinde.

One would think that Rolfe would remember how deceptive women could be. One would think that he could manage to recall that Annelise had just tricked him.

Rolfe stepped to the door of the stables and heard the sound of a woman weeping. His heart clenched and again, he yearned to go to Annelise, to talk to her, to console her, to find out whether she truly had been afraid of him and to discover why.

But the djinn's curse echoed in his thoughts, halting him in his steps.

And let the one in whom he confides,
Lead a killer to his side.

Would she?

Could she?

Rolfe could not imagine as much, but then, he had not expected

Annelise to try to steal a glimpse of him. Was his trust misplaced? Was she like Rosalinde? He wanted to believe otherwise, but had need of proof.

"The only place she knows to find me is in this palace," he reminded Mephistopheles, who was not particularly interested in anything beyond the bottom of his feed bin. "She knows nothing of my transformation or where I go in the day."

Rolfe paced the length of the stables and back, aware that the stars were already fading. "I must leave and watch the palace from the forest." His decision made, Rolfe packed a few belongings. He had only to wish for the things that were not in the stables to have them appear. He was by no means certain that feat would work beyond the palace walls.

There was an abandoned tower not far away that he would use as a refuge. He dared not take a horse, for the steed would be undefended during the day.

"Farewell, my friend," he said to Mephistopheles and scratched the destrier's ears. "I shall return for you when I can." The stallion nosed in his oats, his tail swishing, apparently indifferent. But then, it was comfortable here and Annelise ensured that the destrier was ridden.

Perhaps she would be happy without him.

Rolfe strode toward the gates with his pack on his shoulder. The palace seemed to glow in the light of the moon, as if it were an illusion, and he could not help but pause to look back at it.

The sound of Annelise's weeping was louder and turning away from her distress was the most difficult thing Rolfe had ever done. He reminded himself that Annelise had deceived him, as Rosalinde had done—perhaps also for her own gain.

He could not abandon her completely as she was his lady wife. But Rolfe could and would retreat to a safe distance and watch what Annelise would do in his absence.

It was the right thing to do, he told himself. The prudent choice.

But even knowing that did not make it easy to walk away.

Dawn brought a new sense of purpose to Annelise.

Her husband had shown his true measure and left her for her mistake. He had not struck her or even chastised her much.

How could she regain his trust?

She had already seen evidence of her spouse's agile thinking, as well as his keen sense of humor. Surely half a night of solitude would have calmed him enough to accept her apology. After all, harmony could be found between two people only by discussion and compromise. Annelise was certain he would understand and not be unreasonable. He had been angry and justifiably so, but an apology should set matters to rights.

All she had to do was find him to offer it.

She shivered in the chill of the morning and donned her familiar russet kirtle. It seemed unfitting to seek him out in the new garb he had supplied. She was cold enough to tug on her old, heavy wool stockings, as well. Annelise wished that she had thought to close the doors to the courtyard the night before. She pulled her fur-lined cloak over her shoulders and hurried down the corridor, realizing only after she left the chamber that something was different.

The courtyard had been silent.

The fountain did not splash.

Annelise frowned and stepped into the gardens at the front of the palace.

A large wet snowflake landed upon her nose. She stopped and stared at the garden in amazement.

It had been transformed. The lush plants were disappearing under rapidly falling snow. There was a thin sheen of ice on the surface of the pond, and the red flowers she had grown to love had curled up at the abrupt change in the weather.

It was colder than it had been since she arrived here.

Indeed, the weather seemed to be the same as that outside the palace walls.

What did this mean?

Annelise's heart began to pound with the conviction that her spouse had abandoned her and his palace. She would have no chance to apologize or explain.

She rushed to the stables to be sure. Relief made her knees

weak when she spied all of the horses still in their stalls.

"Good morning, Mephistopheles," she said. "Have you seen your lord this morn?"

The stallion fixed her with an accusing eye, his breath making a white plume in the chilly air. Annelise saw horse blankets with the rest of her spouse's equipment and hastily covered the horses.

Her spouse's equipment. Annelise eyed his armor, wishing she knew more about all the various bits and pieces. There was nothing missing, as far as she could determine. Did this mean that her husband had not abandoned her? Why would it snow, then?

Annelise resolved to check every inch of the palace to find out.

"It is time for our daily ride, Mephistopheles," she informed the destrier, and reached for his saddle. If her husband was still here, Annelise would find him within the palace walls.

And if he were not, she would somehow find a way to open that gate and pursue him.

She would not be condemned without a chance to defend herself.

Annelise quickly confirmed what she had suspected all along.

She was alone.

And she was trapped inside the palace.

If the palace reflected her husband's will, then the weather was an echo of his feelings for her. She had offended him, and Annelise was determined to make matters right. Her husband had left, so she had to seek him beyond the walls.

Where exactly she would seek him once she did manage to leave the palace was a problem to solve later.

First, she had to discover how to open the gates.

As she had noted before, they had no visible means of being opened or closed. There were no handles or bars, no latches or hooks. Annelise knew that the gates opened in the middle, swinging into the courtyard. Each individual portal was both higher than she could reach and wider than she could stretch.

Annelise propped her hands on her hips. This was a djinn's palace, which meant there was sorcery at work. Or there had been, before her husband's departure. She would not consider that she might be trapped forever in his absence.

Words might be her salvation.

"I command the gates to open immediately," she said, summoning as much authority as she could.

There was not so much as a rustle in response. Annelise tried again, with no result. She changed her tone and her wording, but nothing worked.

She knocked on one door and raised her voice. "Let me out!" she cried. "I wedded your lord, as I promised, and now would leave!"

Nothing happened.

"Open that I might follow my lord husband!" she tried, with no success.

Snow continued to settle over the ground and along the top of the wall, burying the palace and garden in a blanket of white.

Annelise kicked the heavy door, cursing whoever had seen fit to design such a solid gate. "I demand to be released!"

No voice came to her ears this time, despite her efforts. "He is not even here!" Annelise wailed in frustration. "There is no reason to keep me here alone!"

The gates did not move.

She brushed her hands and backed away, glaring at the doors. She began to think of them as sentient beings, deliberately denying her will. They might well be, if they had been enchanted by a djinn. "If I must submit to force, then I shall do so." Annelise shook a warning finger at the gates. "Do not insist that you were not warned."

It was midday by the time Annelise had gathered everything she deemed useful. The sun was obscured by clouds overhead and she shivered in her cloak as she approached the gates.

First, she would try to force the lock. Annelise snatched up a dagger and turned on the gates, as though she might surprise them with her tactic.

Of course, there was no sign of a lock.

Annelise peered into the seam where the two doors met, hoping to get a glimpse of the catch. Either the space was too narrow or the doors fitted too well to give her any clues.

She decided that halfway up, at about shoulder level, would be the most logical place for whatever kind of latch these odd gates might have. Annelise jammed her blade into the space as far as she could.

The tip of the dagger snapped off.

The point did not even remain wedged in the door, but fell to the snowy ground so suddenly that Annelise imagined the gates had spit it out.

No matter. She had a bigger blade.

Her husband's quillon dagger was her next tool of choice. Annelise refused to be daunted when it met with the same fate as the first blade.

Obviously, she needed a sturdier weapon.

Annelise hefted the weight of her spouse's broadsword, making no small effort to brace it on her shoulder. She peered down the blade, took aim and dove at the gate.

To her delight, the blade slid neatly into the minute space between the doors. Annelise leaned forward to drive it even farther and savored a moment of elation before she heard the sharp crack of metal.

Then she pitched forward as the tip snapped off this doughty blade, as well. Annelise lost her balance and twisted her ankle slightly. Her spouse's sword fell in the snow, as if it had been spit forth by the gates. She was momentarily glad that he was not present when she saw the state of the blade.

Judging from all the nicks and scratches, it had been a trusty and sturdy weapon for him. Annelise rubbed her ankle as she thought.

The power of Mephistopheles was added to the endeavor. Being a creature of moderate sense, he refused to participate in Annelise's direct assault on the gales. She had the idea that she might ride the destrier at full attack and break them down by throwing their combined weight against them.

Mephistopheles stopped dead an arm's length from the gate on every try. Faced with such a lack of cooperation, Annelise was forced to attempt another method of escape.

She used the destrier to drag furniture through the snow to the wall. Annelise, at times less easily than others, stacked it in an effort to reach the top.

When she deemed the pile to be high enough, she dropped Mephistopheles' reins and scaled it. A chest rocked precariously when she put her weight on it, but she scrambled onward, her heart in her mouth.

She gained the summit with relief. "I will let you out from the other side," she declared as she waved to Mephistopheles and reached for the top of the wall.

It was just beyond her fingertips. Annelise stretched to her toes and strained with all her might, but to no avail.

She could not reach the top.

But she was close. So close.

"One more!" she cried to the destrier. "We need just one more thing." Annelise hurried down the pile of furnishings and led Mephistopheles toward the palace.

A quick scan of the palace showed the perfect choice, a table carved of rosy wood. It was rife with ornamentation, tall and probably quite light.

She tugged the table out into the garden, rolled it onto its back and tied a rope around it Mephistopheles flicked his ears, but obediently hauled it over to the wall.

Annelise's breathing was labored by the time she reached the top. She pulled the table up the last stage, smiling in anticipation.

She was almost free.

At the top, she took one last look over the snow-clad palace and its gardens. It was pretty in its own way, but a prison all the same. Annelise pivoted to face the wall.

She reached up, but the summit was still just beyond the tips of her fingers. She stretched, but it made no difference.

She could not reach the top.

How could this be?

The table she had added to the pile came to the height of her hip. How could it not have brought her closer to the top? Annelise stretched again and was forced to confront the illogical truth.

She was no closer than she had been on the last try. How *could* the top of the wall always be just beyond the reach of her fingertips?

How had the portal opened without a keeper?

Where had the voice that had hailed her originally come from, if there was no keeper?

And if there was a gatekeeper, where was he hidden?

Sorcery. A djinn's sorcery. The evidence surrounded her when she cared to look.

Annelise sat on the table and crossed her arms. She stared at the garden and watched the glittering snowflakes meander out of the sky. Magic was an unsatisfactory explanation. She glanced up and the top of the wall seemed so close.

Maybe she had misjudged the distance. Maybe one more item would make all the difference in the world.

Mephistopheles trailed behind her with even less than his previous enthusiasm. He ambled into the foyer as Annelise sought another piece of furniture that would not be too heavy to haul up the side of the growing pile, yet would give her some more height.

She decided upon a chair and made to pull it away from the wall. It resisted. Annelise pulled harder, and it slipped free so suddenly that she sprawled on her rump.

That was quite enough.

"Curse this place!" she cried. "Curse the wolves and curse the gates and curse my husband and curse this ridiculous wall! Curse each and every one, from today through the end of time!"

Mephistopheles nickered. Annelise looked at the horse just as he lifted his glossy black tail and relieved himself in the middle of the beautifully tiled foyer.

Annelise could have sworn there was a mischievous glint in his eye. She laughed aloud, forgetting her own anger when the destrier's gesture so accurately reflected her own response.

Her laughter might have faded, but Mephistopheles snorted. He glanced about, and appeared to be offended by what he found upon the tiles behind himself. He then strode back through the archway to the garden.

And abandoned his fragrant souvenir.

The sight of the steaming manure on the inlaid floor,

surrounded by tastefully understated opulence—in the wake of her trying day—made Annelise laugh and laugh. Out of the blue, she pictured how horrified Enguerrand would be if he were here.

A tear rolled down Annelise's cheek as she laughed.

She imagined Bertrand de Beauvoir's lips puckering tightly in the disapproval.

Annelise laughed some more.

She pictured Bertrand's mousy wife, desperately anxious to please, scurrying in to remove anything offensive to her husband. Likely that woman would try to cover Mephistopheles' mess with her embroidery, rather than burden her husband with the sight.

Annelise laughed until her ribs hurt

And Tulley? Ah, the overlord would be priceless. She could see the lord's eyes shooting sparks and his neck turning red as he pointed to the offense with an imperious finger. He would bellow a demand to know who was responsible, setting both servants and tableware to quaking.

Annelise thought of the conspiratorial glint that would light Yves' eye and sobered immediately.

Yves was probably dead.

She sat up, her laughter dismissed. She hugged knees to her chest and acknowledged the ache within her heart.

If nothing else, she and Yves had had each other these last two years. Now she was alone again, as she had been for most of her life. Tears welled up in Annelise's eyes and she looked for her discarded veil.

That was when she remembered the book.

As befit her experience of the day, it had vanished as surely as if it had never been. It was not on the table where she had seen it last, nor even in the bed chamber. It was not in the courtyard, so Annelise embarked on another hunt through the entire palace for the cursed book.

It must be her husband's will that it be hidden from her, although Annelise could not understand why he no longer wished for her to break the curse.

One day in the forest, still burdened with the curse of being a wolf, was enough to make Rolfe's anger fade.

Indeed, it was sufficient to make him question his choice to leave the palace.

And his wife.

Annelise had not left the palace during the day, although he had heard sounds of activity within the walls.

He was curious beyond all to know what she was doing.

He knew she was not taking her leisure. That was not the lady's inclination.

No, she had a scheme of some kind. He knew her well enough to guess that. Rolfe could not help but wonder what it was.

Still, he retreated to the tower that night, wanting to be certain of his choice. He could not even see the palace from the high windows, which he had found vexing. The rustle of the wind irritated him as never before, let alone the wail of it in the stairwell of the tower. Rolfe hated that no human sound carried to his ears once he moved away from the palace gates at sunset. He ached to hear Annelise's laughter or the tread of her foot upon the stair.

He spent that night pacing the floor of the abandoned tower, instead of finding peace in his refuge.

All through that night, Rolfe was aware of what he had denied himself. He recalled the smooth, warm satin of Annelise's skin beneath his hand. When he closed his eyes, Rolfe could smell the honeyed perfume of her skin. It was all too easy to remember the taste of her kiss—and long to sample it again.

It was more than the pleasure that he and Annelise found abed that Rolfe missed, though. In his memory, he saw her eyes sparkle, her lips curve and part as they did before she laughed aloud.

He missed her company, her conviction that his cause should be defended, and her faith that she could be the one to do it.

As the moon crossed the sky, it became increasingly difficult to recall why he was denying himself the pleasure of her company.

In hindsight, Rolfe knew he should have anticipated that Annelise would try to look upon him. She was curious. Indeed, that was one trait he admired about her. She solved matters for herself, apparently having learned no expectation that any other soul would show a care for her needs. She had asked him repeatedly to show his face to her, and he had declined.

So, she had found a solution.

It was not that much of a crime, or even that much of a betrayal.

Rolfe stared over the snowy forest and admitted that both hiding himself from her and retreating from the palace had been mistakes. Annelise had not recognized him. He should have anticipated as much. Her years in the convent probably meant that she would not recognize his name, either.

Just before the dawn, he had a troubling idea. What if the bottle offered his dream come true, but he was too fool to take it?

What if love was not merely physical?

What if there were women who, unlike Rosalinde, did not demand concrete gains for the surrender of their favors?

What if he was wed to one? Annelise had declared herself unwilling to marry a man who did not love her. She had seemed confused when Rolfe talked about material comforts in the same breath as love. Was it possible that Annelise was not like Rosalinde?

Could he have misjudged his wife?

Could destiny have brought the one woman to him who could hold his heart captive for all his days and nights? Annelise might be his dream come true, albeit a dream he had not known he possessed.

He hated being without her, though.

And Annelise seemed to know more of love than he did.

Rolfe decided that marriage might be a reasonable place to start a search for love, whatever it was. His mother had professed love for his father, as he recalled, although Rolfe had always assumed she meant the act that begot children. Looking back, he saw that he might have been wrong.

Perhaps Rolfe could convince Annelise to love him.

And why not? She laughed at his jests. She welcomed his touch and took his side. In fact, they were wed, and *she* had been the one to insist that love belonged in marriage.

The sun rose as Rolfe began to form a new plan.

He had found something that his wife would be glad to see.

Due to the curse, he could only show it to her in the daylight, when he could leave the palace.

It was perhaps time she encountered him as a wolf again.

She had, after all, wanted to see his truth.

CHAPTER EIGHT

 day of shouting potential spells had made no difference in the gates. A thorough hunt of the palace and its grounds had not revealed the book, so Annelise retired to the chamber her husband favored in poor temper.

He was not there.

Her venison stew was there, though she had little appetite for it. There was only one portion and she feared that meant he had no intention of returning that night. Did the meal mean that he was not quite so vexed at her? Was it a promising sign? Or did he have a standing order with the palace to see her fed?

Or was he gone, and the palace would see to her basic needs forever?

She waited, but he did not appear.

She ate, but he did not appear.

She paced, partly to keep warm, but he did not appear.

She retired, extinguishing all the lights, but still he did not appear.

Annelise could not sleep without her husband's heat by her side and feared the import of his absence. He could not have abandoned her completely, could he?

How would she apologize if she never saw him again?

And still there was the most vexing question of all: who was

Rosalinde? Why did he utter her name in his sleep? The possibilities plagued Annelise.

Without much else to do, she struggled to recall every childhood tale she had ever heard. Perhaps the secret to the spell of the gates was there, hidden in her own memories.

Every puzzle had a key, she reminded herself. She had only to find it.

The palace grew steadily colder during the night and by morning, winter had settled in with a vengeance. As Annelise had originally thought, the broad arching windows were ridiculous. The wind ripped through them with delight and stirring the drifts of snow that had appeared in the corridors. She had to break the ice on the surface of her bathing water in the morning and was reluctant to abandon her cloak at all. She donned every item of clothing she possessed, her hands shaking with cold, then left the bed chamber. She hoped there was something hot to break her fast.

There was a bowl of porridge, a thin line of steam still rising from it.

But beside the bowl was the missing book.

Annelise hastened to the table and opened the book. The script was still legible, thanks to her husband's touch. She sank down onto the cushion, ate her porridge, and began to read a tale for children.

Surely the book was here for a reason.

Surely there would be a glimmer of truth within it.

Her husband had been cursed by djinn, after all.

There were, there were not, in the oldness of time, twin daughters born to a djinn and his wife. Herein lies the tale of Leila and Kira, twins born to Azima and Azzam. They were matched in looks but not in manner.

This was in the days when man and djinn walked the earth together—one wrought of potter's clay, the other of smokeless fire—in echo of the master's creation. Equal but different, they shared trials and successes, in those times before the djinns were dispatched to the realm beyond the world of men. Good and evil stalked the ranks of both man and djinn in those times, as always it did, and as this tale soon will show.

For Leila, being a child of the night, grew to womanhood with an intuitive understanding of the dark arts, while Kira, a child of the day to her essence, was filled with innocence and joy.

Though both children were fair in their way, the sight of Kira made others feel as though they looked into the warm beauty of the sun itself. People and djinns both smiled when she passed them, even when she was an infant. Unbeknownst to her family, Leila's dark heart grew to nurture a dreadful jealousy of her sister.

The sisters grew, becoming more themselves with each passing day. Kira was good and kind, thinking of others before herself, willing to give the last of what she had to another in need. It was said that diamonds and pearls fell from her mouth when she spoke, and all she gave was returned to her tenfold.

Leila, though gifted, did not have such abundant charms. As she grew older, her jealousy deepened into a dark force that claimed all her attention. She turned to sorcerers' arts to compete with her sister, but though she could oft mimic her sister's gifts, whatsoever is wrought of shadows does not stand the test of time. The flowers she created withered and died more quickly than real ones, while Kira's blossomed with rare vigor and thrived even in adverse conditions.

It was noted by all that Kira was a rare and special daughter and the parents showered affection on their golden child. All this served only to feed Leila's hatred, though none might have guessed unless they looked into her eyes. Accidents began to befall Kira, and as their severity increased, those outside the family wondered about Leila. Kira would not listen to any questions though and would hear nothing said against her twin.

In time the sisters were of a marriageable age, and a young mortal man came calling. He was handsome beyond all, gifted, yet moderate of speech, which pleased the father of the two sisters. He fell in love with Kira as suddenly as Leila fell in love with him. His mortality was not an issue, for the nuptial kiss of a djinn welcomes a mortal partner into the ranks of the immortals. What mattered more was his nature, which was good.

One might easily imagine the jealousy that erupted in Leila once Kira expressed her affections for the young suitor. Leila delved deep into her store of forbidden secrets, and the love of Kira and her suitor was sorely tested in Leila's attempts to drive them apart.

But despite the odds against them, despite the pitfalls laid across their path, the couple's love was of such magnitude that they overcame every challenge. Leila lied and cursed. Her attacks on Kira becoming more overt, but that golden child stepped through the worst calamity unscathed. Each failure made Leila yet more bitter, and she dove deeper into the shadows of arcane sorcery, but to no avail.

It could be said that her spells only strengthened the bond between Kira and her suitor, for a good match faced with adversity will grow stronger to survive.

Meanwhile, the wedding was planned and no expense was spared. Gifts came from far and wide for the happy couple, and the twin's father, Azzam, built a palace for the newlyweds. It was graced with the gifts and the love of all in the community. It was claimed that Kira's smile brought the sun into the central courtyard on the most cloudy day.

Leila, not to be outdone, built a palace so fine that it tugged at the heartstrings of all who came near. Men were drawn to her palace's beauty, like sailors to sirens upon rocky shores, but Kira's beloved was immune. He remained in his new home, preparing for his nuptials, and doting upon his intended.

Leila was infuriated that he spurned her lavish palace. She threatened to cast spells on those who attended the wedding, or those who sent gifts. She cursed a man in the marketplace after he commented on her sister's beauty and that man never uttered a word again. Similarly, those who gazed admiringly upon Kira from afar found themselves blinded shortly thereafter.

When Leila's actions were no longer hidden and could not be denied, the mother of the twins knew that the battle had to stop. Azima knew more than most of the extent of her daughter's stubborn nature. From the beginning, Leila had been a child bent upon her own satisfaction, regardless of the cost to others. Fearing that her spawn might not be amenable to change, however artfully the idea was presented, Azima planned for the worst.

She had hoped to never implement her plan, but Leila had driven her to it.

A djinn goldsmith fashioned a bottle at Azima's demand. He dictated that any djinn released from the bottle would be obliged to grant a gift to whoever was responsible. The resulting decanter was blacker than black, yet impossible to break.

Azima took the vessel home, her heart heavy with what she had to do. She planned to visit Leila in her palace, but Leila would not receive her mother's messengers. Invitations were ignored and even Azima herself was not greeted at her daughter's home.

Fearing disaster, Azima instructed Azzam on the role he must play, should anything go amiss on the day of Kira's nuptials. As soon as Leila dove into the bottle, he was to put the cork in as firmly as he could. Azima reminded Azzam of their responsibility as parents, and made it most clear that all their love would never be enough to control one like Leila should she choose to ignore their appeal for reason. Azima made her spouse swear an ancient oath of uncommon strength to ensure that he would keep his word.

Then she kissed him with great affection and he wondered at the cause. Perhaps even then she knew what would transpire.

On the morning of the wedding, Azima was well prepared, though she hoped Leila would stay away and all her plans would be for nothing. When Kira stepped into the carriage summoned to convey her to the nuptials, Azima darted into the carriage just before it pulled away, even though Kira had asked to ride alone.

Azima found Leila holding a dagger to her sister's throat. Her plan was to substitute herself for the bride, and to cast a spell over the groom so he did not notice the difference until their vows were exchanged. Azima tried in vain to sway her daughter from this foul deed. Leila was resolute and Kira's eyes were wide with terror.

Knowing she had no other choice remaining, Azima pretended to surrender the argument. As they rode, she remarked that she had a decanter at home into which no djinn could fit. Leila scoffed at her mother's inadequate powers, declaring that she would certainly be able to enter the decanter. Azima challenged her to prove it, offering to let whichever daughter could slide into the bottle marry Kira's suitor.

Leila accepted the offer without hesitation. Kira protested, but her mother waved her to silence. The carriage turned around at Azima's dictate to stop at the home of Azima and Azzam. When the women arrived, Azzam fetched the bottle at his wife's bidding and set it in the courtyard. He kept the stopper hidden, as if the bottle did not have one.

Now Kira had been pinched by her mother and understood that she was not to attempt this feat. She walked around it, considered her path, behaving as if the matter were more complicated than it was. Leila, impatient, pushed her aside and slid into the bottle with a cry of triumph.

Azzam revealed the cork a moment too soon and Leila guessed his intent. She tried to leave the bottle, but her mother pushed her the rest of the way in. Leila was overpowered by her mother's determination to save Kira, but, in the last moment, her hand locked around Azima's ankle. To the horror of all, Azima was hauled into the decanter along with her evil daughter.

Azzam hesitated, then recalled his oath and jammed the cork into the bottle with shaking hands. The wedding was held as arranged, for all knew Azima would have desired as much, but the day was less than celebratory for Azzam and Kira.

Despite Azzam's hopes, no one could figure out a way to let one djinn free while the other remained trapped inside. Heartsick, Azzam hid the bottle away, unable to look upon it without guessing what his beloved wife suffered within its confines. It was not long before he died, as a djinn seldom does, his heart broken by his part in the tragedy.

Though Kira looked for the bottle after her father's death, wanting to ensure that Leila was guarded responsibly, it was never found. Kira and her husband lived long lives, then chose to follow the other djinn to their new realm. Leila's palace continued to thrive for a time, drawing people to it seemingly against their will but never allowing any of them to depart.

Over time, the world grew less tolerant of djinns and their kin, forcing those wrought of smoke to hide from mortals. The possessions of the wondrous house built for Kira and her husband were scattered and the house was occupied by mortals. Leila's palace became a source of legends, though the path to it was lost. The story of Leila and Azima passed into legend and no one ever saw the dark decanter again.

It was thus, it was not thus, in the oldness of time.

It was the only tale in the book.

There were many painted illustrations, presumably of Azima and Azzam, Kira and Leila, and Kira's beloved. Annelise found an enormous image of a palace with gardens, a palace which looked much like the one she occupied.

Was it the same palace?

How similar were palaces in the east?

Perhaps this palace had been made to resemble the palace in the book.

Annelise closed the book, her heart chilling with a sudden thought. Could this be Leila's palace? Had Leila given it to Annelise's husband? Why? It said little good about Annelise's spouse if he had won the favor of a djinn as malicious as Leila. That could not be it.

She read the entire tale again, seeking some morsel of

information she could use. The key to this puzzle was proving to be elusive indeed. She shivered and got to her feet, frustrated beyond all, and considered that she should take Mephistopheles for a ride. She imagined that he had become accustomed to her company and the exercise.

She was crossing the courtyard when she heard the subtle creak of hinges.

It could not be! She raced through the palace, only to find that the gates were opening. She watched in astonishment. Slowly, almost reluctantly, the great gates yawned wider and wider.

Annelise ran for the opening. She could squeeze through the space even now and be free. She would flee this palace, seek her husband, even return to Beauvoir if she must.

She was between the opening gates, one foot almost on the other side, when she saw the wolf. She halted in her steps.

She had forgotten about the hungry wolves. This one paced restlessly, as though he waited for something. When Annelise inhaled sharply, the wolf fixed his gaze upon her.

He was waiting for her.

It made no sense. He was just a wolf, a beast incapable of reason, but his steadfast stare made shivers run down her spine. She recalled only too well the wolf that had chased her toward these cursed walls.

Her heart stopped when she saw that this wolf also had one blue eye and one silver-gray.

It was the same beast that had chased her to the palace.

Wolf and woman stared at each other for a moment that seemed to stretch to eternity. Annelise's mouth had gone dry. She did not dare to run lest she provoke his attack.

She took a cautious step backward toward safety.

The wolf snarled and Annelise's heart leaped to her throat. She hurried back, tripping over her own feet as the wolf bounded closer.

"Close, gates, *close!*" she shouted. "Keep out the wolf!"

The gates, curse them, remained ajar.

Annelise ran through the garden as quickly as she could. She could hide behind something in the palace, climb atop a chest, barricade the stables, anything to save her life.

When she reached the palace, she was surprised she had gotten so far before the wolf pounced upon her. Annelise paused and looked back.

Only her own footprints marked the snow in the garden. There was no sign of pursuit.

She saw the wolf pacing back and forth outside the open gates. He snarled, as though agitated, and Annelise grew curious as she watched.

Why had he not pursued her?

Perhaps he did not want to devour her.

What could he want?

The wolf ceased his pacing as though he felt the weight of her gaze. He turned to her and, though he was some distance away, Annelise felt pinned to the spot by his regard. She could feel his stare, just as she felt that of her husband, even when she could not see his eyes.

Unexpectedly, the wolf wagged his tail.

He looked much less fearsome, then, and more like a dog seeking approval. Perhaps the beast did want something of her. Had she been anywhere else, Annelise might have questioned the sense of this thought, but it was clear this palace defied her expectations in many ways.

Perhaps he merely tried to lure her out into the forest because he could not enter the palace. She recalled the man-at-arms' assertion that wolves were wily.

But, Annelise thought, if the wolf could not or would not enter the palace, she could simply ensure that she remained inside the gates. She could approach him, discover whether he wanted anything of her, yet remain safe.

It seemed a sensible plan, even if it felt particularly bold.

Her heart was thundering by the time she reached the gates. The wolf did not even seem to blink as he watched her.

"Do you desire something from me?" she asked.

The wolf's ears pricked up, then he trotted a dozen paces away. He turned and darted back to the gate, then repeated the motion.

Annelise folded her arms across her chest. "You expect me to follow you? You must think me mad." She spared a glance at the darkening sky. "Night will come soon enough and I do not wish to be alone in the forest with a wolf when it arrives." She shivered, remembering her similar experience all too well.

The wolf trotted away and back once more, his feet marking a trail in the snow. Annelise chewed her lip. Every instinct within her demanded that she follow the beast, although she knew it was folly of the worst kind.

Curse her curiosity.

"Why should I trust you?"

The wolf opened his mouth in what looked like a smile. Annelise could have sworn he winked.

That was it. Her mind was playing tricks upon her of the most cruel nature. How could she even consider following a wolf into the forest at night? How could she imagine such a beast could smile or wink?

Evidently, solitude had dismissed any scrap of sense she might have had.

It was odd that both the wolf and her husband had eyes of different colors, one blue and one silver-gray.

Exactly what curse had been laid upon her husband?

Annelise shook her head, dismissing what had to be whimsy.

"This is madness." She could not help but explain herself to the animal. "You are a wolf, a brute beast. You cannot possibly be urging me to accompany you, and I cannot be considering doing precisely that. Go away and leave me alone."

Annelise turned back to the courtyard, but the wolf let out a howl from behind her.

She tried to ignore it, but the wolf barked sharply, then howled louder.

"Cursed creature!" Annelise stormed back to the gates and pushed upon one heavy door. "Cursed gate! Close out this creature that I might be in peace."

She pushed and strained, but the gate was as immovable open as closed. The wolf ceased his howling when she drew nearer, and Annelise spared him a glance.

He wagged his tail, reminding her of the pups the ostler had once bred in Sayerne's stables. Who would have imagined a wolf might have a certain charm?

Clearly, the cold was addling her wits.

Annelise shoved at the door without success.

"A plague on this palace," she muttered, then stepped through the portal to try to pull it closed.

Too late Annelise realized she had stepped over the line the gates made when they were closed. The wolf barked and the portal slammed closed so quickly that Annelise almost had her finger caught between the doors.

She was locked outside the palace's gates.

She spun to face the wolf and propped her hands on her hips. "You did that," she accused.

The wolf wagged his tail as though conceding his guilt, then trotted toward the forest. He glanced back at Annelise.

"You truly expect me to follow you."

He ran back to her, nuzzled her kirtle so quickly that she had no time to pull away, wagged his tail, then bounced along the well-trodden path once more. He waited on a small rise of snow ahead, his posture expectant.

He might have been a puppy waiting for her to throw a ball.

Annelise gave the gates one last shove, already knowing that nothing would happen. They did not budge.

"It seems that I hardly have a choice."

The wolf barked and trotted into the woods. If she was going to keep sight of him and not find herself lost in the forest again, Annelise had to follow him quickly. She picked up her skirts, muttering under her breath, and did precisely that.

The wolf set a killing pace through the forest, yet his path was straight. It was evident he had a destination in mind, and had Annelise not known it was ridiculous, she would have sworn his manner was anxious. He moved so quickly that she guessed it was distant. He glanced at the sky, which Annelise eyed with no small trepidation herself.

The farther they traveled, the lower her confidence that she could return to the palace by nightfall. She was already uncertain that she could find her way back alone. There was no choice but to follow the wolf.

He gave a bark some moments later and she saw his wagging tail. He raced back to her side, gave her a nudge, then hurried ahead to a clearing. Annelise followed him as quickly as she could, then stopped at the sight of blood in the snow.

A carcass had been dragged into the forest to her right and she went to look.

It was a dead wolf, the arrow still lodged in its throat.

It had been eaten by its fellows and there was precious little left beyond the fur. Annelise staggered back into the clearing in revulsion.

But the wolf nudged her again, leading her to the far side of the clearing. There in the snow were the imprints of horses' hooves.

Large shod horses.

Annelise fell to her knees to examine the tracks, the wolf fast beside her. "A destrier," she whispered, her hand hovering above one set of prints. "Fleeing to safety."

The wolf barked as if to agree with her, then pushed his nose into another set of tracks.

"A second horse," Annelise said in wonder, smiling as the wolf sniffed at more tracks. "A third and a fourth. Yves escaped! He rode back to Beauvoir!"

The wolf barked and ran circles around her, apparently sharing her joy. Annelise was so relieved that she felt tears on her cheeks and her throat was tight. She had the curious urge to hug the wolf, but he was no dog.

She turned to consider him and found him watching her again. "How on earth did you know to bring me to this place?" she asked softly.

Once again, he seemed to smile and wink.

Then he barked at the sky and darted to the other side of the clearing.

Annelise understood. It was time to return to the palace. She blew a kiss down the path that Yves had taken, wishing him well, then picked up her skirts and followed the wolf.

Although she quickly realized that he led her in another

direction, she hurried after him, not wanting to be left to fend for herself. Darkness was falling quickly and if anything, the wolf ran more quickly than before.

It was already twilight. Annelise's hems were heavy with snow and her fingertips were chilled. The cold was growing more intense and, in only a matter of moments, the light would fail completely.

She wondered if the wolf was hungry.

She was so very glad to know that Yves had survived. Surely that knowledge was worth whatever her own fate might be this night?

A wolf howled in the forest, not nearly as distant as Annelise would have liked. Her wolf ran back to her, urging her to greater speed. His protectiveness was unexpected and quite welcome. She managed to run faster and he barked approval. She realized why when she saw the outline of a tower above the silhouetted trees ahead. Relief flooded through her at the sight.

Her spirits lifted and her step lightened. If nothing else, she would have shelter this night. With luck, she would find something to bar the entrance against intruders.

The wolf ran back and forth excitedly at the door, then sat to one side as Annelise drew near. It was clear he intended for her to enter but she frowned when she noticed the tower's advanced state of disrepair.

Would she be safer within or without? Annelise considered the crumbling tower, the stars visible in the sky overhead, then looked at the wolf.

"You mean for me to go inside? This place does not look solid enough to last the night." Just saying the words fed her fears.

The wolf barked. He ran in a tight circle around her, then went back to the door, sitting beside it once more. His gaze never wavered from her face.

"What is in there?" she demanded, her voice rising in her uncertainty. "Who is in there?"

Some of her fear must have been audible, for the wolf trotted through the open doorway. He disappeared into the shadows within, reappearing moments later with snow on his snout. He barked and wagged his tail, standing to one side as though inviting her onward. The snow made him look adorable and unthreatening.

Annelise frowned. The forest was already filled with shadows. She could not return to the palace before dark, and she did not know if she could open the gates once there. One last finger of light framed the doorway in gold as though it, too, would invite her to enter. Annelise shivered and wondered whether she would live to see the morn.

"It is evident I have nothing to lose," she murmured and entered the portal.

The tower was made of heavy, square-cut stones, reminding Annelise of the Roman road that passed through Beauvoir. It was clear from the skill of the masonry that it had once been grand, if splendidly isolated. She wondered how old it was and what its purpose might have been.

Silence buffeted her ears as she stepped fully inside and, as her eyes adjusted, she made out the steps of a staircase. It must curve along the wall to the summit. With a wolf at her heels, Annelise climbed the stairs.

The single room at the top was round and possessed four small windows. Annelise was glad to see that the roof was intact. The dying light fanned through one window. The floor was illuminated with its golden gleam, and a sharp line was drawn between light and darkness. What Annelise could see of the room was unfurnished, save for a small lump of textiles beneath the west-facing window.

She crossed the room to examine the pile, lifting the first garment into the light. They were men's chausses, made of a dark wool, and they looked vaguely familiar.

Annelise knew well enough that she had only seen one man's chausses of late. She flicked a glance at the wolf, who settled on his haunches in the doorway, and she shivered to find his gaze fixed upon her. The shadows had claimed that side of the room, and only the gleam of his eyes and teeth were clearly visible.

The hairs on the back of Annelise's neck prickled. There was something about the weight of the wolf's stare, something not canine in his expression, something that made it easy to believe he might be capable of a wink.

He looked almost smug, as though he knew something she did not and dared her to discover it.

Solitude was clearly making her fey. Annelise's hands shook as she lifted a white linen shirt from the pile, then stopped mid-gesture at the scent that surrounded her.

It was the aroma of a man's skin, of a particular man's skin, and her heart skipped in recognition. Annelise would have recognized that scent anywhere in Christendom.

It was her spouse's flesh she smelled.

"Mother of God," she whispered. Tears blurred her vision as she touched the boots resting beneath the shirt.

These were her husband's clothes.

And he evidently had no need of them any longer.

This wolf had devoured him.

Annelise clutched his chemise to her chest and spun to face the wolf, even as her tears began to fall.

"Fiend!" Annelise cried in fury.

She pulled her small eating knife and lunged for Rolfe in his wolf form. He could only admire her bravery, even as he evaded her blow. He bared his teeth and she was so startled that she dropped the knife.

He kicked it so that it clattered down the stairs. He would retrieve it later, but he had no desire to be injured.

"If you mean to attack me, then do not make me wait," Annelise said, her manner grim. She backed against the wall, staring at him in horror.

The last finger of sunlight slipped below the horizon, and the room was suddenly plunged into evening shadows. Rolfe was glad that she would not have to witness his transformation, for he imagined it was as disconcerting to see as to feel. He sighed with relief as he changed to his human form, though his lady's fear was tangible.

Then he stepped into the shaft of moonlight to reveal himself to her. "I shall attack you with pleasure, wife of mine, but not in the way you are imagining."

She gasped and seemed overwhelmed. "You. You!"

"Yes, me."

"But how? Where?" She looked between him and the portal where the wolf had been, her fear evident and her uncertainty clear. She seemed to be at a loss for words.

"Do not tell me that you of all people are speechless, my Annelise?" Rolfe asked. "You will leave me doubting that you are my wife, after all."

She gripped his clothing, clearly still shocked. "But, sir..."

"Perhaps you are not glad to see me, after all."

The lady's lips trembled. Rolfe knew he had compelled her to run quickly and far in the cold and did not doubt that she was exhausted. He crossed the small chamber and caught her close, feeling how she trembled. She leaned her cheek against his chest and gripped his shoulders as she began to weep.

He massaged her nape. "Why these tears?"

"I never cry," she mumbled, though evidence to the contrary wet his skin.

Rolfe stifled a chuckle and rocked her in the warmth of his arms. "Of course not," he agreed.

"My lord," she whispered. "I am so sorry that I broke my promise to you. I thought you would not know..."

"And you were curious beyond all."

"I was." She sighed. "I erred, sir. I wanted to know as much as I could in order to help you."

Rolfe was awed by her words. "And I erred in hiding myself from you, so perhaps we are even."

"Truly?"

Rolfe smiled, though she did not lift her head. "Truly." He tugged at the pile of his clothing that she held tightly. "I shall need these if I am to be decent in the presence of a lady." he reminded her in a murmur.

"I am so glad that you are alive!" She reached up and kissed him, initiating their embrace in the way that fired his blood.

"Yes, Annelise. I am alive," he whispered into her hair. "Surely you did not believe otherwise?"

"But you have been gone all this time. And there was the wolf." She started and tried to stare past him as she dropped her voice to a whisper. Her hands clutched at him. "Is he gone? One attacked my horse, that first night that I came to the palace, and it was terrifying..."

"Hush." Rolfe stroked her shoulder, knowing that when she calmed and began to think the matter through, she would see the answer. "The wolf will not trouble you."

"But he was just there, right inside the door. You must have seen him when you came in."

His thumb slid across her lips, silencing her. He cupped her chin in his hand and tipped her face up to his. "Did I not promise to see you safe?"

The fight went out of her shoulders and she dropped her gaze, demure as he had never expected her to be. "You did." Then she shook her head and he watched as her fear receded. Just as he anticipated, she began to reason through the puzzle. "But why are you without your clothing? And where is the wolf?" She made an exasperated sound. "How did the wolf know to show me that Yves had ridden away? Why did the gates open for the wolf?"

Rolfe turned away to quickly don his clothes as she spoke her thoughts aloud. Her conclusion was inevitable and by the sound, she would reach it quickly. He struck the tinder and lit a fire, but Annelise stared out the window toward the palace, her fingers drumming on the sill.

"I cannot explain it, but every puzzle has a key."

Rolfe closed his hands over her shoulders. He touched his lips to her neck, relieved that her skin was warmer. She shivered, but he guessed it was for another reason. and she shivered despite herself. "It seems I must believe in destiny, after all, my Annelise. I have never been so fortunate as to have known a woman like you before, and yet you are my wife."

"What manner of woman is that?" she asked, her words husky.

"A passionate one," he confessed, punctuating his word with a slow kiss beneath her ear. "A loyal one." Another kiss on her ear prompted Annelise to sigh. "One who would make my battle her own."

"Then you have been unfortunate, sir," she whispered.

"Indeed, I have been, but my fortunes changed with the taking of a bride." He turned her in his embrace but Annelise kept her gaze lowered. "Will you forgive me?"

"Will you trust me?" she countered.

"I will," Rolfe said, knowing it was past time to take a chance. "If you can endure it, Annelise, I will confess the entire tale to you."

"Truly?" She glanced up then and met his gaze.

She gasped, then took a step backward in her surprise. Rolfe knew that the puzzle had found its key.

CHAPTER NINE

nnelise's husband had one blue eye and one silver-gray.

Just like the wolf.

No. It could not be so.

He held her gaze steadily, as if inviting her to make the most remarkable conclusion.

"The wolf that drove me through the palace gates had eyes like yours," she whispered, hoping he would argue with her. He did not. "And that same wolf showed me the tracks of Yves' horse today, then led me to this tower." She looked past his shoulder, just to be certain, but was unsurprised to see that the wolf was gone.

She understood where the wolf had gone, even though all logic fought against it. She recalled snippets of childhood tales about those who changed form. They were chilling tales, told on windswept winter nights and intended to keep children huddled in their beds.

He had confessed to being cursed, but still, it seemed too strange to believe.

"No," she murmured, hearing the doubt fade from her own tone. "It cannot be."

"But it can be," he said with quiet conviction. "Because it is so."

"You said you were cursed."

"Would you not count this fate as one?"

Annelise nodded, still amazed.

"And what do you think, Annelise, now that you know the truth?" His eyes narrowed slightly. "Do you want to leave? Would you prefer to be released from our match than to hear my tale?"

"No," she said immediately and knew it was true. "I want to know all of your truth."

He held her gaze for a long moment. "And if I refuse to tell you?"

"I will leave." Simply saying the words caused a lump to lodge in Annelise's throat. "It must be this night that there is a full confession between us." Annelise was surprised that she had no doubts, even knowing what she already did about her spouse. Despite the unconventionality of their match, this man treated her with more respect and tenderness than anyone she had ever known. She had vowed to help him find a solution to his woes, though she had not guessed their full extent at the time.

"I do not want to leave," she confessed when he did not reply. "Tell me the truth instead."

"And yet it is a fearsome tale," he admitted. "It seems unreasonable that I should share my truth, while your secrets remain locked within your heart."

"I have no secrets," Annelise said, then raised a hand to her lips at the realization that the words were not true.

She had one.

Her spouse shook his head, his gaze knowing. "Why did you cower, my Annelise? I have never shown you cruelty, but you expected it of me. There is a secret behind your fear, to be sure."

She swallowed and nodded. "I do have one secret," she admitted softly.

"And I have one." He offered his hand. "And so, a bargain, wife of mine. Your secret for mine."

Annelise met his steady gaze and knew that the future of their marriage depended upon her choice in this moment. She had never wished to share this tale, and yet, there was no choice. It was worth the price to give her match with this man a chance of a future.

"You will not pacify me with the tale of some hunting romp, sir," she scolded, teasing him in the hope of making him smile. "I will have the tale of your curse or no other."

"I doubt that you could ever be pacified, Annelise." His smile was fleeting but enough to make her heart leap. "Nor would I want you to be." He arched a brow, his admiration for her making his eyes glow. "And your tale must be of equal worth, not a confession that you have always been fond of apple tart."

Annelise laughed. "Fair enough, sir."

He offered his hand to her and Annelise swallowed, then placed her hand within his. His fingers closed over hers, his grip sure and his skin as warm as the glow in her eyes. She felt awareness of him kindle and grow, and she swallowed that she could find him so very handsome, despite his curse. Their gazes locked and held, the small tower chamber seeming to heat between them as she found an answering desire in his own eyes.

Perhaps she would feel less alone if someone else knew her secret.

Annelise took a deep breath. "I take your bargain, sir."

He smiled, then tugged her closer, pulling her into his embrace. "This, my lady, is a wager that must be sealed with a kiss."

His kiss was as passionate and commanding as ever, his touch sending heat and desire surging through her. Nothing could have reassured her so much as her husband's touch, and when he deepened his kiss, slanting his mouth over her own, Annelise knew she had made the right choice.

Rolfe's heart tightened as he watched his bold bride prepare to tell her tale. She composed her features with a care that revealed the importance of what she meant to confess. He granted her the time she seemed to need, feeding the fire and seeing to her comfort as well as he could. Her expression was impassive and Rolfe knew that she was lost in some painful recollection.

It humbled him that she intended to share the tale with him. She could not be giving a performance, as Rosalinde would have done. Rolfe could see that this telling would be painful for Annelise—and her trust bode well for their future.

Indeed, there was much about his wife that fed the admiration he had originally felt for her. He admired her boldness, her outright bravery, the way she lifted her chin when she did not want him to guess at her fear. He liked the passion with which she greeted life, the way she threw her heart into everything she did.

Rolfe recalled the sweet press of Annelise against him. She had been relieved to see him. She had been glad of his survival and the certainty of that launched a warm glow within him. He had been wrong to doubt her.

Rolfe refused to consider the last part of the djinn's curse. No, he would not let a threat keep him from the prize of a marriage filled with trust.

He would not let the djinn cheat him of Annelise.

He sat on the opposite side of the fire, wanting to watch her as she told her tale. Annelise kept her gaze fixed on the dancing flames.

Finally, she began her tale.

"Once upon a time, not that far from where we sit, a woman was given as bride to a lord. I do not know whether she was happy with the match or whether it was simply the arrangement of her parents. Perhaps she did not particularly care who she wed as long as she would be kept in comfort. It matters little what she thought, for the reality was destined to be vastly different from what any woman might hope to gain from marriage."

Annelise frowned and clasped her hands tightly together. Rolfe knew that this was no abstract tale, but was content to let her tell it in her own way. Was she the noblewoman in question? Or was this a tale of her parents?

"Her lord husband, she soon learned, was possessed of a temper. When he did not have his way, he beat anyone he could, and his wife, since she was convenient to his hand, soon came to bear the brunt of his anger."

Rolfe anticipated the direction of the tale. He hoped with all his might that Annelise had not been so abused, but then, he had been certain that she was a maiden when they first met abed.

"At first, it was an infrequent occurrence, and when the lady bore a son to her husband in short order, she escaped his wrath for a goodly time. It was said the lord was in uncommonly good spirits for several years."

This could not be Annelise's own tale, Rolfe reasoned. He knew she had not borne a child. How then did she know this unfortunate lady? It was clear she cared about her.

Annelise shook her head. "But those years passed, and the lady did not ripen with the lord's seed again. Worse, matters did not proceed well between him and his son; soon the boy defied him openly. It was said they were two of a kind, though some insisted the son was more cruel than his father. The lord was furious, however, at the boy's defiance, and began to vent his wrath on both son and wife. The overlord, who was a perceptive man or perhaps one who heard many rumors, intervened suddenly. He arrived at their gates, insisting he must take the son beneath his care. The tale was that the boy would begin his training as a knight, but the father dared not protest too much, as he was owing his tithes to that same lord."

It was a common enough practice for a nobleman's son to be trained for his spurs by another nobleman, though Rolfe imagined this boy might have been younger than was typical.

"The boy also was the lord's sole heir. When the overlord refused to confess where the son would train, this vexed the lord mightily. The tale was that he had not yet decided which of his liege lords would do the honor, but in time, it became clear that the overlord had no intention of sharing the truth with the father. The concession and the secrecy enraged the lord. I have no doubt that the lady bore the brunt of her spouse's frustration after the departure of their guest."

Annelise swallowed. "Of course, the overlord did not trust the father to leave the son in peace, but the violent lord perceived himself to be without issue, an affront to his pride and his fortunes. He demanded another son of his wife, but the lady's womb did not ripen."

Rolfe expected the tale to worsen and he proved to be right.

"When the lord drank—and he did so often—his displeasure made itself known, and the servants would hear the lady cry out in the night," Annelise confessed. "In the morn, she would sport bruises, usually hidden but always noted by her maids. No one dared to interfere, however, for fear that they would bear the weight of their lord's fists themselves.

"The lord accused his wife of all manner of evil, even in front of the servants. She was a witch; she was a sinner; she was an adulteress; she deliberately denied him his sole desire or she was being punished for her sins—and he was the one to pay the price. The lady bore his abuses silently, probably because she did not dare incur yet more of his wrath by challenging him outright.

"Remarkably, despite all this abuse, or perhaps because she knew there was only one way to make it stop, the lady bore fruit once more. The lord, needless to say, was delighted, and made great plans for this son."

Annelise swallowed, and Rolfe watched the light play over her features. Her voice, when she continued, was tight.

"The son, sadly, showed the poor grace to be born a daughter."

Rolfe had a very good idea who that daughter must have been.

The boy then would have been Quinn, taken from the household before Annelise had even been conceived.

She fell silent for a long moment, then finally cleared her throat to continue. "The lord, of course, was enraged by the defiance of this infant and also that of his lady wife. To his thinking, all in his household should have done their utmost to ensure his satisfaction, so he felt that both child and wife had betrayed him. The overlord, though, had sent an armed guard to watch over the lady while she nursed the babe. The lord took out his vengeance upon his villeins, and the land soon abounded with his bastards and his bruises.

"None of those sons were good enough, though, for none bore the stamp of legitimacy."

Annelise flicked a glance at Rolfe, and he did not look away from the pain in her eyes. He could not imagine that this sweet lady had endured a childhood with such a father and not turned out to be much like him. His admiration for her redoubled and he did not hide his feelings from her. She stared into his eyes for a long moment, then swallowed and frowned into the flames once more.

"The armed guard, of course, could not remain forever. When the daughter was weaned at two years of age, the soldiers left." Her brows arched and her voice broke slightly, though she did not look up. She traced a pattern on the floor with her fingertips. "They left the lady and her child alone in that keep with a lord who was good at saving his anger."

Annelise flicked a glance around the barren tower as if recalling her urge to escape. Rolfe saw tears gleam on her lashes. "They say a small child cannot recall events." Her gaze locked with Rolfe's. "They are wrong," she said bitterly. "I recall every moment of that night. It is carved upon my memory so clearly that it might have occurred just hours ago."

She spoke more quickly, and Rolfe hoped that sharing the tale would lessen its power. "I remember the fear on my mother's face when he knocked. I remember the sweet cajoling of his voice as he lied, to convince her to unlock the door. I recall every heartbeat of the time that it took her to cross the chamber, then to lift the latch. Even then, I sensed her doubt." Annelise shook her head. "But I suppose she did not feel she had the right to refuse her rightful husband entry to his own solar. And perhaps she believed he would not harm her in front of me."

She fell silent.

"Your mother was wrong," Rolfe guessed gently.

Annelise nodded. "She was wrong." She looked smaller and more vulnerable, a mere shadow of the bold wife he knew so well, and Rolfe moved to her side. No wonder she had wanted to marry a man whose love she could rely upon! He wrapped one arm around her shoulders and drew her close, then captured her hand in his. She was cold and he felt her tremble at her memory.

"I can see him still as he leaped through that doorway, as drunken and disheveled as ever he was," she confessed, her voice thick with unshed tears. "I can see him lock the portal behind himself, sealing us into the chamber with him. I can see my mother retreating and hear his bellow that she had shirked her obligation to grant him a son." She shook her head and Rolfe saw tears fall.

"And then he began to beat her," she whispered. "It was horrifying to watch, for he derived pleasure from making the pain last. My mother bled, she wept, she cried, she begged, but nothing could turn him from his path. His eyes glowed, I swear to you he laughed. His curses continued until my mother fell to the floor. When she did not move again, he kicked her, but she was utterly still."

Tears streamed down Annelise's cheeks, and Rolfe held her tightly. He sensed that she needed to purge herself of this tale, and he was honored to be the one entrusted with it. He would not risk interrupting her, though his heart ached for what she had witnessed.

And she had seen this a child. It was beyond wicked.

"The solar was silent. The blood seeped from her limp body. I do not know whether she was dead or whether she lingered in a haze of pain." She shook her head, burrowing her face against his chest. "It was odd then, the change I saw in him. He whispered her name, but she made no sound. He bent over her, touched her throat, straightened. The anger melted from his face, leaving a much smaller man. He looked suddenly like the child I was, lost and certainly confused. Then fear flickered across his face, fear that he would be caught at what he had unwittingly done.

"He glanced around the solar, and I remember well the cold dread that clutched my heart when he saw me standing in my cradle."

Annelise's hands grasped fistfuls of her kirtle. Rolfe wished there might have been something he could do to reassure her, yet knew the best salve was to let her talk, and to hold her fast against his side.

"His eyes blazed with anger again and I knew he would kill me, too. Even at that age, I understood that I had seen something I should not, and I feared the consequences. I flinched, I tried to hide in my cradle as I heard him start across the room. I even tried to climb out of the small bed to save myself.

If he had touched Annelise, Rolfe knew he would hunt down her father and force a reckoning from him.

"Then there was a knock at the door." Annelise caught her breath. "He halted and we both stared at the wooden panel. The châtelain had brought the warmed goat's milk my mother had begun to give me at night in lieu of her own milk. 'For the heiress,' the châtelain said from the corridor outside, and the bloodlust faded from my father's eyes."

Annelise exhaled shakily. When she continued, her voice was flat and matter-of-fact. "He had no heir without me and the châtelain had reminded him in the nick of time. I knew then that he would not kill me, but it was only much later that I understood why."

She fell silent and Rolfe felt her trembling.

"Did he beat you?" Rolfe asked, fighting to keep his own anger from his tone.

Annelise shook her head. "Never. I was always afraid that he would. Although truly, I wonder now whether he feared that I might tell my tale out of spite if he beat me." She shrugged. "It ended up that he had not the chance."

"Surely your mother's death was discovered?"

"But it was explained with a lie. My mother apparently had an accident when riding alone with my father early the next morn. I expect he carried her out of the solar and flung her from her horse's saddle in the forest, then lied to all and sundry."

"They must have guessed. Or someone must have seen."

"All feared Jerome de Sayerne and, rightly so, if he would kill his own wife." Annelise took a deep breath. "The overlord, when he heard—and I do not know exactly how much he heard, for even my father could not have silenced all of his servants' gossip— arrived with great haste at our gates. Tulley insisted to my father that a daughter had need of feminine influence in her upbringing. I was consigned to a convent within the week and spent my childhood in the nuns' fine care."

The stress Annelise laid on the word fine told Rolfe her true opinion of the convent life. Still, he was grateful to Tulley and to the sisters of the convent. Their custody had ensured that his lady had not been beaten. He wondered how much of a donation this overlord Tulley had made to the convent, and whether he would desire something of Annelise in return.

Rolfe was astonished that such an experience should have left so few scars upon Annelise. She had trusted him and only now he saw how difficult that must have been for her, and what a measure of the strength of her nature. It seemed that survival of hardship had only forged Annelise into yet a stronger woman than she might have been otherwise. She had a rare determination to savor life, which he could only admire.

A weaker soul might have become bitter or conniving.

Not unlike Rosalinde.

But in the wake of her confession, it was time to make her smile. Rolfe deliberately made his tone teasing. "I must confess that is a difficult image for me to conjure," he said.

Annelise glanced up, a question in her magnificent eyes.

Rolfe smiled down at her. "You in a convent. Silent. Biddable. Spending hours at embroidery." He rolled his eyes and she began to smile.

"You should not have wed me if that was the kind of woman you wanted."

"On the contrary." Rolfe lifted her chin with a fingertip, compelling her to see the truth in his eyes. "I should find such a woman insufferably boring. I have no doubt that she would think me unworthy of rescue, and I know I would be unable to rely upon her aid in any matter of import. I like your passion and your impulsiveness, my Annelise, and I know I shall never desire you to be otherwise."

She flushed scarlet but appeared to be pleased. "The nuns were glad enough to be rid of me when my father summoned me home. Their switch was worn out, after all."

Rolfe did not miss the fleeting reference to her father and felt his eyes narrow. "And why did he summon you? How could he have done as much? Or did your overlord forget you?"

"Tulley did not forget. Perhaps he thought my father had learned his lesson. As to why, my father was considering the possibility of recognizing a bastard son several years younger than me. Perhaps he wanted to see what kind of woman I had become."

"And whether you had forgotten what you had seen," Rolfe guessed.

"In all likelihood." Annelise pleated her kirtle between her fingers. "Tulley escorted me home to Sayerne and he stayed a week. When he rode out, he left two men behind, the tale being that my father had need of more warriors to defend his walls. I do not believe any of us were fooled." Rolfe nodded approval of this Tulley and his schemes. "I tried to avoid my father, but once or twice in that year before he died, I flinched when he approached me. I fear he guessed the truth. He was unresolved as to what to do about Yves when he died."

"I hope your father died as befits a man of his deeds," Rolfe said, and heard the thrum of anger in his words.

Annelise glanced up. "He died alone in his sleep, abandoned by his villeins, his property sliding into ruin about him. He had taken to abusing the holding and the tenants, for lack of any family to bear the brunt of his anger, and they had fled when they could. He was impoverished and the holding was no better than a ruin."

Rolfe felt satisfaction at this. A man who raised his hand against his wife deserved no less. "What happened to Yves? And your older brother?" He pretended to know nothing of Quinn, wanting to know more of what Annelise believed to be true of that man. "What was his name? Did he ever return?"

Annelise held up a single finger, familiar fire in her eyes. "One tale. We agreed to trade tales, one for each, sir. I have not heard yours, yet you demand a second from me."

The lady's opinion of that was more than clear, though Rolfe could not regret his own curiosity. He wanted to know all of her tales and learn her every secret. How many others could have approached marriage to a stranger with as little reticence as Annelise, after having lived the tale she had? Rolfe was astonished that she had not been more cruelly scarred by her father's actions.

He met her gaze and saw an uncommon resilience in those eyes. He felt a glow of pride that this woman was his wife. The trust he had been so reluctant to grant now seemed inevitable.

"Forgive me, my Annelise. I want only to know what has made you the fascinating woman you have become."

She blushed again. "Do not say what you do not mean."

"I never say what I do not mean."

Annelise stared at him as though she did not dare to believe him. Rolfe could not deny the impulse to press a kiss into her palm. "I have never met a woman like you." As soon as the words had left his mouth, Rolfe recognized the resonance of truth within them.

"Not even Rosalinde?" she asked.

Rolfe was shocked. "Rosalinde?"

How could Annelise know about Rosalinde?

What did Annelise know about Rosalinde?

"You call her name in your sleep," Annelise said, her eyes narrowing as she watched him.

"I do?"

Annelise nodded. "Who is she?" she asked, hurt in her tone. "Do you love her?"

"I knew her long ago," Rolfe replied.

Annelise folded her arms across her chest and her expression took on a familiar resolve. "You do not answer my question. Do you love her still?"

"No," Rolfe confessed, because it was true.

"Indeed? To whom do you make love when you touch me?"

Rolfe was amazed. "Annelise!"

Annelise scrambled to her feet and crossed the chamber, regarding him from the other side of the fire. "I will know this truth, sir." She raised a finger. "And it will not replace the telling of your tale."

Rolfe was vexed, then realized that Rosalinde made trouble again, even when she was absent.

He stood and faced Annelise, holding her gaze so she would see that he spoke the truth. "Rosalinde was a woman who deceived me with her charms, then cast me aside. It was long in the past and has nothing to do with what is between us, save that she was the one who taught me to be wary of granting my trust."

Annelise frowned. "Why did she cast you aside?"

"If I am to have but one tale of yours, then you may have only one of mine," he reminded her firmly. "Choose which it shall be."

Annelise, evidently reassured, smiled. "You know which tale I desire." Her eyes twinkled in a most delightful way. "Surely you do not mean to break your promise, sir?"

No. He did not. It was time to trust his lady wife.

"Of course not. A wager made is a wager kept." Rolfe indicated the place where they had been seated just moments before. "Will you join me, Annelise?"

Annelise wrapped her arms about her knees as her husband fed the fire. He frowned as he completed the task and it was clear he was considering how to present his story.

She took advantage of his diverted attention to study him. He was as finely wrought as her fingers had told her during those nights at the palace, and she tingled with the awareness that this man had touched her so intimately.

Who would have guessed that she might have gained so fine a husband by chance alone? It was more than appearance, for he was honorable and kind. He treated her well, he spoke to her with respect, he promised her safety in his presence.

And now, apparently, he intended to explain himself to her, in a manner unprecedented by men Annelise had known.

She could easily become accustomed to such indulgence.

He crouched on the opposite side of the fire and rocked on the balls of his feet, his hands loosely locked before him and his gaze fixed on the fire. "I shall tell you what happened, although you may not believe it to be true."

Annelise knew she would.

He cleared his throat and began without meeting Annelise's gaze. "These past years I have been in Outremer, on crusade, and on my last night there, was given a gift of farewell. It was a bottle of unusual design."

He hesitated, and Annelise asked a question to urge him along. "A gift from whom? And what was inside it?"

Her spouse flicked a glance her way. "I could not know what was inside, for it was sealed. It was the keeper of an inn we frequented. He gave each of the knights in our company a gift. The bottle was said to have the ability to make dreams come true." He shrugged. "I decided that I would give it to my brother, for I was certain he would admire it, in the hope that he might grant me a holding from his estate."

"Because you are the younger son."

"Exactly. Although, I was curious about its contents, I felt it would be unfitting to open it."

That was most appropriate. Annelise smiled and nodded approval. "What happened to the others in your company?"

"We divided into two groups, for we had differing notions of the best path homeward to pursue. I sailed from Acre for Brindisi with two comrades, but as the snow began, they chose to remain in Milan. I wished to be home for the Yule, so rode on alone."

This was consistent with what he had told her before.

"As I traveled northward and it grew colder, I noticed that the wax seal had broken on the stopper. I decided to satisfy my curiosity, as none would be the wiser, and I opened the bottle. Truth be told, I was chilled to my marrow and some *eau-de-vie* would have been welcome."

"*Eau-de-vie?*"

"A beverage made by the Saracens by some skill they hold. It is potent beyond belief and burns all the way down a man's gullet. We call it *eau-de-vie*, the water of life, because it often revives a fallen man, proving that he yet lives."

Annelise nodded, marveling that such a substance should exist.

Her husband's voice dropped. "But there was no *eau-de-vie* inside. There was a djinn."

"The one who owned the palace."

"The very same." Her spouse seemed surprised by her attitude. "I would not blame you if you thought my tale a lie, for I was skeptical of her claim myself."

"Did she not emerge from the bottle itself?"

"Yes."

"Then why were you skeptical? You had seen the truth with your own eyes."

"But it defied belief. One does not expect childish tales to prove true."

"Whyever not? You said that the bottle was unusual. You could not have expected it to contain something mundane, like perfume or water, or even this *eau-de-vie*."

"But that is precisely what I did believe to be inside it," he confessed.

"Then you must have been pleased to have been wrong."

He regarded her for a moment, then leaned closer. "Do you not see that it is illogical for something invisible to change my life?"

"I do not, not at all." Annelise smiled at him. "Of course, matters invisible affect our lives. What of faith? You were in Outremer on crusade. What drove the crusade other than faith?"

Her spouse grimaced. "You are innocent, my Annelise. Greed and a hunger for power are the greater forces there. Otherwise, why would knight and bishop both grasp all that they could in the Holy City itself?"

"You will not convince me," Annelise insisted. "Things unseen can be powerful indeed. What of love?"

"We have loved every night we have been together." He raised a hand to her cheek. "I have seen you and touched you."

"This is but an act to express the emotion," Annelise chided. "Love itself is unseen. It fills the heart."

He was still wary of that notion. "And how do you know it exists?"

"Because I have felt it. I have seen its influence."

"Not in your father's abode."

"No. The merit of love is one thing I learned at the convent. Their love was for the Lord above and his son, but that love gave meaning to their days. They made choices for love, and sacrificed their own welfare for it. Love is selfless and lifts us to selflessness."

Her spouse granted her an intent look. "And this is why you said you wished to wed a man who loved you?"

Annelise nodded. "My father could not have treated my mother as he did if he had loved her."

Her husband considered this and she wondered if there had been no affection between his parents. To be sure, at crusade, he would have seen much of hate and wickedness. It would be easy to lose sight of love when at war.

"What happened when the djinn was freed?"

"Ah, she did not take kindly to my doubts about her nature. She was less happy that a curse upon her compelled her to surrender her palace to me, since I had freed her from the prison of the bottle."

"What did she do?"

"She cursed me." Her spouse's gaze locked with hers again. "She condemned me to become a wolf."

"But you are not a wolf now."

"That is due to the intervention of the second djinn."

"A second djinn? There were *two* in the bottle?"

"Yes, but fortunately, the second had a more kindly manner." He paused and gazed thoughtfully at Annelise. "You truly believe this tale," he said, as though amazed.

"Of course. It makes perfect sense."

"Perfect sense?" he echoed, then flung out a hand. "There is nothing that makes sense about it! Whoever heard of a djinn changing a man to a wolf because he uncorked a bottle? Whoever heard of a man changing to a wolf at all?"

"One hears it all the time," Annelise replied.

"In children's tales."

"And who is to say that they are not true?" she asked. Her spouse had no reply. "It only makes sense that if you insulted her, she would take offense and act accordingly."

"I did not intend to insult her," he said. "She claimed to be a magical, often invisible being who had been trapped in that bottle for several centuries. Clearly, this tale could not be true."

"But you saw her come out of the bottle."

He shifted uncomfortably and averted his gaze. "Yes."

"And you *did* become a wolf?"

"Yes," he acknowledged with reluctance.

Annelise smiled, sensing that his notions of the world were in tumult. "What happened next?"

He paced as he spoke. "I was less than pleased when the second djinn arrived. You see, the first djinn's curse had begun to take effect."

"You were changing to a wolf?"

He nodded.

"What did you say to her?" Annelise almost dreaded his reply.

"I begged shamelessly for her aid." He winked across the fire in an abrupt change of mood that made Annelise's heart flutter. She knew that, in that djinn's place, she would have been hard-pressed to deny him anything he asked of her.

"A women might easily succumb to such an entreaty," she said.

Her husband laughed suddenly, as though she had surprised him. "But not you?"

"I am not certain. You have yet to beg me for anything, sir."

Their gazes locked and held over the dancing flames. He smiled slowly, the expression softening his features and making her heart beat faster. Annelise was not fooled that his had been an easy life. She could see the evidence of his livelihood in the few faded scars that marked his skin. She recalled the well-used but meticulously maintained armor in the stables, as well as the fine warhorse. It was easy to imagine that her spouse would be a formidable foe in battle.

But he smiled for her. He loved her sweetly and tenderly.

And he had given her his guarantee of protection.

It was enough to tempt a woman to lose her heart.

"And what did the second djinn do?" she asked.

Her husband averted his gaze. "She changed the curse slightly and made me a wolf only by day."

"That seems somewhat less than desirable."

He laughed. "It does! I was less than enamored of her solution."

"And you had already begged shamelessly."

His quick glance revealed that the twinkle was still resident in his eye. "But that did not stop me from trying again."

"Yet she resisted you?" Annelise could not help but tease him a little. "Perhaps your charm is less persuasive than might be ideal, sir."

"Perhaps." His eyes glowed and his voice dropped low. "Can you resist me, Annelise?"

Annelise stared into his eyes for a long moment, then recovered herself. "The question is whether the djinn could resist you."

"No. She only granted me some hope of reprieve." Her spouse frowned, but Annelise was delighted with his confession.

She repeated the words he had shared with her.

'Finally, by grace of the powers above,

let this curse be broken by the blessing of love."

"Yes, that is it," he acknowledged, watching her.

"You were the wolf that chased me to the palace," Annelise guessed. "Why?"

"I saw the other wolf attack your steed." He shook his head. "I could not let you perish like that."

Annelise's heart skipped. "You did not even know me."

His jaw set and he stared straight into her eyes. "I am a knight, Annelise. I have pledged to protect those in danger, particularly those weaker than myself. I fulfill that pledge regardless of my own circumstance. It was the only honorable course and I did as well as I could, under the circumstances."

Annelise was ready to abandon her heart to him in that very moment. A man of honor was not readily found in these times, let alone one who stood by his vows, and treated his wife as a thinking creature—never mind one who had shown her such kindness.

He pushed a hand through his hair. "I forgot that the djinn had insisted that the first woman to cross the palace's threshold would be required to wed me."

"A man cursed to become a wolf half the time."

"Indeed." He granted her an intent look. "What manner of marriage is that?"

Annelise knew. She closed the distance between them and reached for him, noting how he watched her, how wonder dawned in his eyes. She let her fingers slide over his shoulders and around his neck. She pressed herself closer, stretched to her toes, and was gratified to feel the accelerated beat of his heart when she brushed her lips across his.

It reassured her to know that he was not immune to her touch.

"I think this might be the best kind of marriage," she whispered, then kissed him.

He caught his breath, but his hands closed around her waist and he deepened their kiss. The heat surged between them and he lifted her from the ground, feasting upon her mouth as if he would never get enough of her. Annelise hoped he would not. When he lifted his head, she smiled at him, loving how he whispered her name.

"I warned you that I meant to win your heart," she said.

He smiled. "You did, indeed, give fair warning, my Annelise."

"And I think the breaking of the curse upon you would be a fine start."

He smiled with obvious reluctance, his eyes glowing as he looked down at her. "Do you?"

"I do. Tell me just one thing," she urged before she kissed him again.

"No. No, Annelise. Ask me no more."

But he halted to stare as she unlaced the sides of her kirtle. He inhaled sharply as she shed the woolen dress, then loosened the neck on her chemise. His eyes brightened when she bared her breasts to view and his gaze fixed upon one nipple as it tightened to a peak in the cold. She lifted his hand and curved it around her other breast, feeling his heart race as he watched the nipple respond to his touch.

"Perhaps it is not so surprising that you believe in magic," he murmured, his words husky. "For you, my Annelise, readily cast a spell over me." Before she could reply, he bent to touch his lips to that nipple. Annelise arched her back and closed her eyes with pleasure.

With an effort, she recalled the one thing she wanted to know most of all.

"Tell me just your name then," she murmured.

He stiffened at her suggestion, then tried to hide his response. Instantly, Annelise knew that she had found an issue.

"I cannot." He released Annelise abruptly and backed away, his expression wary.

This was no good. Annelise was determined to dismiss his curse and she needed his help to do as much. It was promising that he had confided as much as he had this night.

But she would have more.

There was one thing she could offer, one deed for which her spouse clearly had a weakness. Annelise was not above using the weapons she had.

She shook off her chemise, tossing her shoes and hose aside. When she stood nude before him, his heated gaze danced over her. He licked his lips and she smiled.

He wanted her. It was a start, but Annelise needed more from marriage.

She wanted this man to love her.

She was going to ensure that he did. She would break his curse and earn his love. She walked slowly toward him, pulling the pins from her hair and shaking the tresses out, and smiled.

"Then I shall guess your name, husband of mine," she whispered.

His eyes widened. "You cannot. You should not."

Annelise savored how his gaze burned when she stopped directly before him. She immediately set to unlacing the front of the shirt he had donned.

"But I can." She kissed his chest, liking when he caught his breath. "And I will," she vowed, then kissed him upon his mouth. It took him only a heartbeat to respond. His hands found their way around her waist and he lifted her against himself, slanting his mouth over hers in a most satisfactory way.

"Be warned, sir. I am good at solving puzzles," she whispered when he lifted his head.

Her spouse chuckled. Annelise glanced up to see him smiling down at her and the intent in his eyes made her heart beat faster. "I cannot dissuade you, can I?" he murmured.

Annelise shook her head. "No. I like you best as a man."

He laughed.

His shirt was discarded in short order and she began to unlace his chausses, her touch silencing his laughter.

"But Annelise..." he began to argue, until her busy fingers made him gasp aloud.

"Is it Michel?" she whispered. "Antoine? Richard? Gautier? Christophe?"

"No, Annelise." He groaned beneath her caress. "No, no, no..."

"Didier? Bayard? Edouard?"

"Annelise!" he protested when her fingers closed around him. He whispered her name again as she caressed him, and Annelise pulled his head down for a soul-shattering kiss.

It was some time before her husband had enough breath to argue with her again.

CHAPTER TEN

Annelise would have been glad to sleep through the morning, but her husband woke her before the dawn. It was dark and cold in the tower chamber, for the fire had burned down to embers. Their nest within her cloak already chilled with his absence. She reached for him in the darkness, but he evaded her touch and continued to dress.

"It is time to leave," he said with resolve.

Annelise propped herself up on her elbows and gazed around the small tower room. As romantic as their time in this place had been, it was easy to yearn for the luxury they had enjoyed previously at the palace. "This place lacks somewhat in comfort. Could we sleep at the palace tonight?"

Her spouse's lips thinned as he dressed with haste. "No. I dare not return there."

That statement captured Annelise's attention and she sat up, fully awake. "Am I not to see you again?"

"Annelise, I do not know." He appeared to be distressed.

"Why do you not know?" she asked, her alarm rising. "Why not return to the palace? It is much more comfortable than this place—at least it was before it became so cursedly cold. And if we were together, regardless of the snow, we might manage to warm the bed."

He pivoted with sudden interest, his eyes bright. "It is cold there now?"

"Yes, the same as here. The garden is covered with snow. Did you not know?"

"No."

Annelise rose with a sigh and tugged on her stockings and chemise. "It is sad to see the garden. The flowers were so pretty, but I suppose winter had to come at some point."

"Would you prefer it was warm?" He spoke with such intensity that Annelise glanced up at him.

"Of course. There is not a shutter in the place and the snow drifts inside. For all its discomfort, I might as well remain here with you." She fought with the knotted string in her chemise for a moment, then flicked a glance in his direction. "I would rather remain with you in the daytime, sir."

"You cannot." His tone was that of a man used to making decisions and standing behind them. "You will return to the palace for the day."

"Will you come tonight?"

"I am not certain."

Annelise folded her arms across her chest "What if I refuse to go?"

He glanced pointedly at the window. "Then you will not be safe. I have already told you that I take my vows seriously, and I pledged to keep you safe. Get dressed, Annelise, and hasten. We must be back at the palace before the dawn. Make haste!"

Annelise tugged on her boots. She hastened down the stairs, vexed with him beyond belief, and began to retrace her steps toward the palace. She could still see her own footprints in the snow as well as those of the wolf.

Her husband.

His hand closed around her elbow and he hurried her onward.

They strode onward in silence until the palace gates loomed ahead of them. Annelise briefly considered fleeing the prospect of being imprisoned there again.

Then her husband turned to face her, lifting her chin with one finger when she refused to look to him. She knew he would kiss her, and her anger melted at that prospect. His gaze was solemn. He meant to ensure her safety and did not think of her freedom.

"How would you prefer it to be in the palace?" he asked.

"I cannot see how or why it matters. There are many more important issues that we might discuss—"

His finger landed firmly over her lips, and—curse him— his eyes twinkled.

"Warm like summer?" he asked, as though she had said nothing.

Despite herself, Annelise had to smile at his determination, but she smothered the smile as soon as she could. "Not too warm. Like late spring, as it was just after I arrived."

He turned to glare pointedly at the gates and Annelise followed his glance uncomprehendingly. "I wish that it was so," he said, and she recalled that the palace was supposed to reflect his will. Then he looked down at her and smiled so that she could not take a full breath. "I entreat you to take Mephistopheles for a ride for me, please, and give him my regrets for my inattention." He studied her. "Will you?"

"You have yet to entreat me."

His smile was quick and wicked. "Please, my Annelise, see to the welfare of my horse."

"I already do," she replied. "I would rather see to your welfare during the day, sir." He silenced her argument with a potent kiss, one so heated that she nigh forgot her own name. Annelise felt her annoyance with him fade away. She was breathless when he broke his kiss and warm to her toes.

He knocked firmly on the gates. "Open and admit the lady!" he cried.

The gates did precisely that. Did they also obey her husband's will?

There was an intriguing thought.

Her spouse simply pressed a kiss to her brow. "Be good," he murmured, and gave her a little shove toward the palace.

"When will I see you?" she asked.

But he was already gone and gone so completely that she was afraid he had never been there at all. The gates creaked and

Annelise darted into the courtyard, fearful they would leave her locked out in the cold and alone.

Only when they slammed shut behind her did she realize that the scent of the air inside had changed. Rivulets ran across the damp ground, all that remained of the snow that had drifted here when she left. The air was mild and humming with the sounds of insects.

It was incredible. Annelise stared in awe, touching the flowers that only the night before had been bent beneath the weight of the snow. The sky was clear blue overhead and a bird swooped low over her.

He had done this for her.

Annelise laughed and strolled through the garden to the palace, certain she was wed to a wonderful, if enigmatic, man. A steaming bath awaited her, along with clean linen and another kirtle. There were boots of fine leather, boots that would be ideal for riding a horse.

Annelise smiled. Not only did her husband attend to her needs, but he cared about her comfort. He had changed the weather within the palace walls purely to please her.

Perhaps he came to love her already.

She would guess her husband's name. She would convince him to trust her. She would win his reprieve from the djinn's curse.

And then this marriage would be precisely as she had always hoped wedlock would be.

Was Rolfe becoming the same pathetic suitor who had brought gifts to Rosalinde like a hapless pup? He had sworn he would never play the fool again, especially for a woman. Rosalinde had deceived him, as had the first djinn and possibly the second, as well.

As might Annelise.

Yet he had changed the temperature inside the walls of the palace, simply to please his wife. He had entrusted her with the tale of the two djinns and had very nearly told her all about himself.

Was he too trusting?

Or was Annelise worthy of his trust?

Surely, her every thought showed in her expressive eyes.

Rolfe spent the day as a wolf, a wolf pre-occupied with thoughts of a certain lady. Did he dare return to her that night? Would she guess his name or learn more of his secrets?

Would she betray him?

Every instinct within Rolfe told him to go to Annelise, to make love with her, to talk to her, to confess the full tale to her.

But he should not risk it.

He could not risk it.

The djinn's curse warned him of the price he would pay for trusting anyone. What manner of fool was he to doubt what these beings could do, given what they had already done to him?

Annelise was determined to guess his name. What would happen if she discovered his identity in his absence? She had already found his horse and might have seen his shield with his family's insignia.

If she knew his name, she could go to his family and tell them of his fate. If she knew his name, he could not hide from her anywhere.

Nor from the killer the djinn threatened would seek him out.

By sunset, he had chosen his course. He must somehow convince his wife to abandon her determination to know more about him. He did not imagine that battle would be easily won.

He would certainly have to entreat her.

Surely it was only a knowledge of the risk that made his pulse race as he drew near the palace and Annelise, and not the promise of her company.

Rolfe recognized the truth as soon as he entered the palace gates. Annelise was in the long pool lined with blue tiles. She was nude and singing to herself, so beautiful that desire halted him in his steps. Rolfe swallowed and stared at his wife.

Her skin was creamy and smooth, her curves ripe. Water splashed over her breasts and ran over her belly as she emptied an urn over herself. The moonlight made her skin seem to glow, and Rolfe watched the water as it fell over her.

He wanted her.

In that moment, Rolfe realized that he had never wanted Rosalinde the way he wanted Annelise. It was not enough to possess Annelise physically; he wanted to talk to her, to confide in her, to learn every secret that hid within her mind.

This was more than desire, far more.

Could it be love?

He must have made some slight sound, for Annelise turned abruptly. Her eyes widened when she saw him, though she did not speak. Their gazes locked and held for a potent moment, one during which Rolfe forgot to breathe, then she smiled a welcome that warmed him to his toes.

When she crooked her finger and beckoned to him, Rolfe knew he was lost.

He strode, fully clothed, into the shallow pool, with an uncharacteristic abandon for his boots. He could not help but smile when he finally caught Annelise in his arms.

"Waiting for someone?" he teased.

She smiled at him, then her arms slipped around his neck. She was pressed against him from chest to knee, his arms were full of her softness, and the fragrance of her skin rose to tease his nostrils.

"Only you, husband," she whispered. A twinkle glimmered in her eyes as her fingers locked into the hair at his nape. "I guessed that you would come." She smiled mischievously. Before Rolfe could respond, she pulled down his head for a demanding kiss.

Her ardor took him by surprise, as it had once before, then her tongue was between his teeth. Her hands were locked in his hair and her leg twined around one of his own. It seemed that she wrapped herself around him, inviting him ever closer. It was astonishing to realize that she could give him so much more passion than she already had. Rolfe was so overwhelmed by her kiss that it was all he could do to remain on his feet while he savored it.

When she reached beneath his shirt and ran her hands over his skin, he thought the fire she had launched through him might be too much to bear.

Annelise granted him no reprieve, though, for her agile fingers slid into his chausses. Rolfe gasped her name as she caressed him, then met the gleam in her eyes.

"Temptress," he murmured.

Annelise laughed. "I give you no more than you have given me."

It was all the encouragement Rolfe needed. He caught his wife around the waist and lifted her to her toes. "We shall see," he whispered in mock threat. Annelise gasped and gripped his shoulders as his fingers slipped between her thighs.

Rolfe watched with delight as Annelise arched her back in pleasure, and he wondered what had possessed him to sacrifice the sight of her in lovemaking. Her skin pinkened with a rosy flush as she approached her crest; her nipples tightened; her lips parted as she moaned.

Rolfe could not resist her. He kissed her, loving how she responded in kind. He swallowed her moans, savored her trembling, and was enticed by the way she locked her legs about him.

It was magical how her arousal fanned the flames of his own.

Then Annelise tore her lips from his. Her fingers tightened on his shoulders and her blazing golden gaze locked with his own.

"I want you within me," she whispered with an urgency that Rolfe could not resist.

Rolfe shed his boots and chausses, kicking them from the pool. He lifted his wife and her buttocks filled his hands. She wound her legs around his waist and Rolfe was surrounded by her sweetness. Her scent tantalized him, her breasts were crushed against his chest, and her warmth drew him deeper within her.

Rolfe moved slowly at first, but Annelise soon began to echo his rhythm. Her wet skin slid against him in an intoxicating manner. He could think of nothing but his desire, his Annelise. Their lovemaking nigh overwhelmed him; indeed, it was more potent each time and he began to think he would never have his fill of her. He managed to last until she reached her pleasure, but in the moment she cried out, he could wait no longer.

He roared with the force of his release. He strained for the heavens even as he felt Annelise do the same. He gave her his all, his heart warming with the awareness that she was his equal in every way.

There was only they two. Rolfe was barely aware of himself falling to his knees in the shallow pool. He gathered Annelise protectively to his chest and they sank together into the water, their mutual bliss complete.

The man might have invented lovemaking, for all his skill with it.

Annelise nestled against her spouse, more than glad that he had returned to the palace. It seemed quite decadent to embrace in the pool in the moonlight but it was lovely.

If they broke the curse, would the palace disappear? She wondered.

As much as she liked it, she wouldn't mind. She wanted her husband's curse broken more than anything else.

And his heart in her possession, of course.

She caressed his shoulder, smiling at the wet state of his chemise, then kissed his ear. He seemed to be dozing a little, but then, he would have been active in the forest all day in his wolf form.

He stirred and gave her a sleepy glance, then smiled.

"Is your name Ethelbert?" she asked.

He blinked as if startled, then abruptly stood up. The water splashed, but he set her upon her feet, his agitation clear. He even stepped away from her, bending to retrieve his wet chausses. "Annelise! You cannot guess my name!"

She watched him, wondering. "You could just tell me what it is."

"You know that I cannot."

"No," she said with care. "I know that you *will* not. That is different."

He glared at her. "You do not know what is at stake."

"And I am unlikely to know, if you refuse to tell me more," she replied, keeping her tone calm. "Indeed, sir, if I had to guess, I might conclude that you did not trust me."

He shoved one hand through his hair. "I told you about the curse."

"Yes, but I suspect that you confided only half the tale,"

Annelise replied.

His gaze flew to hers and Annelise saw his fear.

"Yes, I see the truth in your eyes, husband of mine. There is more to this tale than you would have me believe, and I would know the truth. How else can I help you?" She raised a hand when he would have protested. "Our lives are bound together, no matter how much you would prefer that they were not."

"Annelise! I do not prefer that."

"And how would I know as much? Surely a woman should know her husband's name?"

He frowned down at his wet boots, then met Annelise's eyes. "I cannot tell you my name."

"Because you do not trust me." She said it, hoping he would deny it, but saw the truth in his eyes. Annelise inhaled sharply. "I must have my freedom, then."

He stared at her. "You mean to seek an annulment?"

"Why? Is that what you desire?"

"No, Annelise." He shook his head with reassuring vigor. "Never that."

"Neither do I," she confessed, taking a step closer to him. She laid one hand lightly on his arm, and saw the uncertainty in his gaze. Someone had dealt a cruel blow to his heart, she was certain. If ever she met this Rosalinde, she would have harsh words for that creature. "But I must be able to come and go."

"You mean to leave?" The notion seemed to trouble him.

"Just for some time during the day. I would ride Mephistopheles in the forest, for example, that he might have a better run." She cast a glance over her shoulder to the palace and grimaced. "I dislike the sense that I am a prisoner, as fair a prison as this might be."

"But you mean to return by nightfall?"

Annelise met his gaze. "Do you not trust me, husband?" she asked deliberately.

He looked toward the gates and did not reply.

Which was answer in itself.

"I suspect that if you do not take a risk, sir, the curse will not be broken."

He heaved a sigh, and Annelise was certain he would refuse her again. But he took a deep breath and turned to meet her gaze with a smile. He bent and brushed his lips across hers. "I would not have you abandon me, my lady," he murmured. "Nor would I see your situation here steal the fire from your eyes."

She smiled, sensing a victory.

"You must be within the gates before nightfall," he said sternly. "Otherwise, my pledge to defend you will be worthless. The forest is not safe for a woman alone in the dark."

His stern manner could not steal her sense of triumph. She knew it had not been an easy choice for him, and she was encouraged that he had decided in his favor. "But I had thought to meet you at the tower tomorrow eve," she whispered. "You had said this morning that you did not wish to return here."

His eyes twinkled. "Do you propose a tryst, my wanton lady wife?"

"I do, sir." She smiled and he laughed.

"If you bring food and a blanket then we will have greater comfort than last night," he agreed and Annelise laughed with pleasure.

"Oh, you will have more of a feast than you bargain for, husband of mine," she teased before she kissed him once more. The familiar heat rose between them once again and she knew with sudden certainty how she would reward him for his choice.

"The bed awaits, sir," she whispered when she had a chance, smiling that she did not have to make the suggestion twice. "I want the chamber lit with candles that I might see you fully."

"It is my desire to see you, my Annelise, so you will find it is already so."

He swung her into his arms and carried her to the bed they had shared on so many nights. Indeed, he loved her with such enthusiasm that Annelise could only believe that her victory was more than half won.

Rolfe was outside the gates the next morning when he felt the change come upon him. He winced as he was transformed to a wolf once more, wishing that he could have remained with

Annelise this day.

By giving her command over the gates, he was trusting her not to abandon him.

The very possibility stole his breath away. He could not imagine his life without his passionate and lively bride. He wanted to keep her captive forever, to ensure that she awaited him, just as she had the night before.

Yet he had realized when she made her request that if he denied her, if he kept her cloistered, that might steal the sparkle from her eyes. Had she not despised the convent, where women lived in seclusion from the world? Annelise, his Annelise, needed to be free to possess the vigor that he so admired in her.

But what would she do with her newfound freedom?

Where would she go?

How could he ensure her safety when she left the palace?

There was only one good solution.

Rolfe would have to watch over his lady by day as well as by night.

Annelise awakened to bright morning sunlight and an empty place beside her in the great bed. In truth, she had not expected otherwise, though she ran a hand over the linens, wishing her husband might be there one morning.

Had he kept his promise to her?

She dressed in haste and raced through the garden, hastening to the great gates. They were closed, but she had not expected them to be standing open.

She took a deep breath, straightened, and hoped. "Open," she commanded.

The gates yawned wide, opening slowly and majestically, revealing the snowy forest to her view. The sky was clear over the forest, and the wind crisp. The sunlight made crystals in the snow sparkle like jewels beyond the walls, and a bird called to its mate as it swooped low through the barren branches of the trees.

He had kept his pledge.

He trusted her.

Annelise clasped her hands together and smiled, her heart

pounding as if it would burst. "Close."

The gates obeyed her once again, and she shouted in triumph.

"I command you to open!" she said.

It worked again. Annelise strode beneath the broad archway of the gates, hesitating only when she made to step over the line where the closed gates met.

That wintry wind stole around her bare ankles, reminding her only too well that the weather outside varied from inside.

What if the gates closed and locked her out?

Annelise retreated inside. "Close," she commanded and the gates did her bidding again. She hurried back to the palace. She donned all her traveling garments—even the wool stockings, which clung to her skin in the heat of the palace— and draped her fur-lined cloak over her arm. Heart in mouth, she returned to the gates.

"Open," she said and they swept wide open. Her heart raced as she stepped through the portal. Annelise realized just how tall the gates were, how broad the entryway, how high and unassailable the palace walls.

She felt very small and wondered whether these massive gates would continue to obey her. She paused to consider the clear line where the snow of the outside world began and the green grass of the courtyard ended.

Annelise took a deep breath and stepped into the snow. It crunched as her foot sank into its whiteness.

As soon as she had taken the second step, the gates slammed behind her.

Annelise stumbled forward a few steps from the force of their closing, then pivoted to find them closed against her again. Panic flooded through her.

"Open!" she cried, hearing the desperation in her own voice.

The gates opened without hesitation.

Annelise lunged back through the portal, clasping her hands together as the gates closed behind her. She inhaled deeply of the garden scent within the walls, then smiled in her relief.

She could come and go as she wished.

Her husband cared about her. There could be no doubt. He had trusted her enough to give her something she desired and that was no small thing.

She would take Mephistopheles for a ride, just as she had promised.

And she would reward her husband richly at the tower that night. Annelise strode toward the stables, planning the feast she would offer to him.

The man would have no doubt that she was pleased.

The wind was crisp in Annelise's face as she rode the destrier. Though it was cold outside the palace walls, it was a fine day. The sky was blue, the snow sparkled, and a contented Mephistopheles thundered through the forest.

She found herself smiling at the destrier's pleasure, for he ran with abandon.

They rode to the east until the sun was high overhead, then Annelise turned Mephistopheles back toward the palace. She would not become lost in this forest again. She kept the sun on her left and followed the imprints of the destrier's hooves in the snow. The sun was warming her shoulders through her cloak when the palace's smooth walls appeared in the distance ahead. She could see the white walls even through the trees.

A surge of satisfaction rolled through her as she urged Mephistopheles onward.

Then Annelise heard the clink of horses' trappings.

How could there be horses and riders at their remote location?

Mephistopheles flicked his ears and slowed slightly at the sound. She peered through the trees, wondering whether her ears had deceived her. They had not, for she caught glimpses of color as someone or something moved back and forth before the palace gates.

Someone waited there.

Perhaps admission had been requested, but there had been no response.

Perhaps a lone traveler sought shelter for the night.

Did the gates remain closed because she was away, or because her husband did not wish this visitor to enter?

How could she return to the sanctuary of the palace without passing the visitor?

Annelise pulled the destrier to a halt. She saw flashes of silver catch the sunlight and spied green cloth. She guessed there were no fewer than four steeds, although it was difficult to see them clearly through the forest.

A man called out and two men responded, their voices making Annelise feel curiously vulnerable.

Voices, not a single voice. At least three men and four horses. Her heart skipped with the realization that she was outnumbered. Annelise peered through the trees once more and saw that at least one man had dismounted.

Clearly, they had no intention of leaving soon.

The sun disappeared behind a cloud and the wind became chilly. The destrier shuddered and she knew he had to be brushed down.

Perhaps they had business with her husband.

She should act as hostess in his absence.

That thought sent Annelise's heels digging into her steed's side. She had a responsibility as lady of the palace. Her spouse would find neither her manners nor her boldness lacking.

And surely no harm could come to her within the walls of a palace so attuned to her husband's wishes?

The men turned as she approached, but their helmets concealed their faces from her view. She rode through the last of the trees proudly, noting the stance of their leader.

There was something familiar about his garb, about that deep green, about the silver diamond emblazoned in the middle of his shield. Annelise struggled to recall, but the details of life before her arrival here were elusive.

Then he doffed his helmet and her heart sank. "Lady Annelise de Sayerne!"

"Enguerrand de Roussineau," she replied with much less pleasure.

"Well met, my lady!"

Annelise might have argued that. She had no desire to see this man again, and disliked the notion of inviting him inside the gates.

She inclined her head politely. "Good day, Enguerrand. What brings you to this part of the forest?"

Enguerrand strolled through the falling snow toward her. His two accompanying knights watched avidly, their trio of squires peering out from behind the party's mounts.

Three men, three boys and six steeds. God in heaven, what would she do?

The clouds gathered overhead with greater speed but Annelise raised her chin proudly.

Enguerrand lifted a gloved hand to stroke Mephistopheles' neck, admiration in his eyes. The destrier snorted and stepped aside. The knight arched a brow as he met Annelise's gaze. "A surprisingly skittish creature for his size."

Annelise smiled as sweetly as she was able. How she disliked this man! It was more than his evident self-interest, for her distrust of him was deep and instinctive. "He is in need of a brush after his ride," she said. "I must not linger."

"He is a markedly fine beast for a lady." His gaze flicked to hers. "Especially one destined for a convent when last we met. Do the nuns ride such valuable destriers these days? Or have you found an accommodating patron?"

The insinuation was most inappropriate.

Annelise felt her eyes narrow. "I do not believe my situation is of your concern, sir," she said. She tugged Mephistopheles' reins, and the steed stepped smartly toward the gates. "I have already asked what brings you this way, yet you have given no response."

Enguerrand bowed low. "It was most churlish of me not to answer, fair Annelise." He folded his hands behind his back and regarded her. "It seems that Bertrand, and hence Tulley, were concerned about your arrival at the convent. No word was returned, you see, and there were doubts as to your safety."

But the tracks showed that Yves and the others had ridden toward Beauvoir. Had they not reached that stronghold? Or did Enguerrand tell her only part of what he knew?

Annelise guessed it was the latter.

"I am safe, as you can see." She sat straighter. "I am surprised that you should undertake the quest to be certain."

"Sweet Annelise, my admiration for you knows no bounds."

Annelise did not reply to that.

"You should have wed me when you had the chance."

"Alas, that opportunity has been lost."

Enguerrand arched a brow. His gaze dancing over her garb, the horse, and the palace gates before them. "What cozy nest have you found for yourself, Annelise?"

His men snickered and her mouth went dry. "Make your accusation clearly, sir."

"I make no accusation." Enguerrand's eyes grew cold. "I have only questions. Yours is lavish attire for a bride of Christ."

"I am not a bride of Christ, after all."

"I thought you chose the convent over me?"

"I did, but matters changed."

Enguerrand leaned forward, his gloved hand closing on Mephistopheles' reins. The destrier nickered and stamped but the knight held fast. "Because you chose to warm a man's bed rather than take your vows?"

"I took vows of another kind," Annelise replied. "I chose my husband over both convent and you."

"Husband?" Enguerrand's eyes flashed. He was sufficiently surprised that Annelise was able to snatch the reins from his grip.

She rode toward the palace gates with Mephistopheles, then turned the horse adroitly. The party of men watched her. Enguerrand's gloved hand clenched in a fist as he glared at her. Annelise did not believe for a moment that Enguerrand had come out of concern for her safety.

Then Enguerrand's dark eyes narrowed, and Annelise knew Enguerrand sought the prize he had desired all along. Quinn must not have returned as yet. Perhaps Tulley grew impatient with the delay. Enguerrand cared nothing for her, and Annelise knew instinctively that once Sayerne was under his hand— if indeed that possibility ever came to fruition—he would have no use for the woman who had brought him the prize.

Should Quinn subsequently return home, even more woe would have fallen upon the sorry bride Annelise might have been. As Enguerrand's wife, she might have shared her mother's fate.

Gratitude flowed through her that she had not been fool enough to accept his offer.

"You are wed in truth?" Enguerrand demanded.

"Do you suggest that I lie, sir?"

He frowned. "No, it cannot be so. You could not have wed another."

"I assure you, sir, that I have done so."

Enguerrand folded his arms across his chest as he watched her. "No. I will need more than your bold assertion to convince me, Annelise."

Annelise tugged her glove from her left hand. The garnet winked as she held it up to view. One of Enguerrand's knights coughed under his breath, evidently impressed with the token. "This is my husband's ring, placed upon my finger at my nuptials," she said. "And this is our home."

Enguerrand's gaze roved over the high walls. "If this place is your home, why then are the gates barred against you?"

Annelise took a deep breath, hoping against hope that the gates would not choose to be fickle at this precise moment. She murmured her command. "Open."

Enguerrand's eyes widened as the broad gates swung back with no sign of a keeper. Annelise rode through the portal. "You were wrong, Enguerrand," she called over her shoulder. "This *is* my home."

She had not expected Enguerrand to recover so quickly. He dove suddenly for the gates and slipped through them before they closed behind her.

"You dare too much!" she said, shocked by his audacity.

The knight, though, smiled. "Fair Annelise!" He gestured to the darkening sky, then to the courtyard of the palace. "Surely you would not condemn my party to a wintry night when your abode is so large."

Annelise had no ready argument for that. Hospitality was a Christian duty.

No matter how much she despised the man.

He could not know that she was alone within these walls.

Surely her husband's desire would protect her?

Annelise hoped as much.

Enguerrand continued with such confidence that Annelise wished she had a reason to deny him. "It is too late to return to Beauvoir before the twilight, and it is said there are hungry wolves abroad this year, since the winter came so early."

Annelise knew she had a responsibility to uphold her spouse's reputation. She cleared her throat. "I apologize for my rudeness, Enguerrand. You must understand that your appearance surprised me."

"But of course, my lady." As he bowed low, his gaze roved, as if he would assess the value of the holding. "There is no need for apologies between friends such as we two."

Friends. The very suggestion made her shudder. Annelise could not bear the thought of having Enguerrand within these walls any longer than absolutely necessary, but there was little choice. Surely first thing on the morrow, he could return to Beauvoir.

Annelise would be certain the suggestion was raised at dinner.

She inclined her head. "I thank you for your understanding. Welcome."

Enguerrand beckoned to his party with a flick of his wrist. He eyed the garden, sniffed the air, then cast a questioning look in Annelise's direction. "May I conclude that the rest of your party chose to remain here rather than return to chilly Beauvoir?"

"No," Annelise admitted, guessing from his tone that he knew precisely what had happened to Yves. "Our party was scattered by a pack of hunting wolves. My husband saved my life."

"How gallant." Enguerrand glanced out over the lush gardens with a thoughtful frown. "And we shall meet your inimitable spouse this evening at the board, I suppose?"

In that moment, Annelise recalled her vow to tryst with her husband at the tower. He would not be returning this eve—and she had to concoct a tale. "Unfortunately, my husband enjoys the hunt this week. I am not certain of the timing of his return."

"Ah, how unfortunate that we may miss him." Enguerrand smiled, clearly thinking the very opposite. "I shall hope for his early return."

Dread rose within Annelise as she commanded the gates to

open and watched Enguerrand's party move inside the walls. She led the way to the stables, wondering what manner of difficulties would result from showing hospitality to Enguerrand.

It was unsettling to have him within these walls, and Annelise knew she would not sleep this night. How could she keep her tryst with her spouse? She dared not risk leaving Enguerrand alone in the palace. Nor could she afford to lead him to her spouse, not without knowing his intent. Would her husband fear that she had no desire to see him? Surely not!

Surely he would see the reason for her actions when she explained.

She would be the dutiful wife, guard his home, and confess all to him as soon as she could.

Perhaps he would come to the palace when she did not appear at the tower.

Annelise would hope for that.

Rolfe was at the tower before the sun even touched the western horizon. The sky was overcast and snow had begun to fall. He bit back his disappointment when he discovered that Annelise was not there.

Of course, she had not arrived as yet. He circled the tower in his wolf form. She knew that he did not change shape until dark, and he had forbidden her to watch his change.

But still Rolfe paced, impatient for night to fall. He worried about her making the journey in the darkness and wondered if he should meet her at the palace gates. But he had pledged to meet her here, at the tower. He had said he would await her and seeking her at the palace might make her believe he did not trust her. The kernel of dread that had lodged within him that morn outside the palace gates had haunted him all the day.

What if Annelise left him?

What if she betrayed him?

What would he do without her?

Rolfe paced as he watched the sky, relief flooding through him when the last vestige of the sun's light was gone and he became himself again. He charged up the tower's stairs and seized his clothes. Hauling his shirt over his head as he crossed the room, he peered anxiously toward the palace.

There was not a flicker of movement in the forest.

But she would come. Rolfe paced the tower room restlessly, haunted all the while by recollections of loving Annelise beside the small fire here.

When next he glanced out the window, the sky had darkened to indigo and was filled with myriad stars.

Still there was no movement in the forest below.

Trepidation rose within him. Why did she not come?

He knew the gates had obeyed his dictate, although he should have expected nothing else. He had watched her in the morning as she tried the gates. Her radiant smile had convinced Rolfe that his choice had been a good one. At the time, Annelise's obvious joy had been enough to dispel all of Rolfe's doubts. Now, in darkness and solitude, he was no longer certain.

What could keep her from his side, other than a lack of regard for him? Perhaps she felt she had no need of him any longer. Perhaps she did not burn with the same desire for his company that he felt for hers.

Every passing moment fed Rolfe's doubts.

He had followed her and Mephistopheles only until she turned back with the destrier. Convinced of her safety, he had retreated to a burrow to sleep in the forest.

What if Annelise had not returned to the palace? What if she had been injured?

Rolfe stared into the blackness as the snow began to fall, and his hands clenched on the base of the window. He had pledged to wait for her here, so to seek her out at the palace would imply that he thought little of her word.

He had chosen to trust the lady and trust her he would. No doubt she had fallen asleep or some such and would come along shortly. He could not imagine how or why that might have occurred, but the possibility that she might be in peril troubled him deeply.

Rolfe would wait until the moon rose, then seek his missing bride.

Until then, he paced the chamber in the tower, impatient to ensure his lady's safety.

CHAPTER ELEVEN

ithin a very short measure of time, Annelise tired of inventing answers to perfectly reasonable questions. Enguerrand asked after every detail, finding the flaw in every quality of the palace. She had explained the lack of an ostler with a vague wave, saying that the man must be slumbering. She excused the lack of squires with the suggestion that they would be along momentarily. Enguerrand's knights had been clearly skeptical as they set their own squires to the task of unsaddling and brushing down their steeds.

She used her husband's tale of quick and silent servants who stayed out of view when they returned to the palace to find a sumptuous meal spread for them in a chamber Annelise had never used before. She could only hope that her urge to see to the comfort her guests was strong enough to have it done.

Enguerrand's curiosity was relentless and his suspicion open. Annelise was aware of the avarice in his dark eyes as he assessed the treasures of this place.

Before they even sat at the board, she had tired of his queries. What was the name of this holding? When had it been built? From whence had her husband's family earned its wealth? How many brethren had he? Why had none heard of their existence in this forest?

Annelise fought to create evasive answers that told her curious guest nothing, knowing full well that the others attended her every word even as they ate.

Soon she would not be able to keep track of what she had said and what she had not.

Sadly, Annelise was not accomplished in the art of deception. Her head throbbed with the effort. Under other circumstances, she might have simply blurted out the truth and let consequences fall as they may, but she had to protect her spouse.

It was illogical, but she sensed that Enguerrand posed a threat to her husband that she could not readily name. And she had no intention of being less than true to the man who had treated her well.

Worse, the snow beyond the walls fell with increasing vigor. When one of the knights jested that they might be her guests for a long while, Annelise had to retreat to the chamber she shared with her husband to compose herself. She wanted nothing more than to be alone, but she did not trust Enguerrand enough to leave him unattended, either.

When she returned, it seemed that even her brief absence had been too long.

Annelise had never expected Enguerrand to find the book. She stepped into that chamber and he saluted her with the tome, malice bright in his eye.

"And what is this, fair Annelise? A collection of secret potions? We have decided that your hospitality here reeks of involvement in the dark arts, for nothing else can explain all we see around us." His men chuckled, though their interest in her reply was clear.

"I do not know what you mean," Annelise responded. She kept her eyes on the table as she slid into her place and resumed her meal.

Enguerrand leaned closer. "It is clear that something most unnatural is at work within these walls."

"Do not be ridiculous," Annelise scoffed.

"Ridiculous? Explain to me if you will, fair Annelise, why the weather within these walls varies so much from outside?"

She swallowed her bite of bread with difficulty, then took a long draught of wine, hoping the delay would give her time to conjure a response.

"It is a trick of the wind," she said, feeling the explanation to be inadequate. She smiled at the surrounding knights, hoping to cajole them with her explanation. "We all know that there are places in the mountains where warm winds are trapped and the weather differs from the surrounding area."

Enguerrand shook his head. "You speak of isolated valleys, not simply the space within a wall arbitrarily constructed."

Annelise forced a laugh. "Who are we to say what is arbitrary and what is by design? Perhaps the builder of the palace simply took advantage of a natural effect." She chided Enguerrand. "Cleverness in choosing a site is not the same as sorcery." The knights murmured to each other, one shrugged, and they returned to their meal, much to her relief.

Enguerrand, though, shook his head slowly. "It is not so, and you know it as well as I." His gaze brightened and she caught her breath. "Why will you not admit as much? Who do you seek to protect?"

"Who would I protect? You see worries where there are none, Enguerrand. Truly, I did not think you were such a whimsical man."

"There is no one else here and only the rumor of your spouse. Is he truly at hunt, Annelise? Or does he hide from his guests?"

Annelise did not trust the gleam in Enguerrand's eyes.

"What does he want to keep us from knowing?" he whispered, before tapping the book firmly. "Is this his collection of black spells?"

"The wine is clearly too potent for you," Annelise said sweetly, and one of the knights chuckled.

"Annelise! I think only of your safety and happiness! Surely you can understand that this situation is most unusual and that my concern is only for you." His eyes widened with mock concern. "If you had fallen into the hands of some sorcerer, who better than me to rescue you?"

Annelise chose not to reply to that. It was time to put this nonsense to rest. She held Enguerrand's gaze and spoke firmly.

"You have nothing to worry about upon that score. My husband is no sorcerer. The man is at hunt."

With that, she bit into a piece of fruit, although it might as well have been wrought of dust for all she tasted.

Enguerrand's fingertips slid over the book. "Then this is not a book of spells?"

Annelise laughed aloud. "Spells? What manner of nonsense fills your head, Enguerrand? It is nothing but a book of tales to entertain children."

The others in Enguerrand's party relaxed visibly at both Annelise's bold tone and her explanation. She reached for the volume, but Enguerrand flipped it open.

"Why then is it written in coded script?"

The weight of the knights' and squires' gazes fell heavily upon Annelise. She saw immediately that the book had reverted to its original form. Annelise would not touch the page for it might change as it had for her husband and that would only feed Enguerrand's suspicions that there was magic afoot.

Instead, she closed the book and claimed it before Enguerrand could protest.

"It is not coded!" she said with a laugh. "This is written in the language of the Saracens. Did I not mention that my husband reads in many languages?"

Enguerrand's eyes narrowed. "Then how do you know what lies within these pages?"

Annelise shrugged as easily as she could and slid the book onto her lap. "My husband has entertained me with these tales on many evenings. I suppose you have only my word as to its contents."

With that, she held Enguerrand's gaze steadily, hoping that she guessed aright his unwillingness to challenge her.

"Do you not trust me, Enguerrand?" she asked pointedly. Her gaze met that of each of the others in turn then she lowered her voice, as if speaking her thoughts aloud. "Why a man would propose marriage to a woman he found untrustworthy, I cannot guess."

The two knights nudged each other, the gesture breaking the tension. To Annelise's relief, Enguerrand cleared his throat and looked away for a moment before glancing over the company. His voice dropped and his manner became confidential.

"You may think my suspicions unreasonable, Annelise, but there have been strange tales afoot of late. Those may well be fanciful stories for children, but these tales are reputed to be true."

"Indeed?"

"Tell us a tale, Enguerrand!" One of the knights lifted his goblet and took a long draught. "A stormy night is a good one for a rousing piece of fancy."

The second companion knight settled back with a full goblet of wine, clearly more than ready for entertainment. The pair had shed their mail immediately, the weather and the wine combining with the evident security of the high walls to put them at ease as men of war were seldom capable.

Night had fully descended in the garden and there was a pleasant hum of insects carrying through the arched and open windows. Had it not been for the company, Annelise might have thought the setting idyllic.

Enguerrand frowned as he gazed into the courtyard. "I am reminded of one tale in particular, told by a bard visiting Tulley's court just the other evening. It was a tale of a vengeful djinn. This minstrel insisted he had been told the tale by the djinn herself when he had the misfortune to cross paths with her."

A djinn? Surely Enguerrand could not know... Annelise set the last of her meal aside, her appetite lost.

"A djinn?" A squire looked confused. "And what might that be?"

"A djinn is an evil and immortal creature, invisible for the most part but able to wreak havoc upon the lives of mortals by choice," Enguerrand said. Annelise watched him through her lashes, noting how he enjoyed telling the tale. There was a definite malice in his manner and she feared his intention. "This one was said to have been of particularly foul temper."

The squire's eyes shone as he listened. Annelise's mouth was dry and she shared little of the boy's enthusiasm, although she strove to hide that fact.

Enguerrand's gaze fixed upon Annelise. "It was said that this djinn had been imprisoned in a bottle before 'once upon a time' and cursed to surrender her palace to whoever opened the bottle and granted her release. The djinn was evidently a selfish sort and schemed all the years she was locked away as to how she would take vengeance upon this unfortunate.

"The bard insisted that a knight returning from the Crusades had acquired the bottle, perhaps in innocence, and opened it near Tulley's estates." He waved. "Perhaps even in this vicinity." Annelise looked down at her trencher. "The djinn was compelled to grant her palace to the knight, but then she took her revenge."

Enguerrand sipped at his wine, clearly enjoying how the men waited in anticipation of his words.

Annelise felt ill.

"What did she do?" asked the squire.

"She cursed the knight and made him a wolf. Imagine, to be condemned to take the form of a wolf when a wondrous palace had been granted to you as a gift!" Enguerrand laughed and Annelise hated him all the more. "The bard insisted that the djinn had forbidden the knight from entering the palace, yet condemned him to prowl around it for the remainder of his days."

His gaze drifted out the window to linger on the splendor of the garden. All eyes followed his gaze, then Enguerrand cleared his throat. "How fortunate we are to wait out the blizzard under such fine circumstances."

To Annelise, his implication was startlingly clear.

"But why would the djinn do such a thing?" demanded the squire.

"It was meant to be a reminder of what he had been," Enguerrand explained. "And a curse most vindictive, for he was doomed to remember his lost state. He was a wolf with the memory of the man he had been, and powerless to change his situation."

"God's blood!" breathed the squire. "That is foul indeed!"

The knight beside him smiled and ruffled the lad's hair. "You cannot believe all you hear when tales are told, boy. Undoubtedly, this bard had need of a warm meal in his belly and concocted the tale on the spot to tempt the lord's hospitality."

The boy looked crestfallen, but Enguerrand held up a finger. "No! Not this time, for he gave us the name of this unfortunate, and there were those in the hall who knew of him."

Annelise yearned to ask the man's name, just as she knew she could not risk it. Enguerrand took a sip of wine, then remarked upon its quality.

"Well? What was his name?" the squire demanded.

"It was said to be Rolfe," Enguerrand said, again watching Annelise closely.

Annelise knew that nothing showed in her expression, for she did not know if that was her husband's name or not. "A pretty tale, Enguerrand, if a whimsical one," she said and lifted her cup to him in salute.

One of the knights snorted. "And a common-enough name. How could any know for certain that the Rolfe of their acquaintance was this same one? Did the bard not supply the name of the knight's estate?"

"No," Enguerrand admitted.

The knight rolled his eyes, muttering "bards" under his breath, and indicated the platter of roast meat. His squire hastened to place the most choice morsels remaining on his knight's trencher.

"But this Rolfe was said to ride a great black destrier," Enguerrand added. "Indeed, Annelise, it was your spouse's steed in the stables that reminded me of the tale." He smiled and she braced herself for whatever he might say next. "Whyever would that beast remain here while your husband hunted?"

"He took another," Annelise said hastily.

Enguerrand raised a brow. "Indeed? I saw evidence of no beast other than the two palfreys and destrier there."

Annelise laughed and lied again. "His favored steed is scarcely here long enough to leave a mark."

The other knights looked less than convinced by her explanation and she tried to think of another subject that might interest the men.

Enguerrand gestured toward the courtyard. "I must admit that this place, with its Eastern air and remarkable clime, also made me think immediately that we had stumbled upon the very place of which the bard sang."

The knights, to Annelise's dismay, shifted in their seats and glanced uneasily about themselves. The candles flickered and the wail of the winter wind could be faintly discerned. It would have been easy—especially under the influence of the wine—for even the most level-headed individual to give consideration to Enguerrand's conclusion.

"Does that mean there is a wicked djinn here?" whispered the one squire.

"Of course not!" Annelise said, laughing again. This time, she feared she sounded a little shrill. "More of the wine?"

Enguerrand leaned forward. "Tell us first, fair Annelise, what is the name of your husband?"

The entire party caught their breath and waited.

The very moment that Rolfe strode through the palace gates, he was aware that something was amiss. The garden still bloomed and the temperature was still warm, but he could hear voices from the palace.

Male voices.

He refused to consider that his lady might have proven herself unworthy of his trust. Rather than revealing himself immediately, he went to the stables to learn about his guests. There were three destriers and three more palfreys stabled there, and the armor of three knights. Only one destrier had caparisons, and they were green and silver, graced by an insignia Rolfe did not recognize.

Three men and three squires! Why had Annelise allowed them to enter? Did she know them? He considered the snow that had been rapidly falling beyond the walls and considered that she might have felt compassion for a company lost in the forest during a storm.

To be of aid would be the inclination of his lady.

Rolfe wondered what they discussed and wished he could hear the conversation at the board. The palace, as he should have anticipated, fulfilled his hope and he heard them as clearly as if they were in the stable with them.

The sound did not improve his temper. It was clear to Rolfe

that Annelise both knew and disliked the one man who spoke the most. Rolfe himself heard how provocative that man was, and disliked him as well, without even the benefit of having met him.

Enguerrand, she called him.

Rolfe wished he knew what lies she had been compelled to tell on his behalf and the earlier part of their conversation filled his thoughts like a memory. So, he was at hunt. That was a clever notion on her part. And she had invited them into the palace out of compassion, though he heard the uncertainty of the wisdom of her choice in her tone.

He wished for heavy garb, such as a man would wear to hunt, and found it at his fingertips. He tugged on the heavy boots and the leather jerkin, then pulled his mail hauberk over it. He pulled on heavy gloves and a thick cloak lined with fur. A small bow hung from his side and there was a quiver upon his back. He donned his belt, with his quillon dagger in its sheath. With a look and a thought, there was blood on the blade. Rolfe raised the hood, thinking he should be embellished with snow if he had just arrived, and found that he was so. He wished for more horses, and a kill for his fist.

As he was walking to the palace with his burden of hares and partridges, he had a thought that might have come to him earlier. He wished for a bevy of servants, eager boys who had accompanied him to hunt, a captain-at-arms, an ostler, and a steward. His wish filled the stables with their horses and trap, and their noise echoed through the courtyard. He wished for two of them to be carrying a dead boar, its feet bound to a pole, to give him a tale for his late arrival.

He strode to the palace, well pleased with his scheme even as he heard this Enguerrand imply that some bard's tale was the truth of Rolfe's palace. It was the truth, but Enguerrand had no right to know it.

He certainly had no right to worry Annelise.

"Annelise!" Rolfe roared, like a man coming home. "What a day! We return in triumph, lady mine." He had a moment to note that the board was loaded with food and wine, and to take satisfaction in the bounty of his hospitality. He noted the three knights, two of which were nearly besotted, and easily identified the one who made trouble for Annelise.

Rolfe decided to let the cur wait. He would ignore him for as long as possible.

"Sir!" Annelise cried, her relief more than clear. She ran to Rolfe, her eyes alight, and he caught her close, swinging her around with satisfaction. She was trembling ever so slightly and he yearned to shred the man responsible for his lady's concern. She reached up and kissed him, then leaned her cheek against his own. "I feared for you in the storm," she confessed, though he knew there was more at root than that.

"Ah," he said heartily. "I forgot myself. I owe you an apology, Annelise."

"But you had a successful day, it appears."

"It was a charmed hunt, to be sure. Look at that boar!" He chuckled. "But you know how I can never leave a matter be. Even the boar was not sufficient to satisfy me." Annelise smiled up at him, apparently also content to let Enguerrand wait. "There was a buck of such majesty that I felt compelled to pursue it. He was clever, though, and wily."

"Even more wily than the boar?" Annelise asked.

Rolfe nodded. "Even so." He sighed and touched her cheek with his fingertip. "I confess I failed to bring you more venison in the end, my Annelise."

"It is sufficient for me to have you home and hale," she said softly, her eyes shining.

Rolfe kissed her again, well aware that their guests watched him with interest. He lifted his fistful of game and called to one of the boys. Annelise's eyes widened ever so slightly as the company of his servants came into view. "Boy! Take these to the kitchens, then all of you, come and restore yourselves. We have had a long day of riding." The servants surged forth, taking their seats at the board, and the hall filled with the sound of their chatter. "But tell me, Annelise, who owns the six steeds new to the stables?"

"We have guests, my lord," she said and gestured to the men. Rolfe pretended to have just noticed them. "This is Enguerrand de Roussineau and his companions."

"Guests on such a night as this," Rolfe exclaimed. "Who would have anticipated as much?" He shed his gloves and shook the hands of the knights, showing no expectation of a reply. He noted that Enguerrand was a little discomfited and was glad of it. "Welcome. I trust you have refreshed yourselves?"

Enguerrand did not move. "I did not catch your name, sir."

Rolfe met the other man's gaze, ensuring that his own was steely. "Rolfe de Viandin."

"Viandin?" Enguerrand raised a brow. "Is that the name of this palace?"

"No, no," Rolfe said easily, distrusting the other knight's interest. "Viandin is the inheritance of my brother, Adalbert, who administers it. It is to the north and west, in Burgundy, near Cluny." He was well aware that this was news to Annelise, but would never have guessed as much from her expression.

"The land is said to be rich there."

"It is a well-established holding," Rolfe acknowledged. "And Roussineau? Forgive me but I am not familiar with it."

"Sworn to the Lord de Tulley, on the other side of the Beauvoir Pass. We mine silver."

Annelise's eyes widened ever so slightly and Rolfe did not miss this hint from his lady wife. "Indeed? How fortunate to have a holding with such wealth to call its own." He moved to sit at the board, nodding to the other knights. Annelise brought him a cup of wine, but Enguerrand was not prepared to abandon their conversation.

"But why do you have a palace here?" that knight asked. "So far from the main road and your home estate?"

"Who would abide beside the main road, given a choice?" Rolfe asked, then turned to Annelise. "Do not tell me that we have civet of hare this night?"

"We do, my lord," she said with a smile. She fetched the dish for him, acting as his squire. He was glad to have her close by his side, for this Enguerrand struck him as a serpent. "It is most fine, but I confess I am glad that you brought more hares."

"Do you have a taste of it yourself, my lady? I know how you like to ensure that your guests are sated first, but it smells wondrous. Did you give the cook access to the spices again?" Rolfe smiled at her and she sat at his left, letting him put stew on her side of the trencher.

"I did, my lord."

Rolfe fed her a morsel, enjoying Enguerrand's growing impatience. He stole a quick kiss, making the excuse that there was sauce upon her lip, and she flushed prettily.

"But your name is Rolfe," a squire said and Rolfe did not have to feign astonishment that the boy was so outspoken. "And you have a palace in the forest, one that appears to be magical, just like the one in the tale. Were you cursed by a djinn? Did you win this palace from her?"

Rolfe stared coldly at the boy, who flushed and dropped his gaze, then sat down as if he wished he could shrink to invisibility. "What is this?" he demanded, letting anger touch his tone.

Enguerrand was either an audacious man or a fool, for he did not retreat. "I heard a tale at Beauvoir of a knight cursed by a djinn, given her palace but compelled to be a wolf. That knight was said to be named Rolfe and was returning from crusade."

"Do I look like a wolf?" Rolfe asked, biting off the words.

"No, but you must admit that it is an extraordinary coincidence..." Enguerrand protested.

"I feel compelled to admit no such thing."

"Sir, you would deceive us all!" the other knight cried. "Explain to us how this palace can be, why it is located in this place, and why the weather is so fine within its walls. Annelise refuses to explain any of it."

Rolfe let there be a long moment of silence. He washed his hands and wiped them with care, then stood, liking that he was taller and broader than his guest. "And so my wife has shown more discretion than you." Enguerrand would have protested, but Rolfe continued, easily speaking over the other man's objections. "You are a guest in my abode, and unless the world has changed a great deal while I was on crusade, that situation calls you to a measure of polite behavior." He gestured to the board. "You have eaten your fill; your companions have drunk a considerable measure of wine, unless I miss my guess; you are warm and sheltered from the storm and your horses are so, as well. Yet you harass my wife with your demands for more. You insult me with your insinuations. And you violate your responsibility to these boys entrusted to your care for training by filling their thoughts with whimsy and foolery."

"I did not harass your wife!"

"You most certainly did. I knew the moment I laid eyes upon her this night that she was upset, and I see no other cause for such a situation than you, sir, and your impertinent questions." Rolfe swept to his feet and took Annelise's hand in his. "You are fortunate, Enguerrand de Roussineau, that I am a temperate man. You may have abused your welcome here, but I will not cast you into the forest in the night. You will, however, leave before the dawn."

"You cannot do this!" Enguerrand protested.

"I most certainly can. This is my abode and you would do well to recall that you are my guest. I feel no compunction in ending my hospitality to you, given the treatment of my lady wife in her own abode."

"But we cannot be turned into the forest in the night! There are wolves..."

Rolfe leaned closer to the other man. "When did you arrive at my gates?"

"Just before the sun set," Enguerrand admitted.

"And as you have noted, this palace is distant from the road. What was your plan for accommodations this night, sir? Did you plan to force yourself into my palace? Did you know of its location?" Rolfe watched Enguerrand flush a dull red. "Or did you, perhaps, mean to seek sanctuary with the Sisters of Ste. Radegund? That is the sole other establishment that I know within any proximity."

Their gazes locked and held, then Enguerrand took a step back and bowed stiffly. "I apologize, sir, if my questions have given offense, either to you or your lady wife."

To Rolfe's thinking, the apology was late and insincere, but he inclined his head. "I accept your apology," he said though. "My palace is distinct and I suppose it is no surprise that its very essence prompts questions."

Enguerrand smiled. "Then we can stay?"

"Oh no," Rolfe said easily. "I am a man of my word, sir." He let his voice harden. "You will be gone by dawn, Enguerrand, or you may never leave this palace alive." He smiled coolly. "Perhaps I do have a trait in common with the wolves, for I do like to hunt." Rolfe's gaze did not waver and he did not blink. He watched Enguerrand consider the merit of defying him, of saying more in his own defense, of protesting anew or of asking more questions. The knight had the wits to abandon all those courses of action and beg leave to retire.

"There is a chamber near the stables that you can use this night," he said, his tone resolute. "The accommodations are simple but fighting men such as yourselves will require nothing more. When I rise on the morrow, sir, I expect you to be gone."

He stood with Annelise, waiting and watching while they left the hall, then wished that the door to those chambers would be barred behind their guests.

Once they were out of sight, Annelise exhaled and leaned against him, her relief evident. "Will they come in the night?" she whispered.

Rolfe shook his head. "The door to the chamber will be barred behind them."

"Good!" She smiled at him, her eyes glowing with such relief that his heart skipped a beat. "I was never so glad to see another living soul," she murmured as he gathered her close.

"Tell me everything about him," Rolfe said. "Every detail you know and every possibility you suspect."

"Of course, my lord." She smiled shyly and met his gaze. "Rolfe."

Rolfe could resist her no longer but bent and kissed her soundly before carrying her off to bed. A simple wish ensured that the hall was cleaned and the servants disappeared, then there was only their great curtained bed and the sweetness of his lady wife.

He decided that her confidences about Enguerrand could wait a few moments, for it was high time that he did remove her garters with his teeth. He had trusted the lady and she had proven herself worthy of his confidence.

Such a feat called for a reward, and Rolfe knew the one his lady liked best.

Annelise was relieved beyond all else. After she had been thoroughly seduced by her husband, she found herself nestled in his lap with candles burning around them. He had eaten little at the board in Enguerrand's presence, so she fed him from the dish of stew that had appeared after their lovemaking and told him about their guest.

Rolfe de Viandin was his name.

He listened avidly, his gaze locked upon her features. She did not doubt that he heard what she did not say aloud about her reaction to Enguerrand's suit for her hand. She told him about the depleted mines at Roussineau and gave voice to her sense that Enguerrand wished to wed her for the sake of Sayerne itself.

"He thinks my brother Quinn will not return from Outremer," she explained. "And if he does not, Tulley may endow the holding upon me."

"Or your younger brother."

Annelise shook her head. "I do not think there was any prospect of that. Yves is young, for one matter, and has only seen sixteen summers. But I think that if there had been any such possibility, Tulley would not have encouraged Yves to seek his fortune at tournament."

Her husband nodded. "That is reasonable. I could not help but note how closely Enguerrand asked after Viandin. He seems much concerned with material matters." He considered her for a long moment.

"There is some other detail, is there not?" Annelise asked. "Some other part of the curse you have not told me?"

He touched his fingertip to her mouth, sliding it across her bottom lip in a slow caress. "I like how you say my name, my Annelise. I should have told you sooner."

Annelise smiled beneath his touch. "Yes, you should have."

His smile flashed. "Say it."

"Rolfe," she said, then kissed his palm. "My husband, Rolfe de

Viandin."

His gaze darkened and he lifted the empty bowl from her lap, setting it aside and rolling her beneath him. He kissed her lingeringly then raised his head to survey her again. "I want to hear you shout it when you find your pleasure," he murmured and Annelise shivered in anticipation.

But she tapped him on the nose. "You, sir, would change the subject."

He smiled but did not argue.

"Once again, you avoid telling me the whole of the truth," she insisted. "Is there another part of the curse?"

He grimaced and rolled to his back, pulling her against his side. His fingers twined in her hair and Annelise braced herself on her elbow to look down at him. He regarded her with admiration. "Of course, there is. You cannot be fooled, lady mine, and I am glad of it." Before she could ask again, he raised a hand and spoke again.

> *"Powers vested beneath the earth,*
> *Hear my words and attend my curse.*
> *Teach this one to respect my powers;*
> *Leave him trapped outside these towers.*
> *Condemn him to howl and prowl near,*
> *This place a reminder of all he held dear.*
> *Mortal ways he shall pursue no more,*
> *Doomed to remember forevermore.*
> *Let the one who crosses this threshold first,*
> *Be condemned to wed him despite his curse.*
> *And let the one in whom he confides,*
> *Lead a killer to his side."*

Annelise gasped. "A killer?"

Rolfe only nodded.

She raised a hand to her lips, thinking furiously. "Surely, he would not..."

"I think he is precisely the manner of man who might think it a good plan to see you widowed. Why, you could be married again before reaching Beauvoir to consult with your overlord, Tulley."

While Rolfe was calm, Annelise was outraged. "The fiend! If he believes that I would accept him under any circumstances, let alone after he did such a feat, then he is a fool..."

Rolfe's finger landed upon her lips, silencing her. "I do not mean to die, my Annelise." He spoke with complete conviction, but Annelise was afraid for him.

"I do not doubt that you could defend yourself well in this form, sir, but what about during the day?"

"I confess that is why I was reluctant to confide in you."

"That is only half the tale," Annelise guessed, and his gaze flicked to hers so quickly that she knew she was right. "What did Rosalinde do to you?"

Rolfe shook his head. "Why should we taint a fine night abed with such discussion? We have already talked about Enguerrand for longer than he deserves. I would hear you make that cry, my Annelise..." He pulled her down for a kiss, but Annelise only brushed her lips across his, bracing her hands on his chest.

"You evade my question again," she charged and he smiled slowly.

"And I am caught again." He lifted a brow, looking mischievous, wicked and utterly alluring. "What price will you demand of me, my lady?"

"The truth."

He made a face and sat up, lifting her into his lap again. "Make a less predictable choice, Annelise," he said.

"Tell me about Rosalinde and then I will," she countered.

He laughed. "Make it worth my while, Annelise."

"I will." Their gazes held for a charged moment and Annelise's heart squeezed tightly at even the possibility of her losing this man from her side. She realized in that moment that she had utterly lost her heart to him, that with his trust, her capitulation was complete. Would that break the curse and ensure that he was a man from this night forth? Annelise ardently hoped as much.

He pressed a kiss to her temple, tangling them together, and she knew he was choosing his words. She had complete faith that he would confide in her and waited patiently.

"Rosalinde was a beauty beyond compare," he said finally. "I met her at the home of my maternal uncle, where I trained for my spurs, near Vézelay. She was a cousin of his wife, so I saw her first at the Yule. She had hair of brightest gold, a lovely sweet face, and eyes as blue as the midsummer sky." The admiration in Rolfe's voice as he recalled this woman made Annelise's mouth go dry. "I had never seen a maiden who was so very beautiful and I was lost with but a glimpse."

Annelise leaned her face against his chest to hide her expression. She reminded herself that she had demanded this tale, and that she doubted it would end well.

"I was astonished when she smiled at me. I thought she was merely polite, but over the following year—at Easter, at St. John's Day, at the feast of the local saint in the parish church—each time I saw her, she granted me encouragement. She gave me a ribbon from her hair the next Yule and I was overwhelmed. At Epiphany, she gave me a kiss upon my cheek."

His hand rose to tangle in Annelise's loose hair. "I was young. I was seduced by a pretty face and a charming smile. I knew nothing of her nature or her heart, but desire burned within me. In hindsight, I am certain she knew it and tempted me apurpose, though at the time, I thought our pairing might be destined to be."

A cup of wine appeared beside the bed and Rolfe took it in his hand, offering Annelise a sip before he drank some himself. "It was Midsummer when we rode to her family abode for her older brother's wedding. I had earned my spurs and would be returning to Viandin after this journey—my uncle had invited me to linger to add another knight to the splendor of their party. Of course, once I saw Rosalinde, all the rest was as dust to me. She sought me out over those three days, time and again. She admired the sword my father had sent for my knighting. She confessed herself to be impressed by the destrier my uncle had bestowed upon me as a gift. There was a tournament to celebrate the wedding, and she tied her ribbon to my spear, cheering for me as I competed."

"Did you win?" Annelise dared to ask. She felt him nod.

"I did. And she claimed a token of my affection as her reward. She led me to the garden where she granted me a kiss that set my very soul aflame."

Annelise blinked, but Rolfe chuckled and tightened his grip upon her. "It was a chaste kiss, Annelise, but my first from a beauty. It was novelty that made it potent, I fear, not the lady's allure or even her amorous skills. I dared to ask for her hand in marriage in its wake."

He fell silent then and Annelise wondered why. She eased back and looked up at him, seeing that he was lost in the memory.

"She changed," he said softly, then shook his head. "The sweet maiden I had seen was banished and in her place was a clerk of stern visage. She demanded to know the precise amount of my wealth and my prospects. I admitted that I was a younger son and landless, that I would have to seek my fortune. I dared to take her hand and confess myself glad that we would have affection between us and that love might light our future."

Again he fell silent. Annelise put her hand over his. "She did not agree?" she prompted.

Rolfe shook his head. "She laughed. She mocked me for such folly. I persisted, despite the change in her manner which worried me mightily."

"You are not a man to readily abandon your path," Annelise said quietly.

Rolfe chuckled. "Not me. I said I would ask my father to entrust a small holding to my care. I said I would ride to the tournaments and seek my fortune. I said I would do whatever was necessary to see her happiness complete." He shook his head. "She told me I was not worthy of cleaning her shoes, that she saw sufficient poverty amongst the villeins of her father's estate and that she would never wed a man who was not rich beyond all."

He grimaced. "I did not believe her. She told me she would wed an elderly neighbor of her father, a baron who had more wealth than he could count. This was a change from what I knew of her, though indeed, I knew little. I confess I remained incredulous that the beauty I so adored could possess such avarice. I saw her eyes glint with malice, though I did not immediately guess why."

"What did she do?"

"She screamed and tore her own kirtle before my eyes. She cried that I attacked her, that my lust had made me indecent. She roused her father's guards and they set upon me, like a common thief." Rolfe's gaze chilled as he looked down at Annelise. "I was humiliated before my uncle and patron, because our host believed his daughter."

"You were not the sole one deceived, then," Annelise whispered.

"I was not, but I never forgot that day, and how my trust of a beauteous maiden led me false."

"Do you fear that will happen again?" Annelise had to ask and her heart pounded as her husband smiled down at her.

"Not with you, Annelise, for your beauty goes to your very marrow." He spoke with conviction and awe, his fingertips trailing over her cheek as he surveyed her. His voice was husky. "You are a marvel, my Annelise, for you have taught me the merit of trust once again."

"Perhaps you were simply waiting for me," she dared to say and he laughed aloud.

"Tell me of destiny, my lady. Tell me our match was fated to be." He lifted his brows. "I do come to consider as much myself." He kissed her so thoroughly that she could have no doubt of his sincerity. It was on the tip of her tongue to confess her love, but Annelise feared he might not be ready to respond in kind—and she knew it would devastate her if he could not do as much.

"And now, Annelise," he murmured against her throat. "I believe we have a task that needs to be done. I would hear you call my name in your pleasure." His eyes gleamed with sensual intent as he looked down upon her and she felt a quiver of anticipation. "Where would you have me begin?"

CHAPTER TWELVE

heir lovemaking felt celebratory to Rolfe that night. Indeed, he wanted to reward Annelise for being so worthy of his trust. It seemed to him that she was more passionate, more giving, more welcoming than she had been yet, and he wanted only to please her. It was a delight to watch her abed and he knew no other woman would ever have such a hold over his attention. Rolfe had never felt so bound to another, and yet, their partnership felt right to him.

When she approached the crest of her pleasure, he smiled in anticipation of her release. She clutched him tightly, gasping and trembling as the tumult made her shake like a leaf in the wind. The gentle touch of her lips to his cheek pushed him over the edge and he held her close as his release went on and on.

She whispered his name and he liked the sound of it well.

Then she whispered three words that shocked him.

"I love you."

Annelise's confession was as soft as a whisper. She was sliding into sleep, dozing against him, perhaps unaware of what she had said. Rolfe was both awed and terrified by her confession. He was honored to have won her heart, but he feared that her love might not survive all of his truth.

The second djinn had insisted that love would break the curse, but Rolfe had little faith in the efficacy of her spells. How abiding was Annelise's love? Would she continue to love him if the curse was not broken? What if she witnessed his transformation? He could not imagine that any tender feelings could survive the sight. The change was agonizing and could not be easy to watch. And he knew well enough that it was one thing to be aware of a truth, and yet another to see it before one's eyes.

Could the price of the curse be his wife's love?

Rolfe hated to even consider the possibility. He could not conceive of a life without Annelise. He tucked her against his side and she sighed as she slept, confident that he would defend her against any peril.

She was right. He would do as much. Rolfe would readily risk his own life to see Annelise safe. But what of love? What of their future? He knew in his heart that this challenge was not yet behind them, though he could not discern a resolution. He listened to her sleep and stared at the canopy overhead, aware of the sounds of the palace around him.

And the threat that was secured in the chamber beside the stables. He did not like or trust Enguerrand and could not wait for that man to be gone. He feared trickery from the other knight, or deception. Rolfe knew that this parting would not be the last of Enguerrand. He suspected that some ploy would be launched that might gain Enguerrand an advantage—and put Annelise in jeopardy. It might even occur before Enguerrand's planned departure.

For Rolfe was vulnerable and he knew as much. He wondered how much Enguerrand suspected of his situation and feared it was too much. With Rolfe's transformation at the dawn, he would be unable to defend Annelise within the palace, so he had to ensure that Enguerrand had departed by then.

It was yet several hours to the dawn. Rolfe knew he would not sleep, not with the other knight within his walls.

Perhaps it was time for his hospitality to come to its end. He disliked being ungracious, but Annelise must be defended from the other knight's malice. Rolfe rose from the bed and dressed quickly, leaving his lady to sleep.

Enguerrand knew there was something odd about the palace. Its location made no sense. The weather within its walls made no sense. The lack of servants yet the provision of every comfort made no sense—just as the sudden appearance of servants with the lord's return made no sense.

The bard's tale had to be true.

But if it was, then why was Rolfe de Viandin not a wolf?

Enguerrand could not reconcile the tale with his host's appearance. Being cursed to take the form of a wolf had been the price of gaining the palace from the djinn. How had he broken that curse? Was their host a sorcerer himself? Or was he an illusion? That seemed a whimsy beyond all.

It was not whimsy that had barred the portal of their chamber from the outside. Enguerrand had tried to leave the chamber, after the rest of his party fell asleep. He was certain that some hint of the truth could be found in the palace, but the portal had been secured.

That meant he was right. Rolfe de Viandin had secrets and they could be unearthed.

And why had Rolfe decreed that Enguerrand and his fellows must leave before the dawn? Such an hour of departure was unknown. There had to be a reason and Enguerrand wanted to remain through the dawn to find out what it was.

His host, however, had anticipated him.

Enguerrand jumped when the portal was suddenly flung open. He spun to find his host silhouetted in the portal, the moonlight shining into the garden behind him. "The storm has stopped," that man said grimly. "You will leave immediately."

"But my men sleep."

"They can sleep at Beauvoir. You should hurry, as there may be more snow before midday." Rolfe stepped into the chamber and Enguerrand saw the determination in his gaze. There was steel in his tone. "I would not have you caught between sanctuaries in such weather."

Such curious eyes the man has. One blue and one silver-gray. Enguerrand had never seen the like and he found Rolfe's steady gaze unsettling. The other knight seemed capable of reading his thoughts or guessing his intentions, and Enguerrand knew he did not imagine Rolfe's disapproval.

"My men will need time to shave and arm themselves..."

"I think less time than you believe," Rolfe said, shaking each one in turn. "Rise! You have a short opportunity to ride for Beauvoir! Make the most of it, lest you meet your fate in the winter forest."

The men stumbled to their feet, their eyes bleary from their indulgence in the wine.

"Boys!" Rolfe roared. "See to your knights, and make haste."

"There is no need to do as much," Enguerrand protested, sensing his host's urgency to see them gone. But the squires scampered this way and that, packing saddlebags and gathering armor, following Rolfe's command instead of Enguerrand's.

"The horses must be tended," Enguerrand protested.

Rolfe smiled but there was no warmth in his expression. "You will find them saddled and stamping to leave by the time you reach the stables," he said smoothly.

What secret did he want to keep from Enguerrand?

It did not matter in the end, for all objections were dismissed. The rest of Enguerrand's company seemed to take on their host's urgency and it was not long before they were riding toward the gates under Rolfe's watchful gaze. Enguerrand tried to delay their departure with fulsome thanks, but Rolfe gruffly interrupted him and bade him make haste.

Their host eyed the sky. "Yes, the blizzard will return threefold by midday. Ride! Ride now for Beauvoir while you may!" He slapped the rump of one destrier as the gates opened and the knights lunged through the open portal. The palfreys followed the stallions, prancing in their desire to run.

Enguerrand reined in his steed with difficulty and eyed Rolfe. "I thank you for your hospitality," he said, his tone acid. "No doubt we shall meet again."

His host smiled. There was something hungry about Rolfe's expression, something that made Enguerrand shiver.

"No doubt," that man said. "But know this, Enguerrand de

Roussineau, you will never threaten my lady wife again and survive to see the next dawn."

"I have never threatened Annelise!"

"Have you not?" Rolfe stepped closer to the gates. "She was fearful when I returned and uncertain of your intent. That is a poor reward for her grace in inviting you to take refuge from the snow."

"I cannot imagine why she should have been concerned," Enguerrand said. "We are old friends, Annelise and I..."

"You are a declined suitor, one whose offer was found inadequate," Rolfe said, interrupting Enguerrand with resolve. Enguerrand did not appreciate the reminder of his failure.

"And what of you?" he challenged. "You keep her imprisoned here, far from society, beyond the reach of her overlord, hidden from her family. Only a dishonest man would do as much." He dropped his voice low. "Or a man with a fearsome secret."

Rolfe laughed. "You are a fool, Enguerrand, to put such faith in the tales of bards. Any man of sense would know that such fables are entertainment alone."

"Any man of sense would know there is something amiss with this palace."

Rolfe stepped closer. "Any man of sense would know when he had exceeded his welcome." The gates began to close and Enguerrand's destrier moved toward the forest of its own volition.

"I will tell Tulley of this!" Enguerrand cried.

"I invite you to do so," Rolfe said. He pointed. "Beauvoir and Tulley lie that way."

He stood there, indomitable and determined as the gates closed. Enguerrand eyed the smooth expanse of pale stone and his conviction that there was more to this situation grew. A few snowflakes fell and he spurred his horse, riding after his party. They were already a good distance away.

But it did not take long for Enguerrand to decide that there might be an easy way to discover why Rolfe wished him to leave before the dawn.

He would linger and watch.

The cursed man had an ability to delay matters beyond

expectation. It was close to the dawn by the time the sound of the party's horses faded. Rolfe could not wish Enguerrand far enough away. He paced in the garden, unwilling to awaken Annelise but wanting to talk to her as well. He had never been so conflicted in the past, so caught between his desire and his knowledge of the rational choice.

He sighed and turned, only to find his lady in the portal in her chemise. "I said it," she whispered. "And you are displeased."

Rolfe strode to her side and smiled. "On the contrary, I am delighted by your confession."

She studied him, those wondrous eyes almost glowing. "But you do not respond in kind. Do you not wish to break the curse?"

"I do not believe matters to be so simple."

"Whyever not?"

Rolfe sighed and bowed his head. "I fear that there are things you could witness that might change your thinking."

Annelise shook her head as he knew she would. "No! Love is true and good. Love is unchanging and steady. A heart once surrendered is lost forever."

"But what if it is not fully surrendered or captured?"

"How can you suggest that my love is not enough?"

He bent and brushed his lips across hers. "I feel the change coming, my Annelise. The curse is not broken, so therefore, love has not broken it."

"Because you do not love me."

"Because your love is not complete."

Annelise's lips tightened, even as she took two fistfuls of Rolfe's shirt and tried to shake him. "Oh, if ever I meet this Rosalinde, I will have words for her!" she said with ferocity.

"What has she to do with the matter?"

"She taught you that women could not be relied upon." Annelise poked a finger in his chest. "I will teach you that she alone could not be relied upon and that you can trust me."

"I do trust you..."

"Not completely, Rolfe. I will wager that love must be reciprocal to break the curse. Because you do not believe, it is not broken." A determined glint claimed her eye. "Tell me what I could do to dismiss the last of your doubt."

Rolfe knew the only reply there could be, but he was reluctant to utter it aloud.

What if his worst fear came true? What if she was revolted by his change and then by him? What if she spurned him and he lost all that he had gained?

At the same time, he felt the dawn's approach just as he always did. Something began to change within him, shifting in preparation for his transformation. Within moments, the sky would lighten and he would have a tail. Then the fur would sprout and his ears would lengthen, even while he was pushed to the gates by some unseen force.

"You must watch," he whispered, knowing that this lady would have the strength to do as much.

What Rolfe could not guess, though, was how she might respond to the sight.

Watch.

Annelise understood precisely what Rolfe meant. She knew from his expression that the transformation must be horrific and saw in his eyes that he feared the sight of it would destroy every shred of love in her heart.

"Does it hurt?"

He nodded once, making no issue of the matter. "It is done soon enough, I suppose, although it feels endless."

She glanced at the sky. "Soon?" she asked, then saw that he had a tail. It was long and graced with silver fur, the tip of a paler hue than the rest.

The first light of the dawn had stolen over the horizon.

The gates groaned as they opened.

Annelise caught her breath as Rolfe's shape altered. As horrible as it was to watch his nose darken and his ears sprout, it was equally fascinating to witness the change.

She stared in amazement as his limbs shortened and his body transformed. She could see the anguish in his expression, then he moved suddenly to the gates as if he was to be flung through them. She ran after him, even as he dropped to all fours and was forced from the palace.

The rising sun painted the palace and the snow beyond the gates with rosy gold light. The stars disappeared, and the wind nudged the barren trees as it, too, seemed to awaken.

Then the wolf turned to fix her with a steady look.

He had one blue eye and one silver-gray.

He was daring her to accept what she had seen.

Annelise swallowed her instinctive fear with difficulty. This was Rolfe, the man who granted her shelter, who made her flesh sing with desire, who spoke to her with an understanding she had never known. This was the man whose ring she gladly wore.

Annelise stepped through the gates with resolve.

The wolf did not move.

She continued, her heart hammering, realizing that she was more afraid of the wolf than the change. This time, he did not wag his tail to encourage her, and there was no resemblance to the ostler's puppies.

This time, it was a test.

Annelise crouched in the snow before him and gazed into those unusual eyes. "I love you, Rolfe de Viandin," she said with conviction. "I love all of your truth, and I know I always will."

He held her gaze for a long moment, as if incredulous, then bent and licked the back of her hand. She reached to sink her fingers into the thickness of his fur and marveled that this was her husband.

Another wolf howled in the distance and Rolfe's head snapped up. Annelise saw the yellow gleam of a pair of eyes in the fading shadows. Rolfe's lip lifted in a menacing snarl and then he barked with vigor.

The second wolf disappeared, abandoning her to seek other prey.

It was clear that in either form, her husband defended her.

Rolfe nudged her elbow with his nose, urging Annelise to her feet. He pushed her toward the gate but she held her ground. "If you are in peril, then I will remain with you," she said, thinking her offer most reasonable.

Rolfe growled in disagreement. He trotted to the gate of the palace, then back to her, effectively telling Annelise what he intended.

She folded her arms across her chest. "I am not going back in there without you."

Rolfe snarled and increased the speed of his pacing between Annelise and the gate.

"No," she insisted. "As long as you remain out here, then so will I."

Rolfe glanced in the direction that the other wolf had disappeared, then growled at Annelise.

She leaned over and tapped him smartly on the snout. "You do not frighten me, husband of mine."

Rolfe dove behind Annelise and pushed her in the direction of the gate with his head. She shook her head at his determination, pivoting to face him.

"I wish to remain with you." She raised her voice. "Close!" she called to the gates and they did. "Let me fetch my cloak and my boots. We will remain together in the forest."

Rolfe backed up, shaking his head from side to side as he did so. He settled on his haunches and dropped his nose to rest on his paws. He looked to be annoyed with her, but that was only fair, as she was irked with him.

"Vexing man."

He exhaled in a low growl, his eyes gleaming. Indeed, the resemblance to him when he was a man and annoyed with her was so striking that Annelise almost laughed out loud.

"Who commands the gates of my palace?" a woman demanded, her voice low and resonant. A shiver ran up Annelise's spine at the sound and she spun to find a dark shadow looming over her. It was a woman, but not a woman, for she was both there and not there. Annelise could see the closed gates through the woman's form, but the force of her glare was not inconsiderable.

Her palace.

The djinn.

Annelise took a reluctant step back. Rolfe leaped in front of her, teeth bared as he snarled at the apparition before them.

The djinn laughed, exhibiting an array of brass teeth. "You

think you are clever, Rolfe de Viandin, because you have been fortunate. Do not imagine that I will permit you to break the curse." She slowly grew taller, until she towered over the walls of the palace and Annelise like a storm cloud. She turned her gaze upon Annelise. "Have you a name, mortal?"

"I am Annelise de Sayerne, wife of Rolfe de Viandin, lord of this palace."

The djinn glared and the fur on the back of Rolfe's neck bristled. "I am the only owner of this palace, not you, mortal, or your companion."

Annelise cleared her throat. "I believe that you have made a gift of this palace to my husband."

The djinn's eyes flashed like lightning. "A loan, and a reluctant one at that. Just because I was forced to surrender it to a mortal man does not mean that he will be at peace!" She swirled, and the wind swept around them, pelting Annelise and Rolfe with cold chunks of snow as she shouted.

> *"Powers above and powers below,*
> *amend the curse that I made before.*
> *My curse may be broken with love's sacrifice,*
> *but only if my palace is as cold as ice."*

Annelise buried her face in Rolfe's fur, her arms flung around his neck. "You cannot change the curse," she dared to say. "That is not fair!"

The djinn laughed. "And when has the world been fair?" She leaned close, smiling so that Annelise saw all her sharpened brass teeth. "I like it warm in the garden." Her eyes shone with malice. "Always, always warm." Then she dropped her voice to a whisper.

> *"Lest this mortal plan for my defeat*
> *Let him truly become a beast."*

"No!" Annelise cried, but the djinn picked her up, forcibly pulling her away from Rolfe. Annelise screamed in protest but the djinn only laughed.

Then she flung Annelise into the gardens of the palace.

The gates shut with a heavy thump, sealing Annelise on the inside and Rolfe on the outside. She heard him howl in frustration, even as she leaped to her feet and ran to the gates. She ran her hands over the portal. "Open," she commanded firmly, hoping they would obey her.

The doors shuddered, though, and did not open. Annelise had the sense that they struggled between two conflicting commands. Rolfe had given Annelise permission to command them, but she guessed that the djinn had made an order of her own. Annelise watched the gates shudder. She thought they might swing inward or even shatter. They fairly bowed with the force bent upon them.

Abruptly, they stilled, leaving her barricaded inside.

The wolves howled of prey in the forest.

A man.

A horse.

Not a company of six horses, but one rider alone.

Rolfe guessed who it might be.

Once Annelise was safely within the palace again and the djinn had vanished, he raced toward the other wolves. He smelled the fear of a horse and the trepidation of a man. He smelled mail and steel and leather and horse dung. He heard a man shout and the barking of the wolves. By the time he reached the pack, they were trotting after the horse. The destrier whinnied and stamped, tossing his head, more concerned with looking back than forward.

The knight in the saddle was garbed in green and silver.

It was Enguerrand, and that he lingered so far behind his company of men could only mean that he had witnessed events at the palace gates.

He knew all of the truth.

Rolfe had no doubt this fiend would use that knowledge against him, use it to make Annelise a widow. He snarled in fury, feeling the raw power of the wolf inside him. Previously, he had been a man in a wolf's skin, but on this day, thanks to the djinn's intervention, he became of the wolf's nature. There was evidence of the change in the manner of the other wolves: instead of easing away from him, clearly sensing that he was different, they welcomed him into the pack. He surged to the lead of the group, snarling and snapping at those who might have fought his ascendancy, and they ceded to him.

He was directly behind Enguerrand.

It was time this knight rode away.

Rolfe barked and snarled, leaping after the horse. Although he had no plan to do it injury, the wolf within was hungry and smelled blood. He snapped closer to the horse's hooves than had been his plan and the destrier bolted. It ignored Enguerrand's attempts to rein it in and raced forward at full speed.

The wolf within roared that the chase was on and leaped in pursuit, teeth bared. The other wolves fell back as the horse galloped through the forest, Rolfe fast behind. Enguerrand was frightened and Rolfe savored the smell of his fear. It gave the wolf more strength to make another leap for the saddle. Enguerrand swore and pulled his dagger. He made to stab at Rolfe, then froze as he stared into Rolfe's eyes. He paled. Rolfe bared his teeth again, and Enguerrand gave the destrier his spurs.

Rolfe cut through the forest when the path bent and he leaped suddenly in the air, knowing he would abruptly appear at Enguerrand's side. The destrier shied and Enguerrand swore again, struggling to remain in the saddle. He threw his dagger at Rolfe, his features contorted in fury, but his aim was poor. The blade sank into the trunk of a tree and Rolfe once again trotted behind the terrified destrier.

He smelled the rest of Enguerrand's company ahead and knew he could not battle six and survive. He fell back, letting the other wolves gather around him, and knew their eyes glowed as they watched the departing knight.

"I will be back, Rolfe de Viandin!" Enguerrand shouted, his courage returned now that he was safe. "I will be back and you will regret your deed."

Rolfe tipped his head back and howled, the wolf within reveling in the sound of the other wolves adding their voices to his. He found his fellows watching him, considering him, deciding what to do about him, and left the pack to review his own choices.

If the wolf within gained ascendancy, would he injure Annelise?

Would he forget her?

Would she forget him?

The book.

Once it was clear that Annelise was trapped alone in the palace, she hunted the book. It was the only reference she had for djinns and their ways. Perhaps there was more to be gleaned from that tale than she had realized. Perhaps there was more to the book than she had seen.

She did not like this new spell at all. Would Rolfe even be able to enter the palace at night? Would he change to a man but be left naked in the forest? How quickly would he become a wolf in truth? What could she do to assist him?

Every puzzle has a key.

The book was in the chamber where Enguerrand and his men had eaten. The tables were cleared and all returned to order, the book reposing alone in the middle of the room. Annelise was reminded of the most ornate Bible in the convent, the one that was kept in a place of honor and only touched by the mother superior.

She opened the book and was confounded by the sight of that foreign script.

Remembering her husband's feat, she tentatively touched the letters with her fingertips. For a moment, nothing happened.

Then the letters shimmered as they had once before, and she could read it.

Thrilled that some matters showed consistency, Annelise read the tale again from start to finish. She could discern nothing in it that was helpful, though. Had she met Leila? It was possible, for the djinn seemed to have a similar attitude. Leila had built a palace and she had been spurned by a mortal man.

That still did not give Annelise any idea of what to do.

A meal had appeared for her while she was reading. She ate a bit of it, although she had little appetite, then returned to the book. What had she missed? Annelise was so deep in thought that when she heard a throat being cleared, she jumped in shock. She spun around only to find a short, plump woman sitting on the opposite side of the chamber.

"Greetings!" The woman waved at Annelise, as if her presence was unsurprising.

Annelise blinked, but the woman did not disappear.

Her kirtle and cloak were commonplace enough, but she wore the most peculiar fur hat Annelise had ever seen. Annelise could not have easily guessed her age.

"Who are you?" Annelise asked.

"I might ask the same of you." The woman laughed and wandered around the chamber, as if she had never visited before. She peeked into the bed chamber. "Oh, that is a fine addition," she mused. "There is nothing like a great bed."

"Have you been here before?" Annelise asked.

"Not for a very long time."

Annelise noticed a faint rosy cloud hovering around her companion and kept her distance. "Are you that djinn again?" she dared to ask. "Or another one altogether?"

The woman grimaced. "Not much of an ambassador for our kind, is she?"

Her expression made Annelise suspect that they shared the same opinion about the djinn, but Annelise was determined to be careful.

"Her?" she echoed.

"Yes, *her*. The troublemaker herself." The woman sighed. "There was a time when I had wondrous dreams for her and what she might become." She shook her head then smiled at Annelise. She waved a hand at their surroundings. "You must realize that this is her palace?"

"And that she cursed Rolfe."

"Oh!" The woman's eyes lit with delight. "You know Rolfe? He is, of course, mortal, but all the same he has a certain charm. Do you agree?"

"Yes." Annelise felt herself liking this other djinn. "He is my husband."

"Truly?" At Annelise's nod, the djinn spoke eagerly. "Oh, that is fine luck, indeed. I had never imagined be would make such progress in such short order. He looked quite grim at the prospect of marriage.”

“What manner of progress do you mean?”

“Progress against the curse, of course, my child!” The djinn shook her head, making the little red balls along the perimeter of her hat sway. “You must know about the curse—after all, you wed the man. Did he not tell you?”

“Of course,” Annelise acknowledged. If she were prudent, this talkative djinn might tell her more about how to abolish the curse.

“I hope he mentioned that I—in a markedly fine spell created entirely on impulse, one that amazes me to this day with its adept little rhyme—mitigated the curse set upon him so that he was only burdened to be a wolf by day. And look at you—you are a fine enough looking woman! What fortune that man has!”

“He has many blessings to count, indeed,” Annelise commented, her tone wry.

The djinn drew herself up taller. “When dealing with our kind, a sharp tongue is markedly less than an asset, though I am surprised to have to remind you of that. Your husband would not find himself in this situation had he been a little less quick to express his skepticism.”

Annelise was not certain that was true so held her tongue.

“You know, he was less than impressed that I could not remove the curse entirely. How anyone could expect that I truly do not know. I thought I did rather well, under duress.” The djinn grimaced. “It was no pleasure to be cloistered with her all these centuries.”

Was this Azima, the mother of the wicked djinn? Or was the confinement in the bottle a common fate for djinns? Annelise did not know.

“I can imagine it would not be,” she said with sympathy.

The djinn met Annelise’s gaze and smiled. “That is a marked improvement in your tone.”

Annelise knew an opportunity when she saw it. The djinn was well disposed to both her and Rolfe; Annelise should make the most of a moment that might be a fleeting one.

She smiled, summoning every vestige of charm she possessed. “Dare I hope that you are Azima?”

The djinn's expression was wary. "I might be."

"And that you might be inclined to aid Rolfe again?"

"Again?"

"Not that I would show any lack of appreciation for your efforts thus far, but the other djinn has returned and made our situation rather worse."

"I can imagine she might." The djinn appeared to be intrigued, at least.

"She has added to the curse and I fear for Rolfe's future."

"Indeed? Tell me."

Annelise repeated the new curse with care.

"Powers above and powers below,
amend the curse that I made before.
My curse may be broken with love's sacrifice,
but only if my palace is as cold as ice.
Lest this mortal plan for my defeat
Let him truly become a beast."

"That is less than encouraging," the djinn acknowledged and Annelise's hopes rose.

"Might it be possible for you to intervene now to help my husband?"

The djinn shook her head. "No, I cannot risk incurring more of Leila's wrath. I think I have done quite enough. We are not supposed to meddle in the affairs of mortals, you know."

Annelise's irritation flared, though she fought against it. "But you and the other djinn are entirely responsible for the situation!"

"Entirely? Oh, I think not." The djinn stood and brushed off her kirtle with such purpose that Annelise feared she would simply vanish.

"How can we end this curse?" Annelise asked as calmly as she could.

The djinn shrugged. "Rolfe's salvation must be earned."

"But how? I love him. I even told him as much and that made no difference."

The djinn considered Annelise for a long moment. "Did it

not?" she mused under her breath, then she cleared her throat. "And what did Rolfe say to you when you first spoke to him of love."

"That a marriage based upon love could not be distinguished from a marriage with the tangible benefits of security, comfort and protection. He said love was unnecessary to ensure a bride's happiness."

The djinn smiled. "And what would be the tangible benefits of your love for him?"

"I meet him willingly abed."

The djinn dismissed that with a wave of her hand. "A whore would do as much and there would be no talk of love."

"I defend his interests and fight by his side."

"A loyal vassal or a hired mercenary might do as much."

"I would break this curse, no matter the price to myself."

The djinn's smile broadened and she raised a finger. "Now there is the measure of love and love alone, when one being cares more about the welfare of another than his or her own self."

What would she give to see Rolfe free of the curse?

The djinn touched Annelise's hand, and the brush of her fingertips sent renewed hope surging through her. "We must all fight for what we believe to be of import, child."

"I am afraid that he will become a wolf and forget me," Annelise confessed, knowing it was true as soon as she uttered the words.

"It is easy to see that Rolfe is blessed with a wife of rare courage and wit," the djinn murmured. "You have the will within you and the means around you to solve all of this. Every puzzle, after all, has a key."

"Surely you can aid us?"

The djinn shook her head. "I have done all that I can."

Tears rose in Annelise's eyes and she turned away. Despite the djinn's confidence in her, she could not begin to imagine how to save Rolfe. She would give anything at all, but there had to be a reason for her gift.

"You will need this," the djinn said.

Annelise spun to find a black bottle cradled in the djinn's

hands. There was something both fascinating and troubling about the dark lights that seemed to move over its surface.

"Do not look overmuch upon it," the djinn advised. "This is the only thing I can grant you that you might need."

"But she—"

"Leila." The djinn's voice was firm, and her gaze grew fierce as she pressed the bottle and its stopper into Annelise's hands. "Her name is Leila." The djinn looked a great deal older than she had at first.

"Azima," Annelise guessed.

The djinn did not reply but turned away, then reached to caress the book.

Annelise dared to guess again. "Surely it is only a volume of children's tales?" she said, suspecting that it was far more.

The djinn looked back at her, and Annelise saw the shimmer of tears in her eyes. "I suppose we are all destined to become tales for children."

Her sadness was clear, but before Annelise could respond, she walked right through the stable wall and disappeared.

There was only a rosy glow left behind and by the time Annelise blinked, it had vanished as well.

She looked down at the bottle in her hands, knowing that she had not imagined the encounter.

Even better, Azima, despite her insistence that she could not help, had given Annelise an idea.

CHAPTER THIRTEEN

nnelise quickly formulated a plan. Jealousy had driven Leila to make her most terrible choices, and Annelise was determined to use that against the wicked djinn. Contrary to the djinn's assertion, though, she did not believe she had all the information necessary to use her plan. She might not know all of the curse as yet. There might be some detail that would change all.

She wanted to talk to Rolfe.

But Rolfe did not return that night. The gates did not open and they would not open. Annelise had no means of knowing whether he was pacing on the outside as she paced on the inside, or even whether he had changed back to a man or not. She hoped he had taken refuge in the tower, but uncertainty gnawed at her.

By morning, she had decided there could be no further delay. The threat of Rolfe changing fully to a wolf was too terrifying a prospect. She could not lose him now!

It was almost as frightening to have to make her best choice, knowing that she and Rolfe would have to live with the consequences for the rest of their lives. Worse, there would be only one chance to trap Leila, and Annelise did not dare to fail.

She thought her scheme had merit.

The difficulty was that she required Leila's presence.

Since the only other thing of import to Leila was clearly the palace, Annelise decided to destroy it, in the hope of gaining Leila's attention.

Or encouraging the djinn to intervene.

By midday, Annelise was ready. The obsidian bottle stood in the foyer, waiting.

She ran her fingers across the inlaid surface of a delicate table she had chosen to destroy first and prayed for forgiveness for what she intended to do. The piece was a work of great artistry, but that meant it had value. Before she could forget that Rolfe's welfare hung in the balance, she dragged the table to the large pool in the garden and flung it into the water. She winced as the top cracked and had to turn away from the water soaking into the wood.

So long as she did not look at the damage, it was more readily done. She cast a carved stool through a blown-glass window, which shattered loudly. There were vases and pots on the sill on the other side, which fell and broke on the stone beneath. She hefted a wooden chest with some effort, shoving it hard against the marble neck of a fountain so that the marble cracked. The top of the fountain wavered, then fell into the water and broke. Annelise cast rugs and pillows in every direction, sending brass clattering to the tiled floor and trinkets smashing against the wall. She screamed and howled as she did so, breaking everything she could move and making as much noise as possible in the process.

Fortunately, she did not have to be destructive for long.

"My beautiful palace!" shrieked the dark djinn, appearing suddenly beside Annelise.

Leila.

As she had planned, Annelise turned to the furious djinn and fell to her knees. "Thank the Heavens you are here!" she exclaimed. "They were destroying all the wondrous furnishings in your palace and there was nothing I could do about it!"

"They?" echoed the djinn.

"Yes, there were two of them, both larger than life. They moved so quickly I could barely keep my eyes upon them, and they were arguing..."

"Who were they? I shall see them cursed for all eternity!"

"I do not think they were mortal," Annelise admitted. She watched her opponent as she tried to appear distraught.

The djinn's eyes narrowed. "How would you know?"

"They appeared as abruptly as you do and their size changed as they argued."

"What were their names?"

"I do not know, but the woman..." Annelise sighed in wonder. "The woman was so beautiful that I felt as though I had stepped into the sunlight when she first smiled at me." She flicked a glance at the djinn. "And you will probably not believe me, but I could have sworn that diamonds and pearls fell from her lips when she spoke. Surely no mortal could be so very lovely."

Leila hissed. "But she was not alone?"

"No, no, she came after he did." Annelise frowned. "It was as if she came to take him away."

Annelise felt the weight of the djinn's gaze upon her and did not dare look up lest she be caught in her lie.

"He?"

"Yes, he came first, and oh, he was so handsome that I nearly lost my heart on sight. He wandered through the palace, not touching anything, calling a woman's name."

"Who? Who? *Who* did he call?" The djinn leaned over Annelise.

"Leila."

"He came," the djinn whispered. She drifted away for a moment, a delighted smile upon her lips. "He came for me."

Annelise almost smiled herself at the apparent success of her ruse, but the matter was hardly resolved as yet. "Then *she* came," she added.

The djinn jumped, then spun to hover close beside Annelise. "So you said. Tell me all! I must know exactly what happened."

"She smiled at me first, but then she saw him. He ran."

"He did?"

"He did. As though he had demons at his heels! She chased him, grabbed him by the hair, begged him not to abandon her. She cried, but he struggled to get away from her, insisting all the while that he loved only Leila."

"Aha!" The djinn was triumphant. "Aha! I knew it!" She flung out her hands and stretched high in the sky. "He loves *me!*" she shouted, her voice so loud that Annelise bent lower and covered her ears.

Abruptly, there was silence. Annelise opened her eyes to find the djinn huddled in front of her, her dark gaze bright.

"Where did they go, mortal?" she whispered.

Annelise was coy. She took a step backward and folded her hands behind her back. "It seems to me that this matter is of import to you," she mused as she stepped away.

Leila darted quickly in front of Annelise, and her eyes snapped. "Do not imagine that I will grant you any favors for telling me this, little mortal," she snarled. "Confide in me or I shall make your miserable life much, much worse."

Annelise did not have to pretend to tremble in trepidation. She pointed one shaking finger at the dark bottle. "She pulled him in there when she heard you coming."

Leila seized the bottle. She grasped it in both hands and shook it. Nothing came out. She peered into its depths, called into it, but there was no response.

She turned on Annelise with suspicion. "Where is the stopper?"

Annelise frowned in apparent confusion. "Why would such a pretty vase have a stopper?"

Leila smiled. The dark cloud swirled about her and narrowed into a plume that surrounded her. When it obscured Leila completely, the cloud dove in its entirety into the bottle, like an arrow sinking home.

Annelise snatched the stopper out of her stocking and jammed it into the neck of the bottle. The decanter shook with force in her hands and Annelise dropped it. Her eyes widened with horror as it rolled about, the fury of its occupant more than clear. She tried to grab the bottle again, but it was oddly evasive.

Annelise prayed that the stopper would hold. What would Leila do to her if she escaped? Nothing good, that was certain.

Suddenly, the bottle stilled.

Annelise waited, but it did not move again. She released her breath slowly in relief and willed her heart to slow its pace.

Leila was contained in her prison once more.

When Annelise took a step to pick up the dark bottle, her shoe crunched in the snow. She looked around, only to find that the palace was gone. It had vanished so completely that it might never have been. A snowy forest surrounded her on all sides.

Annelise's old cloak was cast on the ground just a few feet away, its location roughly corresponding to the site of the room she and Rolfe had shared, where she had left the garment. The new garb Rolfe had given her had vanished into thin air, from whence it evidently had come.

Beyond her cloak, Mephistopheles and the two palfreys glanced about themselves, their trappings and Rolfe's armor scattered about them.

The courtyard was cold.

The palace had vanished, which had to mean that the spell was broken.

Rolfe was saved! Annelise had earned his freedom, just as Azima had said she could. She had found the key and solved the riddle.

She danced in the snow with delight, then considered the position of the sun. Rolfe would appear, free of the curse, and they would ride for Beauvoir and thence to Sayerne. Surely they could reach Beauvoir this night, if they rode hard. The horses were well rested. Perhaps they would reach Viandin for the Yule as he had originally hoped. She would meet his family. Surely Adalbert could not deny his brother some small property to defend.

In truth, Annelise did not desire much more than Rolfe himself. She smiled in anticipation of Rolfe's return as she packed his belongings into his saddlebags and saddled the steeds. She would be prepared for them to ride immediately.

Mephistopheles lifted his head when she was tightening the cinch on his saddle and stared over her shoulder. His ears twitched, and Annelise guessed that her spouse was returned.

"Rolfe!" She spun with a smile.

A lone wolf stood at the perimeter of the forest, his gaze fixed upon her.

Annelise's heart sank to her toes. "No," she whispered. "No, it cannot be thus."

But the wolf began to walk toward her, and Annelise's heart filled with a dreadful certainty. The wolf was so dejected that Annelise knew it could only be Rolfe, and her fear could only be right.

She had failed.

But how and why? Annelise could not have been too late, could she? Surely, Rolfe could not be trapped forever in wolf form? No, he could not have changed fully to a wolf, for he recognized her and his disappointment was clear. There must be another explanation, though she could not think of what it might be.

She had missed some key detail and the djinn's malice had triumphed after all.

"Rolfe!" His name fell from her lips in a whisper.

The wolf slowed even more until he paused a dozen paces away. Annelise stepped closer to him, a part of her still insisting that this could not be her spouse. Perhaps she only hoped it was not Rolfe. The wolf held her gaze, as if daring her to see the truth.

He had one blue eye and one silver-gray.

Annelise had assumed that trapping Leila would make her spells void, but she had clearly been wrong. Should she have trapped the djinn at night, when Rolfe was a man? Did Rolfe even become a man anymore? Curse these djinn and their spells!

No. It was Rolfe who was cursed. Annelise wondered how she would bear to see her beloved like this for every day of their lives, yet be unable to do anything to aid him. She fell to her knees in the snow beside him, feeling foolish. "We will remain together," she told him, even as her tears fell. "We will find a way..."

But there was no way and her voice lost its conviction before she completed her promise.

He sat down before her, understanding gleaming in his eyes, understanding that made her ache with the burden of responsibility. It was so much worse to think that he knew the fate ahead of him. She held him close, savoring his warmth, and wished she was not so cursed with impulsiveness.

She should have waited until the night, when Rolfe was a man, before she trapped the djinn. The logic was obvious to her at far too late a point to make amends.

"Oh, Rolfe," she whispered as her tears began to fall. "I am sorry."

The wolf that was her spouse pushed his dark muzzle under her hand. Annelise sank her fingers into his thick fur and wept.

Rolfe licked her cheek.

It tickled and she pushed him away, but he persisted. He wriggled his nose against her neck and tickled her again while tears ran down her cheeks.

"Rolfe! This is no jest."

But her spouse evidently could not bear to see her weep and was determined to court her smile. Rolfe licked her ear and that tickled even more. Annelise pushed him away, but he pursued her, his tail wagging, his tongue mischievous.

She smiled just a little, despite herself. "You look more like a pup than a wolf," she accused and he barked. He ran a circle around her, then bowed, his tail wagging in invitation for her to play.

"You make a jest of something beyond serious!" She formed a snowball and cast it at Rolfe in frustration. He leaped and caught it in his mouth, then brought it back to her.

He dropped the snowball into her lap and wagged his tail anew. Annelise realized he was trying to encourage her, and she reached out to scratch his ears. "Do you think that we might find a way together?"

He wagged his tail and barked.

"Every puzzle has a key," she whispered and he howled in approval of that sentiment. Annelise felt her spirits rise. "We will go together to Viandin," she said and he barked again, his eyes alight. Then he ran in a circle around Annelise, and she spun to watch him. Mephistopheles eyed the pair of them, while the palfrey that had been attacked by the other wolf appeared to be nervous. When Rolfe licked Annelise's face, she laughed aloud.

She took a deep breath and framed Rolfe's furry face in her hands. She looked deeply into his eyes. "We will find another djinn," she told him. "We will convince that djinn to aid us, or we will find a magician in the hills. It is said there is an old witch near Tulley, and she might be able to cast a spell...." she caught her breath, her doubt rearing again, but she pushed it away. "If you believe, then so shall I," she vowed.

The wolf that was Rolfe seemed to grin.

Then a hunter's horn sounded in the forest.

The sound made Annelise look up in alarm. Why would there be hunters in this remote forest? To whom did this section of forest belong? She doubted it was Tulley.

The horn blew again, the sound echoing more loudly.

"They come closer," she whispered and rose to her feet. Rolfe stood beside her, bristling with attention.

In but a moment, Annelise heard the hunting party crash through the undergrowth and knew they were close at hand. Men shouted to each other and she discerned a cry that made her blood run cold.

"Wolf!"

Rolfe dug his nose into Annelise's knee. He shoved her toward Mephistopheles, his agitation making it clear he intended for her to mount.

"I cannot leave you," she protested.

He snarled, resolve in his gaze.

"But if they hunt wolves, then you are prey!"

Rolfe pushed at Annelise until she was in the saddle. Then he barked and snapped at the destrier's heels. Mephistopheles stamped and stepped sideways, snorting with disapproval. The one palfrey was more than ready to run but Annelise had seized the reins, not wanting to lose any of her husband's possessions. Rolfe kept up his attack, nipping at the palfreys and growling at Mephistopheles until the destrier broke and ran. The palfreys were fast beside him, their ears folded back and their nostrils flaring.

Rolfe pursued them, ensuring that the horses ran quickly. At least they would flee together, Annelise thought with relief. The horses crashed into the forest and toward the distant path.

Annelise clutched the reins. The sounds of the hunting party grew louder and her heart leaped to her throat.

Would they be able to escape in time?

The path became more clear ahead. Annelise thought she would follow it to the left, for the hunting party sounded as if they were to the right. And the left she thought was west, thus heading for Beauvoir.

Annelise glanced over her shoulder to check the position of the sun, only to see that Rolfe had disappeared.

Mephistopheles snorted indignantly when Annelise reined him in. She turned and peered into the shadows of the trees. Was the flicker to her left the silhouette of a quickly moving wolf? What about the one far to her right? Which wolf was Rolfe? Without seeing his eyes, she could not be certain.

The hunting party's dogs bellowed as they found a scent.

Annelise's heart skipped. Where was Rolfe?

She could not leave him to be hunted!

Surely he had not deliberately drawn the party away from her?

That was precisely what her protective husband might have done. Annelise growled in frustration and dug her heels into the destrier's side. She retraced their route, hoping to track Rolfe. To her dismay, the snow was glazed with a crusty surface that left few marks of their passage. She could not tell where Rolfe had broken off and could not identify the point in the forest where she had last seen him.

A hunter burst from the woods ahead of her and Annelise pulled Mephistopheles up short. Her heart sank at the color of his livery.

"Good afternoon, Annelise de Sayerne," Enguerrand said, his voice soft with threat.

Annelise stared in astonishment at the knight she had never expected to see again. "Enguerrand! But you rode for Beauvoir."

"So I did." Enguerrand smiled but it was not a pleasant sight. "Only to discover that there are many tales of hungry wolves this winter. I organized a hunt on the behalf of the Lord de Beauvoir to eliminate the fiends from this forest."

"Surely that is not your obligation."

"Surely any knight of honor would do the same." His smile broadened. "It is not a bad strategy, Annelise, to have a powerful man in one's debt."

Annelise caught her breath. "You think Beauvoir will grant you a prize."

"Or Tulley. In truth, I do not care which."

"What prize do you seek?"

Enguerrand chuckled. "A widow with a holding in need of administration would suit me well. By the way, where is your spouse?" Enguerrand looked to each side and his gaze was knowing as it fixed upon her. "And his palace? I thought it should be nearby."

He knew.

Annelise gestured and told a small lie. "It is easily overlooked in the snow with those white walls. It is a little deeper in the forest."

"Yet you look to have packed all your belongings." He rode around her. "Do you abandon your spouse, Annelise?"

"No, we ride out together, of course, to visit his family for the Yule."

"Yet I do not see the man."

"He had a small errand," Annelise lied. "I am to meet him on the road ahead."

Enguerrand inclined his head, making a small bow even though he was in the saddle. Annelise thought there was mockery in his manner. "Then I shall not detain you, lest that man be concerned for you."

"I thank you." Annelise swallowed. "May your hunt be a good one."

Enguerrand chuckled. "Oh, I believe it will be a fine day. It is said there is a particularly evil wolf with one eye blue and one silver-gray."

Annelise fought to hide her revulsion and was not certain she was successful. "Indeed? I have not seen such a creature."

"Indeed." Enguerrand's voice dropped. "You may rest assured that I shall take that one with my own hand. Beauvoir will be most pleased." The knight arched a brow. "Knowing how your spouse enjoys the hunt, I intended to invite him to join our party."

Annelise forced a smile. "Ah well. Perhaps another time." She gathered her reins, dismissing him with a glance, and saw his lips thin before he turned away.

The dogs were in a frenzy and not far enough away to be reassuring. Mephistopheles stepped nervously at the sound of their barking. Enguerrand spurred his steed and disappeared into the forest.

Too late, Annelise wished she had accepted Enguerrand's offer, just so she might see what was happening. How could she find Rolfe and ensure his safety?

"I wish there was something I might do!" she whispered, knowing there was not.

"Wish?"

Annelise found the friendly djinn perched on a tree branch to her left. The djinn swung her legs and smiled at Annelise. "If it is a wish you desire, I might be able to help."

"You already said you had helped all you could."

"Ah, but that was before you trapped Leila in her bottle again. A very nice accomplishment, I must say and achieved at considerable risk to yourself. Such selfless deed deserves a reward and I, my dear, am precisely the djinn to provide it. You cannot imagine what a relief it is to know that I no longer have to either endure her company or worry about her retaliation. The world is a finer place, thanks to you, so make a wish."

Annelise remembered all she had read in the book. It was gone, along with the rest of the palace.

"You are her mother. How did you decide to trap her in the first place?"

The djinn grimaced. "I was responsible, at least for bringing that one into the world, and I owed a debt to every other being once the truth of her nature was clear. I could not have stepped aside and let the blood of my blood wreak havoc upon the great goodness around us. It would have been wrong." She nodded. "Ignoring one's responsibilities has a way of going awry."

Annelise respected the djinn's choice. It could not have been easy to acknowledge the dark truth of her own child, much less to try to protect the world from her.

The djinn smiled then. "But what will your wish be, child?" She listened, glancing toward the forest. "Think quickly now, for the dogs have cornered something and I have a good idea what—or who— it is. There are limits to what I can do."

Annelise spoke impulsively and quickly. "I wish for a stag of such beauty, grace, and speed that hunter and hound will forget all else to pursue it."

The djinn's gaze was assessing. "I cannot create a living creature from nothing."

Annelise swallowed, knowing what she had to say. The life of her beloved was at stake. "Make me the stag, if you please."

The two women's gazes held for a moment and Annelise imagined that the djinn hesitated. The dogs barked more wildly.

"Quickly!" Annelise urged, and the djinn stretched her hands to the sky. She wiggled her fingers, crinkled her nose and closed her eyes as Annelise watched impatiently.

Just as she was going to urge haste again, the djinn spoke.

"As she wishes, so shall it be.
Make this stag of Annelise."

Annelise felt a tingling pass over her flesh and she slipped from Mephistopheles' saddle. She looked down and saw her flesh darkening to a rich hue of brown.

Hooves grew on Annelise's hands and feet. Her arms lengthened and she found herself on all fours as naturally as could be. A great weight was on her brow and she knew she sported an impressive rack of antlers. Her clothes fell from her and were discarded in the snow as she stamped her hooves.

"That was quite good, was it not?" the djinn asked in apparent awe of her own abilities.

But a dog howled and Annelise did not want to waste her opportunity to save Rolfe. She dashed into the forest, directly toward the hunting party and the dogs.

She had to distract the dogs to save Rolfe.

Even in her fear of failure, she was amazed by the power of the stag's form. It was exhilarating to run at such speed and with such grace. Annelise felt her long legs stretch out, and savored the agility of her new form. She leaped over fallen branches and frozen streams with untold ease. She ran with remarkable speed, her nose catching the scent of dogs, men and steeds ahead.

The dogs spotted her all at once, it seemed. They turned from whatever they had cornered, their noses high as they strained for her scent.

"God's blood, what a creature!" a man breathed. The men in the hunting party turned as one and Annelise fled in the opposite direction with all the speed she could muster. The horses thundered in pursuit, and the barking of the dogs made her pulse race.

She knew how this race would end. There could be only one outcome. Annelise had exchanged her life for Rolfe's and she did not have a single regret.

The dogs gathered around Rolfe, fangs bared. They snapped and growled as they backed him into the undergrowth. Rolfe's heart pounded in his ears as he snarled. He lunged at first one dog and then another, keeping them at bay, though the end of this tale was most clear.

He was vastly outnumbered and when he heard the horses of the hunting party approach, he knew he could not hold them off for long.

But he had to give Annelise enough time to escape.

Rolfe prayed that even now she was riding away. He hoped that Mephistopheles would guess his master's will and carry Annelise out of danger. He knew that she would prefer to join the fray and defend him, but even together they could not win.

He did not want Annelise to witness his demise.

He did not want her left alone to entertain this hunting party in the wake of their kill.

The dogs edged closer, first one then another nipping at Rolfe. Their circle tightened and their eyes glittered in anticipation of the kill. Horses whinnied and men's voices rose in close proximity. It would not be much longer.

He willed Annelise to flee.

"This one is mine!" a man cried and Rolfe feared he recognized the voice.

The dogs backed away with reluctance, growling and whining at intervals.

Enguerrand de Roussineau stepped closer, his dark eyes

gleaming with animosity. Rolfe was shocked to realize that this knight understood fully what he did. Enguerrand knew what Rolfe was; he knew that he would be killing another man, not a wolf.

Worse, he relished the opportunity.

"Ah, wolf," Enguerrand whispered. "You will be the fare at the feast to celebrate my marriage to the fair widow Annelise." He smiled. "I suspect her spouse will fail to meet her this day and I shall be compelled to escort her to Beauvoir with our kill. I wonder how hungry she will prove to be." His voice dropped to a malicious whisper, one that his companions would not overhear. "It matters little. I will have her inheritance all the same, as well as yours, and you can do nothing about it but die."

Rolfe was filled with new purpose, both from the need to defend his beloved and his determination to apologize to her for his doubt. He would not leave this man to claim Annelise as his prize. He would not abandon her to the cruelty of such a villain.

If he or Enguerrand must die, Rolfe knew which he would choose.

The wolf within, cornered and threatened, raged to defend himself. Rolfe let the beast take ascendance.

Teeth bared, he lunged for Enguerrand.

The destrier shied away and the knight cried out in fear. Rolfe had no intention of granting the rogue any respite. Just before his teeth closed on the man's forearm, Enguerrand jerked away. Rolfe's claw grazed the steed's neck. The smell and taste of blood awakened a fury within the wolf even as the horse shied.

Enguerrand shouted and his hunting knife slashed Rolfe's shoulder. Rolfe snapped and twisted, and the knife fell to the ground as his teeth sank into Enguerrand's hand. The knight cried out in pain, flung Rolfe aside and retreated.

The other men circled closer but Enguerrand waved them off. "I said this one is mine," he said through gritted teeth. He and Rolfe circled each other, the dogs whining to join the fray. The fallen dagger glinted in the snow and Rolfe wished he had the ability to use it.

But no. He must work with the weapons he had been granted. In this form, he had wickedly sharp teeth and claws. He was cunning and he was quick.

He had the wolf's hunger.

Enguerrand unsheathed another dagger and gathered up his steed's reins with purpose.

Rolfe circled the steed, snarling, increasing the horse's fear. He had no intention of injuring the horse, but hoped it might throw its rider. He eyed the knight's mail, seeking a weakness. Enguerrand's hauberk hung to his knees, but it was slit on both sides at the hip. He wore heavy leather boots, but no other protection on his legs than his wool chausses.

And for this hunt, Enguerrand had left behind his helmet.

Fool! His bare neck gleamed with promise for a wolf's sharp teeth.

Rolfe leaped suddenly for Enguerrand, latching into that man's thigh. The horse shied, then reared when it felt the weight of the wolf. Enguerrand screamed with pain as he and Rolfe fell from the steed together. The horse stumbled, then fled, abandoning its rider.

Rolfe and Enguerrand battled for supremacy, rolling in the snow, each unable to strike the killing blow.

To Rolfe's surprise, the other knights did not rally to defend Enguerrand. He felt the dogs' attention waver and heard a large creature thunder through the brush nearby. Dogs and horses turned away and the dogs bayed. Rolfe heard them depart in pursuit of some other prize. Left to their own battle, knight and wolf tussled in the snow.

If he accomplished nothing else before he died, Rolfe would ensure that this man could not kill the sparkle in Annelise's eyes.

Enguerrand raised the knife. Rolfe bit hard into his palm before the blade could be planted. Rolfe's teeth slid easily through the heavy leather, and he savored the other man's cry of pain. He bit harder this time, wanting to inflict damage. The taste of the blood made the wolf lust for more. Enguerrand seized the knife in his other hand and drove it into Rolfe's shoulder. Rolfe dove for Enguerrand's chest at the same time that the knife sank home. He dug at the neck of his hauberk with one paw, exposing the knight's throat, and summoned the wolf.

Enguerrand must have realized his intention for he struggled with new force and shouted for assistance. His men were gone, though, and his entreaty fell on deaf ears. He made little sound before Rolfe's sharp teeth were buried in his throat. The wolf bit and ripped and tore, shredding the flesh until Enguerrand fought no more. The villain shuddered, then went still, his blood staining the snow and Rolfe's fur.

It was only when he saw his own blood mingled with that of the knight in the snow that Rolfe recalled that he had been injured, as well. He was shaking and it took no small effort to restrain the wolf again.

But he was a knight in his heart. He would not maul his opponent. Rolfe compelled himself to back away from Enguerrand's corpse.

The baying of the dogs was more fevered than it had been before and he wondered what they hunted with such enthusiasm. Was it the same creature that had distracted them? Despite the pain of his wound, Rolfe trotted in pursuit of the sound as quickly as he could manage.

He was leaving a trail of blood and he knew it, just as he knew the injury turned him from predator to prey.

Rolfe caught his breath in awe to see that the dogs had cornered a majestic stag. Rolfe both admired it and wanted to claim it, with a vigor that was alien to both himself and the wolf.

He was no hunter, and the wolf collected no trophies.

There was something unnatural about the desire the beast aroused within his breast. Perhaps the beast itself was unnatural. Rolfe had an uncommon urge to take this fine creature as a prize, an urge beyond anything he had felt as either wolf or knight. The hunters and dogs clustered there had an unusual gleam in their eyes, as though they were bewitched.

Suddenly they lunged at the stag and it fell, disappearing beneath the pack of hounds. There was a strange shimmer even as the men cried out in triumph and Rolfe heard the dogs whine again.

He could make no sense of it, much less the cursing of one of the men, but assumed the dogs had damaged the prize.

Rolfe was distracted from their hunt because he felt himself changing. He gasped as his own flesh appeared before his eyes, as the fur disappeared, as dark nails rescinded. He stretched and stood tall, noting that the sun was still sinking toward the horizon.

He was a man and in daylight.

The spell was broken! Rolfe did not know how or why, but he was profoundly relieved. If pressed, he would have wagered that his marvel of a wife, his beloved Annelise, had found the key to the puzzle.

He had only to find her.

CHAPTER FOURTEEN

olfe hastened to the tower, hoping that he would find Annelise waiting for him there.

The sight of Mephistopheles and the palfrey standing outside the tower seemed a sure sign that his expectation was sound. Both horses were saddled and the saddlebags appeared to be packed. Rolfe smiled with pleasure that his lady understood his intentions so well. He found his garments neatly folded within the destrier's saddlebags and dressed his wound as well as he was able. It was in an awkward location, but he managed to staunch the blood. He did not want Annelise to see it at its worst. He dressed quickly and took the stairs three at a time, calling for her.

But the tower room was empty.

Indeed, it did not look as though anyone had entered the chamber since he had left it that morning. Rolfe looked out the windows, certain he would catch a glimpse of his wife on some errand outside.

Nothing moved in the surrounding forest.

Where was Annelise?

Rolfe frowned, then went down the stairs to confront Mephistopheles. "Where is she? Where did you take her?"

The steed eyed him for a long moment, then snorted and bent

to push his nose into the snow. He might have been disgusted with his master, though Rolfe could not fathom why.

The sun was sinking toward the horizon. They should depart soon, if they were to put most of the forest behind them before nightfall.

Rolfe frowned. Where could Annelise have gone?

Surely no evil had befallen her while he was battling Enguerrand? The very notion made his chest tighten in fear. Rolfe surveyed his surroundings. Perhaps she had left footprints in the snow. He jumped when he saw the second djinn sitting in a tree, watching him.

She had not been there when he arrived, he was certain of it.

He had learned from his past, to be sure, and was determined to not insult her. "Good day to you, *madame*," he said with a low bow.

She smiled. "If nothing else, you have learned manners from this adventure."

"Then it is over?"

The djinn nodded with an enthusiasm that made the balls on the rim of her hat swing. "That it is indeed. Just as I foretold."

Rolfe bowed again. "I must thank you for your intervention in this matter. It is impossible to imagine how bleak it would have been to spend my entire life alone as a wolf."

The djinn eyed him. "I did not break the spell alone," she said. "Though I appreciate your thanks, you owe the greatest gratitude to someone else."

Something about her tone made Rolfe fear that something was amiss.

"Why exactly did the curse end?" he asked.

The djinn stood up and brushed her kirtle. "It was ended by the power of love, of course."

"Whose love?"

"Why, Annelise's love for you, of course!" The djinn shook her head. "Did you not witness the events of this day?"

Rolfe sensed then that Annelise's absence was a bad omen. "Perhaps you could be so kind as to review events for me."

"You were busy with that troublesome knight, were you not?" The djinn shrugged and took a step toward him. She produced a familiar dark bottle, its cork firmly in place, and tossed it between her hands before Rolfe. "Annelise trapped Leila within the bottle again, which, naturally, is why the palace disappeared."

"But how?"

"It does not matter." The djinn waved her hand and the bottle danced from her grip. Both knight and djinn gasped, and Rolfe snatched the bottle out of the air just before it hit the ground. He handed it back to the djinn, relieved that it had not shattered, and she smiled. "Suffice it to say that Annelise used the tools she possessed to solve that dilemma."

"What will you do with the bottle?"

The djinn eyed the decanter and pursed her lips. "I shall appoint myself as its guardian. There truly is no other way to ensure that it remains corked forever."

"But why would you want to take such a task upon yourself? I had thought there was no love lost between you and the other one."

The djinn trailed a fingertip down the neck of the bottle, her gaze averted. For an instant, Rolfe thought her much older than he had originally believed. "There was a time when we were close," she said. "I owe her no less."

Then the djinn shot a glance Rolfe's way. "Annelise is a most clever woman. I should hope you appreciate that."

"Yes." Rolfe felt a glow of pride.

"Which is why the result is all the more tragic," the djinn said, kindling Rolfe's fear again.

"Tragic? What do you mean? What result?"

"I granted her a wish," the djinn confessed. "It was only fitting after what she had done, but truly, I could never have guessed what she would have asked me to do." Her gaze was fixed upon Rolfe with a steadiness that told him she had finally arrived at her point.

"What did she ask?" His voice was no more than a whisper.

"She chose to become a stag of such beauty that the hunters were distracted from their intent to kill you."

The breath left Rolfe's lungs in shock. Not Annelise! He stared at the snow surrounding him without comprehending what he saw.

It was only too easy to recall the dogs and hunters in pursuit of that stag. Rolfe remembered his own sense that there was something enchanted about the stag to so snare their interest. He thought of the stag disappearing from view as the hounds attacked for the kill and turned away from the djinn. His mouth was dry and he felt raw.

The stag, which was truly Annelise, had been killed.

Rolfe was devastated. His future no longer possessed any promise. His recovery from the spell was no longer an event to celebrate, for the one person with whom he might have rejoiced was lost to him forever.

"She traded her life for mine," he whispered.

"Indeed!" the djinn confirmed, with an enthusiasm that Rolfe found inappropriate. He turned to watch her, incredulous that she could be so cheerful. It was evident that djinns had not hearts at all. "The power of love, of sacrifice, was what ended your curse."

"But Annelise is dead!" Rolfe said, his voice rising in anger. "How can you be so indifferent to her fate? She gave her life for mine!"

"Annelise made her choice," the djinn replied. She pivoted and began to walk away. "As we all must make our own."

Rolfe pursued her. "Is there not something we can do? Can you not make another spell?"

The djinn glanced over her shoulder and her expression was inscrutable. "What is done is done," she said. "You must make your peace with it."

"This is unfair!" Rolfe roared. "It was not Annelise's curse, nor her battle! Why should she be compelled to pay the price?"

The djinn shook her head. "I have told you already that she chose her path. There is nothing else to be done." She lifted her chin. "Perhaps you will be glad to see the last of djinns in your life."

Then she snapped her fingers and disappeared in a puff of rosy smoke.

She was gone.

Annelise was gone.

And Rolfe was more alone than he had ever been in his life. He walked back to Mephistopheles like a man in a dream.

He would never again hear Annelise's laughter.

It was humbling that she had given her all just to see the curse upon him broken.

Rolfe caught his breath, realizing his own mistake. He had never told her that he loved her. Annelise had been denied the one gift he might have given her. Love was the sole thing that Annelise valued and a marriage of love was her one desire. He had never confessed his love for her, thus denying her that pleasure.

Because he had been afraid to trust her fully.

Rolfe was a knave of the lowest order.

He dropped his head into his hands and, for the first time since he had been a small child, he wept. His tears were for Annelise, and for his own folly in not appreciating the marvel of his wife when she was by his side.

Long moments later, Rolfe thought he felt the brush of fingertips on his shoulder. The fleeting touch was so light that he might have imagined it. He did not lift his head, for if the djinn was back, he did not want to know. "Leave me," he muttered, but the weight of that hand landed upon his shoulder.

"It is not so bad a wound as that," Annelise whispered, and Rolfe could not believe his ears. "See? The blood runs clearly. You have bound it but I think it needs a stitch or two. Shed your tunic and chemise, and let me see what can be done."

"Annelise!" Rolfe rose to his feet and seized her hands in his own, unable to believe that she stood before him.

She smiled at him and touched her fingertips to his cheek. "You are not cursed any longer."

"No! And you, my beloved lady wife, are not dead." With relief, Rolfe scooped Annelise into his arms, holding her so tightly that there could be no doubt that she was real. He bent and captured her lips beneath his own, then kissed her with all his love.

Annelise kissed him back. Her arms wound around his neck and she pressed herself against him with a sweetness he had feared never to savor again.

When he lifted his head, she met his gaze. "You thought me dead?"

"The djinn said you had asked to become that stag." Rolfe's heart leaped as he relived his fears. "I saw the hounds give chase! I saw them close in for the kill."

"The djinn came," Annelise said, shaking her head in wonder. "Azima. She said that a good deed should not go unpunished and snatched me away. All I saw was a rosy gold sparkle after I heard her voice, then I was alone in the snow." She frowned. "I thought I was where the palace used to be so I came here in search of you." She reached up and framed his face in her hands, her eyes filled with fear. "I feared Enguerrand had killed you, until I found him."

"Surely he is dead," Rolfe said, fearing it might be otherwise.

Annelise nodded. "There were wolves..." She shuddered. "His men were trying to force them away." She grimaced. "But when I saw that he was lost—not a wolf with one blue eye and one silver-gray—I dared to hope that you had survived. I ran here."

"And I came here in search of you." He kissed her again, still marveling that she was with him and safe. "The djinn told me what you had done." He cupped her face in his hands, his fingertips tracing a scratch on her cheek. He stared down into her eyes, so filled with promise and love, and ached at how close he had come to losing her. "But why would you put yourself in such danger? You should never have taken such a risk...."

Annelise smiled. "Why did you try to lead the hunters away from me, then?"

The answer was so obvious that Rolfe was surprised she needed to hear the words. "Because I had to see you safe." He cleared his throat and held her gaze. "Because I love you, and your survival is of greater import than mine."

She flushed even as her eyes sparkled with pleasure. "I am glad," she whispered. "For I love you so, Rolfe de Viandin." After he kissed her again, she sighed with contentment. "It seems that I wed for love after all."

Rolfe stared down at Annelise in horror as he realized the truth of their situation. "Annelise," he whispered. "The palace is gone. My gift for Adalbert is gone. I am still a younger son, still landless, still without the right to wed. I am beholden to my older brother for all I have and might have." He smiled at his wife. "In truth, I have little to offer you but myself."

"But that is all I want!" she declared. "There could be no other for me but you, Rolfe," she continued. "I do not care where we live or what we eat or what manner of clothes we wear, as long as we are together." She tapped one finger in the middle of his chest and Rolfe's heart began to sing. "My home is wherever you are."

"And mine is wherever you might be, my Annelise." Rolfe smiled and pushed his fingers through her hair, which had loosed itself from her braid. "You will not blame me for wanting more for you, though."

"A life with you is the only life I want," she said with a ferocity that was familiar. "We could live in a hut in the forest and I would be content with you by my side."

She was so solemn that Rolfe had to tease her a little. "So long as there are no djinns," he said and she laughed.

"Or wolves."

Rolfe sobered. "Let us hope that Adalbert will be convinced to grant me some small holding to call my own. I could defend a town on his borders."

Annelise stretched to her toes and kissed him sweetly. "You can do any deed, sir, for you are a knight, a champion, and a man who has defeated djinns."

Rolfe crushed Annelise in his arms and kissed her.

He owed everything to the bold bride whom the Fates had brought to his palace gates. Rolfe vowed silently that he would spend the rest of his days and nights ensuring that Annelise was confident of his love.

"Let us ride toward Beauvoir with all haste," he suggested, even as the sky darkened. "The wolves may be sated for the moment and they will be less likely to attack a moving party." He smiled at Annelise. "I would reach Viandin with all haste."

He was lifting Annelise to the palfrey's saddle when he recalled Marcus' tale. The dark decanter was said to make dreams come true. Was it possible that the djinn's sorcery had another surprise in store?

It had become too cold to snow as their horses climbed the steep road to Beauvoir pass the next morning and the wind was biting. The horses were tired, but they seemed to sense that relief lay ahead. Annelise watched Rolfe covertly as they rode, afraid this might be the last time they rode together and at ease.

Her heart swelled with love for him and she admired the proud line of his profile, the purpose in his grip on the reins. He was the kind of man she had always hoped to marry, yet she feared their union might soon be compelled to end.

There were no witnesses to their exchange of vows, and she knew her overlord was an ambitious man. Would he choose to ignore her marriage to Rolfe, because Rolfe had no wealth or land? Would Tulley care that their match was consummated?

Or would that simply diminish her own prospects?

The silhouette of Beauvoir became clear, feeding Annelise's doubts. Rolfe pushed onward, urging the horses forward when they might have faltered. There was no ready way to Viandin without passing through Tulley's holding and Annelise knew they could not transverse the breadth of that holding without rest.

She did not trust the Lord de Tulley not to turn her presence into an asset.

"Do you intend to spend another night in the cold?" Rolfe asked, his tone teasing as he glanced toward her. "Truly, my Annelise, you slow your palfrey more and more."

"I would prefer we never arrive at Beauvoir keep," she admitted.

"I would welcome shelter this night," her spouse replied. "A place by the fire, a bite of stew, and my lady's smile is all I need to be content."

Annelise could not summon the smile she knew he wished to see. "Beauvoir keep is Tulley's abode, on the border of his lands."

"So you have said before. Perhaps they will have word of your brother, Yves."

"It was here that Tulley tried to compel me to wed Enguerrand."

Rolfe granted her a look. "But he cannot do as much now."

"He could accuse you of foul play."

"Nay." Rolfe shook his head, his manner adamant.

"Enguerrand was a villain and he threatened my lady wife with violence. He endeavored to kill me. I merely defended us both."

Annelise bit her lip. Rolfe did not know how demanding Tulley could be.

She jumped when his gloved hand fell over her own. He had slowed the destrier to ride beside her and leaned closer as he tightened his grip over her fingers. "Tell me what you fear, Annelise," he invited, his gaze searching hers.

"That Tulley will not acknowledge our match, for he did not arrange it."

"But we have consummated our marriage."

"I fear that might only diminish my future prospects."

"Nay," Rolfe said with conviction. "You are my wife and will remain so. I will fight every authority, from here to Rome and back again, to see that you remain so."

"If Tulley believes Quinn to be dead, he might send me back to Sayerne, to be its lady."

Rolfe nodded, untroubled by this prospect. "Then we shall govern it together and be good vassals to him." He smiled at her. "We would have a holding then."

Annelise winced. "I should hate to return there at all." Sayerne was too filled with dark memories for her to find any happiness there and she knew it well.

And she did not trust Tulley.

Rolfe raised his gloved hand to her cheek. "All will be well, my Annelise," he said softly. "I promise you as much."

"The choice might not be yours to make," she whispered, but he winked at her with a confidence that could only feed her own.

"Do you know something I do not?"

"Only that Quinn de Sayerne is not dead."

"You know my brother?"

"I fought with him in Outremer." Rolfe lifted a finger when she might have protested. "And contrary to all that you have been told, he is a fine and honorable knight. I would trust him with my life." Rolfe smiled. "It seems that you siblings have much in common, more even than the hue of your eyes."

Annelise was astonished to silence and more than a little

skeptical.

"Hail, gatekeeper!" Rolfe called for they neared the barred gates. "We seek shelter this night of nights!"

"We offer no shelter to travelers," replied the gatekeeper. "But should you have coin for the toll, you are welcome to pass."

"But this lady is from a holding pledged to your overlord," Rolfe insisted. "Surely a place might be found for a loyal vassal?"

A slot in the gate slid open and the gleam of eyes appeared in the darkness beyond. "Who is she?"

"Annelise de Sayerne."

"And you?"

"Rolfe de Viandin."

Viandin. Annelise frowned to herself, temporarily distracted from her concerns. It was odd that the name of that estate now seemed familiar to her. She was certain she had heard the name of that estate before, but could not recall where or when.

There was activity behind the gates and a flurry of whispers. Footsteps echoed as someone evidently ran across the bailey to the keep itself.

Annelise watched the snow gather on the pine trees around the gates and wished she could make this moment last forever. Rolfe eased Mephistopheles closer and claimed her gloved hand, lifting it to his lips. His eyes shone, one blue and one silver gray. "Believe, my lady," he urged her in a whisper, then kissed her fingertips.

Annelise wanted to believe, more than anything in all of Christendom.

The gates opened then, as if to prove her husband right.

"The Lord de Beauvoir grants you welcome, Rolfe de Viandin and Annelise de Sayerne," the keeper said, his tone more friendly. "Indeed, the Lord de Tulley awaits the lady in the great hall."

Tulley was in residence. It was the worst possibility Annelise could have imagined. She swallowed, knowing the moment she dreaded was upon her, but kept her head high. They rode through the gates and dismounted in the bailey. Squires came to lead the steeds to the stables, vowing that all three would be brushed and fed.

Rolfe took Annelise's hand, clearly intending to escort her to the hall, and she was glad that he would be by her side.

But the guard at the portal raised his hand before Rolfe. "The lord requested the lady come alone."

Annelise glanced at Rolfe, knowing her trepidation showed. He smiled, obviously intending to reassure her. "I shall see to the horses," he murmured, his gaze warm upon her. "No doubt Mephistopheles will welcome some attention from me."

Annelise could not repress a smile of her own before her husband turned away. She took a deep breath as the guard led her toward the great hall. As she stepped into the shadows of a corridor, Tulley's annoyed tone carried to her ears and her heart began to pound.

Rolfe waved off the squires and brushed down his steeds himself. This was a task he had missed, for the rhythmic motion helped him to compose his thoughts. He thought of Annelise and his love for her warmed him to his toes, prompting him to whistle as he worked. He knew she feared the worst, but he hoped for the best—and he would do whatever was necessary to ensure their future together.

She would believe him soon enough.

"You are in fine spirits for a knight feared to be lost forever," a familiar voice said from behind him.

Rolfe spun around, not believing his ears.

But he was right. His mother, Hildegarde de Viandin, stood at the end of the stall.

Her ebony hair was just tinged with silver, just as it had been when he had left Viandin. She stood as straight and proud as he remembered. Indeed, she might not have aged a day since his departure. Her sapphire wool kirtle made her eyes look a more vivid hue and accented her slender form.

She had eyes like his, one blue and one silver-gray.

"Mother!" Rolfe said in amazement.

She twirled a piece of mistletoe in her fingers. "Surely you have a kiss for your mother after all these years? It is the season, after all."

"Of course!" Rolfe stepped to her side and pecked her on both cheeks, holding her shoulders in his hands. She felt smaller to him and a little more frail. "What are you doing at Beauvoir? Why are you so far from home?"

His mother ruffled his hair affectionately, as though he were but a boy and not a man who towered a good foot taller than she. "I feared to never lay eyes upon you again," she whispered and her voice wavered.

"I wrote! Did that company of troubadours not arrive at Viandin? I confess they were not the most likely to be reliable, but I had few choices..."

"They came but it was months ago. Why did you take so much longer?"

Rolfe had no good reply for that, at least not one his mother would believe.

She eyed him, then smiled. "How many maidens have you seduced on your journey?"

"Only one."

"Truly?"

"Truly."

"My good son." She studied him and her strength seemed to falter. Rolfe thought he saw a tear gleam on her dark lashes. "When they said a Rolfe de Viandin had come to the gates, I could scarce believe my ears...."

Her voice broke and Rolfe gathered her into an impulsive hug. "I am here, Mother, and as vital as might be." He felt her shaking and held her tightly. It was not like his mother to be overcome by emotion and he wondered that she had changed so much in his absence.

Finally, she pulled back a little and looked into his eyes. Her hand ran over his shoulder as if she could not quite believe he stood before her again. "You were never so quick with affection before."

"You never seemed in need of it."

"How else have you changed?"

Rolfe smiled. "In a thousand ways, Mother."

"Aye, that is the way of war," she said softly and held his gaze for a long moment. When she took a step back, her voice was crisp, which he found more familiar. "It is a long way to Outremer."

"Aye. It is." Rolfe picked up the brush and turned back to his task. "Yet here I am, hale and hearty, and on my way home, none the worse for wear."

"On a different steed."

"Alas, Sebastien did not take well to the heat."

"He died?"

"I sold him to a knight returning to Paris when it was clear he suffered overmuch, and bought this destrier instead, for he was bred in Outremer." Rolfe paused in his task. "I wonder if Sebastien might be found and purchased again. He was a fine creature."

"You do not have need of two destriers," Hildegarde said, as pragmatic as ever. Rolfe acknowledged that he might not be able to afford two. She followed Rolfe into the stall, eyeing Mephistopheles warily. "Could you have found one any larger or blacker? He looks as fearsome as a demon."

"Then you will well appreciate his name."

"Indeed?"

"It is Mephistopheles." Rolfe grinned when his mother frowned in disapproval and she rapped him sharply on the shoulder with the mistletoe.

"It is most unfitting to ride a beast cursed with such a name! Ill fortune could only dog your footsteps! Have you no regard for your own welfare?"

Rolfe smiled to himself, knowing immediately that his mother and Annelise would agree on more issues than this. "And have you no regard for your health?" he retorted cheerfully. "What madness has you far from home in the dead of winter?"

His mother's face fell, and Rolfe knew that something was amiss.

"What is it? What is wrong?"

"I came to seek you out, but the snow stopped us here. I would have ridden all the way to Jerusalem if need be. Bertrand, you may know, trained with your father, and he offered my party accommodation for as long as required."

"But why did you leave Viandin in this season? Surely nothing is amiss there?"

"No." Hildegarde cleared her throat and looked away. She watched the posey as she tapped it against the side of the stall. "Viandin runs as ceaselessly as always it does."

Rolfe watched her as he waited, puzzled.

She glanced up at him, dismay gleaming in her eyes. "Last fall, Adalbert took the ague."

"But he is recovered?"

To his dismay, his mother shook her head. "He is dead, Rolfe."

Adalbert dead. It was impossible to believe. Rolfe swore softly and stepped away. The homecoming he had anticipated would not occur. Adalbert would not stalk out to the bailey, complaining all the while about his lot. They would not shake hands, as they always did when Rolfe returned home. They would not look into each other's eyes for a silent moment and see the admiration each had for the other.

Adalbert would not wink. He always turned away after that wink, bellowing for the ostler and the cook, complaining heartily about the trouble caused by those who arrive unexpectedly at the gates.

He would not have the opportunity to plague Rolfe with questions. Rolfe realized how much he had been looking forward to sharing his adventures with his older brother. Usually, they talked so much that their meal became stone-cold before they had taken more than a bite.

It was unthinkable that Adalbert was not at Viandin.

Rolfe cleared his throat and his words were husky. "He did not suffer?"

"It was quick," his mother admitted. "Too quick in one way and too arduous in another."

Rolfe's shoulders sagged in relief, but his mother was not finished. She laid a hand upon his arm. "I have not the will or the strength to administer Viandin, Rolfe, though I have endeavored to do my best in your absence." Her voice was low with concern. "I hope you will not be disappointed in my efforts when you take the reins of the estate."

Take the reins? Rolfe turned to look at his mother for a moment.

She smiled at him. "You are heir, Rolfe," she said. "Viandin is yours."

All the breath left Rolfe's lungs. He was no longer a landless younger son, but Lord de Viandin.

He had something to offer Annelise.

His mother frowned as she continued. "I must apologize, though, for despite my finest efforts, I was unable to procure a bride for you."

"I told you, Mother, that I had met a maiden. She loves me and I love her..."

"Whimsy!" his mother said. "Even Bertrand tried, without success, to convince a local noblewoman, name of Annelise de Sayerne, to take your hand. I fear that young women are less enamored of matches made without a meeting these days, though I do not know why they should imagine themselves above such sensible solutions." She patted Rolfe on the cheek even as he marveled at her words. "Perhaps the ladies have need of a taste of your own charm."

Rolfe's lips twitched at her confession. They had tried to match him with Annelise? He was the other suitor she had deemed unfitting? It was the threat of wedding him that had driven her to the convent...and hence to him?

The coincidence could only make him laugh aloud.

"Rolfe!" His mother frowned at him. "I should hardly think the matter amusing. Despite the insult that witch Rosalinde granted you, you will have to consider marriage, whether you have the inclination or not. It is part of your responsibility to Viandin to ensure the bloodline continues...." She suddenly fell silent and glared at Rolfe's hand. "Where is your ring? Surely, you did not lose the token I granted you?" She caught her breath and took a step back. "Surely, you did not sell it?"

"No, Mother," Rolfe said with a smile. "It was used to seal the vows between my wife and I."

"Wife?"

"The maiden I spoke of."

His mother exhaled in a hiss. "You married? Without consultation? Without any consideration of her lineage or suitability..."

Rolfe silenced his mother with a touch. "The lady's name is Annelise de Sayerne."

Hildegarde's eyes widened, then a reluctant smile curved her lips. "Well, does that not take all?" she murmured. "I always knew you had the devil's own charm. Evidently, you have his luck, as well." She tweaked Rolfe's ear and he abandoned his brush, beckoning for the ostler to finish the task.

"Come, Mother. There is someone I would like you to meet."

"I should think so," his mother retorted. "A wife, And without telling me first." Her manner was indignant, but the sparkle of delight in her eyes revealed her true feelings. "At least she has the wit to love you. That shows her good sense."

Hildegarde and Annelise would get along just fine. Rolfe's step was light as they left the stables.

All had come right, just as he had promised his lady wife.

Annelise was shown to a room to one side of the great hall. She glimpsed the boughs of cedar hung in the larger room and realized that it must be very near the Yule. She had lost track of time in the djinn's palace. Would it be possible to reach Viandin in time for the festivities? She hoped Tulley did not intend to delay them.

That lord's bright gaze locked upon her as he pivoted to face her.

"Come in, Annelise," he said, as emotionless as ever.

Annelise swallowed her fear and obeyed.

"I had understood that you were to join the Sisters of Ste. Radegund a short time ago," the overlord said. His gaze flicked over her garments. "Without my permission, I might add. But you do not wear nun's garb."

"I did not return to the convent, sir." She spoke more demurely than was her inclination. This man held her future in his hands, and Annelise had no intention of annoying him unnecessarily.

"Why not?"

"Our party was beset by hunting wolves, sir, after we had lost our way. The man I travel with granted me refuge."

Tulley arched a brow. "Indeed. Yves returned here with the others. I sent him on to France, to fight in the tournaments."

Annelise bowed, relieved to hear these tidings. "It was his fondest desire, sir."

"Yet he was concerned about your fate. He feared the wolves had taken you."

"I was more fortunate than that, sir."

"Indeed." Tulley leaned closer. "But why did you abandon Sayerne in the first place? I did not grant you leave to do so."

"But you summoned Quinn." Annelise shuddered. "I could not simply await him there."

Tulley's gaze turned assessing and he settled back in his chair. "You have no reason to fear your brother."

"It seems to be only good sense, given the tales I have heard of Quinn's cruelty."

Tulley arched a brow. "But from whom did you hear those tales?"

"From my father."

His gaze locked with hers, as resolute as ever. "A man we both know to be of somewhat unsavory character."

Annelise saw in Tulley's gaze that he knew what had transpired at Sayerne all those years past. "You knew!" she breathed. "You knew and yet you did nothing."

"On the contrary, I did all that I could!" Tulley's tone was savage. He pushed to his feet and paced the room, his frustration evident. "Law maintains that a man cannot be accused of a crime without evidence or witness, Annelise. There was neither! I had no option but to send you away and secure your safety, and that was what I did."

Silence reigned while Annelise came to terms with this news.

"So now you would compel me to return to Sayerne."

Tulley looked surprised. "Why would I do that?"

"Because Quinn is not home and I am the only other legitimate child. I am not a fool, sir, so pray do not treat me as one."

Tulley smiled before he sobered again. "Trust me, Annelise, even if that were the case I have learned my lesson about leaving a woman—heiress or no—in charge of an estate. No, I would find a man I could trust and grant the estate to him on the condition he wed you.”

Annelise parted her lips but Tulley raised a finger imperiously, commanding her silence.

“But that prospect is not before you. I have had word that Quinn will shortly return home to claim his legacy.” The overlord fixed his gaze upon Annelise. “Which leaves the issue of what to do with you. Perhaps Quinn had best resolve the matter.”

“I will not wait for my brother, regardless of what you deem his character to be,” Annelise said. “I have made my own choice...”

“I would never have permitted you to wed Enguerrand de Roussineau, regardless of how appealing his entreaties might have been!” Tulley jabbed his finger through the air at an astonished Annelise. “I was absent for but a month and all nearly came awry. I would have seen that match annulled, if I had to ride to Rome myself to make it so.”

“Truly?”

“Truly.” Tulley spoke with vigor. “The line of Roussineau is so badly tainted that the only sensible course is to let its seed die out.” He inhaled. “I should not say it aloud, but praise be that fool rode to hunt. The wolves have saved me a great deal of trouble.”

“I never wanted to wed Enguerrand,” Annelise admitted.

“Truly?”

“Truly.” Annelise smiled as her overlord considered her.

He frowned. “Perhaps you should return to the convent. Although, I would be more inclined to spend coin upon a dowry than a convent donation.” His gaze flicked to hers. “At least then your allegiance could yield tangible benefits.”

At that meager encouragement, Annelise took a deep breath and unclasped her hands. Tulley, who missed very little, immediately spied Rolfe’s ring upon her left hand. He rose to his feet again, his eyes flashing. “Tell me you did not wed without my permission.”

“I did, sir.” Annelise swallowed. “It seemed only fitting, sir, especially as the knight and I were sequestered alone together at night, and he had saved my life.”

Tulley exhaled, his gaze falling to the ring again. "And who performed the nuptial mass?"

"We exchanged a pledge with each other," Annelise replied. "I have heard that such vows hold weight."

"Yes," Tulley admitted to her relief. "Among villeins, that practice is prevalent enough. Who might this knight be? Is the match fitting?"

"He returns from Outremer where he has been on crusade."

Tulley's eyes gleamed. "I find these credentials promising, but has he a holding?"

"No, my lord," Annelise was compelled to admit. "He is a younger son."

Tulley frowned at her in disapproval. "Impetuous," he muttered. "And what is his name?"

"Rolfe de Viandin."

"Rolfe de Viandin! Let me see that ring."

Annelise showed it to the older man, who threw back his head and laughed. "Annelise! This was the knight you refused!"

Annelise blinked. "I do not believe as much, sir..."

"Yes, you did. Bertrand said that when he presented Hildegarde's offer for your hand in marriage to her son, you declined and chose the convent instead. Hildegarde's son is Rolfe de Viandin."

Annelise was astonished.

"And he is a younger son without a holding no more, Annelise," Tulley continued. "His brother has died."

"How terrible. He will be disappointed by the loss."

"But not by the gain, if he is a man of good sense." Tulley fixed her with a look. "Is he?"

"Yes, sir."

"That is good news indeed." Tulley's eyes gleamed with amusement and satisfaction. "To think that I feared I might not be able to encourage you to make this match. It is a good one, Annelise, and an alliance I deem most fitting for you."

Annelise raised her hands to her mouth, not daring to laugh in her delight. Then Tulley grinned and Annelise could not help but smile in return. She sobered then, recalling her manners. "I am sorry to hear of Rolfe's brother's demise…"

"And his mother Hildegarde will undoubtedly welcome your condolences."

"His mother?"

"She is here, Annelise."

Annelise's heart leaped for fear that Rolfe's mother might not approve of her.

"What is it?" Tulley demanded, his gaze as shrewd as ever.

"I hope the lady does not take affront that I dared to wed her son without her permission."

"I shall ensure that she does not." Tulley eyed her. "In fact, we should make the most of this opportunity to see your vows exchanged again before witnesses."

"My lord?"

Tulley crossed the chamber with purpose, claiming Annelise's elbow. "Come along, Annelise. Bertrand will summon the priest and the hall is festive. We shall see those vows of yours exchanged again this very night and duly celebrated. I want none to question the alliance your spouse and I will make."

Annelise could scarce believe her good fortune. How could she have doubted that all would come right in the end? Tulley escorted her into the great hall and she saw Rolfe on the far side, with an older noblewoman. She had dark hair and as Annelise stepped closer, she saw that the woman had eyes just like Rolfe's. One was blue and one silver-gray.

Would their children have such eyes? She could not wait to know for certain.

"Rolfe! We are to be wed this very night!" Annelise ran across the great hall and he swung her into his arms with a grin.

"We *are* wed, my Annelise," he corrected and punctuated his words with a kiss. "And we shall stay that way forevermore."

Indeed, Annelise could not have hoped for greater promise than that.

EPILOGUE

It was in the fall of 1102 that Annelise's labor contractions began.

Rolfe was banned from the solar at Viandin and found himself in the hall with little to do but wait. His wife's cries made him cringe, but he avoided both drink and companionship. He paced the length of the hall and back, time and again.

Childbirth carried no small risk and he feared for Annelise's welfare. Rolfe recalled every moment he had spent with his beloved wife and knew that there had not been enough of those moments to satisfy him. She had taught him so much about love, given him a faith in the unseen, shared with him her passion for life and all its joys.

He had so much, but he wanted only more.

Twilight crept into the hall and lengthened the shadows. A servant silently lit the candles then departed, leaving Rolfe with his concerns. Annelise's cries reached a new crescendo and Rolfe stared upward, his mouth dry.

If he should lose her this night—no, he could not think of it. His mother's voice, low and reassuring, carried to his ears as Annelise's cry subsided.

Rolfe shuddered to think what his wife endured.

And what had he given her in return? His love, his commitment, his protection. The balance seemed rather thin to Rolfe, especially in light of this night's ordeal. A new mother deserved a gift, but Rolfe knew well enough that Annelise would not care for jewelry or other finery.

He must grant her a gift from the heart. It must be intangible, to show her that he had learned the value of things unseen. It must be something she could not hold but that might make her life more complete.

Rolfe thought of Sayerne. He had sent a message to Sayerne in May when the company had vowed to meet again. Annelise had been so ill early in her pregnancy and he had not wanted to risk a long ride. It would have taken them a week to reach Sayerne, and he had feared she might lose the child. He could have gone alone to see his comrades, but had not wanted to leave her in her distress, even in the care of his mother.

Perhaps it was time to invite Quinn to come to them.

Rolfe distracted himself that day with the task of writing an invitation to Quinn. If he could heal the scar of Annelise's past by uniting brother and sister again, that truly would be a gift worthy of his bride.

He had no sooner sealed the missive and placed it into a runner's hand than Annelise screamed with greater vigor. Rolfe muttered a curse and lunged up the stairs to the solar. His mother could not keep him from the chamber in such a moment. He would be with Annelise for the last of her ordeal.

Annelise awakened as the first rays of the sun slanted through the solar window. The room was lit with a rosy gold glow, its hue reminding her of the good djinn. Without Azima's influence, she and Rolfe would not be so happy together.

Even better, she had given Rolfe a son.

Annelise was tired and sore, but so filled with joy that she was more content than ever she had been. The midwife had cleaned both Annelise and the chamber before leaving a few hours earlier, then Rolfe's mother had retired, as well. Annelise had been left alone with her husband and son.

She had slept, but Rolfe, she knew, had not.

Even now, he rocked his son at the foot of the bed, the sunlight glinting in his dark hair. Annelise watched him make faces at the babe for a few moments before he realized she was awake.

"Sleep well?" he murmured.

"How could I not, with you standing guard?" she whispered, not wanting to startle the baby. Rolfe smiled and she saw the exhaustion in his eyes. Her heart swelled that he had been with her at the last and most difficult part of the delivery. His strength had made the pain easier to bear. Their gazes locked for a long, potent moment, one that made her hope she could soon consider giving him another child.

Then the babe let forth a healthy cry.

Rolfe flicked a glance downward at their son. "Do you think he is jealous?"

Annelise laughed. "I think he is perfect."

"Not as perfect as his mother."

"He might be hungry." She opened her arms. "He did not take much the last time."

Rolfe lowered the babe into her embrace, so gentle that the child might have been made of spun glass. Annelise was awed by the tiny burden of their son and could scarce believe their good fortune. Rolfe sat beside her, his hand beneath the weight of the babe so that she could unfasten her chemise. His other hand brushed over her bare shoulder and along her cheek, leaving her flesh tingling in the wake of his caress. She nestled the boy against her and urged him to the breast. She thought she was clumsy with the task, but Rolfe watched her with glowing eyes, his confidence feeding her own. The babe settled in to suckle, and Annelise met her husband's gaze.

"Thank you for coming at the last," she whispered. "I cannot tell you how much it helped."

Rolfe captured her free hand within his own. "I could stay away no longer."

"Despite your mother's demand?"

Rolfe's lips quirked, but his gaze was warm. "It would take more than that to keep me from your side, Annelise."

"You said before that I would be safe while in your presence."

"That is a pledge I mean to keep forevermore, my Annelise."

The heartfelt declaration brought unexpected tears to Annelise's eyes. Her grip tightened on his hand and he leaned forward, concern in his eyes. "What is it?"

She shook her head and her tears fell. "I am simply so happy," she confessed. "I never imagined that I would have a husband such as you, or a home such as this, or a family." She sniffled and bit her lip in an effort to control her tears. "To have all three and so much love, it defies every expectation. This is what I have always wanted and you have granted it to me."

"It is no less than what you deserve." Rolfe moved closer and the welcome weight of his arm slipped over Annelise's shoulder. He leaned down to whisper in her ear, his hand still cradling hers. "You had a family before."

Annelise shook her head. "No, I had no family, not after my mother died. I will not accept that man as a part of my life. If I had a family, it was at the convent."

"But I thought you did not think as those women did."

"No." She sighed. "We had little in common, but they were good to me. They gave me a home and for that I will always be grateful, even though that life was not for me."

"I am relieved to hear it," Rolfe teased and she smiled at him.

The babe stirred against her breast, then opened his eyes to gaze upward. To Annelise's shock, his eyes were the same amber hue as her father's. She gasped and Rolfe's grip tightened around her.

"What is amiss?"

"His eyes are the same as my father's." Annelise whispered, then looked into Rolfe's gaze. "What if he has inherited more than the shade of his eyes from Jerome?"

Rolfe's finger flew to Annelise's lips and his touch silenced her. "Annelise," he said in the low tone that always reassured her. "Our son has your eyes."

"But it is more than his eyes," she admitted, staring down at the tiny child. "What of the rest? I would hate to know that such evil flowed through his veins because of me."

"But you share nothing of your father's character."

"What of my brother Quinn? He was said to be worse than my father. Perhaps it is a curse upon the men alone!"

Rolfe gave her a little squeeze. "What of your brother Yves? There are men in your family who do not share your father's curse."

Annelise shook her head again. "Yves was only a half brother. It could be that his mother's goodness overwhelmed my father's evil. My mother, it is more than clear, was dominated by Jerome in every way." She straightened and looked Rolfe squarely in the eye. "No, you, our son and your mother are my sole family. That is more good fortune than most have to call their own."

A considering glint lit Rolfe's eye. "I told you before that I knew Quinn de Sayerne."

"But you never mentioned as much again."

"You never spoke of him again, either," Rolfe said. "Though I think it time to put your ghosts to rest."

What did that mean?

She might have asked, but Rolfe changed the subject. "What shall we name him?" He tickled the babe's chin and the child squirmed. He belched with a volume that surprised them both into laughter.

"I do not know. Do you have a family name you would like to bestow upon him?"

"Let me think upon it." Rolfe kissed her on the nose, and then lingeringly on the lips. "Take your leisure this morning, Annelise."

"I should like to wash and dress."

"Then I will send the maids, and the nurse for our son, as well."

"Your mother will doubtless come to visit, too."

Rolfe smiled, his gaze lifting to the portal where Hildegarde already stood. Annelise smiled and beckoned to her, and it soon became clear that grandmother and mother were equally smitten with the boy's charms.

A week and a half later, just before midday, Rolfe entered the solar. Annelise knew immediately that he had a scheme or a surprise, but expected that he had thought of a name for their son. His mother had declined to provide any suggestions, insisting the task was not hers, and had left the solar but moments before. Annelise was just lacing her kirtle when Rolfe arrived. Her maid tied the knot and secured her girdle, then carried the baby off to his bath.

"What mischief have you been making?" she asked with a smile.

Rolfe grinned. "Me?"

"Yes, you. You have the devil's own glint in your eye."

He folded his hands behind his back and strolled to the window. "A messenger delivered something for you today."

"For me?"

"Yes. It was a twisted little root that I have asked the gardener to plant in the herb garden you favor."

"What kind of root?"

Rolfe spun to look at her, his eyes gleaming. "One from Outremer. I sent word to a merchant in Lyons when we first returned to Viandin, and he finally had success in locating it."

Annelise clasped her hands, guessing what he had obtained. "Those flowers. The roses!"

Rolfe smiled. "Yes. Now you shall grow a shrub of your own."

"But not an enchanted one," Annelise scolded in a teasing tone. "Do not even think of cutting all the blooms to cast across the bed!"

Rolfe laughed and she launched herself into his arms.

"Thank you," she whispered. "But you had no need to fetch me a gift for bearing you a son. He is my son as well, and his presence gives me joy."

"No, that was not my intent," Rolfe said. "This is a nuptial gift that took much longer to acquire than I expected."

"And a welcome one all the same," Annelise whispered as she lifted her lips for his kiss.

Rolfe only just touched his lips to hers. "Your gift for bringing our son into the world awaits in the garden as well, but it is not the rose."

Annelise blinked, but one glance told her that Rolfe was not going to tell her more. She crossed the solar and looked out the window.

A knight strolled there. His cloak flicked in the wind, but it was difficult to see him clearly because of the plants and the sunlight glinting off his mail. His auburn hair, so like her own in shade, gleamed in the sunlight and she took a step back from the window.

He was too tall and broad of shoulder to be Yves, and his hair was not of the same hue of gold. Indeed, he moved like a man older than Yves.

His cloak fluttered and Annelise went cold when she realized it was the robust wine color of Sayerne's standard.

An older knight from Sayerne could be only one man.

Annelise pivoted to face her husband, only to find that he was watching her closely. "You did not," she whispered.

"Did not what?"

"Invite my brother Quinn to visit." Annelise was hot with trepidation.

"Of course, I did."

Annelise's mouth went dry. What would she do? What would she say?

"What did you tell him?" she asked. "What does he want?"

Still worse, what would Quinn do and say?

Would he silence her so that she could not tell anyone else of their father's crime? It was too easy to imagine that a son and heir would not want the truth of her mother's death to come to light.

"Annelise," Rolfe said. "Quinn is our guest."

"Guest?"

"Yes. I invited him to visit." He crossed the room and gripped her shoulders. "Annelise, I know how you feel, just as I know your feelings are unjustified. It is time you learned the truth." His voice echoed with the force of his conviction, and Annelise could not help but glance into his eyes.

He was so convinced that he was right, that she had nothing to fear.

"You are wrong about Quinn," he insisted. "Trust me."

Annelise returned to the window, watching her brother. "You summoned him without telling me."

"Would you have approved?" Rolfe's thumbs traced soothing patterns on Annelise's shoulders when she did not reply. "A discussion with Tulley at Beauvoir confirmed what I had suspected since you confessed your tale—Quinn and your father argued over the abuse of your mother."

Annelise spun to face Rolfe. Could this be true? Clearly he believed it to be.

"Quinn sought to defend her until Jerome threatened to cast Quinn out. Tulley intervened, for Quinn was young, and took the boy under his own protection. He never imagined that your mother would bear another child."

A lump rose in Annelise's throat. "But how could Quinn abandon her there? He had to know that my father would raise his hand against her again. What kind of man, or even boy, would leave his mother undefended?"

"Perhaps you should ask him that yourself."

Annelise's mouth worked for a moment. "I cannot do this."

Rolfe pulled her into his embrace, and Annelise did not resist. She closed her eyes and leaned against his chest as his fingers slid into her hair.

"Where is my fearless bride now?" Rolfe teased softly.

Annelise shook her head. "I am afraid," she admitted in a small voice. "What if he has charmed you? What if he wishes only to silence the truth about my father's crime once and for all? What if it is all a ruse?" She could not bear to think of having her happiness threatened, much less the welfare of her child—or her husband, or his mother.

"What if I am right and you have another brother to rely upon?"

Annelise pulled away from Rolfe's warmth and met his gaze. "I was the only witness and you are the only one in whom I have confided the tale."

Rolfe cupped her face in his hands. "There is nothing to fear, Annelise. You wanted proof that our son is not doomed to repeat your father's crimes. That proof awaits you in the garden."

"But what if—"

"Do not imagine that I would let anything befall you now, wife of mine," he said fiercely.

Despite herself, Annelise smiled at the reminder of his pledge to protect her. She straightened and looked toward the window.

Rolfe was right. It was time she confronted her fears and put the past to rest.

She took her husband's hand. "Will you come with me?"

Rolfe closed his hand over hers. "Do not imagine that I would be anywhere else."

The knight in the garden spun around at the crunch of Annelise's footsteps on the gravel. His boots were splattered with mud, as were his chausses and his cloak. He looked as if he had ridden in haste, without care for his garb.

Was that because Rolfe had summoned him?

Did he want to make amends so badly as this?

His gaze locked with hers, and Annelise found herself staring into eyes that were familiar, yet not. Quinn's amber eyes were so like her son's, so like her father's, yet filled with a compassion unknown to Jerome de Sayerne.

That gave Annelise the confidence to approach him. Rolfe waited behind as she crossed the garden one step at a time. Annelise had never met a man who could keep his true feelings from reflecting in his eyes, and Quinn's were so warm that she felt her doubts melting away.

He smiled a slow and encouraging smile, one that reminded her of her mother. It was a marvel to her to see the echo of both father and mother in his features, as well as a faint reminder of her own son's face.

"Blood of my blood," he whispered, as though he could not believe she was before him. He dropped to one knee before her and took her hand in his. "Annelise de Sayerne, I am most pleased to finally make your acquaintance," he said, and brushed a kiss across her knuckles.

"As am I to meet you, Quinn de Sayerne."

Quinn smiled up at her, his gaze dancing over her features. "You look so much like her," he whispered.

Annelise's heart skipped a beat. "Who?" she asked, knowing all the while who he must mean.

"Our mother, of course." Quinn shook his head as he studied her. "But there is a strength about you that she never had. I can see it in your eyes, feel it in your grip." His fingers tightened on Annelise's hand before he rose. "I am sorry that you were forced to learn that strength so early and while so alone."

"Why did you leave her?" The question fell from Annelise's lips with less grace than might have been ideal. She hoped her question did not sound like an accusation. "How could you have abandoned her? You had to know that he would strike her again."

Pain filled Quinn's eyes and he looked away. His voice, when he spoke, was strained. "She would not come." He cleared his throat and looked back at Annelise with new intensity. "She refused to leave him. We argued long over the matter, but she insisted that I was only a child and could not understand. I believe now that she feared no other man would have her, that Jerome alone could see her sheltered and fed."

"She was wrong," Annelise whispered. "You should have forced her to leave!"

Quinn's expression turned sad. "She refused, Annelise. And Jerome swore before Tulley that the beatings would stop. Tulley insisted that I leave immediately, that I accompany him that very moment." He shook his head. "There was nothing I could do but hope for the best." His voice faded. "I was only a boy."

With that heartfelt confession, Annelise knew her fears had been unfounded.

Quinn intended her no harm. He, she could already see, was the complete opposite of their father. He was so still, so thoughtful, so resolute. There was not a line of cruelty in his features or demeanor. Her overwhelming sense was that he was kind and just. That Rolfe thought highly of him could only mean that Quinn shared her husband's honorable nature.

Annelise claimed his hand, seeing how he blamed himself and how the responsibility was not his to bear. Her vision blurred with unexpected tears. "You could not have known."

Quinn frowned. "I could have known, if Tulley had sent word. For whatever reason, he told me nothing of what happened at Sayerne, though he kept a close eye on my whereabouts." His gaze bored into Annelise's own. "Perhaps he feared that if I had known the truth, I would have challenged my father more seriously."

"And what would have been the harm in that?"

Quinn grimaced. "I was too young to rule Sayerne well, especially after our father's lax administration. Even now, if I did not have Melissande at my side, the task would be insurmountable."

Annelise must have looked puzzled, for Quinn smiled slightly. "My wife, Melissande d'Annossy. Tulley did us the great favor of insisting we wed. She awaits in the hall, for she tires easily now that she is with child." His eyes twinkled. "I think you might have much in common with her."

Annelise recognized the name of Sayerne's highborn and reputedly beautiful neighbor. But because of Annelise's years in the convent, the two women had never met.

"What would I have in common with your wife?" Annelise asked with a smile, for she knew he teased her.

"Your doubt of my character," Quinn replied with a smile of his own. "It took me many months to convince her that I was as different from our father as could be. He left a long shadow, did Jerome de Sayerne."

Blood of her blood, as he had said. She and Quinn shared a legacy—one that had had its pain, to be sure, but the bond between them would be greater for it.

Annelise did not relinquish her grip on his hand. "Then we shall create a new legacy," she said with conviction. "One so bright and noble that Jerome's shadow will be eclipsed, perhaps even forgotten."

Quinn smiled slowly. "Yes. Yes, Annelise, let us do that." He kissed her fingers again and bowed to her, then turned and escorted her to Rolfe's side. Quinn shook Rolfe's hand with hearty vigor. "I thank you, Rolfe. Who would have thought the company of rogues and angels would have brought me a sister so fine?"

They laughed together at what was obviously a familiar jest.

Rolfe's gaze landed upon Annelise. "Yes, fine she undoubtedly is." He extended a hand to her and she moved to his side, her heart swelling with joy.

She had another brother, a family both past and present. This was more, so much more, than she had ever dreamed she might call her own.

And she had Rolfe to thank for it all.

"If you will forgive me," Quinn said. "I would see that Melissande is at ease." He bowed again then strode to the hall, his concern for his wife clear. Annelise smiled at the sight, very glad that both she and her brother had made matches of love.

She had to hope that Yves would fare as well.

"I have thought of a name for our son," she said to Rolfe. They walked slowly and she leaned upon him, savoring the heat of the sunlight.

"Yes," Rolfe murmured, trying to hide a smile and failing. "I imagine it is the same one I always thought fitting."

"You always intended to name our son Quinn?"

Rolfe only winked in response, and Annelise could not help but laugh aloud. "But you said nothing to me!"

"A wise man knows when an idea must be his lady's own," he teased.

Annelise laughed at the truth in that, then sighed with satisfaction. "Oh, Rolfe, you have made me happier this day than I imagined I ever might be. Thank you."

Rolfe turned to face her, cupped her face in his hand. She stared into his eyes, one blue and one silver-gray, both gleaming with heartfelt sincerity, and forgot her newfound brother.

"Surely I owe no less to the woman who so completely enchanted me with her love," he murmured. "You cast a potent spell from our first meeting, our Annelise."

"This is one spell from which you will never wriggle free," Annelise threatened with a smile.

Rolfe laughed as he pulled her into his embrace. "I will not even try," he vowed. He smiled down at her. "I think Marcus might have been right, after all."

"Marcus?" Annelise frowned in confusion before she remembered. "Oh, the man who gave you the dark bottle."

Rolfe's smile broadened. "The one who insisted it had the power to make dreams come true," he said with satisfaction, then bent to claim her lips in a possessive kiss.

And Annelise could only agree.

AUTHOR'S NOTE

The wild roses that are native to Europe are flat with five petals, much like wild roses elsewhere in the world, and bloom in shades of white and pink. Roses with more petals derive from flowers that originated in the Middle East. Rolfe is a bit before his time in bringing roses back from Outremer—it was Thibaud IV who brought the red Apothecary Rose, or Rose de Provins, to France on his return from the Seventh Crusade in 1250.

These roses were cultivated extensively near Thibaud's château in Provins, outside Paris, and were renowned for their strong fragrance and rich color. Although not as rounded as the cabbage roses bred in the nineteenth century, Provins roses are sufficiently different from the native wild rose in hue, scent and shape that Annelise—not a gardener, by any means!—would not have realized they were the same flowers. The shrub grows about knee high and these roses spread with enthusiasm by underground suckers. They are hardy and I grow them in Canada.

A medicinal preserve was also made from Provins roses in the Middle Ages, leading to their name Apothecary Rose. There is also a striped variety, with deep pink and white stripes, named for Henry II's mistress Rosamunde. A tisane is still made from the hips—which are the seed pods that ripen in the fall—and it is an excellent source of Vitamin C.

In the late thirteenth century the red rose was associated with the Virgin Mary and the purity of her love. As her cult grew in popularity throughout the Middle Ages, so did that of the Provins rose. Eventually, the troubadours linked the blossom to more secular love, and the red rose evolved into a symbol of romance still recognized today.

Read on for an excerpt from the next book in the Rogues &
Angels series of medieval romances by Claire Delacroix.

One Knight's Return
Book #2 of Rogues & Angels

The *Rogues & Angels* series of medieval romances continues with the tale of Quinn's return home to Sayerne—and his arranged marriage by Lord de Tulley to the beautiful heiress Melissande d'Annossy. Too late Quinn discovers that his lady wife not only believes him to be the same manner of villain as his father, but that her heart is already lost to another man. Can this rough knight win his lady's reluctant heart? Or is he doomed to lose her when her beloved returns?

An excerpt from
ONE KNIGHT'S RETURN

A husband?" Melissande d'Annossy kept her tone temperate with difficulty.

Lord de Tulley was looking older than when last she had seen him. Though his blue eyes still sparkled bright with intent, the lines were etched more deeply in his brow. He looked smaller, but no less determined.

Melissande held his gaze with no small measure of resolve. She knew it was Tulley's right to choose her spouse since her father was dead. She supposed she had been foolish to hope that he had forgotten his obligation since he had not insisted on her marrying before this point.

"Yes, Melissande." Tulley leaned back in his chair as he regarded her, his bright gaze appraising. "You are still young, but it is time we saw you wed."

Melissande had a feeling that Tulley did not intend to secure the match that she desired. But nothing was gained by silence, as her sire had often said. Melissande cleared her throat. "Dare I assume that you have found Arnaud de Privas?"

Her lord snorted in a manner that was a reply in itself. "I have already told you to put that childish whimsy behind you."

Melissande stood taller. "A pledge is not whimsy."

Tulley braced his elbows on his desk as he resolutely held Melissande's gaze. When he spoke, his voice was low and compelling. "If your sire were alive, he would have seen that childhood pledge dismissed long before now. There is more at stake here than you might guess, Melissande."

The implication that she could not understand the repercussions of her choice annoyed Melissande as nothing else could have done. Her chin shot up and her tone was less temperate when she replied. "My word is at stake and that, sir, is of immeasurable value to me."

Tulley frowned. "My lands are imperiled by your insistence upon this nonsense," he countered. "Annossy is a point of weakness for me, as long as you administer the estate alone."

"My lord, you promised me the opportunity to administer Annossy alone and prove my abilities," Melissande replied. "I had hoped that you might have invested me with the seal of my father's estate by now."

"And I am glad that I have not taken that step, given these recent attacks upon Annossy!" Tulley said with heat. "The marauders know the holding is governed by a woman alone and have probably guessed that you have not been invested with your family's estates officially. You know as well as I that their actions reflect their perception of weakness."

"I am not weak!" Melissande protested. "My father saw me well trained, sir. The villeins are satisfied and the tithes have been beyond expectation. Annossy is well-ruled..."

Tulley interrupted her. "But not sufficiently well-defended."

Melissande's lips tightened. She could make no argument, for her estates had borne the brunt of the attacks, precisely as Tulley maintained.

"I hold these lands for the king by grant of the Count of Burgundy and should any of them be lost, my own position would be compromised," Tulley continued. "You know that I cannot risk that. The attacks upon Annossy compel me to make a choice, Melissande."

Melissande stood, hands clasped, and wished she had been born a man.

Tulley continued. "Whatever you or I or even your villeins might think, these bandits perceive the weak link in my holdings to be Annossy. I will not risk any loss for the sake of your pride. I might let you temporarily administer your family holdings, but I will not invest you and break openly with tradition."

Melissande saw the warrior that the Lord de Tulley had once been, and appreciated anew his reputation as a man who would see his will fulfilled against all odds. She regarded him silently, recognizing that she would have to cede to his bidding in this.

If she had been a man, she would have openly defied him. If she had been a man, there would have been no criticism of her administration. If she had been a man, she would have chosen her own mate freely. Or taken no spouse at all.

"But..."

"But nothing, Melissande," Tulley said. "This situation has continued for too long now and the time for action has come. You will wed and, as befits my right as your liege lord, I will decide to whom."

Melissande straightened and dared to ask what she most wanted to know. "I understand that you regard my childhood vow to Arnaud childish whimsy, but might he not be considered? It would please me to keep my pledge, my lord."

That was an understatement in the greatest extreme. Her word was her bond and that was a source of pride for Melissande. Tulley's brow darkened, though, and Melissande knew to dread his next words.

"Do you think, child, that after all these years I would ignore what I know to be important to you?" he demanded. "I did seek out that rogue Arnaud whom you inexplicably hold so dear."

Tulley had sought out Arnaud? Melissande regarded the older man in surprise. Her heart skipped a beat at the possibility that Arnaud would be her spouse, though the lord's tone was surprisingly disparaging.

His next words surprised her even more.

"It seems he has taken a wife himself."

"A wife?"

Tulley's eyes narrowed as he surveyed her. "It would appear

that your loyalty has been misplaced."

No! This could not be. Arnaud would not break his pledge.

There could be only one explanation. Tulley was trying to deceive her so that she would agree to his plan.

"That is untrue!" Melissande declared before she could consider the wisdom of that accusation.

Tulley eyed her coldly. "The source was reliable beyond doubt," he said. "Apparently, Arnaud wed Marie de Perricault a year past."

"Marie!" Although Melissande had not seen the older woman in years, she remembered her testy manner. "Arnaud would never wed Marie and break his word to me! "

"But he did exactly that. I would suggest you come to terms with the truth, Melissande." He cleared his throat. "I appreciate that you spoke hastily and out of disappointment but it would be folly for you to repeat such an accusation."

"Even if your source is deceived in this?"

Tulley gave her a warning look.

Melissande took a steadying breath and forced her hands to unclench. "All these years, you have treated me with respect and honesty. Please do not abandon that path now, my lord."

Her heart began to pound as Tulley said nothing, his regard impassive.

"Tell me that you did not find Arnaud," she suggested. "Tell me that you refuse to seek him out for whatever reason, but do not lie to me about his fate. I know that I must do as you dictate. Do you think that deception will reconcile me to your will?"

The lord's lips tightened. "If you do not wed my choice, you will forfeit your holdings to me."

"This you cannot do!" Melissande protested. "Annossy is my family's ancestral holding."

Tulley arched a brow.

Melissande was too infuriated to stop. "Should you wrongfully take Annossy from me, I shall see your word tested. I shall appeal to the king himself!"

"Whose authority is thin this far from Paris," the lord responded. "Do you think that he will test his relations here over the pleas of a landless noblewoman, however beauteous she might be? Remember that you are not even invested with the estate. Annossy is mine to grant as I see fit and it was only by my grace that you have administered it these five years. I could easily make an argument that your refusal to wed threatens the security of my estates." The lord settled back in his chair again. "Do you truly imagine that he would take your side?"

Melissande stared at her shoes and reluctantly faced the truth of her situation.

"I took a vow," she whispered.

Tulley arched a brow. "And now you will take another."

His gaze was resolute.

Melissande would be wed, regardless of her own will.

At Tulley's command.

Soon.

And likely to a man whom she did not know.

A man who would seize her holdings and consign her to the bedchamber, as the law fully granted him the right to do. Melissande could imagine no worse fate than this.

"At least, you have seen the wisdom of holding your tongue," Tulley muttered.

Everything her father had built would be stolen away from her and there was nothing she could do! Melissande forced herself to remain calm, so that she might learn the worst. She took three deep breaths before she trusted herself to speak.

"Who would you insist I wed, sir?" she asked.

A rap at the door to the lord's office interrupted whatever Tulley might have said. The lord smiled, his welcoming expression prompting Melissande to glance toward the portal.

A knight filled its frame. No, not a knight but a renegade. Foreboding crossed over Melissande's heart and the room, which had seemed too warm just a moment past, suddenly chilled.

No, her first impulse had to be wrong. This had to be some man-at-arms in Tulley's employ. A messenger or a mercenary. His arrival at this moment was nothing but a coincidence.

But still Melissande looked.

He was tall and broad of shoulder, though his travel-stained garb made him look rough and dirty. His mail glinted in the candlelight, half-hidden beneath a tabard with a torn hem. A well-worn cloak was tossed over his shoulders, its hem stained, and his thick leather gloves were scuffed from years of heavy wear.

He removed his helmet with a grunt of satisfaction and ran one hand through the length of his untrimmed chestnut hair. It was wavy but clearly unclean, falling to his shoulders. There was stubble on his chin and a streak of mud across his cheek.

Melissande was certain he must be plagued with lice, and took a step back.

He must have sought out Tulley to pledge his blade to that lord's service.

Melissande's mouth went dry with the sudden certainty that the châtelain would never have shown him here while she remained, if that had been the case. The vagabond would have been left to wait in the hall.

She feared then that she knew who this man must be. But surely Tulley would not wed her to such a barbarian?

"My lord," intoned Tulley's châtelain. "Quinn de Sayerne, son of Jerome de Sayerne, as you requested."

Son of Jerome de Sayerne! That detail dismissed any possibility of Melissande greeting this man with the slightest favor. She regarded him with shock and distrust. Trust that lecherous serpent to have spawned a son of no greater merit than himself!

She had believed her troubles over when Jerome finally died. Melissande had never suspected that Jerome had sired a mercenary for a son. She recalled Jerome's determination to join Annossy and Sayerne under his hand only too well. Her stomach churned as she stared at the new arrival and recalled the thievery Jerome had initiated against her family's holdings.

Now the son would finish what the father had begun.

Indeed, if sire and son were cut from the same cloth, it was not unlikely that this man was behind the recent raids on Annossy.

Surely, Tulley would not compel her to wed him.

But one glance at her overlord's expression sent Melissande's heart sinking to her toes.

Quinn de Sayerne would be her husband and, if she did not miss her guess, their vows would be exchanged without delay.

One Knight's Return
Book #2 of Rogues & Angels
Coming soon!

ABOUT THE AUTHOR

Bestselling and award-winning author Deborah Cooke has published over fifty novels and novellas, including historical romances, fantasy romances, fantasy novels with romantic elements, paranormal romances, contemporary romances, urban fantasy romances, time travel romances and paranormal young adult novels. She writes as herself, Deborah Cooke, as Claire Delacroix, and has written as Claire Cross. Her Claire Delacroix medieval romance, *The Beauty*, was her first book to land on the New York Times List of Bestselling Books.

Deborah was the writer-in-residence at the Toronto Public Library in 2009, the first time TPL hosted a residency focused on the romance genre, and she was honored to receive the Romance Writers of America PRO Mentor of the Year Award in 2012. She's a member of Romance Writers of America, and is on the RWA Honor Roll. She lives in Canada with her family.

To learn more about Deborah's books, please visit her websites at:
http://deborahcooke.com
http://www.delacroix.net